JANICE GENTLE GETS SEXY

Mavis Cheek worked with the art publishers Editions Alecto for twelve happy years before becoming a mature student at Hillcroft College for Women where she graduated in Arts with Distinction. Her short stories and travel articles have appeared in various publications and her first book, *Pause between Acts*, won the SHE/John Menzies First Novel Prize. She is also the author of *Parlour Games* and *Dog Days*.

Acclaim for *Janice Gentle Gets Sexy*

'Delightfully funny' – *Woman's Journal*

'Miss Cheek writes in a breathlessly jaunty style juggling her formidable cast of characters with the dexterity of a professional conjuror ... It is impossible not to be enthralled' – Carla McKay in the *Daily Mail*

'Amusing and original' – Maureen Lipman

MAVIS CHEEK

JANICE GENTLE GETS SEXY

PENGUIN BOOKS

PENGUIN BOOKS

Published by the Penguin Group
Penguin Books Ltd, 27 Wrights Lane, London W8 5TZ, England
Penguin Books USA Inc., 375 Hudson Street, New York, New York 10014, USA
Penguin Books Australia Ltd, Ringwood, Victoria, Australia
Penguin Books Canada Ltd, 10 Alcorn Avenue, Toronto, Ontario, Canada M4V 3B2
Penguin Books (NZ) Ltd, 182–190 Wairau Road, Auckland 10, New Zealand

Penguin Books Ltd, Registered Offices: Harmondsworth, Middlesex, England

First published by Hamish Hamilton 1993
Published in Penguin Books 1994
5 7 9 10 8 6 4

Copyright © Mavis Cheek, 1993
All rights reserved

Grateful acknowledgement is made to the following for permission to reprint previously published
material: Penguin Books Ltd for extracts from *Piers the Ploughman* by William Langland, translated
by J. F. Goodridge (Penguin Classics, 1959, revised edition, 1966), copyright
© J. F. Goodridge, 1959, 1966; and for an extract from *The Canterbury Tales*, translated by Nevill
Coghill (Penguin Classics, 1951, 4th revised edition, 1977), copyright © Nevill Coghill, 1951, 1958,
1960, 1975, 1977; reproduced by permission of Penguin Books Ltd. Gerald Duckworth & Co Ltd
for the poem 'Distance' by Dorothy Parker; reproduced by permission of Duckworth. Estate of
Richard Aldington for the poem 'Epilogue' by Richard Aldington; reproduced by permission of
the Estate of Richard Aldington

Printed in England by Clays Ltd, St Ives plc

Acknowledgements

Boundless gratitude to both Kate Jones and Henry Dunow, my
anchors in the storm.

For Fred and the Fountain

Then you will come to a hill, Bear-No-False-Witness. Turn right away from it, for it is thickly wooded with bribes and bristling with florins. At all costs gather no blossoms there, or you will lose your soul.

William Langland, *Piers the Ploughman*

Chapter One

MORGAN P. Pfeiffer, known in the New York publishing world as Midas, was a presence. He made his very big, very bare desk look very small. He imposed. Ms Rohanne Bulbecker, slender as a willow, fair as a lily, youthful as a nymph and tough as an extremely old boot, faced him sitting at her full height. Ambition glowed out of her.

'The late Mrs Pfeiffer was very fond of Janice Gentle books. Do you know Janice Gentle's work, Miss Bulbecker?'

'Certainly,' she said crisply. 'She writes romantic novels.'

'She does.'

'And sells extremely well.'

'She sells enviably well. She is a bestseller *par excellence*.'

Rohanne did not flicker as the lilt of French became lost on his lips. 'She certainly does.' A little light dawned. 'You intend to offer for her? I am sure she would come to Pfeiffer's if the price was right.'

He shifted in his seat. He removed the ash from his cigar pensively. 'Mrs Pfeiffer had one criticism of Janice Gentle's books.' He looked at the photograph of Mrs Pfeiffer, deceased, on his desk. This time Rohanne was certain the slight noise was a sigh. 'They contain no sex, Miss Bulbecker. Mrs Pfeiffer was much disappointed by this. She felt that they ought not to . . . ah . . . stop short of the . . . er . . . act. I speak plainly.'

'You do.'

'I would like to publish Janice Gentle. Very much. I would like to have a Belinda Jane Pfeiffer memorial imprint.'

Rohanne had the merest tickle of excitement somewhere around her belly button. She pushed on it hard with her hands. When she spoke, her voice was even. 'And you would like me to secure her?'

'Poach her, I believe the English call it. Sentiment aside, it makes very sound business sense.'

'It certainly does,' agreed Rohanne Bulbecker, who always preferred to set sentiment aside.

'Others have apparently tried to persuade her and failed.'

'Why? What makes her resistant to the proposal?'

Morgan P. Pfeiffer shrugged. It was a gesture of genuine loss. 'I have no idea.'

'What did she say?'

'*She* did not say anything. Her agent spoke for her.'

'Her agent?'

'Sylvia Perth.'

Rohanne wrinkled her brow for a moment. 'I know the name. We've not met. Who does she represent?'

'Solely Janice Gentle.'

'So why did Sylvia Perth refuse?'

He shrugged again. 'It is clearly not money. Our offer was substantial. We have not been able to talk to her directly because Janice Gentle is recluse. Nobody even knows where she lives. It could be London, it could be anywhere in England. It could even be *Scotland* . . .' He said this last as if it were on a fairly accurate line with Mars. 'Sylvia Perth has total charge and Sylvia Perth is adamant. The answer, she says, will always be no.'

'Sounds like bluff to me. Sounds like she's trying to push up the offer.'

Morgan Pfeiffer shook his head. 'Set aside the money to be made from the book, there were all kinds of marketing-synergy inducements. Janice Gentle would have become a very rich woman.'

'If it is not money, what else could it be?'

He shrugged. 'All I know is what Sylvia Perth tells me. Janice Gentle does not *wish* to get sexy . . .'

Rohanne Bulbecker undid the button of her snappy red jacket, adjusted the collar of her pristine blouse, put her hands on her hips and leaned forward in her chair. Anyone used to dealing with her would recognize the signs. 'No?' she said. 'Then I shall just have to persuade her, won't I?'

2

Out into the cool spring air went Rohanne Bulbecker. There was nothing in the world she liked better than a challenge, the tougher the better. Metaphorically she raised her standard high and marched back to her office to think.

'Janice Gentle,' she said to herself, 'Janice Gentle gets sexy? Come on Rohanne. You can do *that*!'

Chapter Two

JANICE Gentle is travelling on a morning rush-hour tube train somewhere between South Kensington and Holborn. She wears a stone-coloured mackintosh and clutches a plastic bag to what remains of her lap now that her bulky body has managed to squash itself into a seat. Since it is a summer's day of drizzle, the atmosphere in the carriage is made even more unwholesome by the smell of wet fabrics in their various stages of uncleanliness. The herded inmates of the rattling cell seem not to notice the steamy stench and sit or hang strapwards imperviously. They have the glazed appearance of wooden marionettes until the doors slide open to revive them. Even those who read newspapers or books look slack-bodied and unreal, and unlike the travellers of old they neither swap stories nor take pleasure in each other's company.

Only Janice seems alert and on the look-out. She has the wide-eyed look of a fearful but hungry animal that must hunt but would prefer to hibernate. Behind her glasses those pale, blinking eyes of hers rove the compartment, searching the faces of her fellow travellers, appraising their physiques, considering their demeanour. It is a restless seeking, from which the seeker takes no pleasure. Here is no lonely middle-aged woman in need of company and conversation. This seeker is unhappy to be here, very unhappy indeed.

In fact Janice Gentle finds the whole experience near to torture and wonders whether torture would not be preferable. You can, after all, have a scream while it is going on and nobody minds. But here, in this place, you must not make a sound. Only sit and rock and wait. It is its own little world in which you neither acknowledge your companions, nor talk, nor break the mode of

4

isolated being. Only those who must be here are here. The others, the freewomen and freemen, come nowhere near until this time is past.

Janice is here because she has to come. As some must sip seven times from seven glasses before going to bed at night in order to survive the dawn, as some must always bow to a full moon for safety, so must Janice Gentle make a rush-hour tube journey as prelude to beginning a new book. She cannot remember how she first began to need the process, but now, several books on, it is the lodestar, the foundation, and nothing can begin without it. It is not an entirely futile superstition, as arguably are the water and the moon, for, in the tradition of both illustrative and literary creators from Hogarth to Fielding, Picasso to Joyce, Janice draws from life. Her characters she takes not from the street but from the tube, and only when she has found the absolute physical specimen for each character required, can she take herself back to the silent, beige blandness of her Battersea flat, and begin to write in its colourless, closeted tranquillity.

This morning she has her eye on a bright Little Blonde with glistening, early-morning pink lips, which move very slightly as she reads. By coincidence she reads from one of Janice Gentle's own books; this is not an unusual occurrence since Janice Gentle's work is popular. Indeed, Janice Gentle's work is always in the bestsellers' list and there is no doubt that were she to lean across the gangway divide and prod the Little Blonde on her sharp little kneecap and say, 'I am Janice Gentle,' the Little Blonde would be overwhelmed and say *ooh* and *ah* and *oh* through her pretty, pink mouth. '*Ooh ah and oh!*' she would say, 'I have read *all* your books. I think they are really good.' And she would be astonished that one so fat and plain could create such things.

Janice does not do this. Janice likes anonymity. Besides, Janice is not wholly aware of just how successful she is. She knows that she produces a good many books, she knows that she cannot rest on her laurels no matter how much she would like to, because she knows – or *thinks* she knows – that she has not made enough money to stop yet. Janice has a positive reason for wanting to get to this point. A Quest, a Seeking that will require a great deal of money. According to Sylvia Perth, agent and friend, the day of successful fiscal achievement is still a long way off, though it is, of course, getting nearer. Frequently and kindly she gees up the flagging Janice. 'You are only as good as your last book,' she says. 'So come along, dear. Let's get our heads down, shall we? I've got to have *something* to offer your publisher in a few months' time . . .'

So – always – the successes of the past are over. So – always – it is time to begin the gruelling process again.

There is some pleasure to be drawn from seeing the Little Blonde Secretary Bird holding her book, since, though unworldly, Janice is not without feeling. That primly perfect face wrinkled its small nose and made a little moue of disgust as Janice squeezed into her seat opposite, and Janice knew that she need look no further for her anti-heroine. Perfection sat opposite her, perfection that was so unflawed as to be dead, perfection that was so very insensate it deserved to die. Janice had never had any of her characters die before, but it was an engaging concept. She studied her anew. Or maybe she could just be seriously damaged? A fall from a horse, perhaps? Victim of a low-hanging branch? A crack of her spine and ever after wheelchair-bound? No – wheelchairs had a kind of kudos, not like in the days of Heidi's Klara. Nowadays it was quite apparent that life did not stop in a wheelchair, nor did love and happiness. Better to make her bedridden, then. Mentally Janice wipes her hands. Yes, that'll do nicely for her. And no bedside scenes of contrition, either, to soften the case. In real life, she opined, such things scarcely happened, anyway.

It was such touches of reality which made her books so popular even among the graduate classes. If Janice Gentle wrote about romance, she wrote about it pragmatically; readers could say 'I know what you mean' to the page they were reading, identifying with the inner experience even if the outward experience were remote. If Janice built castles in the air with her books, she also offered a credible means to climb up to them – for those

6

who were interested. Those who were not interested could bypass the occasionally esoteric word, forget about the quotations, and go straight to the heart of the story.

For essentially Janice Gentle wrote stories. Men and women stories reflecting desire and reward. She could combine the unreal (a Newmarket stud and a heartbruised millionairess) with the real (what are we in the dark of the night when we sit alone but sisters and brothers under the skin?) without losing touch with reality. So, the Little Blonde piece of perfection will be stuck paralysed for all eternity as punishment for her insensitivity – unless Janice decides to be kind and let her die in the end. Everybody likes to see wrongdoing suffer as they like to see virtue rewarded. The Little Blonde will suffer for her sins. The way Janice is feeling this morning that seems justice. She really does hate going out in the world, avoids it wherever possible, has given herself up to be organized and controlled by Sylvia Perth and likes nothing better than to scuttle back to her retreat as soon as possible. Janice has given up on society. These tube journeys and the resulting books are the price she pays for conventual seclusion; it is unlikely that the dainty creature opposite will receive a more kindly end. Janice is not disposed to be kind.

Unaware of her fate, and only uncomfortably conscious of Janice's gaze, the Little Blonde Secretary Bird looks up. She shifts her tight little bottom in its sketchy lace knickers and pulls down the hem of her neat black skirt. People of more than a size twelve should not be allowed on the Underground in the rush hour. So thinks the Little Blonde Secretary Bird, giving the ample form of Janice one more fleeting glance of shudder before she quickly dives back into the pages of her book. She loves a good read and is one of those Janice Gentle fans who ignores the rope ladder and goes straight for the castle every time. She also skips the longish words, passes over the quotations from poets long dead and takes comfort that all will be well in the end. She feels that this is just as life *should* be; others who read it feel that this is the way life never will be, but it would be *oh so nice* if it were. Janice Gentle, with some mysterious and unerring skill, manages to make her work appeal to the credulous and the sceptical alike. An anomaly in the world of books, one that many have tried to emulate, one that none, it seems, can.

It is a tiring business, this research. On the train by eight-thirty, not off again until ten. And sometimes the whole upsetting procedure has to be repeated the next day if the spark of inspiration fizzles out or if it is successful only in part. This happens. Sometimes she can see the most perfect character and yet not find its twin or its foil. The process cannot be forced. Janice knows this. It is depressing, but unavoidable. Sometimes she has to go out several times.

She removes a sandwich from her plastic bag and chews on it meditatively. The hero could either be that tall, thin chap further down the car or this square-jawed mid-thirties strap-hanger opposite. He, focusing momentarily and in some horror at what he sees – Janice biting into the sandwich has not quite negotiated the ham successfully and a piece lolls out of her mouth like a dead snake's tongue – turns away, bumps the knees of the Little Blonde Secretary, apologizes (a rare moment of intercompart-mental intercourse), and they smile at each other. Fleetingly, it is true, and perhaps not with their eyes, but a smile, a connection. For a picosecond they are human together. Janice notices, feels this is somehow fortuitous, and decides. The thin man down the line is too thin, too peppery-looking. Square Jaw will do very well. Heroes – she bites again – are much more difficult than heroines. Somehow men do not seem to give out their personalities as freely as even the most static of women.

She settles back and spreads a bit now that the seat to her left is vacant. The rush hour is thinning and it may be that she will have to start all over again tomorrow, for she has yet to find a heroine. She checks the height of the square-jawed chosen one. Good, she thinks, he is quite tall so there should not be too much of a problem matching him up. Ever since she became fixated on a very short but remarkably beautiful olive-skinned chap (just right for the Eastern Diplomat she needed at the time) she has been wary. Finding a match for him at under five foot four was

8

not at all easy, for she was wise enough to know that all women, if only in their fantasies, like their partners to be bigger and stronger than they. Of course, it was possible that men *also* – if only in their fantasies – liked their female lovers to be ditto, but this did not concern her. It was women she wrote for and – happily – it was women who bought and read her books.

Sylvia Perth had told her. 'Janice,' she said, 'almost all fiction is read by women. Chaps read other stuff, so don't you worry about them. You carry on writing just the way you do and that will be absolutely fine.'

So, there could be no heroine towering over her olive-skinned hero – and that had been hard. This was the crux of the problem of her creative shibboleth; it could never be broken. If it were – even once – then everything else would tumble to the ground. The Eastern Diplomat had taken three dreadful journeys before she found the right match and she felt miserable at the prospect of similar difficulties now. She unwraps a Mars bar. Two more mornings of torture like this, especially if the wet, warm weather continued, would be –

'Excuse me.'

A well-bred, firm-toned female voice.

Janice looks up.

Tight lips, a strong, fine-boned face framed in a red-gold fringe, below which there are flower-blue eyes that say nothing. Remainder of hair held close in an uncompromising chignon. No lipstick, no rouge, refined bearing with the smell of lemons and honey about her. Graceless clothes; pleated skirt, plain white blouse, indeterminate brown coat and unadorned black pumps. Janice remarks to herself that the coat is not summerweight and yet its owner does not even glow. She also sees that the ankles are small, the wrists delicate, the curve of the neck graceful. This is not raw-boned gracelessness but imposed, surface only. Early forties perhaps, but not difficult to picture her younger. Janice blinks and half smiles, she nods, moves her bulk and the crackling plastic bag, and goes on chewing her chocolate bar. She continues to look sideways as she does so. Good, very good, she thinks.

9

'Thank you so much.' Superior politeness as if the one giving thanks is in fact saying, *Be grateful to me*. Cold. With fire lurking somewhere within.

Janice is intrigued.

An idea shapes in her head.

She chews faster, shifts her position to see better. Waits.

The idea grows in her as the woman arranges herself in the seat and adjusts her clothes to avoid encroaching on Janice's side. Janice spills everywhere, well into her companion's space, yet the woman manages to avoid any physical contact at all. There is something engaging about that isolation. She takes one more long, slow sideways look before daring to decide. But yes – yes, yes, yes – it is right. Easy to see her as she is now and as she was once. Fading red-gold beauty. Lines of experience, lines of regret, perhaps? And a hardness somewhere. Perfect, perfect, perfect. Janice wants to write a retrospective novel for which red-gold and her artificial, self-imposed dullness will be the very epitome of Phoenix rising. In fact, that might very well be the title of the book.

When the red-gold woman brings out a *Church Times* and begins reading it, Janice feels that her cup of invention is full. To create a romantic heroine from a vicar's wife – flaming hair, scorched hopes – is the beguilement that she seeks. Without such beguilement Janice Gentle could never complete a sentence let alone a whole book. Now she has what she needs.

Red Gold, who will be eternally happy.

Little Blonde, bird-like, bird-brain, who will be driven by boredom and disappointment towards a bitter, wretched end.

Square Jaw, whose even features resembled the Before in an Alka-Seltzer advertisement, will become a solid and desirable force – one who will be forgiven and loved.

The tale is set.

Janice can go home now, for her day's work is fairly done.

Genius, born out of such disparities.

Genius.

*

It is of course genius that Janice Gentle has. Her works have
been likened to Jane Austen, they have been likened to Enid
Blyton, they have been likened to Grimm. They have been
discussed in sentences that breathed the names of both Richardson
and Danielle Steele, they have been reviewed in *The Times*, they
have sold by the yard in airport bookstalls. She is read by the
wives of both Oxford dons and Oxford butchers, for she writes
of that which touches the human condition most, that unfashion-
able, elusive item on which turns the world. She writes, at the
core, about love. 'Stone walls do not a prison make/Nor iron bars
a cage . . .' Janice may be recluse, she may have little experience
of the commodity, but it does not stop her understanding it.
After all, she has never been sat upon by an elephant, but she
knows that if she were it would hurt. Life may pass her by, but
she is not hampered in letting her own small experience fly free.
Indeed, very possibly, it is the life passing her by that helps.

She herself had been touched by love once and it made a
profound, if inconclusive, impression. Until she found Dermot
Poll again writing about the condition was preferable to seeking
more of its reality. And so she did. Calliope, beautiful-voiced
Muse to a thousand epic poems, had blessed her sister with the
gift of words (every woman has something if it is only smooth
elbows), and Janice, alone and heart-bruised and severely into the
pleasures of eating, used her gift well.

Sylvia Perth was right. Ninety-three per cent of her readership
were women, princesses to pauperettes, taking the romance with
as large or as small a dose of salt as they chose. They were loyal,
enthusiastic and read her avidly.

Of the seven per cent remaining, this was almost entirely made
up of men who, so far from having romance on their minds, were
accused by their womenfolk of not having it anywhere within
their vocabulary of understanding – not even so much as tucked
away in an armpit. They read Janice Gentle as one might read a

textbook, looking for a solution and a set of rules. And they came away, usually, as baffled as they had been before, the enchantment of the genre being beyond the ken of fact-finding man.

From Sydney to Stockholm, Dubai to Dundee, Janice Gentle's books were very much in demand. She had made a lot of money and spent little. She had spent little because her personal requirements were scant and also because she did not know that she had made a lot. Had she known how much she had made it is unlikely she would have been taking a tube-train journey this morning at all, it is far more likely that she would have been lying on a settee with her feet up, eating and waiting, waiting and eating, until the Quest she could at last set going produced results, and her Crusade could begin.

But only Sylvia Perth, agent and friend, confidante and publisher's go-between, loyal fan and devoted accountant, knew exactly how much money Janice Gentle had made from her books, and for reasons of her own, for the present, she did not feel it necessary to enlighten her.

*

Back now towards home, mission accomplished.

The Little Blonde Secretary has left the carriage already. Square Jaw and Red Gold remain. As the train pulls into the station and Janice steps out, she gives one last backward look at her intended characters. Yes, yes, they are both perfectly right, especially the colour of that hair. If she is skilful she can make much of that as it turns from its chignon into flowing silver-streaked fire. But she will have to be careful. Distinguishing sentimentality from romance is a thin line and the descent into bathos is never far away.

Sylvia once brought her a whole pile of books which, she said, were trying to replicate Janice's style. Janice read one or two and winced – it was as if the writers had stripped a tree bare of its fruit instead of taking selectively, or had demanded that each tree carry all the fruits of the universe just to be sure . . . Square Jaw may well release that chignon of blazing hair – very possibly Red Gold will be young and beautiful again. But whether that beauty is in the eyes of the *world* or whether it is only in the eyes of her *lover* – that is the question which counts. As a mother looks upon her new babe which to the world resembles a potato and which to the mother resembles a cherub, so, Janice instinctually knows, do lovers look upon lovers. How else could the plain and the ugly be loved? And that is a thought which is dear to her. She believes it utterly.

It is this thin line of integrity, buried almost without trace, to which her readers subliminally respond. '"Love,"' says Janice, '"is Nature's second sun."' '"Love,"' says Janice, '"looks not with the eyes but with the mind,/And therefore is wing'd Cupid painted blind . . ."' Both quotes from Elizabethans, which is annoying since Janice's heart is set in times before them. Indeed, Janice considers Elizabethan literary arts a mere dilution of the golden age that passed before. But they are apt quotes all the same. She has many more stored away, all of which she keeps buzzing in her head as she writes so that they flavour, always, the text.

Back, then, to Battersea.

After her first book was published, Sylvia Perth said gaily, 'Janice, my dear, you can now afford to live anywhere you choose. Right in the centre of town if you want to.' But Janice had chosen Battersea. Battersea suited her very well. The area she chose suited her very well. Sylvia Perth it did not suit. In vain did she try to persuade Janice at least to select the *best* part of Battersea. 'Why not near Albert Bridge – so close to Chelsea – or Prince of Wales Drive . . .? But not here, dear. Not in this bit. Why, it's practically *Nine Elms* . . .' But Janice did not mind that at all and the apartment block was right. Built in the 1950s in that strangely dull cube-like manner, it was unremarkable. Neither large nor small, neither smart nor dowdy. And with no architectural features at all. It just was.

Of course the area had changed in the years since she moved there. Young upwardly mobiles had discovered the river, provender shops had discovered the young upwardly mobiles, and it had all got rather fashionable. But not in Janice's bit. Here, due to bomb damage, the buildings were too new to knock down, too dull to become desirable and too off the beaten track to appeal to any but the drear of heart or those to whom surroundings are frivolities. Hence the shop on the corner still sold ordinary items like digestive biscuits and standard tea, having no market for *langue de chat* nor Lapsang, and hence its owner still wore an overall and liked to chat to his customers. Janice avoided the place whenever possible, preferring the supermarket, where the only exchange required was a grunt of apology as your trolley ran over a foot and where the act of shopping was so detached that there was no sense of shame at whatever you stuffed in your shopper.

The corner-shop man attempted to look unmoved by Janice's requirements, but he was a singular failure at it. If she said four packets of custard creams, his brows shot up and his eyeballs fairly rotated in his head, and all the while he would keep his voice even, saying, slow and deliberate, '*Four* packets of custard creams, six Mars bars, six fudge fingers, two pounds of butter, one pound of cheese,' in a never changing rhythm that made the whole seem like a litany of disapproval. Nothing she ever bought there tasted quite so good as things she bought elsewhere that were free of the stain of his glance. Neither did she very much like the way he glanced at her. His look held too much interest, too much human *bonhomie*, and Janice would prefer to efface herself from such involvements. She would like, so far as the world was concerned, to avoid existence until the time was right to emerge.

As dogs grow to look like their owners and owners their dogs, so Janice Gentle had grown towards nothingness rather well. All excepting her size, of course, and that was just one of those anomalies that occasionally spring up in life. If our presence in the world can be described with a colour, then Janice Gentle was

14

beige. Her skin was pale, her hair nondescript, her eyes indeterminately light, and bloodless her lips. Her body, naked, was not unlike porridge or, more kindly, not unlike a Rubens without its rosy tints and the light of wickedness in the eye. She had never lain on sundrenched beaches taking the hue of honey or the glow of chestnuts from the sun, and though some poet or songster might call her flesh milk-white, it was, in fact, rather an unwholesome paleness, like the skin of one who has stayed in the darkness too long.

No man had lusted for her so far as she knew, no woman had sighed to have her curves. No child had rested on her ample lap nor settled its head within her shelving bosom. Janice's sensual delights were all taken by mouth, and that was the way she liked it. She wore a loose, long cardigan that draped her form as unbecomingly as a dust sheet on a thirties suite, she wore regulation spectacles of unremarkable design, and her hair was held back in a plain rubber band and washed once a week on Thursdays. She weighed fifteen stone, stood five feet two in her bare, spreading feet, was an absolute virgin and looked the same in her twenties as her thirties, her thirties as her forties, in which latter category, just, she now resided. Since coming to Battersea Janice Gentle had kept her life neutral. Other women looked upon her as a sad creature compared with their stylishness; and those feminine-hearted ants scuttling beneath her minuscule fifth-floor balcony would look away sorrowingly and in disgust should they chance to raise their heads and catch sight of her mottled cellulite taking the air.

Men did not pity her, for men did not notice her. So far as men were concerned, Janice was invisible – so plain as to be erotically unuseful, her intellect not strident nor colourful enough to be considered a threat. Apart from the corner shop they left her alone and unremarked, for which she was content, and she hoped it would ever more be so. Until her Quest and Crusade, of course; when they were completed, things would have to be different. Meanwhile she had her books and her beige, beige world. And that was all she sought.

**It had,
however,
not always
been
like that . . .**

Chapter Three

MRS Gentle, deceased, had nothing to thank men for. In her opinion she had done her woman's duty by life and she had not received her due. Mr Gentle had absconded when Janice was a little thing in plaits and had broken his wife's nose into the bargain. Mrs Gentle wore this broken nose as the martyrs of old wore their whip marks, for until its receipt she had been a proud and orderly woman prepared to accept and forgive much for the cause of neighbourly propriety. She had received it standing in the street in her nightclothes, clutching four-year-old Janice's hand while the four-year-old clutched her teddy. Mrs Gentle had been patiently waiting for the episode within her home to pass and thought the midnight street was the safest place to wait while Mr Gentle rampaged. So long as they kept quiet no one would know. Janice, whose dressing-gown and pyjamas did not keep the cold away, began to sob and wish to be held where the warmth would feel nice. Mrs Gentle, who had kept her step whitened and her privet tidy and whose nets had never let her down, felt this was the very last straw. 'Eat this and shut up,' she said, handing the child a sweet that happened to be in her raincoat pocket. It was a Clarnico toffee and its sugary smoothness did the trick. Somehow Janice felt warm again.

Mr Gentle, spotting his wife and child from the upstairs bedroom where he was breaking the last of Mrs Gentle's china fancies, and seeing that this pleasurable activity was coming to an end, ran down the stairs, out into the street, and brought his fist into an equally satisfying collision with the cartilage of his wife's nose. The child howled afresh, her mouth now empty, and blood dripped on to her teddy bear. Mrs Gentle, caught off guard and momentarily released from her dignity, yelled for pity, yelled for vengeance and yelled for succour. Neither of the first two was available and the third came late, for the Gentle household lived in one of those polite streets where if you saw someone fall down you looked away, allowing time for them to get up again lest they be embarrassed by your noticing. Mr Gentle ran off into the night, and when succour did eventually come, it provided a sugar lump for the sobbing Janice, as well as strong, sweet tea for her mother. The sugar lump had the same pleasing effect on little Janice as the Clarnico toffee had done and she was soon very soundly asleep.

There were several incidents in that house in the years that followed, though Mr Gentle did not officially return. But no matter what he occasioned on his brief revisitings, Mrs Gentle never again ran out into the street. On the whole the humiliation of sharing her plight with her neighbours was worse than bearing it alone, and she kept herself to herself after that.

On Janice's seventh birthday Mr Gentle made his last appearance. He left the house with pieces of birthday cake embedded in his hair and cuts to his face from the broken window through which he had thrown it. His departure was rapidly followed by an hysterical line of seven-year-olds who had witnessed whatever it was that had happened. Janice stood on a chair at the front-room window watching them go. Then she helped her mother pick up the broken china and apply Elastoplasts, and took her teddy to bed, along with a large chunk of the iced cake, from which she picked clean the garden detritus before chewing her way slowly through it. They did not entertain again after that. Although the years rolled by with no more visits by Mr Gentle, the safest way forward seemed to be to stay self-contained and to live orderly, quiet lives. And they remained in that house, in that street, since that was what you did.

When Janice Gentle began growing hair and curves and found herself crying a great deal for no reason in particular, Mrs Gentle told her to watch out. 'You keep away from men, my girl,' she said, shaking her moppet to give emphasis, and she pointed at her splayed nose. 'Look at what I got. Never trust any of them and if you do, well . . .' – she shook her head this time instead of the mop – 'just make sure you get your fist in first.'

So Janice, being an obedient sort of a girl, obeyed and steered clear of the opposite sex. She became academic, a bit of a blue stocking, tipped by her teachers for great heights, Cambridge, should she choose, for the world in which she immersed herself was the world of six, seven, eight hundred years ago. The change from a land to a money economy, the demise of the feudal system, the growth of town and city, increasing secularization, the birth of a middle class . . . She read all she could of the medieval romances. She loved the prose and the poetry and the clear ideas expressed of right and wrong. Guillaume de Lorris's *Roman de la Rose*, Piers the Ploughman's search for the ultimate truth in Langland's everyday setting, Abelard and Héloïse, Dante and Beatrice, Christine de Pisan who wrote with such beguiling simplicity and yet was mistress of the art of the court as well as mistress of her own life by virtue of her pen. *L'amour courtois*, from its roots in Provence to its spread throughout Europe, fascinated and delighted Janice both for the lyricism it inspired and for its ideals: love should be a thing freely sought and freely given; marriage is no excuse for not loving. Chivalric love, the highest achievement. This was the core of it. And out of this was spawned a great literature and art, a philosophy with rules and theories in which no woman was demeaned nor lover spurned if he obeyed them. Only through love, said the poetry of the troubadours, can man become virtuous or noble, and indeed – as Janice delighted to discover – even the very principles of Provençal grammar and metre were based upon the noble laws of love.

Courtly Love, the perfect ideal, the golden age of chivalry with its civilizing effect upon manners, became for Janice Gentle the golden age of history. *Vous ou Mort* was, she felt, the correct, and only, undertaking for love.

She refuted Castiglione for his latter-day belief that in *The Courtier* he had encapsulated it all. 'Castiglione was a hundred and fifty years too late,' she wrote in an essay, 'and his own weaknesses barred him from understanding the purity of what had gone before him. He, like the Elizabethans, took Courtly Love and bastardized it, killing the parent Provençal and burying it under a mawkish effluvium of sentiment, conceit, artifice and plagiarism. As the Pre-Raphaelite Brotherhood was inspired by Giotto and went on to make bad, naïve paintings despite the greatness of their inspiration, so did Castiglione become inspired by *l'amour courtois* and go on to write an intolerable pastiche. In the next pages I intend to illustrate this with evidence drawn from early source material – from the courts of Blois, Flanders, Brittany, Burgundy, England, and from the writings that abounded among the troubadours and the trouvères of France, the minnesingers of Germany and the *dolce stil novo* of Italy . . .'

It was this essay which won her the scholarship to Cambridge. With little encouragement from her mother and even less from herself, Janice declined to go. One thing to sit in a very small sixth-form class of girls and discuss Petrarch; quite another to be away from home, in a strange city, with new faces belonging to both sexes, and not fear giving public voice to her views on the *Judgements* of Marie de Champagne. Janice Gentle abandoned the idea. In any case, she told herself, her mother was getting old and frail and ailing, and Janice was required to stay with her. Mother and daughter colluded and Janice stayed, very firmly, at home: Janice to continue her studies by post and to attend the occasional lecture on her favourite subject, Mrs Gentle to sew and settle herself into the role of fragile parent. Janice stepped up her intake of food and rounded out considerably, finding, as in the past, that it was cheering to munch away the hours. They had a small income from Mrs Gentle's deceased maiden sister, and the house was theirs. With caution and low expenditure they existed very well, caution and low expenditure being the major legacy left to them in their experience of Mr Gentle, disappeared.

For Janice's twenty-first birthday Mrs Gentle made a special effort and produced a birthday cake. The first since, well, she could hardly remember. Could Janice? Janice could, just as she knew her mother could, but she forbore to say so. Instead she opened the parcel her mother handed to her, out of which tumbled a coat of myriad colours, product of many hours' boudoir struggle by Mrs Gentle: a ravishing item made up of long-squirrelled-away remnants and the cut-up remains of what had once, in the good days, been Mrs Gentle's not unstylish wardrobe.

Janice was astonished at its colourful variation and brightness. It made her think of Chaucer's Madame Eglentyne in her pretty cloak and her coral and green gauds. Generally clothes were not something which interested her, she being somewhat well-covered for mini-skirts. This, however, was a delight; it flared around her plumpness without feeling restrictive, and she slipped it on the very next night when she went out to her Literary Society. It uplifted her spirits. There was something jewel-like about it, something that made her feel she glowed like a detail from an illuminated manuscript, something altogether fitting to her ways. It continued to uplift her as she left the Adult Education Building to catch her bus home. It was a rainy February night, bleak and cold, dismal and forlorn, but Janice did not feel any of these things. As she mused over Thomas Campion (1567–1620) and his absurd notions of Astrophel and Stella and Sir Philip Sidney's even more conceited tribute to the starstruck pair (making a pun with his own name, of course – *very* Elizabethan to riddle-me-ree rather than delight in the distancing of self and controlling the form), she looked pink-cheeked and happy. There was something altogether delightful about being snuggled into this soft, bright stylishness. She looked quite radiant, like a beautiful feminine ball in her contentment. Such is the power of clothes.

Dermot Poll coming out of the Bell and Bugle public house stepped swaying into the drizzle and shivered. A young Irishman with a pale (despite the Guinness consumed), appealing face and damp black curls, he embraced the night in sentimental mood. His wife, somewhere behind those low lit windows of the hospital opposite, had just been brought to bed with his first son, and

Dermot Poll was prepared to be in Love with the World. Everyone in the Bell and Bugle had loved him and he had assuredly loved them. Now it was the turn of the rest of humanity to experience his emotional beneficence. It being rather a bad night, however, the rest of humanity seemed to have stayed indoors. Only one human figure graced the darkness. Janice. And when he saw her, head bowed against the rain, body glowing radiantly against the shadows of the street – Madonna, Life-Bearing Womanhood – he felt a rising desire to worship.

Janice, still mulling over Thomas Campion and whether his apologia for classical metre was a useful piece of information or not, was concentrating. As she tried to recall some lines of his *Astrophel*, and not muddle them with Sir Philip Sidney's, she was wholly absorbed and did not notice the approach of the rapt young Dermot. Concentrating was an attractive facial arrangement for Janice in those days. Her large, pale eyes, unseeing, had a misty quality, and the line of her mouth was puckered in a rather delightful way. In a low voice she attempted to recall the verse exactly.

> 'Hark, all you ladies that do sleep;
> The fairy queen Proserpina
> Bids you awake and pity them that weep.'

Janice paused, unsure of the next line. Dermot paused, entranced. What better for a son of Erin, with a belly full of beer and his potency so recently made flesh, than to hear beautiful words in the night?

Janice recollected what she had forgotten, and continued.

> 'You may do in the dark
> What the day doth forbid;
> Fear not dogs that bark,
> Night will have all hid.'

Dermot remained entranced. 'Night will have all hid . . .'

But not from Dermot Poll. He saw and he was conquered. Oh how he needed to worship. To worship was a requirement that was becoming acute. Woman. Birth-giver, God's unsullied creation. He fell to his knees before Janice and lifted up his shining, pretty face so that the light from a shop front near by illuminated him.

'Oh Queen of the Night,' he said, 'you are colour and you are magic. I have come to worship you and you have captured my heart.'

The emotion spilled out of him. A Father. A Man. And here was Woman. Woman who looked undeniably pregnant, full with seed, the highest state of feminine being.

'My heart,' he said, 'is yours, Fair Lady.' And he offered himself in the purest sense.

Janice took this very well. She did not run away nor scream, for threat was not in the air in those days. A stranger bending his knee to her on a wet pavement was, however, unusual, so she looked down at him and gave a hesitant half-smile, revealing a pair of pretty dimples.

'Ah, Mother of God, the Night Queen has dimples,' said Dermot to the empty street.

'Perhaps you should get up,' said Janice, 'for your knees must be quite wet.'

But Dermot, as much feeling the gravitational pull of the Guinness as the overwhelming thrill of the moment, stayed where he was. Janice continued to be unafraid, so she smiled at him again. Smiles from girls to sober men are pleasing. Smiles from girls to inebriate men are bewitching. Dermot Poll was duly bewitched and said so.

Janice blinked, astonished. Modern men were philanderers and brutes, were they not? Yet this one knelt before her like some knight of old.

Courtly Love, she thought, and she whispered aloud, 'Love unto Death.'

'Is that more of your poetry, O Lady of Colours?'

'What?' said Janice, who had already gone back in time to see it emblazoned upon a courtier's shield.

'More . . . of your poetry?'

Janice, obedient, heard this as a request.

'Well,' she said, 'it is not the sort of poetry I really care for you to see, but of its kind it has a certain ring.'

Dermot nodded encouragingly. What did it matter what the vision said, so long as she stayed here in the dark and the cold with him? It was infinitely more joyful than being alone.

So Janice continued with Campion, realizing that this sort of thing was some people's preference.

'"This night by moonshine leading merry rounds/Holds a –"'

'Moonshine!' Dermot Poll felt indignant. 'This is not moonshine . . .' And indeed, he felt quite convinced it was not. He took her hand, in its woolly glove, and kissed it chastely. On the whole he was enjoying himself and was now firmly entrenched in the undemanding role of lyrical enslavement.

Janice blinked again. Something stirred within her. A little urge to reach out and touch his face with her other woolly glove, an urge she resisted. Very possibly he might bite after all. Courtly Love, she found herself saying, first made its appearance in twelfth-century poetry, term probably originated in Islamic culture, original European tenets set down by Guillaume de Lorris before 1240, but . . .

Vous ou Mort . . .

Vous ou Mort . . .

It just kept getting in the way.

Dermot Poll looked about him for inspiration. He wanted to go further, he wanted to see signs, give symbols, but he had nothing. And then, like a miracle, he saw. He rose from his knees, clasped the hand he had so recently kissed, and led its owner, as if she floated, towards the lighted shop window near by.

'See,' he said, gesturing towards an enormous satin heart that rested in the window. 'A sign . . .'

She looked cautiously from Dermot to window and back again. She looked unconvinced. It was therefore Dermot Poll's absolute requirement to convince her.

'You are my heart's delight,' he began to sing, placing his free hand McCormack-like on that area of his anatomy.

Janice's eyes widened even further, though whether at the sentiments expressed or at the manner of their expression he could not tell. So he stopped singing and spoke to try it both ways.

'You are my heart's delight,' he said, 'because you are colour. You are radiance. You glow like an exotic flower and I wish to worship you.'

Janice's heart bumped again.

'A picture made of jewels,' he continued, quite caught up in the joy of it all.

Book of Days, thought Janice excitedly, *Les Très Riches Heures* . . .

'In your lovely coat, your magical, magnificent, momentous coat, you are blessed with the beauty of a rainbow. Ah, I could sing to you all night . . .'

Janice stared, no longer able to hear above the rushing in her ears the pumping in her body.

Dermot Poll, exhausted both by metaphor and by passion, loved the world and all creatures in it. 'I love you,' he said, making a grand, all-encompassing gesture. 'And I worship your womanhood . . .'

Christine de Pisan, in her fourteenth-century study somewhere in the ether, said, 'Do not listen.'

Thomas Campion and the Court of Gloriana said, 'Hark.'

It was scarcely a contest. Gloriana was yards in front.

This, then, was what she had been avoiding for so long. This, then, was true and real and beautiful. She stroked her coat. How wrong her mother had been. How unlike Mr Gentle this beautiful, poetical young man was . . .

Dermot watched entranced as her hand slid over the swelling of her belly.

She looked at him, saw the enchantment in his eyes, and saw that this, her gallant, spoke a truth so strong that it trembled. Indeed, she noticed, from time to time his voice became quite indistinct with the burr of emotion. How could she *not* believe? How could she *not* let him worship her and love her if he wished?

Poor Janice. Fatal trust. *Vous ou Mort*. She offered herself up.

'Tell me who you are,' she said. Her eyes never left his beautiful, shining face as she spoke. This was love, she was convinced of it. It was beautiful and real.

'My name is Dermot Poll,' he said. 'I come from Skibbereen.' His eyes grew moist. 'And one day, when I have travelled the world, I shall go back there. But meanwhile, O lovely creature, this' – he looked at the lettering in the shop window, he smiled at her, a warm smile, a blind smile, a smile that belonged to the absent Deirdre – 'is St Valentine's Eve.'

'Yes,' she breathed, skirting the voice in her head, which was her own, her former, now deceased, academic persona, which said, 'Valentine, martyr, date unknown, legend lends no credence to connection with lovers . . .' Instead she smiled and exhaled a sigh with the involuntary huskiness that befitted such romance.

'Tomorrow, then, is St Valentine's Day . . .' he breathed.

Janice disregarded the faint, last whisperings of her blue-stocking ways, which pointed out to her that this was tautological since he had already said, had he not, that this was St Valentine's Eve?

Dermot Poll remembered that he could sing. Through the mists of this impassioned sensibility he recalled that it was by singing he earned his living. The Irish Balladeer, beloved at over-sixties clubs everywhere, the popular high spot at many a silver wedding, doyen of a dozen Irish clubs up and down the Kilburn High Road and beyond . . .

He burst forth, his lungs leaping readily to the task. 'I'll walk beside you through the passing years . . .' he warbled into the damp dark night and Janice Gentle's ear.

Janice Gentle continued to believe. If anything, her believing deepened. Dermot Poll was now singing for all the women in the world. Janice listened, entranced. When he had ceased, she whispered, 'Do you really think you love me?'

Deirdre had said that on the night of their first physical union, nine months since and four months before they were wed. It was an emotional remembrance. He said the same now as he had said then.

26

'Love you?' he said with passion. 'Love you? I will love you for ever. I will never leave you. And if ever we are torn apart, I shall come looking for you, or you for me. Though I go to Australia, America, China even, I will find you again or you will find me. Now kiss me, darling . . .' Janice had become Deirdre. Dermot was beginning to be very muddled.

Janice, cautious, desiring, restrained and obedient, leaned towards him and planted a kiss upon his pale, damp cheek. It felt strangely alluring, exotic, tight, cool and with the slightest rasping from the stubble lightly sprouting there. It was essence of man-liness after Mrs Gentle's slack and sweet-smelling pinkness.

'I think perhaps I love you, too,' she said, astonished. 'You will come to see me tomorrow? You really will?'

'But of course. And then I travel the world.' He burst into song again. 'Each and every by-way . . . and did it my way . . .' Dermot was looking up at the sky as he spoke. He was lost in the dark clouds, a traveller.

'I shall wait for you tomorrow after dark,' said Janice eagerly. He reached out his hand and, still looking up at the veiled sky, ran his fingers over her contours, lightly and not concernedly touching her round shoulders, her plump breast, her generous belly. 'I love this shape,' he whispered to the firmament. 'This shape, round and full, is the essence of Woman.'

Janice blinked slightly as the hand slid gently over her bosom, but finding it was all right and nothing else was expected of her (thus finally disproving Mrs Gentle's maxims on men), she relaxed. She saw them travelling the world together, a troubadour and his Lady. Arterberry Road and its unpleasant associations put down at last.

Dermot Poll swayed a little. She, too, felt like swaying, swoon-ing perhaps, in the joy of it all. Chance encounter: Dante on the bridge seeing Beatrice, Abelard coming to lodge in Héloïse's house, Dermot finding Janice on a bleak February night in south London.

'I will wait for you,' she said with conviction. 'If necessary, I will wait for you for ever.'

27

'Ah,' he replied, and clutched at her arm for support. 'I will come to you tomorrow when the mists of morning have yielded up the moon.'

'Thirty-two Arterberry Road,' she said. 'Opposite the pillar-box.' He repeated it dreamily. 'Valentine red heart . . .'

To be absolutely sure, she wrote it down for him on the back of a sheet of paper torn carelessly from her notebook, which thus destroyed two hours' work on whether or not the grasping Lady Fee of Langland's *Piers* was really a representation of Edward III's mistress, Alice Perrers. Now she abandoned what had once been so totally absorbing for this new wonder in her life.

She who had never been kissed and who had never sought it began to hope that he would kiss her, began to hope it very much indeed. And before her bus came along, too. But he did not, and in a way she was content with this, for whatever all that side of things was, it had no place here (as indeed it had no place for the ladies of *l'amour courtois*) and might or might not come later if Destiny allowed.

His last words to her were 'Farewell, O brightener of the starless sky', and her last sight of him was from the top of a 77A double-decker. A young man leaning up against a lighted shop window that held red sticky paper hearts in abundance. She waved and watched him, starry-eyed, until the bus turned a corner. What she did *not* see was how he very slowly and rather elegantly slid down the length of the window and crumpled peacefully into a sleeping position just as the tail-lights of the vehicle disappeared. Nor did she know that the piece of paper which flapped through the gutter and kept up with the ponderous pace of the bus for a time, held cogent arguments both for and against its being Alice Perrers, on one side of it, and her own, now illegible address, on the other.

How could she know any of that?

Any more than she could be aware that the memory of this great moment in her life remained the merest dim flicker to the young man asleep on the pavement – for what is the registering of memory to the experience of a policeman's toe-cap prodding him in the rear? Besides, he was a romantic, not a fool. And when a man has fathered his first son, he would do well, as Dermot Poll intended, to recognize his priorities. All the same, such fleeting images and words that did remain before he tucked them away were pleasing. He felt, by the memory of her response, by the trace of an image of her smile and the light in her eyes as he had kissed her hand and touched her fulsome body, that he had *made that girl's day*. He felt proud of himself. To have done that and to have fathered a son as well. Ah! Is this not happiness?

Janice waited all day with her hair in curlers. She hummed and she sang and she was strangely cheery with her mother.

'Spring, spring, spring,' she sang, for although it was dreary February she felt very much that spring was in the air. Every activity that had once been so mundane was now filled with significance. She dressed herself after teatime in her brightest colours – fiery oranges with rich brown whirls that streaked through them like chocolate. She removed her curlers, set up her station on a chair by her bedroom window (at the front of the house since Mrs Gentle preferred the silence at the back) and sucked her knuckles in anticipation. She tried to read, first *The Paston Letters* and then – as she thought more fittingly – Christine de Pisan's *Oeuvres poétiques*, but these soon fell by the way. It was no longer her books she sought, it was Dermot Poll, for there, she was sure, lay her future.

Midnight and beyond. Every step in the street, every movement of a tree or distant sound of a bicycle or car, every motion of a shadow made her start and believe it was he. Lurch, bump went her heart, which had not calmed down once since her encounter at the bus stop yesterday eve. But gradually, gradually, throughout the long vigil, she began to fear the unthinkable, pushing the unthinkable away each time it surfaced, time and again bringing the memory of his words to bear over the rising anguish that he was never, really, going to come. Not until the morning darkness lifted and real life moved beneath her window again, did she yield herself up to the misery of knowing that the rising anguish had won. Dermot Poll was never going to arrive. She had got it all wrong, been confused, should be somewhere else, waiting for him in another place altogether. Australia, America, China had taken him. They had met too late. He had lost her address, he had broken his leg, he had . . . he had . . . Rattle, rattle went such thoughts. Even now he was roaming the streets searching. She ran out into the dawn – out along Worple Road, up towards the Ridgway, flying tears and hair streaming down Christchurch Hill.

Everywhere she could feel his presence, nowhere could she find him. She waved her arms from the gates of Holland Gardens, looking into the yellow distance of the creeping dawn. She walked home, vowing on the way that she would find him one day, wherever he was. At Raynes Park Station she found a sixpence and put it in the chocolate machine. That helped, that soothed, and with it she fed the shape that he loved. She sucked on it, savouring it, for the short walk home. Then she put away her orange and brown finery, dressed herself in an old beige sweater dress, and lay with her aching heart on the top of her virgin's bed.

'I shall never wear colours again,' she said to herself. 'Not until I see Dermot Poll.' And she fell asleep to dream of palfreys and pilgrim lovers and herself and Dermot Poll on a ribbon road in moonlight, horse to horse, hand in hand.

'Dermot who?' asked her mother in the morning.

Janice told her.

Mrs Gentle raised her eyes to heaven above her battered nose. 'Irish!' she said. 'As well as being a man. Can't trust either.' She looked at her daughter. 'I warned you, I warned you, didn't I?'

Janice turned over and slept again. When she woke she drank tea and ate toast with melted cheese and butter on top. 'So this is love,' she said to herself, through the crisp and oily mouthfuls, and she thought that for the first time she really *understood* courtly lovers of old, who were willing to die for their joy.

After Mrs Gentle's death it might have been correct to put on the certificate, 'Primary cause: meticulous daughterly attention. Secondary cause: heart failure.'

Certainly by the time the Grim Reaper called, Janice's mother was probably more than ready to go. For years she had watched her daughter become gross and pale, as unhealthy-looking as a slug in hibernation. The peaceful closeting of their life together had given way to an uneasy proximity of necessity, and was dull. Very dull indeed. Television, what to eat, radio, library books and bed being the order of things, although in summer Mrs Gentle did a little pottering in the postage-stamp garden. But it was not enough to sustain life. Mrs Gentle, though unsure of what was to follow, appeared to breathe her last with a sigh of profound relief. What she was going to could certainly not be any worse than what she was coming from, and listening out for the rustle of a biscuit packet from the kitchen or the chink of spoon on bowl from Janice's late-night bedroom was something she would be more than happy to shed. Her last words to her daughter were 'Brighten up a bit, Janice – there's a dear. And for goodness' sake find yourself something to take your mind off things.'

By 'things' Mrs Gentle meant food. But Janice took the suggestion at its word. She had better get something to occupy her now that Mother was gone. But what?

It took her three months of solid writing and by the time she had finished she felt she had been wrung dry. There were she and Dermot Poll, reunited – recriminations, vindications, vengeances all accounted for and dealt with, the clear, pure light of being ahead of them. Companionate, harmonious, his journeyings done, coming to rest with her in a love that would last until Death divided them.

Ah, she thought, when it was finished, if only it were really and truly like that, how happy I should be. She never lost hope that one day either he would return to find her, or she, travelling life's highways, would find him.

She put the manuscript to the back of a drawer, where it might have remained had not the maiden aunt's annuity dried up, a factor not at first noticed by Janice's bank, which went on paying bills and cash for some time before the mistake was recognized. The bank manager was particularly annoyed about this, since he was about to retire and wished to get all the ends tied up properly. Janice Gentle was the only black mark on his copybook. After he met her he was not surprised. Decidedly overweight, he thought, and possibly retarded. She sat there, heavy as a sack of potatoes, putty-faced and expressionless. He persevered. He did not seem to be making much headway. He had explained that she was in debt. He had explained that she needed to earn some money. He had not explained the bank's culpability, because it was not appropriate. Nevertheless, he wished to get the difficulty dealt with to save any ... er ... further investigation by his successor. Miss Gentle did not seem to recognize the urgency of the problem, and he had made little progress in the matter of a job.

'Well,' he said with an exasperated raising of his hands, 'what *do* you do?'

Janice was feeling very confused. Men in suits with demanding voices were not her usual experience. She was watching his gold signet ring, which he twirled as he spoke, and she had become mesmerized by the motion, forgetting to listen. She looked at him dumbly. Did he mean what had she been doing in the last five minutes? Or the last five years? Or what? Perhaps he meant her daily routine? Perhaps this was social chit-chat, ice-breaking? She decided it was conversational and went for her daily routine.

He stopped her when she got to the bit about washing her hair on Thursdays. 'I do not mean activities of a personal nature,' he said testily. 'I mean how have you occupied yourself since your mother' – he was too irritated to euphemize – 'died?'

'Oh,' said Janice, glad to have something positive to say. 'I have written a book.'

'What sort of book?' He was sceptical. Could one so fat and dull really have achieved such a thing?

'Um,' said Janice, 'a story.'

'I see. Good, good. Well, well. Now, then.' He picked up his pen, unscrewed the cap and prepared to write. 'And how much have you been paid?'

'For what?'

'The book?' His pen was fairly itching to begin.

'Nothing,' said Janice. 'It's in a drawer at home.'

The pen nib splayed. 'Well, it's no good there, is it?'

The upshot of this meeting was that Janice should go away and consider her position – both with regard to the immediate and pressing concerns of her debt to the bank, and with regard to the future concerns of making a living. Janice should then return the following week with some clear ideas. Frankly, he thought, after she had gone, the likelihood of her doing any of those things was remote. The issue preyed on his mind. Only three more months to go and bright and bouncing Barnfather would be sitting in his chair, and he didn't want bright and bouncing Barnfather dining out on this. It was extremely irritating and took far too high a profile, as he kept telling himself, but if he wanted to hold his head erect in the golf club he needed to find a solution.

A day or two later, enthroned in the *en suite*, and having become bored with rereading the Harpic bottle, which celebrated the fact that his wife's preferred toilet cleaner contained sodium hypochloride and should not be allowed to enter the eyes (and who, he wanted to know, would want to put it anywhere near their eyes but a mental defective?), he brought Janice Gentle back to mind. He reached for one of the magazines his wife kept to while away the evacuatory hours, and flicked through it. A competition caught his attention and, with the juxtaposition of Janice Gentle and the page, a possible, if remote, solution raised itself. The competition was for a 'first novel by a yet unpublished woman writer'. Well, Janice Gentle was certainly that. Why not? It was a chance. He tore out the page, took it to his office, got his secretary to ring her – he being weary of any further encounters – and request delivery of the manuscript. Janice, not much inclined to relinquish it, was reminded that she had a responsibility to do so, and did. The secretary scooped it from her unwilling hands and passed it on to the bank manager, the bank manager passed it on to his wife, and she, in turn, passed it on to her daily. Both women thought it was wonderful. The bank manager's wife liked the lack of smut, the daily liked the romance of it, and the bank manager, who did not read it, sent it off to the magazine.

It did not win. It did not even qualify.

The magazine immediately put it on the reject pile because it was handwritten; the rules specifically stated it should be typed. And, lest detractors bemoan this as a cavalier approach to literature, they should first be made to sit in a silent room attempting to interpret spider scrawl and backward slopes day after day after day. Despite Janice's manuscript being reasonably legible, on the reject pile it remained. And would have done so for ever were it not for the bounty of England's temperate clime.

The judge of the competition, her task completed, rang for a taxi after her final meeting with the magazine's editor. The winner had been chosen and a lady from Bournemouth was about to be honoured for her nineteenth-century tale of a shepherdess made good.

It was raining.

The judge, in years to come, had reason to bless this English phenomenon. While she waited for the taxi, she grew fidgety and began sifting through all the failed manuscripts – rejects, non-qualifiers, plagiarists. She picked out one at random, then another, then a third. She expected to laugh or at least to smile deprecatingly. It was something to do and a literary agent, for such was the calling of the judge, is never more at home than with a manuscript in her hand and half an hour to kill.

In Bangkok the trishaw drivers positively thrive, burgeoning like desert blooms, during the heaviest showers. In Madrid, given a cloudburst, you can scarcely move for taxis. In Venice, for some quaint reason, even the water taxis are not averse to helping a stranded pedestrian when a flood descends on San Marco. Interesting, then, that in London this particular mode of transport seems to shrink and wither when the finest drizzle appears. 'Not for ages, love,' said the taxi company to the judge when one of their number was requested – and ages meant ages. Sylvia Perth, for she it was, settled back to wait, with nothing but a whole pile of rejected first novels for entertainment.

The rain continued and, true to their word, the taxis of London did not come. But Sylvia Perth no longer cared. She was reading, suddenly, with that rapt avidity that Muhammad the Wolf might have experienced when first he lighted upon the Dead Sea Scrolls (had he not been illiterate).

And when, eventually, the snub, black-nosed creature did condescend to appear, its driver was much discomfited to be met not by a hair-tearing wreck, but by a freshly lipsticked, uncritical female, who, contrary to his expectations, was not at all put out that he had taken so long to arrive. She even tipped him to excess when he finally set her down on the pavement outside thirty-two Arterberry Road, so that he was forced to say with civility, 'Would you like me to wait, lady?' And to receive the gracious, smiling reply, 'No thanks. For I may be some time . . .'

Chapter Four

JANICE Gentle makes her way back to Battersea, feeling relieved and positive. Relieved because her characters are delineated, positive because she always does feel positive about going home. There is another reason for these twin emotions. She can now telephone Sylvia Perth, who has been waiting in heavy silence, and say that the deed is done, the book is afoot, decisions have been made. Today she will invite her over for tea, she decides, and tell her. Another little ritual. Sylvia Perth awaits the summons to Janice's tea-table as a relative to the reading of a will, outwardly tranquil, inwardly afire with impatience. All Janice knows is that the announcement is long overdue and that Sylvia Perth has shown a touch more agitation than usual during the six months or more that she has been waiting for teatime to be announced. Well, teatime is here at last.

On taking the timely decision, some of Janice's positivism dies. She has nothing in. Which means she will have to buy something in. Which means the tribulation of the corner shop. She sighs. She really is *not* good with people. In fact, she is very bad with people. She recalls its proprietor and shudders. Sometimes she thinks she will brain him with his own bubble-gum machine, and quite a lot of the positivism dies in her as she approaches the door. She takes a deep breath, enters, and at the same time decides that she will not, she is determined, be enticed into conversation. Whatever he says to her, she will remain mute apart from giving her order. 'Two packets of chocolate digestives, one cut loaf, a pot of raspberry jam, four scones and a half a pint of thick cream.' That is all she will say. She will repeat it if called upon to do so but she will say no more than that.

Alas, on entering, she stumbles.

'Enjoy the trip,' he calls.

She clamps her mouth shut. The bubble-gum machine stands innocently beside her. It would only take a minute . . .

'Nasty out again,' he says.

She gives him her order.

'Ah,' he says, 'sweets for the sweet.'

She stares at him.

'Raspberry, did you say?'

'Raspberry,' she repeats.

'Hot one minute and wet the next.' He shrugs. 'July? Never like this years ago. Greenhouse.'

Janice places jam, biscuits, loaf and cream in her bag and waits for the scones, silently.

'Six?'

'Six,' she repeats. She is not going to make the mistake of saying he is wrong. And what, really, is a couple more scones here or there?

'I thought you said four.'

'Six, please.'

She runs a plump hand over the bowl of the machine, looking at the fading wrappers of its contents.

'Brown or white?'

'White scones,' she says.

'I prefer 'em myself. All this brown stuff tastes like rope, eh?'

'Yes,' says Janice. 'It does.'

And then she shuts her mouth with a snap, but it is too late. She has begun to converse and he takes it up keenly.

'Course, I remember when they used to put little wooden pips in the jam to make it *seem* like raspberries.'

'Really?' she says, and sighs.

'That's how the Co-op came into being, you know.' He rests his hands on the counter in waxsome mood. 'To improve the standards of food. Of course, nowadays . . .' He is off.

Janice awaits patiently, putting her mind to more engaging things. She remembers, more cheerfully, that she has chosen her triumvirate of characters. She is here to buy tea for the ritual of beginning, and she wonders, as the history of modern social retailing unfolds before her, where her triumvirate will take her, and where she, in turn, will take them.

*

In the office of her Boss Masculine the secretary with blonde hair, pink lips and a daintily turned ankle stands. The man has dandruff on his dark lapel and two warts on his left hand. His face is tired. She hands him a cup of coffee and wishes he were like the boss in her magazine story, the one called Hugo. Hugo would look up abstractedly with his darkset eyes, and momentarily his guard would slip and she would see the real man behind the tough façade. Something would have begun between them, but she would not, yet, know what. But the Boss Masculine does not look up and behind him there is no mirror to reveal – perhaps – a broadset body with powerful shoulders, only a sales chart awash with blue pin flags. She takes a sheaf of papers from the side of his desk and departs. Only her scent remains in the room, vying with the stale tobacco smells. He lights his third tipped cigarette that morning and puts through a call to Birmingham. His wife is to have an hysterectomy next week and the unspoken hope between them both is that their long-dead sex life will be revived. Perhaps it will be a medical miracle, though he has little hope of this. The hospital has given him a book on how to cope with a woman whose womb has just been removed, and it has depressed him. Convalescence can, it seems, take months and requires patience and gentleness. He seems to have run out of both commodities over the years. He sighs as Birmingham comes through, picks up the telephone and lifts off into his dynamic businessman role. It is the one he is best at, the last saving grace of his life. He has failed pretty badly in the marital one.

The Little Blonde Secretary beyond his door also sighs. In her magazine it discusses the all-engulfing multiple orgasm as a Woman's Right, which makes her feel anxious about herself. An

38

unusual experience. There is also another article, as yet unread, on how to avoid the trap of boredom in your marriage: 'Yes, it can happen even after six months.' This makes her doubly anxious and doubly convinced that it is best left unread. She fingers the cover of her Janice Gentle, which also sits in her drawer. Here there is no such thing as a physical description of the all-engulfing multiple orgasm. Only at the end of the book, when the right couple are united, when good has won over bad (which will reliably happen, though with many a twist and turn on the way), only then will it begin to express itself. The Little Blonde Secretary has her own concept of what it is like, this desirable state of paradise: it is like the sea breaking wave upon wave as a sun-tanned male face with even, white teeth and an expression of tenderness places his warm, moist lips upon her own. Then there will be three dots on the page which represent the fulfilment of the dream. The unfamiliarity of this experience is somewhat explained to the sighing secretary because Derek goes pink in the sun and has slightly buck teeth. When he kisses her, there are no dots at the end of the line to express what comes next. His hand reaches straight up her nightshirt and between her legs, and it is no use calling, 'Dot, dot, dot . . .' for he never reads, anyway. He is too busy mending the window sashes or cleaning out the gutters to pick up a book. Mind you, she thinks tidily, at least they get it over with quite quickly nowadays.

She removes the anxiety from her own little shoulders and places it firmly upon Derek's. Which feels much better. It is his fault. She then turns her attention to the magazine menus. Steak au poivre and pavlova, fish kebabs and mango ice-cream. Too exotic to contemplate. She closes the magazine, remembering that she is defrosting the cod steaks, and wonders if there is any cheese left to make a sauce. Derek won't mind. He's not fussy about his food. The man in the magazine photograph above the recipe is looking up with a loving smile of appreciation at the woman who is lighting the candles. She wonders if they have a smoke alarm. In their house Derek has fitted two. He points them out to people. It is proof that he cares.

She sighs and closes the magazine. Now the house is finished, they can start entertaining properly. At least, they thought it was finished, but this morning, looking around the bathroom while he was scrubbing those prominent teeth of his (she made sure that he gave them a thorough going-over, morning and night, so that at least when they came popping through his damp lips they were shiny bright), she had to admit to herself that the lilac walls had been a bit of a mistake. Perhaps a fresh coat of paint would be sensible. But nothing more than that. She is getting to the end of her tether with all their improvements. So noisy, so messy – she is *forever* wiping down the surfaces.

She decides to keep the recipe page for the time when the house is completely ready for entertaining (how she looks forward to showing it off when it is all absolutely perfect) and to read the article on orgasms quietly at home before Derek arrives. Maybe it will solve the problem, once and for all, of whether she has had one or not. She knows she ought to have had one because she is young, pretty and married . . . Correct in every detail . . . Very probably she has.

The Boss Masculine calls her in for dictation. She shuts the magazine away in her drawer and goes in, wondering as she seats herself opposite him why on earth his wife doesn't buy him Head & Shoulders like she buys Derek. She cannot, really, feel entirely sympathetic for his wife. The Little Blonde Secretary Bird feels that, in some way, the hysterectomy must be her fault. If a woman cannot look after her husband's dandruff, then she probably cannot look after her womb properly, either. She could just about tolerate the warts, but the *dandruff* . . .

Derek is on the telephone ordering a new bathroom suite. He will surprise his wife of six months by redoing the entire thing single-handed. It will keep him occupied and save them hundreds of pounds. He will put the money towards a loft extension too. There is mounting excitement as he states the catalogue numbers to the plumbers' merchants. The taps will be the crowning achievement. Won't she love *those*? French with ceramic handles.

Really nice. She likes nice things. He puts down the phone and rubs his hands. He just can't *wait* to get started.

*

Square Jaw is only marginally recovered from the repugnant sight of a staring fat woman untidily eating a ham sandwich on the tube. He was already feeling grim and angry, having yet again left his girlfriend in tears, propped up in bed and snuffling into the duvet cover. 'Sorry, sorry, sorry,' he said without actually meaning it. 'For Chrissake,' he had wanted to shout (but didn't), 'what's a bunch of flowers, anyway?' They'd been more or less living together for two years. Surely there came a time when such trifles were unimportant? And there she sat, making him feel guilty again with her indisputable argument, primly delivered as usual, about it being important to her and therefore important in its own right. Well, what about all the things he *did* do? ('Like what?' she said, the bitch, and he couldn't think of *one* at that moment.) Did she want him to be like Pavlov's dogs? See Melanie, think giftwrap? When he bought her things, he liked to do it spontaneously. It wasn't his fault that the spontaneity was rare – she'd wiped a lot of it out by being too demanding – but it was real when it came.

He walks very fast in the drizzle, his legs swiping viciously at the air, his shoes banging into the pavement angrily. One of his feet, which should have made contact with hard stone, plunges into a dip full of water. He is merely splashed, but a female leg is drenched. He looks up. A pretty girl, and pretty angry, under an umbrella. He apologizes, she glowers.

'I should bloody well think so,' she says.

Hmm. Very pretty. He smiles. 'Won't happen again.'

She smiles, too. Girlish. Knowing. Establishing her sex. And then she moves off.

He is cheered. He is fed up with Melanie and her miseries. And there are plenty more fish in the sea. After all, he is not unattractive – that girl's smile said so. He thinks he might turn around and rush after her, thrusting flowers into her hands like they do in that silly advert that Melanie thinks is so sweet. Might well have done, had not, had not – he stops, and then continues on his way – had not, he thought, the memory of the girl's first outburst come back to him. There was something altogether Melanieësque about her. '*I should bloody well think so.*'

Ah, no. Stay safe with what you've got. At least the sex wasn't bad. And regular, got to give her that. He'd go over to Melanie's that night and offer to get a take-away. That was the sort of thing he did and never got praised for. *He* went out in the pouring rain to collect the stuff, *he* paid for it and quite often refused to let her go halves. Well, tonight that's what he would do, and pick up the bill for it. That'd show her he was making the effort. Bugger the flowers.

Square Jaw's Melanie has finally got out of bed, bathed and put on her make-up. She surveys the puffiness of her eyes unhappily. Then she cheers up. He *must* have seen how much she would love him to give her a token now and then, a little romantic something just to say he had been thinking of her – even a tiny bunch of violets would be so touching. Of course he would now, now that he had seen her unnecessary misery, added it to all the other times of unnecessary misery. Such a token would reverse it all. He must understand ... Anyway, she hops out of the bathroom feeling quite happy again. Anyway, the sex had been very good indeed last night. He couldn't forget that, could he? Good sex is a positive asset, a *definite* asset, but not – surely – something to take for granted? She gives sex ('Freely, freely,' she tells herself) in return for love, and he gives love in return for sex. Simple as that. Only she would like to *see* or *hold* some tangible evidence of it sometimes. That's all. Not much to ask, after all ...

By the time she is dressed, she is absolutely positive that it will be all right. She will ask him over to her place this evening and cook something really nice – not one of those dreary take-aways again. She hums as she pulls his duvet straight, hangs up his jacket that lies crumpled on the floor, rinses out the mugs and wipes the ring from the bath. She leaves with the door of the flat making a familiar click behind her. She runs down the stairs and out into the morning street feeling much happier. This time, she decides, *this* time, it is all going to be just *fine* . . .

*

The vicar's wife from Cockermouth is in London for a conference on rural poverty. The vicar was told by the bishop that somebody had to attend, and the vicar thought that Alice might like the change. She was a grand helpmate, unwavering of sacrifice, and he just could not go, could not be in two places at once, though he did not really like the idea of her going back to London alone. She had never revisited it after their marriage and had never suggested that she wanted to, though when they first met there, Alice had loved the place, told him so, said, 'I could never leave it; London is my home.'

He was still astonished that, apparently, their love had changed her impassioned need for the capital, though when she first made that statement they were still only acquaintances. He had fallen for her straight away, keeping the secret to himself, certain that one so dashing and vital would never return such feelings for him, a mere underling on the baby slopes of Synod. She had been so pretty, so bright, so alive. Was still so pretty, but the sparkle, the joy, seemed to have gone out of her, just died overnight back in the London days, long before he declared himself and brought her to Cockermouth. Growing up, she had called it, Alice Grows Up. And it was sad to see how her dazzling eyes had grown dull.

Perhaps she missed the high life? She never once said that she did. When they met, she was private secretary to a distinguished politician – travelling with him, entertaining for him, important. Cockermouth could hardly compete with that. Indeed, it was a source of some amazement to him that she had showed such alacrity, such eagerness, when he first nervously suggested they attend a concert together – she being so pretty with her red-gold hair and her merry blue eyes. He had thought himself far too dull compared with the exciting life she led within and without the House of Commons, but apparently he was not. And how proud he had been, despite his church's edicts on the subject of deadly sin number one, and humbled too, by her instant, almost *desperate*, attachment to him. Indeed, he had expected that a great deal of wooing would be required to win her, had consulted books on the subject stealthily at the library, but in the year of their courtship and the subsequent years of their marriage very little had been asked – in fact *nothing* had been asked – of him in that line at all. He rather wished it had. He rather liked that sort of thing, a little courtliness, a little gallantry, the tokens of love and desire.

Once she got quite upset when he brought her a small gift, a powder compact with her initials entwined; she said such things were unnecessary, that she had hardly expected it of him, that in future he really should not bother, for in the compass of their marriage such things meant very little, and she hoped she was above that kind of indulgence now. She did not need tokens, nor gifts that were useless. She did not contemplate using face-powder ever again.

Disappointed and confused, he said he thought the whole point *was* their being unnecessary, but he had complied – just bought slippers or secateurs or some such for Christmas and birthdays and turned away from the pleasing foolishness. He had chosen a good wife, he felt, and one who had thrown herself into the pastoral role quite as fully as he had. And if he sometimes wished that he could do something silly, like have champagne in bed with her or brush her glowing hair, he forbore. She had never denied him her body, their marriage was still real in that sense. Only sometimes, sometimes, he felt that in their lovemaking her body was all that she *did* yield to him, that there was another dimension, somewhere far away, denied . . .

He no longer sought it. It was likely that he was merely being romantic. She called him that. When he suggested brushing her hair or having champagne, she said, half smiling, that it would not be seemly for a vicar. He demurred, she mocked him playfully but with underlying rigidity, saying that he had better beware or she would insist on their only using the missionary position, which, she believed, was the correct and only way for God's intended. He laughed, acknowledged the superficial joke, registered the determined underpinning – and bought the secateurs. Then he bought lambswool slippers and moved tentatively on to records – she liked opera in the old days. *Der Rosenkavalier*, *Turandot*, *Tosca* pleased her but did not move her. Then he bought *Faust*, which had brought tears to those brilliant blue eyes. A puzzle. What was it that the ambitious anti-hero touched that those fluttery lovers and tragic heroines had not? No more operas, she had said, so he bought her a new bicycle, wishing it could have been a red sports car with white leather trim.

He hoped, he said, that she would be safe in London. She reminded him, tartly, that she used to live there – and in a flat on her own near the House of Commons, too. So he was reassured. Since they never talked about the past, he tended to forget the glamour of her life before him.

At the station she told him not to wait about in the wet to wave her off, so he said goodbye at the entrance, pecking her cheek and thinking in his heart what he could not say aloud, which was, How pretty you look, and hurry back, I shall miss you. He would have liked to give her some token – a buttonhole from the garden, perhaps – and say something lovely like, 'Be home before this fades . . .' But he knew better. Instead, he handed her his new copy of the *Church Times*, which, since he had had not yet read one line of it, was a genuine sacrifice of love.

On the tube the vicar's wife from Cockermouth eases her pleats again now that the fat woman next to her has gone and feels that she is doing quite well at being a Christian. After all, she has managed to sit in that particular vacant seat when there were others, and the obese woman eating was clearly some kind of . . . er . . . *eccentric*. It was precisely the sort of act for a good Christian. Alice spends most of her life doing penance like this.

45

She hates gardening, so she gardens. She hates children, so she runs the Sunday school. The smell of the Community Hall tea-urn and its incessant dripping makes her feel sick, so she takes charge of it whenever the opportunity comes. It makes her feel better, atones. The old blacksmith in a nearby village once told her that to deal with his arthritis he would thrust his arms into a bed of nettles. It did not cure, but it gave a new, more immediate pain to think about. The garden, the children, the disgusting tea-urn are her nettles and she will not let Arthur soften them with loving tokens. There was a price to be paid, and for twelve years she has been paying it.

Twelve years since she has been back to London.

The train rocks on through its newly refurbished stations. The *Church Times* slips from her lap. She forgets the unpleasant image of fat woman eating and lets the rhythm of the carriage unwind her like a massage. She strokes a small hand over the smoothness of her chignon and her eyes are alight with a view of the past. She looks at her watch: she could make the first half of the conference and the lunch and then get someone else to cover for her this afternoon. She would like to see him again, just once, and she could get to the House for Prime Minister's Question Time. He would be there, on the front bench, supporting his leader. To see him in the flesh again would be . . . would be . . . She touches the pleats of her skirt nervously. Even a newspaper photograph or his sudden appearance on the television screen still makes her heart beat faster, her brain go to water. Pushed to the back of her dressing-table drawer, wrapped in yellowing tissue-paper, she keeps the few things, the few tokens, the gewgaws from that time – removed from their love nest on the day his appointment as junior minister was announced. (She took them out this morning, looked at them, the compact, the trinkets. Did she put them back? Did it really matter?) A minister's women, it transpired, like Caesar's wife, must be above suspicion. His wife was, that sour-faced madonna. Alice was not. A junior minister's secretary could be clever and personable. A junior minister's secretary must not also be desirable and a lover. What had once excited him, kept him for so long, was her willingness to be an instrument for his pleasure, a receptacle for his romantic notions – roses, perfume, silk. And suddenly those very things were undesirable, dangerous to his progress. Ambition had been made of sterner stuff. Fool that she was, she had not seen that it was all a game to him, and real only to her. How well, how very well, he had played the lover's role. Unreal, detached, amused, while she . . . she had – she reaches down to retrieve the paper, scrumpling it in her fists – she had *believed*, fuck it, *believed* . . .

Her face burns, her mouth is dry, her heart beats with delirious ferocity. She begins to smooth the paper out again. To return it to him in that condition would be too cruel.

*

Janice Gentle enters the lift of her apartment building with a sigh of relief. Home again. In her head she repeats the title, *Phoenix Rising, Phoenix Rising* . . . Sylvia has suggested quite firmly that a one-word title would be a good idea – they were, apparently, fashionable – but, says Janice to herself, *Phoenix Rising* is *two* and I can't make it any less. Sylvia Perth will just have to see that for a change. Janice feels a dim little surge of something. Irritation? She couldn't be sure what – as much to do with that man in the corner shop who had gone on for ages before she had managed to escape him as to do with anything else. Nevertheless, she does feel *irritated*. Sylvia would look at her and wait, and Janice knew she would eventually comply and the title would be singular as suggested. But *Phoenix Rising* felt so very right. Why couldn't she stick out for it just this once? Sylvia was wonderful, supportive, kind, always interested. Opposing her wishes would make Janice feel extremely guilty, but all the same, all the same, it was irritating, irritating, *irritating*.

Again the tiny flame niggled at her placid inner calm. This was disturbing, disturbing and very unusual, since her relations with Sylvia Perth were always of a cordial nature, not to say a little apprehensive, and always respectful. Sylvia was, after all, the person who *knew*. And if Janice *knew* anything, it was that she was nothing without Sylvia Perth.

One-word titles, she muses, and runs through a string of them in her head. As the lift ascends, they seem to drop from her like dead flies falling down the lift shaft, useless and out of sight, none of them owning a barb with which to hook itself securely in her brain. '*Phoenix Rising*,' she repeats to herself as she lets herself in, '*Phoenix Rising*.' It will have to be that. But will Sylvia Perth let her?

She closes the door, feeling weary and annoyed, and takes the foodstuffs to the kitchen. Does she *really*, she asks herself, need to go through this performance every time there is a new book to begin? The tube journey, the people all jostling, the contact with that horrible world outside her door? Why doesn't she just *invent* her people? Other writers probably do, so why not her? She butters some bread and cuts a wedge or two of cheese and waits for the kettle to boil. She licks her buttery fingers. *Why* put herself through this ghastliness? She makes tea and while it brews she pours off the top of the milk into her cup. She enjoys that first drink which is creamy and rich and rolls smoothly over her tongue like a coat of silk. After the first mouthful she feels cheered. That is just the way it is. She undertook to abide by the rule and – she carries her cup and plate back into the living-room – that is what she must do. It is her integrity which is at stake. Integrity . . .

Well, she *could* call it that, she supposes. But she really doesn't want to. And why should she have to? Why, come to that, should she have to write any more books at all? And if she *does*, couldn't she at least have the right to choose what she calls them without needing permission? Not that Sylvia Perth would see it as that. She would see it merely as giving advice, sound advice. Well, a small, rebel flame comes leaping up again, has her advice been so sound? Janice Gentle dwells on this momentarily, decides it is a question best not put, but feels bothered by it, all the same.

And then she stops, sets down the cup, sets down the plate, puts a piece of cheese in her mouth and smiles as she chews.

Perhaps if she were a bit less amenable with Sylvia, if she were to ring her now and be a bit offish, then she might get her way about the title. She has never done such a thing before but ... hmm ... it might be worth a try. The irritation rises again. Anyway, why not? It's her book, after all. Even if Sylvia does do all the donkey-work and pay all the bills. Surely she has some rights in the choice? After all, she's the one who has got to get her head down until it aches. Sylvia Perth will be very nice and visit her, and telephone from time to time, and say that she is available whenever Janice might need her. But the plain fact of the matter – Janice takes an *enormous* and really quite savage bite from her bread – is Here We Go Again. Another book, another chunk of time out of her life. And always she has believed that each one would be the last. Would this new one be any different? It certainly should be. Time is rolling on for Janice. She has a Quest to pursue, a Pilgrimage to make, and the only thing that stands in her way is the need to have a substantial supply of money in her coffers. Every book she has written so far has been supposed to fill these to the brim. They have not. Always a good reason, of course, and Sylvia does her best, but her reassurances that perhaps after the next Janice need never write again are wearing a little thin. Indeed, at the very beginning that is what Sylvia Perth told her. She remembers it distinctly. And it has still not come about.

Sylvia said, Janice remembers it clearly, that she need never write anything again after her second book, if she would only *finish* it.

Writing being a hard, labouring agony, and her being as virginal as a nun, she began to call the products of her craft her children by way of a little, maidenly joke. Sylvia took it up and henceforth Janice Gentle's books were always known as her babies. And there seemed to be more and more of them as the years went by – quite a teeming womb, in fact. Looking back, she is still not *quite* sure what happened to all those promises of Sylvia's, but their failure to hold was no one's fault but the public and the publishers. Both Janice and Sylvia had nothing to be ashamed of. It was, really, out of her friend and agent's hands.

Nevertheless it became, 'We need a third.' What else could she do but comply? 'We need a third.' And, smiling, Sylvia, dipping her hands into her Gucci bucket bag, brought forth temptations.

'Look,' she said, 'I remembered how you like them.' From its depths she took a gold box adorned with ribbons bearing a crest and the legend 'Chocolat Dufours'.

'Oh,' said Janice, enraptured, 'how kind of you.'

'And what is more,' Sylvia Perth smiled conspiratorially, 'they are all for you. Now, grit your teeth and write on, my dear. A third book is essential.'

Janice munched and Sylvia departed. Ever since then it seemed a foregone conclusion that Janice still had a long way to go before the Seeking could begin.

'Money,' said Janice a year or two later. 'Have I made enough yet?'

'Not yet, I'm afraid, dear. Is there anything, apart from the Thing' – Sylvia bared her teeth – 'that you need?' And, as was customary, Janice merely shook her head.

Janice Gentle appeared to have no tastes or desires beyond the most basic kind, and Sylvia Perth was intrigued to know what this odd, reclusive pudding of a woman could ever possibly want to buy. It had taken all Sylvia's persuasion to get Janice to sell her mother's house and to begin negotiations on a flat somewhere further into town. And even then Janice had insisted it should be in Battersea. They had taken a taxi to look at properties around Harrods and Kensington Town Hall, and the fool of a driver had gone along on the wrong side of the river. Janice, looking out, suddenly said, 'This is the place,' and that had been that. No amount of persuasion made any difference. So if Battersea was the kind of place she wanted to live in, and if she was as happy with that dreadful hutch-like place as she seemed to be, it was hardly surprising, mused Sylvia Perth, that Janice asked for nothing beyond her keep. But, oh dear, it was such a *waste* . . .

'Dermot Poll,' said Janice Gentle dreamily.

Sylvia raised her eyebrows. Lord, she was off again.

'I'm pretty sure that somewhere along the line that night I

missed something he said. I *thought* he was going to come to me, but ... well ... I must have got it all muddled. He probably arranged a meeting somewhere else. He probably waited there all night, just as I waited all night for him ...'

Her voice rose, her eyes filled with tears, the pain was quite real to her, and Sylvia was embarrassed. She wiped the wetness beneath Janice's eyes with her Venetian lace handkerchief.

'There, there,' she said, 'we'll find him for you. Don't you worry.'

'Did you use those private detectives?'

Sylvia Perth replaced her hanky in her Anastasie pochette, snapped it shut, and said smoothly, 'Of course. I told you that they had no luck. And *that*, I am afraid, is why we need another book. As I told you, dear, they cost so much, so very much nowadays ...'

'Skibbereen was a clue. He came from Skibbereen ...'

'Yes, dear, and Charlie Chaplin came from London. But he didn't end up there. Do you see?'

'He mentioned Australia, America, China ...'

Sylvia nodded. 'I know, dear. So we need lots and lots more in the kitty before we can do anything about it. So buck up and let's get started. Shall we?'

Janice ceased the tears. What good would they do? What was needed was action, creativity, to provide. After all, did those queens of Spain and France flinch from raising the finance to fight *their* crusades? They did not. And neither, therefore, must she.

'You don't think he will have forgotten me?'

Sylvia looked at Janice. Above her considerable bulk the only relief from beige and buff was the pink rosette of her nose and the misty red rims of her eyes through the steamed-up glass of her spectacles. 'I don't see how he could, my dear,' said Sylvia Perth with feeling. 'I really don't see how he could.'

It was at this point that Sylvia Perth felt the first tightening in her chest. She sat very still for a moment, and soon it passed. She stood up. 'Good luck, my dear,' she said, straightening her little

Dior skirt. And she went out into the air to breathe slow and deep and remind herself to stay calm.

Janice Gentle wrote on.

Sylvia Perth kindly took over the management of all Janice's affairs, for which Janice was deeply grateful. She no longer had to deal with accountants, publishers, taxmen, bill-paying, the general public, bank managers (particularly bank managers), the media – not anybody. Sylvia was even able to sign things for Janice, which saved a great deal of what Sylvia called *fuss*.

Fuss was something, in any case, that Sylvia Perth wished to avoid for her own good, too. Fuss made her breathing difficult, fuss made her chest tighten, fuss brought the occasional pounding in her ears as if the ocean itself were closing in. Fuss, as the years drew on, seemed ever lurking and a most debilitating nuisance.

'Just leave everything up to Sylvia,' she said the last time they met. She placed an Alfredo-gloved hand upon Janice's pale head and patted it. 'You must not worry any more. Just keep on writing. It's the only way. And don't forget, it really would be helpful if this time you could give it a one-word title. That's what they like nowadays.' She lit one of her Turkish cigarettes so that Janice was wreathed in the blue-grey smoke like an unblinking houri. 'Who knows if this next one won't do the trick. And then' – she gave Janice a wicked little smile – 'it will be Dermot here I come . . .'

She breathed the smoke out generously and it eased the remnants of the tense, odd feeling in her chest. 'How I envy you your isolation, Janice,' she said. 'Sometimes I wish I could lock my door and throw away the key. I *love* this calm solitude, this undemanding colour scheme, this lack of busyness and ornament. How I should like to live somewhere like this and make myself a home – but then, I can't. One of us has got to be out there on the road, hasn't she?'

Janice nodded, immediately feeling guilty.

Sylvia gave a martyred grimace. 'It must be wonderful to be incommunicado and have everything done for you . . .' And leaving Janice with that thought, Sylvia Perth buttoned her little Ungaro jacket and departed.

Janice knew Sylvia was right. She always was. It was wonderful to be here, protected, alone. And it was the next best thing to retiring to a convent, which, had she lived long ago, she would have preferred. But still, with Sylvia Perth in the role of Mother Superior and her Battersea apartment more or less enclosed, it was the nearest she could get, and it would do very well. Besides, she couldn't really be a nun, or they might not let her out again to find Dermot Poll. She picked up her calendar and selected, with a pin, the day of her first tube-train outing. There was no point in delaying the beginning of the process any longer.

The pin had selected today – and with the law of Sod continually in mind, it was the first day of rain for six weeks. But it was over. Concluded successfully. And that – she eyed the scones happily – was *something*.

*

Before telephoning Sylvia she crosses to the word processor and removes its cover.

The only thing that comforts her is that somewhere, wherever he is, Dermot Poll is growing older, too. She has kept that roundness that he so admired (not at all hard to do). So he will certainly be able to recognize her when the time comes. And as for her, why, she would be able to pick him out on Brighton Beach in a heatwave. Of that she is absolutely sure. Dear God, she thinks, has not this waiting gone on long enough?

Impatience and crossness flare again. She cannot help it. There is a limit, she thinks, to the amount of time you can keep a love alive without its object before you. She switches the machine on aggressively. She makes notes – notes about the characters, a plot sketch – and then she goes back to the beginning of the file and titles it. 'Phoenix Rising,' she types in bold. That makes it real. It's in the machine now. Sylvia Perth must simply accept it. If Christine de Pisan was allowed to choose her titles six hundred years ago, surely, by the laws of emancipation, Janice Gentle should be allowed to choose hers today?

She dials the familiar number, keeping her eye very firmly on the screen. Just for once Janice intends to assert herself.

*

In her office near Claridge's Sylvia Perth has been giving an idealistic young author a pep-talk. And while the idealistic young author has been upturning her pretty flower-like face to the desk, perching Sylvia has been attempting, with moderate success, to look down the neck of the idealistic young author's blouse.

Sylvia is fifty-four. She has spent most of her working life persuading publishers to publish books enthusiastically, and authors to write them in the same spirit. Sometimes she wondered whether the two kinds even occupied the same planet. But now she represents only one author, Janice Gentle, from whom the pickings have been gratifyingly good. Sylvia Perth feels that she has given up quite enough of the joys of ordinary mortalhood to be compensated in this way. She has given up the possibility of marriage, children, friendships, in pursuit of her career, and she has absolutely no qualms about either her business methods with her author or her attempts to look down the blouse of the young woman opposite. 'I might be a smutty old dyke,' she says with wry amusement to herself, 'but at least my author is pure and honest and squeaky clean.' She rather likes the oppositional comparison and the dot, dot, dottiness of the activity left unsaid. Janice's books have a purity about them which makes Sylvia – who, in many ways, and despite objectively knowing otherwise, views herself as rather soiled – feel better. By this one act of honour in representing Janice she feels she has bought herself many pardons. In other words, though she would never admit it to a living soul, the only thing Sylvia Perth is involved with that feels clean and wholesome and good is Janice Gentle's books. And when she is approached, as she has been recently, to take them from their shell of honesty and inject them with a vein or two of gratuitous smut, she takes a warm, righteous pleasure in refusing. Not that sex in literature offends Sylvia Perth, for literature reflects all manner of life, but she is wise enough in the world of books to know that the best of such writing is organic and that you had as well try to attach a dried flower to the glass over a Chardin painting as to put a hot-bed scene in one of Janice's books. Since Janice constantly refers to them as her children, it would be like offering them up for paedophiliac rape. The goose was laying golden eggs. Why on earth risk a change that could seriously lead to dross?

There were other reasons why Sylvia preferred to leave things unchanged – reasons not at all connected with literary integrity, reasons which Sylvia chose not to contemplate and which she kept tucked well away in the darker recesses of her most private mind.

Sylvia sighs. How pretty is the idealistic young author, and what indulgence it is to listen to her tinkling away about whatever it is she *is* tinkling away about. She might be able to do something for her, she supposes, put in a good word somewhere; there was always the possibility of future gratitude. Temptation creeps up Sylvia Perth's spine, but she suppresses it. She has already made one error of judgement at lunch today with a beautiful ash-haired American girl – a cardinal Perthly sin, that was. No, no, she had better stick to just looking on from a distance. She is lucky to have a preference for breasts, for in a male-oriented culture there is never any shortage of *them*.

The idealistic young author pauses for breath. To be in the presence of a real-life literary agent who seems interested in her work is wonderful. She does not normally smoke but accepts one of Sylvia's strange-looking cigarettes with a flourish of abandon and leans forward for it to be lit.

Sylvia momentarily loses mental equilibrium and asks, 'Are you married?' The idealistic young author looks surprised. Since she was at that point setting out her views on the meaning of meaning, it seemed a substantial non-sequitur. The cigarette gives her a kind of confidence; Sylvia Perth has screwed up her eyes against the smoke and is smiling encouragingly, sleekly.

The idealistic young author also screws up her eyes, though of necessity rather than design, and says, 'Married? I should think not. I'm only twenty-three and I want to express myself through my writing.'

Sylvia puts her hand on her chin and nods sagely. 'Well, quite,' she says.

'It is experience which counts. Every possible, conceivable, *imaginable* experience . . . At the centre of the voyage of literary discovery is oneself . . .'

Sylvia has lost track completely of what is being said. After the words 'imaginable experience' she has given herself up to a wonderful fantasy in which hand-warmed massage oil makes an appearance.

'. . . break new ground, push out the boundaries.'

'Oh yes, yes,' says Sylvia, though in quite another connection.

Good heavens, thinks the idealistic young author, we are getting on well. 'May I come again?'

Sylvia, to whom this phrase has arrived a little early in her fantasy, returns to the real world. She faces a pair of round, dark, *ingénue* eyes and says the first thing that comes to mind. 'You have immense talents.' She looks at the girl's chest. '*Immense.*'

'Really?' says the girl, leaning even further towards the pinkening dampness of Sylvia Perth's face.

Sylvia leans towards her and taps the delicious scrubbed rosiness of her cheek with her fingertip as if to say, 'Naughty, naughty . . .' They are practically nose to nose when the telephone rings.

It is Janice Gentle.

'Yes? What?' she snaps down the phone.

The irritation which subdued itself a little as Janice dialled surfaces again at the abrupt snappishness of Sylvia's answer. 'Sylvia, it is Janice.'

Sylvia immediately takes her eyes off the delights before her and concentrates, as much as she can, on her caller. 'Janice, my dear.'

'I wonder if you could come over for tea?'

'Certainly.' Sylvia looks at the pretty flower-like face upturned towards her, rosy and keen. 'When?' The agent flicks open her diary. The idea of dinner is still buzzing about in her head.

Janice's little irritation flares. 'Now. For *tea*.'

Sylvia understands the signal. Just for once she hesitates. 'Not tomorrow?'

Janice is astonished. She had expected, as ever, instant response. She is ready to do battle for her two-word title. By tomorrow both the impetus for that, and the scones, will be stale.

The little irritation becomes a bonfire. She tears with her teeth at a paper wrapper from a chocolate in the bowl she keeps by the telephone. Sylvia sent them. Sylvia is always very good at sending Janice little treats. She sinks her teeth into the centre. It is gritty. It is marzipan. The confectioner's mistake, not Sylvia's. Nevertheless, Janice hates marzipan. It was beneath the icing on her seven-year-old's birthday cake the day that Daddy left. She spits it out. The horrible taste lingers. The vexation grows.

'As a matter of fact, Sylvia,' she says, 'I've got a real problem with the title . . .'

Sylvia tries to bring herself back to the matter in hand. 'Just a moment,' she mouths to the idealistic young author, and to Janice she says, 'Well, dear, you don't really have to worry at this stage, do you? Why don't you just get writing and the title will come later . . .?'

Janice, raw with the series of irritations already, is made more so by the dismissiveness. Sylvia always acts as if it is so *easy*. 'Actually,' she says, 'I am so stuck and so fed up and so – well, so *something* that I don't know if I shall ever write again. I may well go into retirement. I think I've had enough of it all. Yes . . . very possibly . . . I have had quite enough. You see I – hallo . . . hallo? Sylvia? Sylvia . . .?'

. . . But Sylvia has put down the phone. Janice has never spoken to her like that before. Janice is benign, bovine, bonded. Sylvia must go, fly, be there. *Now*. What are the twin orbs of sensual delight and fantasies about warm rosemary oil compared with this? No more Janice, no more rosemary oil, anyway.

In complete confusion the idealistic young author reels as the air before her nose is rent by whirling agent, and the scent of Arpège mixed with attar of roses. Like the flying saint of a

Tintoretto, Sylvia Perth exits. As she goes, she says something, but her companion cannot swear to its identity. It may possibly be that she is wishing her *good luck*.

Sylvia picks up her coat. Her heart, once so light, is now heavy. The impassive blonde at the reception desk looks up, smiles, says, 'Goodbye,' in the elegant way she was taught at finishing school and appears to notice nothing unusual, also a skill learned at finishing school. In years to come she will marry someone very rich and very well bred, and when she finds him in the afternoon shrubbery with the nanny she will apply these same skills and take her tea alone.

Sylvia Perth frantically hails a taxi. Her face has darkened to the colour of a plum and there are spots dancing before her eyes. She sinks into the seat. She is deeply afraid.

Janice is feeling contrite and she has put out the scones, jam and cream.

While she has been setting out the repast, Sylvia Perth has been caught up in traffic, and having palpitations. Sylvia is not having an easy menopause and has a tendency to get very warm under stress. She is very warm and very, very stressed at the moment. Eventually exhausting her store of expletives, which were good enough to make the taxi-driver blush, she leaves the cab and sets off on foot. At that precise moment the traffic clears and Sylvia is left standing on the kerb, twitching with fury, flapping her arms, mouthing obscenities and looking like an immaculate bag lady. The palpitations scarcely diminish when she finds another cab, and she sits in it with her chest feeling as if it were bound in steel. Her breathing exercises do not work.

What has happened? What has gone wrong? From where has Janice Gentle suddenly got this new-found streak of resistance? At the very thought of it the pain tightens and only the shallowest of breathing is possible. 'Janice!' she cries. 'Janice! I am coming. Wait for me!'

Janice presses her entry phone and awaits the noise of the click to say Sylvia Perth is inside the building. At least the lift is working today.

She is feeling even more contrite, since two of the scones have now disappeared. Still, Sylvia never eats very much, anyway – though how she can resist it . . . Janice sticks her finger in the cream and then licks it. She waits to hear the whine of the lift and the noise of the doors sliding open. She takes another swift scoop of the cream and she smiles. All her crossness and irritation have melted away and she is looking forward very much to seeing Sylvia's face when she tells her that all is well, that the new baby is on its way, that she is resolute about the title but apart from that she is ready and poised to begin . . .

Come on, she thinks, hurry up or – lick, lick, lick – all the cream will be gone.

But Sylvia Perth never arrives. At least, not in any useful condition. The lift doors slide open, but instead of stepping out, Sylvia Perth rolls out. Purple-lipped, white-faced, in the last twitching spasm of her death throe and on her way to meet that great publisher in the sky.

Her body lies between the lift and the passageway and the doors close and open, close and open, confused by their inability to go on their way. Slide, bang, they go as they hit Sylvia's torso; slide, bang, as they try and try again. And Janice, waiting, lost for a moment in the opening sentence of Red Gold's first words – 'It seems a very long time ago that I was kissed beneath the apple tree on that blossom-scented night . . .' – is disturbed.

The rhythmic thudding from the hallway is disturbing. That Sylvia has not yet rung her doorbell is . . . disturbing. She goes to her apartment door, opens it and looks out. What she sees is also disturbing. Seriously disturbing. What she sees makes her let go of the scone she holds, which falls cream side down (Sod's law yet again) and brings her back from that balmy night in early summer (does apple blossom actually smell? Check this), and she gasps.

The unthinkable has happened. A thing most terrible in its potential effect. Sylvia Perth, agent, financial adviser, friend, counsellor, upright woman of the world and guiding star, is rolling around on the floor and, it appears, stone cold dead.

Janice, first picking up the scone, pads across the passageway and looks down. The doors go on with their rhythmic dance, using the rolling torso like a punching-bag. Janice kneels and puts a creamy finger on Sylvia Perth's cheek. There is no doubt about it. Even the latest exhortations by *Harper's* or *Vogue*, whose advice Sylvia had valued so much, could never have recommended blue lipstick, parchment cheeks, demonic eyes. And the tongue – how extensive these things are when distended – the tongue, lolling, is red. Too red.

She sits back on her haunches and stares. A little bit of cream plops down from the scone on to Sylvia Perth's cheek. Janice scoops it up with her finger. Absently she licks it clean. It tastes of face-powder. Janice stares. The unthinkable, indeed. Sylvia and Janice, agent and author, intertwined, interdependent: Sylvia, total guardian of Janice and all that she is; Janice, total protégée of Sylvia and nothing without her. So close that not a leaf, let alone another agent or publisher, can come between them. Sundered now, for ever, by the Great Leveller.

Impossible, unbearable, unthinkable.

But true all the same.

The cream cloys in her mouth.

Who will protect her now?

Janice Gentle's agency, so prized by Sylvia Perth, so defended from attempted coups, so utterly, utterly the property of one woman alone, is, quite suddenly, up for grabs.

Chapter Five

SYLVIA Perth died a martyr to retail therapy.

Through her relationship with Janice Gentle she had learned to worship and accrue the beautiful things that money could buy. She dreamt not of love but of objects, she yearned not for friendship but for possessions, tangible items that never let you down (and if they did, you could return them and get your money back – unlike a wasted life). Love was a singularly hollow affair, a specious deceit, and Sylvia had no time for it. Vowing eternity one minute, vowing murder the next.

Even had she broken her rule and gone for dinner with flower-face, it would not have been love that she sought, for love required feeding, time, attention, care, *sacrifice*, and Sylvia Perth delighted in having a life that required her to give up nothing. The gap that non-existent love had left in her was easily filled with nice things. Nice things were Sylvia's DNA. The prospect of a life without them was too cruel, too barren, for Sylvia to contemplate. When Janice Gentle had her innocent little flicker of rebellion, it was experienced by Sylvia as the very heat and jaws of hell itself. No Janice Gentle books, no more beautiful things. And, worse, if it went any further, if the *truth* got out, if those things only known and hidden in the darker recesses should shine forth, why, they might actually take all the beautiful things away . . .

Christ, thought Sylvia Perth, as she scrabbled out of the taxi-cab and stabbed at the door button, La Doughbag might just mean it. Stab, stab, she went again, mad at herself for having got sidetracked by mere passing fancy. That it was entirely her own fault made her passion ten times worse. Janice Gentle was not known for her flippancy. She had her big, spreading feet planted firmly on some damnably honourable medieval floor, and what she said she usually meant.

Panicking at the lift, waiting for it to descend, Sylvia could feel the sweat of fear breaking out. She pressed the button again. It wasn't as if, she muttered hysterically, the silly cow ever *wanted* to spend much of her money, anyway. Stab, stab. It wasn't as if she had taken anything away, *not really*, from that lump of obese immobility. There was nothing, nothing at all, that Janice Gentle had wanted for, *nothing*. Whereas she, Sylvia, was all splendid exuberance for the finer things. *She* understood Imelda Marcos even if nobody else did. Why not have a million pairs of shoes if it pleased you? At least shoes didn't stab you in the back, at least hats didn't slip down and strangle you, and money had no barriers of age, sex or religion – at least, at least it was *something* to make you feel really good.

The lift took an age. Sylvia Perth contemplated using the stairs, but she felt very tired. Why the devil didn't Janice move somewhere better? Across the water? Chelsea or Knightsbridge or somewhere refined. Battersea, I mean – punch, punch at the button – *Battersea*. And in a flat that looked as if it were owned by the council. Style and money – Janice would never have much of either. And anyway, she didn't *want* them – not at all. The only thing Janice had that she treasured was an old chest with a lurid old coat in it – that and her appetite. Whereas she, Sylvia . . .

She relaxed. She could hear the lift at last. She smiled and breathed out and waited for the tension in her chest to flow away from her. Once she was with Janice it would all be fine. She had a way with Janice. She made her happy, gave her what she wanted, listened to her rambling away so pottily about that Dermot Poll and soothed her whenever she showed signs of agitation over finding him. She hoped it wasn't all to do with that again. If Janice Gentle found Dermot Poll, it would break her illusion, and with the illusion gone . . .

Sylvia thought of the antique Beshir she had set her heart on, and her palpitations increased. To lose it all now was unthinkable, not fair. After all, what had she done? Nothing. She had taken nothing that Janice could possibly want. Indeed, she had given her all the things she wanted in the world: her inviolable home, her impenetrable privacy, her comforting food and an occupation that kept the dream alive. Dreams were never worth realizing, anyway. They were things that kept you going while they were unattained and always disappointed when they were reached. Find Dermot Poll and Janice Gentle would probably cease to want to live. In a way, Sylvia argued to herself, she had been doing Janice a kindness by *not* helping find Dermot Poll for her. Let the dream live on for ever. Her books gave her a route through life, didn't they? Though Janice wouldn't see it like that. But they gave her an interest. Find Dermot Poll and she would certainly cease to write. And if *that* happened it would lead directly to the thing Sylvia – twinge, twinge – feared more than anything . . .

*

Sylvia had not meant to start borrowing from Janice Gentle's income. It had begun quite innocently. Sylvia Perth deducted her own percentage, just as any literary agent must, and the rest had gone into an account for Janice. Since Janice was not at all worldly in such matters, it had seemed sensible, indeed imperative, for Sylvia Perth to have control of this account for the dispensation of the various moneys required to make Janice's life run smoothly. The problem was that Janice required so *little*. And the other problem was that she made so much. It was only a shift of emphasis that made Sylvia offer to be responsible for everything, and Janice had been heartfelt in her gratitude. Who would *not*, Sylvia said to herself time and time again whenever conscience poked out its ugly head, given half the chance, like to abrogate those responsibilities? And who would not, if finances were to hand, pay handsomely for the service? The only discrepancy, so far as Sylvia was concerned, was that Janice did not exactly *know* that she was paying, though initially she had only to ask and Sylvia would have told.

It was after the second book that things, or rather Sylvia's fingers, got a bit stickier. Sylvia had worked very hard on her author's behalf and she felt the imbalance of reward rather keenly. After all, if it had not been for her, Janice Gentle would never have got published in the first place, would have remained, for ever, in Arterberry Road. Put like that . . .

And thus into the treacle well Sylvia Perth's fingers went.

By protecting Janice Gentle from the outside world, Sylvia Perth also protected herself from discovery; but it did not help her heart, that insular organ, which rebelled against the deceits and joined with conscience to form an unhealthy alliance. Sylvia had her ways of countering the stress and, as many do, thought herself immortal. The spending went on, the delights of possessions increased. It was beyond endurance to imagine it all being taken away.

She was very cautious with regard to Janice and the world outside her cloister. Over the years she had managed to deflect any attempt by members of the publishing world to make contact, and nowadays it was accepted that Janice Gentle was recluse and would always be so. Business was conducted through Sylvia Perth as her agent, and the situation was one of perfect accord. Occasionally this harmony was broken by some brash newcomer who thought he or she might move the pieces around on the board a little, but always it ended in defeat. Janice colluded with Sylvia in her anchorite existence, so it was based on free will. There were no chains, no hedge of thorns, no locked tower to be breached, and Sylvia could rest, almost, assured.

Almost, because there were always new contenders to the lists. For Sylvia these joustings were little more than pleasant interludes, although occasionally she felt she was required to be on her mettle. As with the Bulbecker woman today. Very intelligent, very positive and no bull-shitting. She had admired that at once. And they had enjoyed the lunch, both eyeing each other and talking of other things.

With coffee, Ms Bulbecker said, 'We both know what we are doing here.' And Sylvia, in her usual cat's-game way, replied, 'Well, I know why *I'm* here. I'm here because the langoustines are the best in town and you are paying.'

Sylvia Perth looked at Rohanne Bulbecker and Rohanne Bulbecker looked at Sylvia Perth.

Sylvia Perth shook her head. 'No, dear,' she said, 'no.'

'One book,' said Rohanne, holding up her freshly manicured finger. 'One book with that extra dimension and not attempting to dictate whatsoever . . .'

Sylvia smiled, cat-like. '"Extra dimension" is rather a mouthful, don't you think? Surely we can say the word sex?'

'Sure!' said Rohanne Bulbecker hopefully.

'But the answer is still no.'

'May I ask why?'

'Janice Gentle is not interested in writing about sex. She wishes to continue to write as she chooses.'

'Money?'

Sylvia shook her head. She tapped the end of her cigarette so that ash fell into the spent bodies of the langoustines. It was designed to be provocative.

Rohanne pictured Morgan P. Pfeiffer sitting at his desk, impassive, waiting. 'I should like to meet Janice Gentle and talk to her about the project. And to say, face to face, how much we admire her over there; how very keen Mr Pfeiffer and I are to work with her. Would that be possible?'

'Impossible,' Sylvia said. 'Janice never gives interviews. Everything is conducted through me. Put it in a letter and I will make sure she sees it.' She stood up. 'I have to go. Another appointment, I am afraid.'

Rohanne stood up.

'A very nice frock,' said Sylvia Perth.

'Thank you,' said Rohanne.

'Armani, I think?'

'Perhaps I could call her?'

'Afraid not. She distrusts the telephone.'

'Then I will write.'

They shook hands.

'I can be very persistent,' said Rohanne smiling. She watched her combatant moving away with irritating confidence. She put one of her fingers into her mouth and bit off the end of a much prized Bulbecker nail.

'And we,' said Sylvia Perth, also smiling, 'can be very impervious.' She walked away, still smiling, and said from the door, 'Over my dead body, I always say.'

And Rohanne, staring at her ragged fingertip in misery, thought that really wasn't such a bad idea.

*

Sylvia Perth tried not to remember those fateful words as she waited in the lobby of Janice's building. 'Damn the lift,' she said, having no energy to say worse, '*Damn*, and *damn*, and *damn* it.' At each outburst she kicked the closed doors until, like some avant-garde version of Ali Baba, they slid open, the lift appeared and Sylvia Perth caught her breath, clutched at the pain beneath her breast, and entered her tomb. She leaned, half fainting, against the steel wall and for some reason, though she feared she knew why, images of the past floated into her mind.

Her mother, Mrs Perth, in her pinny and turban, reading the trade papers for seaside novelties with which to stock their shop. Never turning away a travelling salesman in case he should have any fresh trumpery tucked among his wares. Mrs Perth bought the new plastic buckets cheaply when the fashion for tin was just turning, Mrs Perth bought Taiwanese rubber shoes when the custom was for raffia, and her decisions were sound. She was the powerhouse. Sylvia saw her sitting at the round chenille-covered table in the back room smoking Weights and making notes on the back of an envelope while Mr Perth made jovial banter with the customers and did the display. Whenever Sylvia thought of those days, which was not often, she knew it was not her mother's talent with novelties that she despised, it was her mother's small-mindedness, her parochiality, her lack of breadth in exploiting such a talent. Tin buckets and rubber shoes, indeed. Tawdry, tacky, parvenu . . .

She saw her father, Mr Perth, duster in one hand, Boy George

T-shirt in the other, laughing as a customer selected dog turds and hot sweets. And then Mrs Perth again, who, after his death, retired to the centre of Birmingham, having seen, as she said, quite enough of the open horizon. She would not sell the shop, only lease it, since she was contemptuous and unbelieving that the lure of the Costa del Sol would endure. Skin cancer proved her right and, with a last triumphant flourish, she went back to her trade, bought tin buckets now that plastic was outcast, raffia instead of rubber, and did very well. Now she lived in self-paid-for comfort in an old folk's home suburban to Birmingham. Sylvia saw her mother as she was now, and saw herself on the rare occasions she visited her, dressing down for the part of humble daughter, struggling into a chain-store frock and shoes, buying low-brow chocolates as advertised on TV, bringing with her the latest Janice Gentle in *paperback* – a double-edged irony which Sylvia enjoyed – travelling by bus from the station. These were her extreme moments of penance and a goodly reminder of how not to end up.

Mrs Perth's insight deserted her when it came to her daughter. She never suspected that she had become rich, as she never suspected the truth about Sylvia's unmarried state. She saw her daughter as comfortably well off and dull to drabness, seldom free to visit her, being tied to London to earn her wage.

'If you made more of yourself,' she said through a montelimar on Sylvia's last visit, 'there's still no reason even at your age why you couldn't get yourself a well-to-do husband. One who could help you a bit with the business. No reason why you shouldn't get on the gravy train.' With sticky fingers she picked up the paperback of Janice Gentle's latest. 'See this? *She's* a winner. Better than that Betty Cartland woman. Bit realer, bit more meat to it, I always feel as if I *know her* people. They could live next door, really. Do you know a Janice Gentle book once made me *cry*?' She nodded her head in personal wonderment. 'Thanks for bringing it. Chocolate?'

Despite the pain Sylvia chortled: discovering the truth might kill her mother off, too. Hah, hah, that'd be ironic . . .

She gasped. The cell seemed airless. Rohanne Bulbecker. First her voice, then her face floated, swam into the closed-in space. Why ever had she said those final words to her in the restaurant?

'Over my dead body, Rohanne. Over my dead body, Rohanne Bulbecker, *dear* . . .'

Ho, ho . . .

Ho.

Chapter Six

Over Sylvia Perth's dead body Janice put several slightly used tea towels, the first things which came to hand. She had wedged the lift door with one of Sylvia's handmade Corizon shoes, and from below the lift shaft came the sound of a frustrated would-be ascendant. Janice never had, and certainly did not now want, social confrontation with any of the other tenants or their acquaintances, so, having done all that she felt she could under the circumstances, she went back into her own flat and pushed the door to. The screen of the word processor blinked at her, mocking. *Phoenix Rising*, it said, and Janice felt a terrible emptiness in the pit of her stomach.

As she passed the table with the scones, she picked one up and bit into it, which calmed her a little. That, at least, had a sense of reality. She looked at the jam but it no longer enticed. Its redness was a bit too lurid and alive; apricot, she found herself thinking, it should have been apricot, a far less angry and disturbing colour. As she shuffled across to the telephone, she wondered why she had never thought of it before. Apricot. Pale scones, white cream and the gentle, translucent gold of a precocious fruit.

She telephoned the caretaker with no idea of what she would say and waited for him to speak first.

'Yes?' he rapped out loudly.

Janice jumped. 'My agent has just died halfway out of the lift,' she said. 'Fifth floor. Could you come up, Mr Jones?'

Then she dialled the emergency services, thought Ambulance, but said Police, and went back to the table again, waiting and listening as she chewed and swallowed, hoping it would all go away.

Mr Jones, who had been pickling onions, thought it was his hearing-aid on the blink again. He stirred the chillis and peppercorns into the boiling vinegar and hoped that the sieved raspberries with which he was experimenting would colour the onions as positively as they had coloured his fingers. Sighing, he turned the pan down to simmer, and picked up his tool-box. By rights he ought to stop and put on his boiler suit, but it was a warm day. Tenants, he thought, tenants! There was always something. He knocked the handle of the pan slightly and it slopped some of the vinegary juice on to his bag and his shirt. His already darkened brow darkened more. He looked extremely fierce.

Out of his basement door he came, slowly, grudgingly, and with the hot odour of acidic onions wafting around him. At the front entrance to the building he paused to look up at the sky, took a deep breath and closed his eyes, enjoying, just for a moment, the afternoon peace which should have been his by rights. He took another, deeper breath and felt rather uncharacteristically that life was quite good after all. And then he changed his mind. He remembered the raspberry juice, he remembered being disturbed, and he resumed his fierceness through closed lids as the tranquillity was violated by the ear-splitting sound of a siren (nothing wrong with the batteries, after all) and the protesting squeal of hard-pressed brakes. He winced, and then winced again as something jabbed him in the ribs. He opened his eyes and met an excited pair, shaded by a cap of authority, which stared poppingly into his. A voice, thrill-edged, spoke rapidly and with a hint of Transatlantic Patrolman.

'Where is it, then? Come on. Where's the body?'

'What body?' said Mr Jones, not unreasonably.

Sergeant Pitter looked at the tool-box and noticed its owner was sweating, he saw that the hand which grasped the tool-box was bloody. There were also suspicious stains on the tool-box itself and on the man's garments. Oh, joy of joys. His heart, a somewhat depressed organ for most of the time, leapt within his breast. This was no hoax call from a bored housewife – this was *real*.

'You do not have to say anything,' he began (more joy, how he had longed to utter those words), 'but anything you do say may be . . .'

Mr Jones, anxious about leaving his pickling spice in too long, turned on his heel. He had done nothing wrong, his conscience was clear and he could not make head nor tail of what the policeman was saying. It was probably raffle tickets. It always *was* raffle tickets. Well, poking him in the ribs and being aggressive about it weren't going to get *him* digging in his pockets. And if the raspberry extract simmered for too long, it would be jam. He entered the block of flats swiftly. Sergeant Pitter danced after him.

'Cover the back entrance,' he said to his driver.

'Thinks he's 007,' muttered the constable, but he went to try and find one.

To Mr Jones Sergeant Pitter continued excitedly, following him in, '. . . may be taken down and used in evidence . . .'

'Ah, Jones,' said a tall, thin man with a walking-cane and a respectable air. 'Lift's up the spout again.'

Mr Jones lacked humility. 'Use the stairs, then,' he said peremptorily. Afternoons were definitely supposed to be his quiet time.

'Now, look here, Jones,' said the respectable man, waving his cane, 'you know perfectly well my leg's dicky.'

It was beyond even Sergeant Pitter's hopeful imagination that this could be an impromptu exchange between felons. 'Excuse me, sir,' said Sergeant Pitter sadly, 'do you know this man?'

The man tapped his cane, prepared to speak, but Sergeant Pitter had gone, trailing the shadow of the absenting Mr Jones.

'Who are you?' the sergeant puffed at Mr Jones's resolute backview. But in his heart a creeping despondency told him that he already knew. The evidence for a trained police officer was overwhelming. This was not, after all, the Boston Strangler. This was a genuine caretaker, and the sweat, like his own, was to do with the air temperature and sudden exertion. No doubt the redness had some legitimate source, too. He followed him, keeping his distance, for despite his disappointing reassurances about normality, the man smelled very strange.

On the fifth floor Janice peeped out as she heard footsteps approaching. She too was sweating, both hot from the day and cold from fear. The point was, she argued to herself, that Sylvia Perth was now deceased. No amount of standing around and debating cause and effect would change that. It was the ultimate truth and required nothing further than its acceptance. Therefore, she was not going to communicate with any of these people. She was no good at it, didn't want it, and despite the fact that Sylvia Perth had been on her way to visit her – well, she hadn't exactly *arrived*, had she? Therefore, she – it – was not Janice's responsibility. She did not want responsibility, she did not want participatory dialogue. That was why supermarkets were so nice. Perhaps, she thought, she could just say, 'There it is, take it away,' and go back into her own safe world to mourn in peace. It was, you might say, but the shell, the soul having clearly departed. Nevertheless, if Janice was a poor communicator, she was not a fool. She would have to say more than this, and besides, there were her tea towels to consider. She wished she had never taken the things out there now. In any case they looked shamefully incongruous and by no means freshly laundered.

At the penultimate turn of the stairs a depressed Sergeant Pitter paused and listened. There was no doubt about it, the plodding Mr Jones was whistling. Sergeant Pitter became even more depressed. The caretaker would not whistle unless he were innocent.

'Stop that,' he called.

'Eh?' Mr Jones turned, confused.

'Stop that whistling,' said the sergeant tersely. And he wondered how Mr Jones could apparently continue the noise while not moving his lips.

'Eh?' said Mr Jones again, and he tapped his earpiece. The whistling stopped.

'That's better,' said Sergeant Pitter, feeling more secure now that the authority of his uniform had apparently had its effect.

'Just round here, officer,' hazarded Mr Jones. 'Next landing.'

They turned the corner and the policeman's heart sank.

There was no body to be seen. Merely a pile of laundry sticking out of the lift doors. Tea towels, by the look of it. A hoax? A joker? Someone would pay for this. He looked up and saw a door move infinitesimally, caught the gleam of a bespectacled eye peering out, a bespectacled eye that was not without a hint of guilty rectitude. He pounced.

'Gotcha,' he cried, hauling Janice out into the corridor, or attempting to. But she was heavier and larger than the crack in the door suggested. *Much* heavier, *much* larger and, more to the point, unwilling to be moved.

He felt his back go ping, muscles spasmed, the pain was savage. He released Janice's Rubenesque shoulder, sank to his knees and, crawling, turned himself round. And it was in so doing, as Mr Jones whipped off the tea towels, that Sergeant Pitter came face to face, quite literally, with his first stiff. Big red tongue, livid cheeks and popping, accusing eyes. Sergeant Pitter attempted to retreat on all fours.

'What about the kiss of life, then?' asked Mr Jones.

Sergeant Pitter retreated even further and bumped up against Janice's legs. 'Do you know this person?' he began, attempting to swivel his neck to address the quivering Janice . . . And then he fainted.

Janice let out a hearty scream. Not for the sight of her once living agent, nor for the sight of Mr Jones attempting the kiss of life on her once living agent (part of a caretaker's job, first aid to the injured), but because she had a presentiment that this whole episode was the beginning of the end of her peaceful enclosure. Janice could not *quite* mourn for Sylvia, for she had been too afraid of her, but she could mourn for the passing of her protection, her greatest gift.

Well, nothing was to be gained by standing out here and getting caught up in all this.

She moved swiftly.

Mr Jones gave up and replaced the tea towels. Sergeant Pitter murmured in his unconsciousness. Janice slipped back into her apartment and closed the door, but not even the pale familiarity of her apartment soothed her. She picked up the jam dish and washed the contents away down the kitchen sink as if she had been the murderer. Then she tidied away the table and the things that had been set out for two, switched off the screen's insistent eye, and waited on the settee for the knock to come, with a Mars bar and Chaucer's *Criseyde*.

Double solace.

The entrance by Troilus into his lady's chamber while Pandarus pleads the hero's case, she reads. A favourite piece of Janice's. And she sucks heartily at the chocolate bar.

> This Troilus ful soone on knees hym sette
> Ful sobrely, right be hyre beddes hed . . .

Momentarily she allows herself to transpose Troilus for Dermot Poll but buries the thought of it immediately. Their union had begun with the purity of a lily flower and who was to say it might not stay that way? Like the chaste love of Dante and Beatrice? She reads on. It is all much safer in books.

Reading *Troilus and Criseyde* serves only to increase Janice's vagueness about sex. In practical terms Janice was comfortably vague. Sometimes when she was sitting in the bath she would look down, past the three large rolls of white flesh, and observe that mysterious place, deep in a forest, without being at all privy to its secrets. She tried not to think that in order to get *her* both parents must have experienced this thing at least once. But this was such a disturbing notion that she usually pulled out the plug at its inception and let the thought vanish down the gurgling waste. One day, she always vowed, one day . . . In the meantime her books did not contain any reference to it because she did not want to get such an important thing wrong. Love she knew, for love was within her. But sex? She knew it not. And she had no desire to invent it.

She reads on, still waiting for the knock, still taking comfort from Troilus, who placed his faith in love so strongly that it reflected itself back upon him, sweetly blinding him from the truth that its object would finally betray. The bedroom scene, Janice Gentle thinks, is one of the most enchanting in fourteenth-century literature. As a matter of fact, thinks Janice, she had rather hoped Sylvia Perth would take the role of Pandarus in the bedchamber herself and sort of *throw* Dermot into bed beside her, as Pandarus threw Troilus in next to Criseyde, once Janice had located him. Now *that* isn't going to happen, is it? She sighs. Life has been seriously unkind, considering that all she has ever really wanted is to seek, to find and love and worship back.

'But al shal passe; and thus take I my leve.' The noises outside continue. At least, so far, the knock has not come. '. . . thynketh al nys but a faire,' she reads. 'This world, that passeth soone as floures faire . . .'

Yes, she thinks, that is the tragedy. That the world is so potentially fair, yet made so ugly. A deep and tragic beauty. She is best set apart from it until the time comes when it will bloom for her. Christine de Pisan knew this; Langland knew this; Chaucer knew this. Life is a journey in which the valiant banner of beauty must be flown. She will not write of ugliness. How brave, she thinks, those Canterbury pilgrims were, travelling the ancient and dangerous byways with only their stories and their small number to keep them safe. But she will also be ready to travel when the time comes. Alas, it seems more remote than ever. With Sylvia Perth gone, to whom can she turn? And where can she get enough money to continue this Quest of hers? (She remembers the bank manager and shudders. Never. Never. No. No. No.) At least the travellers of yore knew exactly where they were going. Janice doesn't even know that yet. At least Canterbury Cathedral was accessible, even if footpads and forests made it tricky. And at least they all had enough money sewn about their persons. Janice doesn't know how much, if any, is at her disposal. She sits on, hearing the noises outside, wishing they would go away, waiting for the demanding knock to come as Gothic souls might wait for Armageddon. And she decides to do the only thing possible in the circumstances.

Nothing.

After all, Sylvia Perth turned up magically upon her doorstep all those years ago. Why should not another? It is as likely as anything else.

She continues to read, turning her mind from the hubbub beyond her door. On the page all is serene and elegant. *Vous ou Mort*. What are the oaths and scuffles in the corridor to that?

Janice sits silent, save for the flicking of a page and the slightest murmuring of the words as she reads. Across the room the machine sits silent. It, too, is waiting for a spark that will kindle it to life.

*

The Little Blonde Secretary puts the cover over her machine, tidies her desk and takes her bag to the Ladies'. She puts paper all over the seat and does a little pee before coming out, washing her hands, and fluffing up her hair. She peers at her eyebrows, which need tweezing, she thinks, and returns to her office. Through the half-open door she sees the Boss Masculine, cigarette in mouth, telephone at ear, brush one of his shoulders with his free hand. Disgusting, she thinks, and heads for the homeward tube, her little metal heels clacking quickly along the pavement. A workman gives her a wolf whistle, to which she returns a haughty look. All the same, she takes it as her due. She takes care of her appearance and cannot grumble if they wish to show their appreciation. She is feeling slightly miffed since the plain (and slightly smelly) girl who works the switchboard has announced today that she is having a baby. The Little Blonde Secretary was surprised to find out that she was married at all, really, given that hairstyle. Clack, clack, clack, go her heels and she clitters down the station steps in a trice.

'Guess what?' says Derek, forking in whole lumps of fish and swallowing almost without chewing. 'I've ordered the suite for the bathroom and you should just *see* the taps.'

'Chew, Derek,' she says.

He begins to describe them. He smiles as he does so. Out come those teeth again with little bits of fish attached to them.

'When you have finished what is in your mouth, Derek,' she says.

He gulps and begins describing them again. Brunel, when first he beheld the joys of ironwork, could not have been more enthusiastic.

The Little Blonde Secretary Bird feels better. She likes Derek to be occupied. Nobody else will have anything like those taps since they are newly over from France. When, one day, their home is complete and they begin to entertain, people will be very, very impressed. It's a shame they haven't had much opportunity to see their friends since they moved here, but what with one thing and another there just hasn't been time . . .

'Lovely,' she says, and adds some water to the teapot. On the kitchen table is a note she had made to herself. It says, 'Eyebrows!' and is underlined several times.

Derek pushes his plate away and begins reading the catalogue for extractors. He will watch *Coronation Street* first (she likes him to digest his food properly) and then begin measuring up.

*

Square Jaw is humming to himself as he makes his way out of the Rawalpindi and back to the car. He has bought lamb pasanda, chicken mughlai, Bangalore okra, special dhal, stuffed paratha and plain nan (remembering that Melanie prefers these to rice). With a selection of relishes, and mango ice-cream. His heart is once again light. He is doing the right thing. He is courting her as she asked. Is he not?

Melanie is also humming. She has decided to push the boat out after all and makes fish kebabs, steak au poivre, and pavlova. The magazine menu also suggested mango ice-cream, but it is not a fruit she cares for. Besides, there is quite enough to eat and, she simpers into the fish marinade, they don't want to be sitting up eating *all* night now, do they? He will understand from all this what she means by tokens of love. She smiles and hums again. Won't he?

*

Red Gold has persuaded Mrs Lovitt to cover for her in the afternoon. 'I have something to deliver to Lambeth Palace,' she says, 'and I need to wait for a reply.'

If you are going to lie successfully, she remembers him saying before a television interview, then lie outrageously.

Mrs Lovitt is impressed. Lambeth Palace!

'I wish I could say more,' whispers Red Gold, 'but I am sworn to secrecy.'

Mrs Lovitt's eyes bulge. She practically genuflects. And only from Cockermouth. Truly the Church is taking a serious approach to the North–South divide. Mrs Lovitt is from Guildford and has had nothing to do directly with Lambeth Palace *ever*.

Red Gold slips away. She intends to call into a department store first and use their make-up.

Her heart beats painfully.

Her hands tremble.

Love.

She could almost faint with the prospect of the wicked act before her.

No, Arthur, she says, when his sad face invades her excitement, I have been a good wife and have atoned for not loving. This is my reward. Just one look, one meeting perhaps (her desire for this is too powerful not to hope), and then, no more. Just this one thing. To see him again, to talk to him. What harm can it do? Just this once?

*

When the ambulancemen came to collect the body, they found there were two. One very dead, one alive and groaning. The

78

corridor was warm and airless. Mr Jones stood to one side to let them pass. They sniffed.

'Been here some time by the smell of it,' said one.

The other put a clean white handkerchief to his nose and nodded.

Mr Jones picked up his tool-box, stepped over the body and stood close to them. He was interested in what they had to say.

'Must have been here for days. Phew!' They spoke in unison and with some relish.

'On the contrary,' said Mr Jones with dignity, feeling in some way this was an aspersion on his efficiency as caretaker. 'It has only just occurred.' He stepped closer. They recoiled anew.

'Christ,' said the one with the handkerchief. 'It's him.'

Warm air, closed-in corridors, body heat and pickling vinegar create an odour not unlike the rotting of corpses or unwashed feet. Mr Jones was asked to leave the area and he did so thankfully. His onions called. From the slowly cooling body of Sylvia Perth came the fragrance of Arpège and Ottoman roses. Breathing free again, the ambulancemen advanced on the injured policeman and made as if to tend to him. Good manual training made sure that the living were always dealt with first. Sergeant Pitter whimpered as they made to move him, and suggested they should deal with the corpse first. He wanted time to build up to the idea of going anywhere; at that precise moment the corridor floor and his position upon it seemed the best and only place to be, and he was rather afraid of bursting into tears or something disgraceful if this comforting space were taken from him.

They carried Sylvia Perth with her mingled scent of Arpège, roses and death juice very gently down the stairs and settled her comfortably in the ambulance. Then they went back for the injured policeman. Without enthusiasm he heard them returning slowly up the stairs. He had just found a position in which the pain, though acute, was bearable, providing he bit the end of his tie and thought of Mrs Pitter's marmalade pudding. The mind plays useful tricks when the body is under siege. The two ambulancemen came on resolutely and stood over him. He relinquished the pudding, though not the tie, and looked at them.

They returned the look and both had the simultaneous thought that they had seen this officer before. But where? The one scratched his head, the other looked inquiringly. The policeman stared from one to the other with pleading eyes.

'I know you'll do your duty by me,' he said, and also wondered where he had seen them before.

It was the phrase 'do your duty' that gave it away. Light dawned for the two ambulancemen. The last time Sergeant Pitter had uttered that phrase in their presence it had been under very different circumstances and in a very different tone of voice. Then it had been said with intimidating sarcasm shortly before PC Pitter, the energetic police recruit eager for promotion, had stove in their placards and upturned their emergency-fund stall. FAIR PAY FOR AMBULANCEMEN their placards had said before being ground into the pavement by an exceptionally well-polished boot. Twelve weeks of no pay, the vilification of politicians and the tag of killers by default in the tabloid press left a deep impression. The dispute may have been years ago but the memory was fresh for ever in their minds.

They nudged each other to affirm recognition and narrowed their eyes.

'It *is* him?' said the one.

'It is,' said the other.

'Right?' said the one.

'Right,' said the other.

They rubbed their hands and spat on them. Sergeant Pitter did not altogether like that gesture. He had seen it once or twice preceding a particularly gruesome wrestling match. With some embarrassment he found himself saying, 'Be gentle with me.' They spat, rubbed, advanced again and bent towards him.

The screams were pitiful. Janice, despite being on the fifth floor and putting a cushion over her head, could still hear them as they issued from the depths of the ambulance itself. Only Sylvia Perth remained unmoved. Mr Jones turned his hearing-aid off. What with the screams and the chatter of the gawping crowd that had collected about the ambulance, his brain felt quite spongy. The gawping crowd thought that at the very least the policeman had sustained serious injury in the course of his duty, and lost all sympathy when the ambulancemen told them he had pulled a back muscle. If that was the kind of cowardly reaction a sergeant of the Force gave for something so trivial it was no wonder danger walked the streets.

'Blimey, mate,' said a generously proportioned woman of late years, 'try having a baby . . .'

Another woman tittered.

A third guffawed.

The law was seen to be weakened.

'Help!' cried the sufferer from the depths of the ambulance.

Its driver revved and made for a pothole in the road. Sylvia Perth, untroubled, bounced.

'Help!' cried Sergeant Pitter.

But none came.

After traction treatment and a short spell at home under Mrs Pitter's feet (during the course of which she withdrew both marmalade pudding and conjugal rights), Sergeant Pitter was never – quite – the energetic young officer of his fancy again.

When the ambulance drove off, Janice, who had retrieved her head from beneath the cushion and was peeking out from her balcony, felt a profound sense of relief. She also felt, with a mixture of hope and certainty, that she had been permanently reprieved from that chilling rap at the door. Now all she could do was wait. And hope. She looked at her postcard of Christine de Pisan depicted as she knelt before her queen and patroness to present her book.

How smilingly the wimpled queen accepted tribute. How delightedly her entourage of ladies looked on. The young widow had supported three children and a mother by her pen. Janice felt she was being just the teeniest bit weak by hiding herself away. And for one wild, glorious moment Janice wondered whether she could do something similar with Queen Elizabeth II? But she decided against it. It didn't seem very likely that they would find a little workroom for her in Buckingham Palace. Best wait here, then. She picked up her Froissart. Something was bound to turn up.

Chapter Seven

ROHANNE Bulbecker was lying under a man when the telephone call came.

'Excuse me,' she said, reaching out her arm and picking up the receiver. 'Roll off. I need to breathe.'

Outside the window, far off below, came the sound of Broadway traffic. The cultivated attending the Carnegie Hall or attempting to. The man listened and felt he was really beginning to get to know Rohanne. He concentrated on recalling the hoarding that had recently been erected near his apartment of a big-breasted woman with parted wet lips advertising toothpaste. He had to do something to maintain nether activity.

Rohanne was certainly exciting. Even if she did do things like throw him over for a telephone call at a time like this. And she was looking more and more excited as she gripped the phone. 'Do you really think there's a chance? Oh *God!*' she writhed pleasurably. The man watched a little nervously. 'That would be so wonderful ...' She held the telephone away from her and apostrophized towards the ceiling. 'So *excruciatingly* wonderful!'

Herbie cleared his throat. He wasn't sure if she had finished on the phone or not. And, anyway, there were limits. What was going on, anyway? Fortunately there was something erotic about it all. Even the telephone ... 'Rohanne,' he said firmly, 'are we going to continue, or what?'

'I want it, I want it. Oh *God*, how I want it!' shrieked Rohanne Bulbecker, undulating into the rumpled sheets, still clutching the telephone.

It was hardly Herbie's fault that he misinterpreted this. Rohanne could be unpredictable (red wine with fish, dislike of Lloyd Webber musicals), so it was not at all unlikely that she might wish to continue their coupling while still on the telephone. Women had a right to their fantasies just as he did. With renewed vigour he leapt back into position and enjoined himself anew like a dowel into yielding wood.

At the other end of the telephone in a quiet room in Bloomsbury, Rohanne Bulbecker's London connection reeled and put down the telephone. He was a fastidious, celibate man and given to obedience. When someone shrieked, 'Get off, damn you,' twice down the telephone to him, there was little he could do but oblige. He shook his neat, unremarkable head and wondered at folly. So far as he knew, his information about Sylvia Perth's death and the freeing of Janice Gentle should have made Ms Bulbecker very happy. He had been retained by her when she was in London and instructed to keep his ear to the ground (he winced at the paucity of such language), his eyes open and his mind on the job (wince, wince), for which he would be well paid. Now here he was reporting to her exactly what she wanted to hear and she had reacted like that. Even more grateful that he had no emotional involvement with either unpredictable women or difficult men, he let himself out of his service apartment and walked down the road for a curry in solitude.

He decided as he nibbled his onion bhaji that he would, after all, become a monk. A quiet order somewhere in Malvern would suit him very well. With sudden certainty he knew that he could never, under any circumstances, be associated with the book business any more. If you were going to have popular fiction – he plucked at the crispy batter – then Janice Gentle was not bad. Indeed, given what you quite often found nowadays, she was remarkably good. He rather admired the way she managed to get to the heart of things. You could detect some real emotion despite the somewhat hackneyed settings she chose. And her characters were soothingly human ... And – fair play – like Henry Miller, she could write; she had a natural rhythm, a delicacy, a sense of the poetical tucked within her somewhere. He was not at all surprised that Pfeiffer wanted her. She had class. He sighed. All that would probably go now. Janice Gentle would get sexy, no doubt of it with Rohanne Bulbecker in pursuit. And he had – still bound into the modern measure of the earth – accepted the silver. He held the bhaji aloft and pulled a face of painful regret. Judas money. Janice Gentle wrote with a sweet, direct line all the way back to the first flowering of literature. Chaucer, Pisan, Langland, Boccaccio. From now on all that would go.

Suddenly he was very glad Rohanne Bulbecker had shouted down the telephone. Suddenly he saw the way. Suddenly, though he might in reality be sitting in a London high street, he found himself on a metaphorical Road to Damascus. A phrase heard at a publisher's drinks party recently had offended his delicacy so much that he had, until this moment, refused to remember it. Now he did, and it made him shudder. Commodity publishing. Books as packaged, marketed products. About as inspiring as vacuum-packed ham, and with just as much water added. The clean and sterilized robe covering old whore's petticoats. The old whore being bread and circuses, for who but a fool nowadays would give *hoi polloi* the chance to read what might inspire them to set high their sights? The pen had lost its universal bite and had become no more than the Soma of *Brave New World*. He looked across at the waiter, patiently sitting while he finished his starter. He was reading a newspaper, small, easily handled, quickly digested (rather like chips), none of its paragraphs longer than four lines . . .

Well. He would have no more of it. If Ms Rohanne Bulbecker changed her mind about his getting off the telephone and called him back wanting him to pursue the issue further, he would refuse. That, at least, in atonement he could do. He very much liked the idea of atonement. He should have got out of publishing years ago, when Higgins's eagle first landed . . .

The waiter, looking up suddenly, was distressed at the look of painful regret and hurried over, anxious to know what was wrong with the bhaji. He waved him away with an elegant gesture of blessing. Already, in his head, he was tonsured and beatified. He sipped his lager as if it were mead. Crap was invading everywhere. He had promoted some of it, and now he was ashamed before his God. And Janice Gentle. If there was one thing that slick cat Perth had done, it was to defend her popular kitten. Now she had gone – well, no one was going to leave *that* kind of prominence alone. Babbittry, Babbittry – all was Babbittry. Popular fiction. Pah! He banged down his glass in disgust. He had had quite enough of popularity. Look where popularity led to – stringing up blacks and putting gays in hospital. No, no, he had betrayed them all, from Dante to Woolf, from Petrarch to Joyce, betrayed those who believed in *quality* literature for all. He must now atone.

If he *must* atone (which he knew he must), then it would be suitably fitting to do it in an itchy robe under ascetic conditions in the heart of those sublime, inspiring Malvern Hills. They had found a hair shirt under Thomas à Becket's ritual finery: the discovery had made men fall to their knees and weep. He popped the last of the onion bhaji into his mouth. Now that *was* a telling image . . . He would pray for those who had turned their backs on literature and taken the primrose path towards pap. He would pray for them hourly and hope that it got no worse. It couldn't – could it? Whatever the answer, he was best out of it . . .

'And leaves the world to darkness and to me . . .'

He thought lovingly of the beautiful Rupert. So golden, so fair. He was glad that such a prince had died young. What was wrong with seeing death as a purifying romance? Flanders trenches need not necessarily debase the beauty of the dead lying amongst those blood-red poppies. Rupert had looked up, not down. Heroism, lyricism, beauty . . . poetry. That was what counted, the poetry of the soul, the spirit beyond the body, the romance, the utter, utter *romance* of the mighty line. Everybody used to read it. Nobody said it was too bloody difficult and they couldn't understand it and please could they have something a bit lighter. Why, the very defeat of War as a Popular Pastime came from the pens of poets: Sassoon, Owen (another beauty), Hardy. Where had the popularity of such writing gone? Brooke. His mind would keep returning to Brooke – he was so *extraordinarily* beautiful. He smiled regretfully. No more of that, either. He must do penance for the thought.

He wiped his fingers – Pilate-like, he thought. Poetry. He had asked a young man about his views on poetry in this very restaurant a while ago. A nice-looking young man with a strong, square jaw, who was waiting to collect a take-away. The chap was educated, well spoken, apparently cultivated, yet he merely said that he didn't know anything about the stuff – absolutely nothing. And smiled as if he had said he didn't know how to get to Catford by bus. And, oh dear, the temptation to offer to read him some had been acute – but overcome. No. He had chosen celibacy. Henceforth, celibacy. To remember the words of love must be enough.

If Janice Gentle must get sexy, he would wash his hands of it. That the pursuit of religious belief had become mingled with the pursuit of romantic love in the flowering of the Chivalric Ideal seemed acceptable, understandable, forgivable. Innocent, even. But to replace it with the crudity of sexual sentiment? Wretchedly base.

He observed his lager, held it up. Why look through a glass darkly when all around were longing for the strip light to come on? No mystery. Anatomy rather than feeling. Bones but no breath. Perhaps he should record this passing like the monks of old? He smiled at the thought. Aelfric, Caedmon, the Venerable Bede. How could they know what they had started? He smiled and placed a thin line of *raita* on the edge of his plate. The souring of what was once sweet. The conundrum of the modern age. Pfeiffer begat Bulbecker, and Bulbecker would beget Gentle. And who would stop them? Him? Ah, no. He could do nothing, *nothing* . . .

Malvern, then, and the verses of Gerard Manley Hopkins in a cold, white cell. As far removed from the bathos to come as he hoped was heaven from hell.

His chicken mughlai was brought to the table. He looked at it with clasped hands and spiritual wonder. It was probably the last rich dish he would eat in his whole life and it smelled delicious.

He began to eat. Rohanne Bulbecker could damn well do her damnedest all on her own. He would have no more of it.

'Flesh fade, and mortal trash/Fall to the residuary worm . . .'

He picked an almond out of the creamy sauce and sucked it.

The waiter hovered anxiously.

'God bless the spirit of humanity, if not its works,' he said.

The waiter bowed. The mughlai was obviously all right.

'Behold,' said his customer, bowing back. 'I see the clear light of bliss.' He smiled at the waiter. 'Did you ever read a poet called Gerard Manley Hopkins?'

The waiter returned the smile, bowed again and withdrew. The English were very strange. Why should he know about *their* poets when he had fine poets enough of his own?

Ms Rohanne Bulbecker sat up in bed and redialled the London number unsuccessfully. Herbie she had consigned to the Manhattan stars. She had hit him on the shin with her Filofax, a good aim, and now she sank back among the pillows and tried for the second time to recall her London connection. This time it rang but there was no reply. An onion bhaji was being nibbled, a life decision had been taken, and Ms Rohanne Bulbecker, rather like her London prey, stood alone.

She pushed aside the telephone, drew up her long white legs, rested her dainty chin upon her perfect knees, and thought. She was an intelligent woman. She realized that her screeching must have offended her London connection, and she also realized that there was no time to redress his umbrage. Besides, he had told her all she needed to know. Sylvia Perth was dead. Janice Gentle was back on the market. Action. And off the bed she tumbled.

'To London. To London. This time to win,' she sang, reaching for her suitcase, scrabbling among her clothing, cursing her ragged nails for catching in everything she touched. Since her lunch interview with Sylvia Perth, she had done nothing but bite them down to the quick, wait for them to grow, and bite them again. Loathsome, and a sign of deep personal distress. She smiled to herself. She contemplated her hands and no longer felt distressed. Soon, very soon, she would be able to grow them back again. Perhaps the nails would be even longer and more beautifully shaped than before.

She folded her black biker's jacket, rolled up her leather trousers and threw in her Ray-Bans. Looking threatening was quite useful when you were endowed with a gamine blondeness, and she would rather wear leathers than have her hair shorn or her nose professionally broken for the blessing of being taken seriously. Sometimes her attractions were a positive disadvantage. One of the things she rather liked about Herbie was that he didn't seem to mind what she looked like – travel-exhausted or ready for the ball. But she sure as hell wasn't going to tell him that. Love was next stop disaster, and life was far too inviting to get caught up in its snares. She shivered. Look what happened if you did.

All the same, she wished he had thrown the Filofax back instead of just limping off like that. Still, it was the third date and about time he got his marching orders. Men, like fish, in Rohanne Bulbecker's opinion, should not hang around too long.

She snapped her case shut and rang Morgan Pfeiffer. 'Sylvia Perth has died,' she said, 'and I am going to London now to find Janice Gentle.' Everything was arranged and with a light and happy heart, Rohanne Bulbecker set off.

As she retrieved her Filofax from the door, she thought again of Herbie. How *could* he think she wanted sex during a telephone call? Men!

Not bothering to wait for the elevator, she whistled her way down the stairs feeling very happy indeed. Success was waiting for her. Too bad about her London connection but, really, it didn't pay to be quite so fastidious in this day and age.

Chapter Eight

I N Skibbereen Dermot Poll grunted and moved his head with annoyance. His chin rasped against the grey sheet that was tucked around his neck. He turned on his side and swore. 'Shite and more shite,' he groaned. 'Wouldn't you think they'd fly their planes somewhere else? Why it's scarcely the morning . . .'

He pressed his buttocks into the ample female behind that was Deirdre, and she too grunted. What she grunted was difficult to distinguish, but the gist of it was clear.

'Pig yourself,' he retorted, and pressed his head further into the pillow. The smell of it was strong. 'If you cleaned up a bit, I'd be less of a pig – even were I a pig, which I am not.'

This time what she grunted was perfectly distinguishable.

'And you,' he murmured comfortably, and slept anew.

Outside in the passageway their son, Declan, tiptoed past the door. He was a man now and he was going to seek his fortune in London. And not like the others, either – it wasn't to be the building site for him. Oh no – he could sing, he had his guitar, and he had thirty-eight Irish pounds in his pocket. He pushed open his father's pub door and went out into the beautiful fresh air. Swirling behind him came the stale unwholesome atmosphere of last night's revelries. That was the last time he would sing for that drunken lot, with their tears and their anger and their patriotic, meaningless sentimentality. He inhaled long, wonderful breaths of the sea air and took the road out of Skibbereen towards freedom. And, unlike his father before him, he had no intention of ever coming back.

Dermot slept on, rank-breathed, raw-chinned, greasy from sleep and odorous of excess, unaware that more waves were breaking all around him than the silver horses on the shores of Skibbereen.

Rohanne's plane, diverted, roared on over the green beauty of Erin, but she never looked down nor gave it a thought. On her lap was a Janice Gentle book and her calculator. When she pulled this deal off it would be like the Phoenix rising once more.

She drummed her fingers on the book jacket. According to the captain they were just flying over Dublin waters. She looked down but could see nothing save greenness and sea in the morning mist. All that Ireland meant to her at that precise moment was an irritating addition to her ETA.

Chapter Nine

SYLVIA Perth had been put on trial for her obscene sin of dying in a public place without first giving statement of intent, and being unoriginal enough to have done it of proven natural causes. The case was closed and Sylvia Perth's remains were released for interment. The media showed little interest in this small death since a member of the Blood Royal had been discovered in a massage parlour and there was a summer heat wave – 'Phew Wot a Scorcher' – both of which news items put the demise of one female literary agent into the shade. Happily, for Janice (though sadly for the Royal transgressor), she was left completely unpursued by the Hounds of Wapping.

On she waited, quietly, calmly, in her cloister of beige, certain that something was bound to turn up.

The police, in their inquiries regarding the reason Sylvia Perth should have been in the apartment building at all (and perhaps fired by the 'Sexy Royal in Oily Romps' headlines), decided that just about the only natural thing in Sylvia Perth's life was the cause of her death, and that very probably she had been visiting the apartment building in Battersea for 'Lezzie Perves in Girlie Romps' activities, not literary ones. Despite their inclinations this was not a punishable offence, though it was, of course, disgusting, and without the iron zeal of Sergeant Pitter the matter was given only a cursory investigation.

Door-to-door inquiries provided no serious leads (the only non-alibied female, being fat, bespectacled and, so far as they could tell, three quid short of a five-pound note, was left alone). Mr Jones forgot everything because he wanted to get on with life. His hearing-aid came in very useful if his forgetfulness seemed in question. Sergeant Pitter could not think beyond his pain to what caused it in the first place, and, all in all, the parties concerned in the 'Dead Body in the Lift' episode appeared to be potty.

The pursuance of potty people was not the issue concerning the Great British Public at the time. They wanted law and order restored; they wanted their girl guides and aunties to walk abroad at night without being mugged, raped, terrorized; even the traditional criminal classes were indignant at the nasty turn things were taking. Despite governmental pressure for more and younger and larger exposed breasts in the tabloids, the natives were becoming restive. The police were told in no uncertain terms to catch a few big-time bad eggs and made the mistake of catching out a captain of industry in a rather large city-based fraud, thus embarrassing rather than enhancing the Government, with whom (possibly metaphorically) the captain of industry was intimately involved. It was no time to go pursuing perverts unless they were perverts in high places. All in all, the reputation of the law enforcers was at a very low ebb. The women of Battersea were not surprised. As one remarked to the other while waiting in the launderette, 'If a policeman's going to burst into tears and call an ambulance just because his back aches – well, I mean to say . . .'

Since she had no way of mourning beyond the immediately accessible, she had put the cover on her word processor. Before doing so she contemplated erasing everything to do with *Phoenix Rising* (especially the title), but did not. Somehow it seemed right, a connection with Sylvia, to keep it all in there, even if it would never now be used. There had been no word from anyone about a funeral, and Janice was not sure she could have faced one anyway, but since she had not taken part in such a ritual, in a sense Sylvia Perth was still with her.

Christine de Pisan tried to encourage her. 'When I started to write, things were a great deal tougher. Those *witty* lordlings publishing their *blastanges de femmes* all over the place against my sex, I can tell you. And very popular they were, too. Of course I succeeded in countering the defamations in the end and published my *Cité des dames* in praise of women – to great acclaim, actually. So I can't really feel a lot of sympathy for you. Not really, I'm afraid.'

Janice spooned in chocolate mousse miserably. It's all very well for you, Christine, she thought, but you're *dead*. Janice was undoubtedly alive. Very much alive. Signs of forthcoming patronage were not. She was still but a lady-in-waiting. She glanced at the covered screen and wondered, very hard, whatever would become of it all.

*

In Croydon Derek gave a loud whoop of joy as the Vent-Axia unit slipped perfectly into the hole he had made. Not many men could have done that straight off, he thought to himself, and he felt very manly. It had been the same when he made the cellar steps. Bingo! They had slotted in just like that. But when he had called his wife to see the six-stair miracle, she hadn't shown as much enthusiasm as he would have liked. 'I hope you haven't made too much mess' was all she said, which was rather unsympathetic given all his efforts. He had taken half his annual leave to do the job. And although to him making cellar steps was as good as a week in Torquay – still, she might have been perkier. You wait, he had thought irritably, you wait until you need to come down here with your hands full. You'll be jolly glad of a decent stairway then.

So much for the cellar. Perhaps the Vent-Axia would be different. He turned on the switch and the softness of its whirring was music to his ears. He stood there for a little while basking in the achievement, and then he called his wife. He called her again. He called her from the top of the landing but still no response. Suddenly he felt extremely cross; he'd been working in the bathroom up here since after their evening meal and she hadn't come up once – not *once* – to see what he was doing or to bring him a hot drink. Other wives did that sort of thing. Ken at work had only been saying so today – and what's more, Ken at work

94

went out to the pub twice a week with the lads. Derek had never done anything like that, being happy to stay at home and do things about the house.

Eventually she called up to him. 'Not *now*, Derek,' she said. 'Can't you see I'm *busy*?'

Surely he had a right to feel hurt? Creating a non-damp atmosphere, *and* one that removed unpleasant odours (and it certainly hadn't been an easy job), was something he had done for both of them. Usually she would be very encouraging, but just recently she had been, well, less than her efficient and supportive self. She'd said something about the receptionist where she worked, but he had lost the thread of it. It would have been all the same if *he'd* said *he* was busy. After all, what was a moment or two to pop upstairs and admire what he had done? He looked with some pride at the Vent-Axia again.

As he had pointed out to Ken at work, a diamond ring might well be for ever, but with the wrong fitting in the plughole it could soon slip off and be lost for ever as well. Hah hah! He was always thinking of things to make everything function more perfectly. She liked that, didn't she? Then why couldn't she leave off whatever she was doing and come upstairs for a moment to say so? Women were a mystery. He would bloody well go to the pub like Ken had suggested. He tried out the Vent-Axia one more time before going downstairs; it worked a treat. Then he stood at the open front door very pointedly, with his anorak thrown carelessly over his shoulder, and declared rather tersely that he was going *out*.

Perhaps she would call him back? 'Bye,' she said from the kitchen. She had her Van Morrison turned up and was humming to it.

'Will you be having a bath later, then?' he called.

She put her head round the kitchen door. 'I always have a bath, Derek, every night,' and she was gone again.

Something had definitely got up her nose. He smiled over his teeth. Well, with the new unit installed it couldn't be *that*, now could it?

He tried to close the door loudly but the new Softaslam fitting meant he couldn't. Everything was against him. Even the building inspector, who had said there just wasn't room to extend the loft. Derek had been so disappointed. He'd got himself all geared up for it. The Vent-Axia had been a little bit of compensation for them both.

By the time he reached the gate his crossness had evaporated. Hallo? What was this? One of the hinges not quite right. He'd have to fix that. Indeed, now he came to think of it, the whole fence looked a bit dodgy. Perhaps that's what he should do this weekend. He set off down the pavement, swinging his anorak and calculating the amount of wood required, and felt quite cheerful again.

The Little Blonde Secretary sighed with relief. She had cleaned the bath after Derek, hoovered up all his mess – in the bathroom, along the landing *and* in the bedroom for heaven's sake – and now she was soaking in their nice, new big bath. A faint whirring above her head made her look up. A new plastic object stuck out from the wall, ugly and irritating. The steam rose towards it, it whirred even louder. She tried to lie there with her eyes closed and think nice thoughts, which is what that article on relax your way to beauty had said, but she couldn't. It sounded like there was a dentist drilling away in the room with her. Oh, for God's sake! She got out.

As she dried herself and put on her nightshirt, she thought that *surely* she had the right to feel angry. First, his mess left all over the place (was he blind or what?); and second, here she was, the first time for ages, alone in the house and able to enjoy the peace (no drills, no smell of paint, no hammering) and he hadn't even done the job properly, because, whatever that thing was up there, it was making an awful racket and obviously needed attention.

She did her nightly face cleanse, taking particular trouble with the pores at the side of her nose. These – she peered more closely – seemed to be getting a little larger. Perhaps she should get one of those face-steamers she had seen advertised. As she plucked away at a few odd stragglers around her eyebrows, she gave a sour little snort; better not tell Derek she was thinking of buying that sort of thing or he'd volunteer to build one. But she *did* like everything to be nice about herself; if you looked nice, then you felt nice, and if you felt nice, then your life was nice. How that plain telephonist at work could actually be pregnant, looking the way she did was – well . . . The Little Blonde had no intention of letting herself go, *ever*, because once you did – she shuddered – it would be impossible to get the niceness back. That woman in the tube the other day, for example. *Gross*, absolutely gross . . . No wonder she stared so hard at her. Envy. Not surprising. *Gross*.

She read a Janice Gentle for a little while in bed, and when she felt drowsy she curled up her legs, snapped out the light and fell prettily and daintily asleep to dream of exotic places, beautiful clothes and a man who was faceless but who didn't seem to be Derek at all, because he was – odd, really – a dentist.

Derek, returning a while later, slipped in beside her and reached for that nice curving bit she had at the bottom of her stomach. He tried to wake her by squeezing it, but she rolled away and brought her knees up to her chest and slept on. Ah well. He turned his mind to the satisfying new addition in the bathroom. 'And what did you think of my little surprise, then,' he murmured happily. 'I see you had a bath. Good, isn't it?'

He ran his tongue over his teeth. He had forgotten to clean them. Oh well. If she couldn't come and look when he wanted her to, why should he do what *she* wanted all the time? He closed his eyes. Ken was probably right about being able to reuse some of the existing wood for the new fence. He pushed his back up against hers. As he dozed off, he reflected that he wouldn't mind a bit of the other – a little reward for all his efforts – but she was far away now and he couldn't imagine that she'd be pleased to be woken up just for that. Ah well. He put his hand on his own private bits. They'd die down soon enough. He yawned – what with the beer and everything – and, feeling very contented, he snuggled himself further into his wife's sweet-smelling posterior and drifted off to sleep.

*

Square Jaw was lying awake and feeling sorry for himself. He felt misunderstood and undervalued and the dry-cleaning hadn't removed all the marks of the take-away she had up-ended over him. There were no two ways about it, women were neurotic and whatever you did was wrong. They could be taken in by the contrived notion of a bunch of flowers and other such devices, while when you *did* do something nice they'd say it wasn't what they needed. Then if you asked, 'Well, what do you need?' they'd say, 'If I have to tell you, then there's not much point.' As if you were a bloody fortune-teller or something. Well, that was it, certainly it so far as Melanie was concerned. He could get sex any time without all this fuss. He just had to go to a club or something. There was always plenty of it flying around, and you were all right, providing you used condoms. Not that he particularly fancied sex much at the moment – he didn't seem to fancy anything much – but, then, the weather was oppressive. Of course he was all right during the day, because he had his work, which concentrated his mind completely, but apart from that the stuffing seemed to have gone out of him.

Naturally enough it was going to be a bit hard at first, but he was looking forward to being single again. It would free him up for all kinds of things. In the evenings it got a bit difficult, but he managed to watch television or go out. Last night he had been to see a film someone at work had said was really sexy, *The Unbearable Lightness of Being*, but it had depressed him rather than excited him. And one or two lines that the woman said reminded him of – well, they sounded familiar, anyway. So he came out again and didn't see the end. Sentimentality. That was all it was. It was also disturbing to see them making love like that. It hadn't made him horny so much as – well, a bit low-spirited, really.

Sex was what cornered you, it was sex that gave you a need for a relationship. If it weren't for that, he would probably never look at another woman again. They set snares for you with their curves and their smiles and the way they were so accommodating at the beginning. Anyway, he had put all *her* stuff – scent bottles, nightie, flannel, hair-dryer, make-up, clothes (a surprising amount) – into a cardboard box and shoved it under the bed. He certainly wasn't going to sit around being reminded of all that shit, nor of *her*. If he found himself wondering what she was up to, he soon stopped. What good did that do? Chewing things over in your mind didn't help – he wanted to bury it all and just forget. He sniffed his jacket. He could definitely still smell the lamb pasanda, and he was sure he still had some in his ear. God – *women*. Melanie's face was suddenly in his head. What was she doing? He went and had a shower and turned on the hi-fi loud. He didn't want to know. He thought of that woman in the tube train, the fat one with the piece of ham lolling out. Who was to say Melanie wouldn't end up looking like that, anyway? What he must do was keep himself busy, fill up his time so that he didn't find himself alone and having to *think*.

Melanie had done several things. She had hit the bottle alone. She had gone out to a wine bar and felt wonderfully in control as she flirted, and the man had been lovely really, saying all sorts of nice things and being very complimentary, but suddenly she didn't want him and refused, very firmly, when he asked to take her home. 'You're mad,' said her friend Becky, 'he's really nice.' Melanie thought to herself, So was the other one once. And she went home, sorrowing alone.

Then she had sat with girlfriends, talking it all over, paring it down to the last little detail, working out what *he* felt, why *he* said this, did that, until, eventually, shaking their heads, they declared that The Way Men Were was impossible to deal with and that Melanie had had a lucky escape. It didn't feel like that when, the next night, in an unbearable rush of needing, she had driven past his flat and seen him getting into his car looking haggard. At first she felt pleased, then she cried, for his haggard appearance probably meant he had been living it up, burning the candle, sleeping with loads of women. She suddenly wanted to know if this was true, and dialled all but the last digit of his telephone number before hanging up. She *didn't* want to know, just as much as she *did*. She had cried during a film, cried in the office, cried at home, in the car, even cried in Marks and Spencer when she saw the orchids, because they were the flowers he had brought her on their first date. The only thing that sustained her was that this terrible separation gave him time to think and understand what had gone wrong – as long as *he* was confronting it, as long as *he* was thinking about it. As long as he was, then surely he'd understand . . .?

*

In the garden in Cockermouth Red Gold was leaning on her gate, looking harassed and being talked at very earnestly by a headscarfed woman of slightly older years.

'There is too much sin,' said Headscarf.

'Or not enough,' said Red Gold defiantly, and then immediately colouring, both for the little thrill she felt and for the effect the statement was likely to have.

'That is hardly the observation I would expect of a vicar's wife,' said the shocked woman questioningly. 'What do you mean?'

Red Gold thought quickly. 'I mean,' she said, her tone suitably humble, 'that the less sin there is in the world the more righteously can the majority condemn the weak minority who sin and whom the Bible tells us to love.'

The headscarfed one's jaw dropped. There was something wrong with that but it sounded very plausible.

The vicar approached. His eyes were on his wife, on the curve of her neck, on the line of her arm, on the shape of her hand as she brushed it among the blue delphiniums. Near to the hand that brushed the flower-tops was another, gloved, clasping and unclasping the top of the fence paling. It raised itself in greeting, to which he responded with similar gesture. His wife did not look round.

'Good morning,' he said to his discomfited parishioner, 'you look startled.'

He took his wife's hand and pressed it to his lips unselfconsciously, a gesture of connection, a little piece of loving; something had made her tense, he could tell from the way she was standing.

'Your wife thinks that there is not enough sin in the world.' The parishioner was not amused. Either by the statement or by the hand kiss. Apart from anything else, the parishioner was privately in love with the vicar herself, rather as she had been with his predecessor. As the woman who did most of the flowers and polished up the brasses, she had a right to love her vicars secretly. Part of the private love was feeling sorry for him, seeing him as a man made unhappy by his married mate. When he kissed his married mate's hand like that, it was hard to sustain the pity, and if that went – well, it might be the love to go next.

His wife removed her hand. Surreptitiously she rubbed where he had kissed it; it was not that kind of kiss that had been in her thoughts. He put his hand on her shoulder, lightly, and felt her stiffness. He wanted to say that her eyes matched the flowers and to lie down with her in the daisy lawn with the morning sun warming them. God, who knew everything, would just have to accept that he had thoughts like this. She did not know, his parishioners (perish the thought) did not know, it was only between himself and his God. He touched the bone of her shoulder, and he knew that if he followed it downwards it would lead to the soft delight of her breast. He smiled appeasingly at the headscarf, who had raised her nose and stuck out her chin and was waiting, the onus on him, to hear a rebuttal.

'That,' he said gallantly, 'is because she knows I like to be kept busy. And now I am afraid that I must whisk her away. We have the donations to count before Sunday and I have no head for figures . . .'

The vicar's wife trailed her hand back and forth across the tops of the flowers, watching the pollen dust scatter and the fading pods fall to the ground.

There was *not* enough sin in the world. Half an hour of it last week, and she was still savouring every minute, every second. She had gone into Body Shop and made up her face (trying not to look too closely as she did so: little red lines from the cruel northern winds, puffy tissue around the dulled eyes, mouth grown thin – no longer the rose he had called her). She had brightened herself up with a scarf worn as she used to wear it, thrown around her shoulders – casual elegance, not the sort of thing she indulged in nowadays. Funny, all the same, how the scarf had just fallen into place immediately. A latent skill, London scarf-throwing, one which you apparently never lost. It was almost as if she were being reminded that another life existed, that this life was still there if she wanted it, still there . . .

During Question Time in the House she did not listen but watched him. Characteristically, he had his arms folded, his long legs stretched out and crossed at the ankles. She remembered the body beneath the blue serge and how it looked and felt naked. From a distance he looked only a little changed – perhaps fleshier, perhaps greyer, perhaps more formal, but still him. She thought that if she closed her eyes, she could smell his smell again. Love me, she sent the message across the House, love me one more time . . . Only once more, and that will be enough.

They had a brief tea. He asked her if he was forgiven, he kissed the palm of her hand (that, she wanted to say now to Arthur, is where you kiss a woman's hand – not the cold, bony back of it, but the fleshy, warm softness of its centre. Fool). She lied and said she was terribly, terribly (the language of the thrown scarf coming back, too) happy up in the northern country. That Arthur was a dear, that her garden was beautiful, that . . . And then she had looked him in the eyes, defiantly, and said, 'I should like to go to bed with you one more time,' and he had said, so that her heart leapt and the place between her legs tingled, 'Only *one* more time?'

In the taxi back from Fortnum's she took his hand and kissed the palm of it as he had done hers, then she slipped it beneath her heather mixture handknit, under her plain cotton brassière (oh for the lace and teasing bows of yesterday, the oyster satin, the peachy silks), and for a brief moment yielded herself up to the searing experience of passion rekindled, until they reached the top of St James's, where they parted.

'Is it possible?' She stood on the pavement, holding the open window of the cab, so that it would not go until she was ready.

He knew what she meant.

He called her his dearest Alice, and it was as if the years had been wiped away. Her breast tingled. She looked at his hand, long, sensitive white fingers, curved and properly kept nails, and she thought with surprise of where it had recently been; they looked so innocent, those fingers, *he* looked so innocent, this Establishment Man.

'Let me know in advance next time you are coming down.' He said it cautiously.

She was rapturous.

During the last part of the conference she could not stop smiling and chuckling to herself, which caused Mrs Lovitt a great deal of confusion since the final session was about child abuse.

She arrived home, back to being Alice again. She told Arthur all the minutiae of the trip, including a description of the fat female eccentric whom she had sat next to in the tube.

'London seems to be full of madness,' she said, but she said it happily. She wanted Arthur to make love to her that night, but he did not come to bed for a long time. She suddenly remembered that she had left his *Church Times* in the tearoom. It was probably that which had offended him – he had been strange when he met her at the station.

Downstairs Arthur sat sipping malt whisky and wondering why his wife had come back wearing perfume and make-up, and why her eyes, always blue, looked as if she had changed the batteries in them, so brightly did they shine and sparkle now. She misses London, he consoled himself; she should have had a child, he consoled himself. He did not want to think beyond either of those. Nor why, in a desperate search for a collar stud (or was that true?), he had come across a powder compact and other little fancies in the back of her dressing-table drawer. He thought it was the one he had bought, but it was not. It was much finer. And it had a message of enduring love entwined with her and another's initials on the lid. He sipped on, the book of *Piers the Ploughman* and his open Bible forgotten at his side.

Chapter Ten

JANICE opened the window of her little balcony, but there was no air, only the midday heat and the smell of cars and tarmac. She was beginning to panic. Nothing had happened yet. This morning she had received her monthly cash delivery from the motorbike messenger, which seemed chillingly normal. Perhaps she had dreamt it? Perhaps Sylvia Perth had not died at all? Below her she saw Mr Jones in his boiler suit retreating down his steps. He would know, but she didn't want to ask. What could she say? 'Do you remember anything of a peculiar nature happening here recently?' Suppose he said no? Would she then go on to jog his memory? 'Something odd. In the lift, hmm? A body or anything?'

Hardly.

Yesterday, drawn by an urge that was stronger than the fear of madness, she had telephoned Sylvia's apartment. She had neither visited it nor telephoned it before, but Sylvia had given her the information to be used in emergencies. Well, this *was* a very real emergency, and though she had no expectation in mind, she dialled – quite unprepared for the shock of hearing Sylvia's voice.

'I'm sorry that I am not able to take your call right now. Leave a message and I will get back to you.'

Janice swallowed. It was as if she had not gone away at all, as if she had not ever died, as if she was still there, chic, bright, alert, a living thing. Janice ate a pound of maple Brazils while considering this phenomenon. She reached no solution, save it just felt *wrong*.

After that she rang the number several times, always to hear that voice, firm and alive, making the image of the torso in the lift seem unreal and remote . . .

*

Erica von Hyatt leaned against the scratchy, embroidered scene of Khomi (beautiful sloe-eyed adulteress) pursuing Khani (sacred bell-girl disguised as a boy), and wondered what to do for the best. What little food there had been in the flat she had consumed, and she was now down to a packet of halva, a tin of dried milk (rapidly diminishing), half a tin of coffee and a few dried pomegranates, which might or might not have been put there for decoration. There was also a highly ornate drinks cabinet, into which she had so far made only furtive dips, but that could change if nothing else happened soon.

'Do not answer the telephone,' Sylvia had said, 'and I will bring you something nice when I come back tonight.' Well, that had been so long ago that Erica von Hyatt had lost count of the days. She was not altogether disturbed by this, since life in general was a series of broken promises and fraying ends – but, all the same, she had not expected it to go on for quite so long. On the one hand it was much pleasanter here than hanging out in Piccadilly, on the other it was boring. The telephone had been going non-stop and the persistent whine and whirr of the answering machine had become like a coda in her life. Click, whirr, click, pause, whine, whine, whirr. She knew it very well and it took quite a lot of self-control not to throw it to the floor and stamp on it. She had placed a couple of sequinned cushions over it, which helped, and after the first couple of days the ringing eased off considerably. Only very occasionally now did it ring, and she almost didn't hear it any more.

The silence in the apartment was nice, and she had done a great deal of what she called luxury sleeping during the time she had spent alone, an enjoyable experience, but she wished she could go out now and then. Alas, if she did, she would not be able to get back in. It was tempting, though. She had found a ten-pound note and some coins in a drawer, and she knew that there must be a food shop somewhere round about, though the view from the window showed nothing but posh grey street. Perhaps she could just slip out, leaving the door on the latch and risk someone taking the opportunity to burgle the place? But supposing Sylvia came back and found it deserted? She would be angry and throw her out for showing such carelessness. Erica von Hyatt did not want to be thrown out just yet. She wanted to enjoy cleanliness and peace and quiet for a little while longer. Living on your wits was all very well and good for the adrenalin, but it was no compensation for stretching out on a couch and watching daytime television. *That*, Erica guessed, was what *real* women did.

Her stomach rumbled. Even around Eros there had been food, for Chrissake. If not from the tourists, then of the in-house variety: stolen fruit, the odd end of bread, a shared grimy cheese paring, all passed around with the same communal solicitude as a damp-ended joint. She did not question Sylvia's prolonged absence much. Erica von Hyatt had been left on her own a lot by her real mother before taking to the streets, and by a series of other mothers and fathers, all of whom had forsaken her sooner or later. Passing on was just a part of life, something you did when you had to do it. In her turn she had moved on from her own daughter when the time came. She had produced her, held her, kissed her a couple of times, and then left her in a doctor's waiting-room; you couldn't keep a baby on the streets. Erica had decided to stick to women after that. You didn't get pregnant and – on the whole – they weren't violent. Leaving Dawn (called that because she was born at dawn) at the surgery made Erica von Hyatt feel that she had been a responsible mother, no matter what those sentimental dossers might say. She *was* responsible, really. After all, she had looked after herself on the streets for years, and she was twenty-seven (or possibly twenty-eight, things got a bit fuzzy) and nothing really bad had ever happened to her. She'd been beaten up, locked up, even raped a couple of times, but you dealt with those things as part of the common lot. And you passed on, politely if possible, when the time came. She knew how to take care of rape nowadays. You just told them you had AIDS – it wasn't hard to believe when she was in her street gear

– and they backed off smartish. She was pretty sure she hadn't. There had been no more men after Dawn and she didn't do hard drugs. That really was for the birds. And you just looked out for yourself.

Sometimes though, like now, she played with the idea of being taken care of for ever, but people always buggered off in the end. Like this one would. But she couldn't have buggered off yet. Not leaving Erica here and with permission. She'd return. For the moment this was OK. A little bit of peace. Something must have come up unexpectedly. Well, Erica von Hyatt could wait.

She stretched, enjoying the freshness of her smell. No one had really damaged her on the inside, and on the outside she still looked great, better than most when she had a chance to clean herself up. Some people were just strong. She was. She liked herself because she could get through anything, and she liked the way she looked because it was part of the getting through. She kept her naturally fair hair very long, because when she did get the chance to wash it, it was really lovely. Her face looked more healthy than some of those secretary tarts she saw rattling their way along the morning streets. Her waist, hips, bum and thighs were all just as neat as when she left home, and, if anything, her knockers had improved since the baby, got bigger and stayed bigger – not gross or anything, just a decent size. Dawn would be about four now and she'd be *really* happy. Erica von Hyatt knew this because she knew exactly who the father was and he had a sunny nature just like she had a sunny nature, so Dawn would be the same. Erica was known as Mona Lisa among her peers, but the priest who ran the crypt sanctuary told her it wasn't very accurate because the Mona Lisa smiled in a sort of sad way, whereas Erica smiled with a sparkle. He had kissed her on the forehead after saying this and she – generously, she thought – had offered him one despite his gender, but he had jumped like she'd bitten it off. He told her she had to learn to separate the kinds of love there were in the world and find the one she wanted.

She was still thinking about that one. But in the meantime – she stretched lazily – in the meantime there was this little number here and she'd hang on to it for as long as possible. Nowhere was safe for ever, but this one was safe for the moment. It was warm, really luxurious if a bit on the small side, sustaining and, more to the point, she had got it to herself.

Of course the owner would come back some time or other, but that wasn't really a problem. Erica judged that little would be asked of her beyond the favours of what her body could do, and that was never a problem either, you just let yourself into overdrive for that, coasted through it where possible, and if it got more sophisticated and dangerous, then you got your head to-gether quick and went along with that, too – only with more awareness. She doubted if there would be anything like that here. Sylvia had been quite kind, and younger than many, with a body that was all right – if a little slack. Erica ran her hand over her stomach, quite good still, not slack at all. She doubted if she would ever reach the sort of age when it would go droopy, but she didn't feel bad about that – it just made sense to live for the moment. And for the moment this felt good. Occasionally she allowed herself to dream that this was her real home, but it made her feel quite maudlin, so she quickly stopped. Real homes were what other people had – the respectable people. She would never be one of those and, well, really, when she looked at them, she wasn't altogether sure she wanted to be. They all said one thing and did another. Anyway, fantasies about home were best left alone. In a way she was looking forward to the real owner of this place coming back. That would stop the fantasies. Sometimes they got quite painful.

Erica thought about it, sucking on the individual pomegranate seeds as she did so. The main thing about this one was that she was rich without, apparently, that streak of meanness which often accompanies the state. They had eaten a really nice meal that first night, delivered, which was very posh. It was quite spicy and very filling, and afterwards they had mucked around in the bed for ages with scents and oils and stuff. All quite nice, really. And although the woman had held on to her very tight in the night, an aspect that Erica found difficult, being used to sleeping alone, she could put up with that for a while. No, no, Erica von Hyatt was not about to lose it all just for a bit of temporary hunger. She was not going anywhere unless she was told, absolutely, that she had to. So she would wait. She had been told to wait, and she would wait. She stuck out her pretty chin with an unselfconscious gesture of determination; she was an invited guest and just let them say she wasn't. She would eat the halva, drink the coffee, risk another pomegranate and, if nothing had changed by the time she had done all that, she would think again. But the answer would be the same. Stay put. Why look a gift horse in the mouth when the time passed so easily?

She might have yet another long, scented bath (that was another thing that was good here: the bathroom was crammed with potions and scents and all sorts of pretty, smelly things, like jewel-boxes with their colours and shapes), and then she would change the robe Sylvia had given her for another from the wardrobe. There were thirteen there, Erica von Hyatt had counted them, and they were all very beautiful – they made you feel good just wearing them. Then she would watch TV, read another of those yukky books Sylvia kept on her shelves, and perhaps be a little bolder with the bottles in the cabinet. She might even open the Jack Daniel's, which looked rich and golden and interesting. She had often dreamt of having a place like this to herself – and now she had. And what dream lasted for ever? While she had it, she would live it, and when it was over, why, then she would move on. No hard feelings. Why should there be? Hard feelings got you nowhere and spoiled your enjoyment of what was happening here and now. Before and after were things out of reach. Today was real. Today was all that counted. And today was being very nice to her. She put another pomegranate seed in her mouth and sucked it with pleasure. Life could be worse, after all, and she repeated to herself that whatever happened, she had been invited here and told she could stay. Whatever happened, even she, destitute Erica von Hyatt, had rights. She yawned and stretched at the pleasure of it all. Sylvia Perth would be back one day soon and in the meantime – well, in the meantime she would simply get on with the dream. Pity that the telephone broke into it from time to time, but, well, you couldn't have *everything*, and at least she knew there was no point in answering it since it certainly wouldn't be for her: she did not exist.

*

Square Jaw rang Melanie's number. It had taken several attempts and two glasses of white Rioja to make the call, and he wasn't sure why because, after all, he was only ringing her about her things in the box under the bed. He presumed that she would be needing some of them, or he wouldn't bother to ring. It felt very peculiar needing courage before tapping out that familiar number. He let it ring for a long time. After the build-up, it was hard to believe there was no reply. He replaced the receiver and felt relief. He hadn't really wanted to speak to her, anyway. He wondered for a moment where she was but put the thought from his mind very quickly. None of his business.

*

Red Gold jumped and Arthur looked up sharply from his notebook. She had catapulted rather than moved in her usual deliberate way and answered the call with a voice he had never heard. She turned her back and he watched how her shoulders sagged as she put the receiver down on the table.

'It's for you,' she said and left the room.

*

The Little Blonde Secretary removed her yellow plastic gloves and put them away neatly in the bucket under the sink. The house was clean and shining from top to bottom and she had two Marks and Spencer stuffed chicken breasts in the oven because it was Saturday night. She felt at peace with the world. Derek came through the back door, having removed his shoes in the porch.

She was pleased that he remembered and decided that he was a good husband really, had been very responsible since she told him about all that upstairs mess. She smiled at him encouragingly and said, 'Well done, Derek,' looking at his socked feet. He smiled back. She would have kissed him on the cheek, but he had not shaved. Instead, by way of illustration, she rubbed the very tip of her index finger down her chin, shaking her head.

The chicken breasts were very nice, they both thought, if a little too spicy. They had a glass each of Lambrusco and put the rest away in the fridge for tomorrow. Then they went and sat on the new settee in the newly cleaned front room and watched the final episode of a Jeffrey Archer serial, which they both found very exciting. Later Derek made them a milky drink and they went to bed. She slept well and so did Derek, though both had disturbing dreams, which they put down to either the Lambrusco or the Jeffrey Archer, and in the morning Derek's chin was stubbly again.

*

Erica von Hyatt had developed a taste for Jack Daniel's mixed with milk and taken slowly in the bath. The source of the milk was her own streetwise cleverness. Bottles of it were delivered to the other flat in the building downstairs (semi-skimmed, alas), along with orange juice and yoghurt. Hearing the chink of the milk float had been one of life's better joys. Too much cushy ease had blunted her edge. Out on the street she would have had no compunction, would not have thought twice, about lifting the necessaries of life from the doorsteps of the Good Bourgeoisie. Here, with her comfortable trappings, she had momentarily lapsed into responsible citizenship. A foolish slip. So, quick as a dart, silent as a shadow, her golden hair streaming behind her, the rustle of her soft, pink robe scarcely disturbing the air, she had run down the stairs, even as the retreating milkman's rubber soles were still audible, and stood poised, thinking.

Three bottles of milk, one carton of orange juice and a packet of six yoghurts. Riches!

What she thought was this. If I take it all they will be watchful in future. If they are watchful in future, my source will dry up completely. If I take only the minimum I need, they may not notice. If they do notice, they will think the milkman has shortchanged them.

What she did was this. She took one pint of milk. She slid her thumb nail along the polythene packet containing six yoghurts and took two. She left the orange juice, deciding its loss would be too noticeable. In general, her experience showed that people with plenty were not blindly open-handed, but if you were careful, and took only a portion, very often they didn't notice its loss at all among what was left. So the orange juice had to stay.

The owner of the flat did not notice since his female companion took the remaining items in. He, frowning into the business news, was impervious to the contents of his refrigerator, as he was also, now sated, impervious to her dewy eyes and the curves of her naked body beneath his shirt. She made the coffee as discreetly as a geisha, poured milk on to the muesli, and dreamt of gaining a status beyond that of girlfriend by appointment.

Thus the Have gave to the Have-Not without suffering. Almost the basis of successful modern charity – with the exception of allowing the giver the knowledge that he had given, and therefore providing him with the pleasure of a warm glow, which would, of course, have made it perfect.

One yoghurt is as good as a feast to a shrunken stomach. A third of a pint of milk taken straight from the bottle, bountiful nurture. With black-cherry flavour reserved in the fridge for the morrow, Erica von Hyatt was happy again. With two thirds of a bottle of milk to play with and Jack Daniel's glowing in his Arabian-carved homestead, Erica von Hyatt could live a little. And that, to be quite honest, was as much as she had ever asked.

Chapter Eleven

GRETCHEN O'Dowd had been with Sylvia for years. Man and boy, Sylvia used to say if she was feeling humorous. Gretchen did not mind. Over the years they had developed a comfortable companionship: Sylvia the mistress, Gretchen the servant. Neither inquired into the other's life beyond that. Gretchen ran the country home to which Sylvia came for weekends, and their lives were smoothly semi-detached. Gretchen was grateful and Sylvia was released from responsibility; it was like keeping a large, dependable, loyal dog in the country and no more rigorous in its expectation than that. The brief fling that had united them was almost forgotten history, and if they shared a bed occasionally it was more to do with human hot-water bottling than passion or desire. It was as close as Sylvia chose to move in a relationship, and Gretchen was not ungrateful for its peace.

They had met at a publishing party where Gretchen was serving the drinks in a neat little black frock with a white pinny and a bow in her hair. In those days she shaved her legs and bleached her moustache and, though rather square in form, had a young woman's air about her. When Sylvia acquired her Queen Anne house in Oxfordshire with its substantial garden, Gretchen was the perfect solution – strong, healthy, amenable and not of a possessive nature. She installed her, paid her a basic wage, and knew that she could trust her completely, for Gretchen had been bruised by life. Who had not? Sylvia wanted to know. 'Stick with me, dear,' she suggested, 'and you need never worry your –' She was about to say, 'pretty little head,' but thought better of it, given that it was beyond any realms of reality, and substituted the more sensible 'self again . . .'

Gretchen's father had been a boxer. He had two requirements of any offspring. The first and most important was that the offspring should be a son and therefore made in his own image. Failing that, the offspring should be a daughter and made in an image as far removed from his as possible. Gretchen, perversely, was neither. She was a daughter with the physical attributes of a son. Her mother, a florist, was also disappointed. Where was the pretty, golden-haired child with delicate fingers and an eye for colour that *she* required? Still in her ovaries by the look of it.

Gretchen did her best to be a good androgyne. She learned to box and she learned to arrange flowers. Had she been a son, in the prevailing climate of New Men she would have been lauded and honoured; as it was, she was a she and was not. A little confused, she began to make her own way in the world.

When her father passed out of the ring and immediately passed on, the floral tributes had been delightful. The neighbours in East Grinstead still talked about the cortège, and tried to recapture its charms whenever one of their number died. Unfortunately for Gretchen, the neighbours in East Grinstead also still talked about her and what they called her Perversion. At fifteen she had fallen in love rather heavily with one of her peers, and a teacher had found them at it in that quintessentially adolescent place, the bike shed. Unfortunately it was an all girls' school, and the peer in question was called Wendy. Wendy was saved from Perversion by coming absolutely clean and saying she would never do it again (which Gretchen was hurt to discover was not the truth), and Gretchen was permanently committed to hellfire by saying the opposite. So far as she was concerned, it was pure love and the only way, and she was much muddled that truth (which was supposed to be the ultimate Good Thing) should suddenly be so ultimately wicked.

Mrs O'Dowd, still basking in the admiration of her neighbours regarding the cortège and optimistic about a settled and respectable future now that the insurance had paid up, was not about to chuck it all away. As her daughter's oddity was apparently founded on unchanging rock, it was time for Gretchen to leave home. With a ten-pound note and an air of dazed acceptance, she was dispatched to London. Her moustache had come on considerably in the years from pubescence to maturity, and she was even more confused to find herself quite proud of it – though the world told her it was the brand of her sin and should, along with leg hair, be removed.

Her paternal aunt in London read tarot cards and occasionally held seances in polite people's houses. Gretchen lived with her and housekept for a time until she fell in love with a barmaid who had come seeking guidance about whether her husband would ever pay maintenance or not. The barmaid, married for fifteen years, one son, lapsed husband, was a trifle bored by men since she had her pick of the pub's clientele. For a time she turned her attentions to Gretchen, who loved and served her slavishly. But such slavishness became boring too, for it provided no grit.

'There is nothing worse,' said the barmaid one night, 'than being loved too well. The trouble with your sort of woman in our sort of relationship is that you never hit out. Frankly it gets very dull with all your tender loving care and understanding. What I need now and then,' said the barmaid metaphorically, 'is a bit of dash, perhaps even brutality. A bit of thrust, a bit of poke – even a punch on the nose wouldn't come amiss . . .'

So Gretchen, being down to earth and of a literal nature, duly punched the barmaid on the nose, forgetting that she was the sturdy daughter of a boxer now deceased. The barmaid, unwilling to accept complicity in the act of violence and with her face very much rearranged, terminated the love affair, and Gretchen, sadly, for she had loved her buxom partner dearly, moved on. There would always, she knew, be a place in her heart for barmaids.

She gave up the notion of love and decided to earn a living for herself. She ceased her unfeminine ways – dealt with leg and arm and upper-lip hair – and, though it by no means felt like an *honest* living, waitressed. Now she learned what life on the other side was like. Her bottom was pinched, hands wandered up to her thighs when her own hands were too full of glasses to do anything about it, obscene suggestions were whispered in her ear by wine-breathed men in dinner jackets, and she was frequently grabbed from behind while doing the washing-up. In the end the long-suffering Gretchen had had enough. When a wandering hand goosed her for the umpteenth time at a publishing party, she dropped a large tray loaded with dirty glasses, looked the perpetrator firmly in the eye and, in the astonished silence of the room, gave him a right hook that had the air of Zen it was so pure and so fine.

'I'm sorry,' said Gretchen to the floorbound perpetrator, 'but I don't like men pinching my bottom.'

'Looking like you do,' said the floorbound perpetrator, 'you should be grateful for what you get.'

A hand reached under Gretchen's elbow, she was steered out into the Berkeley Square evening, and Sylvia Perth said, 'Well done, dear. What is your name? Let us go for a little walk.'

Sylvia had just acquired the house in Oxfordshire. It was at the beginning of her financial perfidy with Janice Gentle, and she wanted somewhere to keep completely separate from her London life – partly for the fun of it (when one game got dull she could switch to another), and partly for the serious aspect (if the perfidy was revealed one day, she would still have a home here). It was understood that, should anything befall Sylvia, Gretchen would inherit everything, and this worked to a perfect accord. If you know you are going to inherit something, you look after it especially well. Sylvia could trust Gretchen utterly. And Gretchen was content to sit and wait very happily with her knitting and her television, knowing that she was secure for ever. She knew nothing of London beyond how to contact Sylvia there if necessary, and she knew absolutely nothing of Mrs Perth's existence in Birmingham.

In Oxfordshire Gretchen was able to be herself, inclusive of moustache. And, in a reaction to the bows and pinnies of her waitressing days, she never wore anything designatedly feminine again. If anyone thought about it at all, they thought of her as masculine, but given the changing of the seasons, the farming and the pruning, the repainting and stabling that was going on all around, no one had much time to worry about sexing their neighbours. Pigs, yes. Horses, yes. Human beings, no.

Whenever it came to it, and it almost inevitably would, since there was a difference of more than twenty years between them, Gretchen O'Dowd planned to give Sylvia Perth a wonderful funeral. Memories of her father's last great day had made a deep impression on her, and she knew that she would be able to do the flowers a treat. Since in life Sylvia asked so little of her, it was a pleasing notion that in death Gretchen would be able to do her this final public honour.

Of course she had not reckoned with the responsibility falling upon her shoulders quite so soon. Yet, in those dark days following Sylvia Perth's decease, it was the planning of this that kept her spirits up. The garden was beautiful, a mass of summer flowers, and the wide stretch of lawn was perfect for a marquee. At last, and in her own right, Gretchen would be able to enact the one experience that the privacy of their sporadic life together had denied her. Having the neighbours in.

*

Nobody knew the whereabouts of Janice Gentle.

Rohanne had received a rather sharp telephone call from Morgan Pfeiffer early that morning which gave her cause to panic.

'Miss Bulbecker.'

'Mr Pfeiffer?'

'We had expected confirmation of signing by now, Miss Bulbecker.'

'Soon, Mr Pfeiffer.'

'You have not yet located Janice Gentle?'

'I am close, Mr Pfeiffer.'

'Good, Miss Bulbecker. And you will fax me a copy of –'

'The signed contract? I certainly will. Very soon. Mr Pfeiffer, I am almost there . . .'

'Would that I were,' she said, when she put down the phone. If ever there were a time for the calling up of friends, lovers, allies, it was now. Rohanne had never felt quite so near to defeat or tears, nor felt quite so alone. But her rule was absolute: to the world you showed only the face of success; whatever went on between you and your mirror in the dark, silent hours, you kept strictly to yourself.

Be resolute, she told herself, and slipping into her leathers and her Ray-Bans, she set off for Sylvia Perth deceased's office. She would try that dimbo of a secretary one more time before making her way to Dog Street. There must be some lead somewhere. It was all beginning to feel distinctly like one of those ancient fairy stories in which the damsel in the castle awaits rescuing by the courageous and bold. Well, Rohanne had never been short of either attribute. She wondered what Janice Gentle actually looked like. She had been able to trace no pictures at all. From the tone of her writing, she thought, as she hailed a taxi in Brook Street, she might well look like the princess in the thorn-covered tower.

*

Gretchen O'Dowd decided to be brave about it. She had told the Powers That Be she was not the next of kin (far too honestly, with hindsight), and the Powers That Be therefore refused to discuss the release of the body to her. Worse, they refused to give her any further information over the telephone. To their question 'Who are you?' Gretchen found herself answering in some confusion, since who she was was rather undelineated. She could hardly say companion, friend, housekeeper, sometime lover to this brusque voice. If she could have just simply said wife, it would have been better, but she was, after all, talking to authority, and it was a lie. She compromised by saying that she had known Sylvia Perth for many years and that she was her close companion. The voice at the other end of the telephone grunted.

'Well, what can I do?' she asked.

'Get in touch with the deceased's solicitor, if I was you.' And he gave her the address.

Gretchen knew that once she got Sylvia Perth (she couldn't yet think of her as a body) back with her in Oxfordshire everything would be all right. Perfectly all right. Honour would be done and then life could go on once more . . .

There was no doubt about it, Gretchen would have to go up to London and see the legal people herself to sort everything out. Sylvia Perth must come back to her, it was only right and proper. Gretchen felt uncharacteristically positive about that. She made an appointment, the first available, for late that afternoon, and then, feeling restless, she decided to set off immediately. She had keys to the office and keys to the Dog Street apartment, and she was curious about these, having never visited either. She would go to the office first, then she would go to Dog Street. After that, she would visit the solicitor. A positive plan for the day helped considerably. There was nothing worse than feeling inadequate at this one moment in her life when she had planned to be so utterly and supremely the opposite. She ran a damp finger over her moustache and felt comforted. It was always there when she wanted it.

*

Janice Gentle packed various compartments in her clothing with a variety of little sustenances, picked up her carrier bag and, taking a deep breath, summoned the lift. She had to use it again one day, and today, when she was bound for Dog Street, seemed the most appropriate occasion. There had been no news or hint of a funeral, and Janice had privately made up her mind that, in the manner of those who would once put pennies on dead men's eyes, her grieving duty was to go to Sylvia Perth's apartment and switch off her answerphone, since there was something altogether indecent about the way Sylvia's voice continued while her life did not. But most certainly, she was not going by tube – Janice Gentle was going to walk there. It was a sunny day, she had plenty of time, and the tube would conjure up far too many memories to be worthwhile.

The lift did not arrive. She thought about reporting it but decided not to. It would mean engaging Mr Jones in conversation, and he might, as was the way of people, wish to bring up their previous and last encounter. She tiptoed past his basement door and noticed in his rubbish bag a quantity of jars containing what looked remarkably like innards pickled in their own blood. A strange man, she mused, and best left.

*

Gretchen O'Dowd was just locking the door behind her when the postman handed her a letter.

'Morning, Mr O'Dee,' he said, 'another lovely one. How's the missis?'

Gretchen was going to say, 'Dead,' but thought better of it. 'In London,' she said.

'No wonder you two get on so well,' he said, 'with her never here.' And he went whistling on his way.

She tucked the letter into her pocket and followed the postman's example. There was nothing so pleasant as these Oxfordshire lanes in high summer – the fussing pheasants darting around in the hedges, the cooing of pigeons, the crowing of rooks, and above her, wheeling and diving and squealing for attention, the plovers. She stopped to admire their antics. Brave birds. They would do anything to protect their young. She liked these best. Behind the beech trees and blackthorn, a farmer was harvesting. He waved, she waved back.

'Morning,' she said.

'Morning. How's the missis?'

'Dead, I'm afraid,' she replied. It never mattered how you answered him when he was perched up there. The noise of the tractor drowned everything. Sylvia used to stand at the edge of the field and wave and smile while saying disgusting things, to which he would merely nod and smile back. Gretchen felt it was rather cruel, really.

'Good, good,' he said, and waved again.

In town, before boarding the train, she visited Mr Mole the undertaker. A few preliminary words on the subject of Sylvia Perth's remains were necessary. There was something prestigious about being in charge of a corpse and its ceremonials, and Gretchen was quite enjoying her growing sense of status and the prospect of a proper burial.

Mr Mole was heartening. 'We can make quite a lovely ceremony out of it, don't you worry, sir. And this coffin is our best. Our very best. It doesn't do to skimp on the handles, either. Oh, not at all. You must have the right accessories. You know what the ladies are, they do like to have the right accessories. I don't expect your good lady was any different?'

Gretchen, remembering how Sylvia valued her appearance, thought Mr Mole was wonderfully understanding. 'I want the best, of course,' she said. 'That coffin and those handles . . .'

'And the pure-white silk lining?'

'And the pure-white silk lining.'

Gretchen jotted down the prices and went on her way. The people in the big house had a garden party last year with a marquee. How she had envied the festivities . . .

*

Morgan Pfeiffer leaned back in his chair and pressed the ends of his fingers together. He looked pleased. Rohanne Bulbecker was hungry. If anyone could bring home the bacon, it was her.

On the other side of his office a weasel-faced man in a shiny suit put down the extension telephone, fingered his Rolex and returned the smile. This was Stoat, President of Marketing, and he was known to boast that he had never read a book in his life. He was, however, supremely good at packaging, and he was breathing deep for Janice Gentle, breathing deep and waiting to spring.

'Encouraging, Mr Pfeiffer.'

'I hope so, Stoat, I hope so.'

'Blue skies now,' said Stoat, 'blue skies all the way . . .'

*

On the train up to town and much buoyed by her enthusiastic encounter with Mr Mole, Gretchen O'Dowd dreamt on. A pity she had lost contact with her mother. She would have quite liked to have sent her photographs of the event. After all, she didn't hold a grudge against her for the ten-pound note and the spiritualistic auntie. Indeed, the reverse, she was rather grateful. At least when Mrs O'Dowd got senile dementia or merely became enfeebled with age, she wouldn't have to do anything about it. Her conscience was quite clear. That ten-pound note had been severance pay. Wherever Mrs O'Dowd fetched up on the rocky shores of life, Gretchen would not be obliged to put out a raft to save her. And that was a comforting thought.

Gretchen O'Dowd was looking forward to being financially independent. Money, she felt, would overcome many of the things that had been a burden to her, including, very probably, her personal proclivities and even her moustache. Sometimes she felt positively ashamed of the things she had done to remove or disguise it in the past. With her own Gold Barclaycard she was unlikely to be rejected for a little extra hair here and there. She fingered the area above her lip. If anything, she thought, it might be nice to darken it a little, make a feature of it, like some women changed the shape of their eyebrows or curled their lashes. Why not? What was one piece of facial hair to another? Why darken it? Why not bleach it pink? Or turn it multicoloured? Why, who knew what she couldn't do from now on? Anything she liked. Anything at all. It was a wonderful thought, like a dream come true . . . Dear Sylvia. She would miss her. But there certainly would be compensations.

She watched the neat countryside gradually change into urban sprawl and saw herself, after the black-plumed funeral, happily ensconced with some nice young woman. They would knit together, have long, hearty walks through muddy byways enjoying the plovers, discuss television programmes, watch old films, and eat delicacies that someone other than herself had prepared. The nice young woman could even continue with her bar work now and then – if she really wanted to . . .

It was a lovely vision, and the man sitting opposite her in the train could be forgiven for finding his proximity to the blank-eyed, vacant grin of a moustachioed woman (who periodically licked the tip of her finger and made a kind of Hercule Poirot gesture to her upper lip) discordant. Every so often Gretchen, unknowing, would mouth a word or make a gesture as the vision of the rosy future grew more real in her head.

At the point where she extended an inviting but empty hand towards her carriage companion and said beguilingly, 'Another smoked salmon sandwich, dear,' he got up and left. What *was* this grudge the Lord of Travellers had against him? Only recently he'd suffered the disgusting sight of one of the urban deranged on a tube train sucking at a piece of ham as if it were their own wayward tongue. He felt still very fragile about Melanie, and wasn't sleeping at all well nowadays – he seemed to travel around the bed and wake up empty-armed or, worse, hugging the pillow.

*

Erica von Hyatt, a little bleary-eyed from sleep but with her wits otherwise intact, sat up in bed. That was the noise she had been waiting for. The milk float. She needed a new plan for survival since the person below didn't seem to be having any further deliveries. The note in the milk bottle said, 'No deliveries until further notice.' Too open-ended for Erica; it could mean weeks. She rolled out of bed, grabbed the ten-pound note and shot out of the flat, leaving the door ajar. She caught the milkman as he was about to depart from the floor below.

'Could you,' she said, 'begin an account for the flat above?'

'Cash down?' said the milkman.

'Of course,' she replied primly, fluttering the money and feeling virtuous. Curious to be one of the legitimate paying multitude. She savoured the legitimacy. 'What can I buy?'

He told her. It sounded so good she felt herself start to dribble.

'Have to start tomorrow, though. Got to get the order in first.'

'Oh dear,' she said.

'Sorry, love,' he said, 'but that's the way it has to be . . .'

It crossed Erica von Hyatt's mind to overcome this difficulty in the best way she knew how, but somehow, what with the money making her feel real, the nice clean feeling from the bath and the robe, and upstairs being so specially hers, she didn't really want to disturb it all by doing that. Instead she held up a haughty hand to silence his apologies. 'I quite understand. But can't you at least let me have some milk?'

'One pint I got,' he said cheerfully. And, thinking for a moment, he added, 'I got a cut white loaf I can spare.'

'Butter?' she said hopefully.

'No butter. Chocolate milk drink? Could do you two of them.'

Her stomach gave a series of joyful rumbles. 'Fine,' she said. 'Thank you very much.'

Sated on bread dipped in chocolate milk tinged with Jack Daniel's, and following a long scented bath and a change into the pink robe with silver tassels, Erica von Hyatt spread herself on the damask ottoman and slept the sleep of the contented. Like a princess she lay, her golden hair laid out upon the coral softness of the pillows, her mouth half smiling, humming to herself as she dozed off and slipped into her twilight pleasure of food and warmth and time-being happiness.

*

Gretchen O'Dowd was a little surprised at the pale sparseness of Sylvia Perth's office. The whole was decorated in black and grey, offset by white or cream. Gretchen found it all rather intimidating, but then she had always found Sylvia intimidating, so she was not *altogether* surprised. Apart from a large blood-red couch at the far end, there was no colour at all. The outer room was not much better, containing little more than a light satinwood desk, pine shelves containing reference and telephone books, a tweed-covered typing chair and a near-dead unrecognizable plant. If she had hoped to find out a little more about her deceased employer and friend, she was disappointed. The only thing you *could* say about the place was that it was *completely* different from the English antique style of their Queen Anne house with its tapestry-covered dining chairs and carved oak settles. Odd, thought Gretchen, I always thought she liked *that* kind of furnishing.

She crossed to the couch, which stood out like a wound. She touched it. It was velvet and very soft. The curtains, sateen-grey, were half pulled against the sunlight. The room was monochrome, soothing, particularly if Gretchen avoided the throbbing colour of the velvet by lying back on it. She did so. The journey had been quite a long one and the day was warm. She closed her eyes, she breathed deeply, she slept.

*

Mrs Lovitt wrote to the vicar of Cockermouth with a substantial donation taken from Guildford's general fund. The committee had agreed that, if the mighty were taking such a positive interest in the problems of Northern poverty, so should they. She stressed in her letter that Mrs Vicar had not broken one word of her confidence about her visit to Lambeth Palace, and she hoped that the notes taken on Mrs Vicar's behalf while she was away from the afternoon part of the conference were useful. If *not*, perhaps he would like to write to her directly for clarification.

*

The Little Blonde Secretary Bird collected her magazine and hurried down the tube-station steps. On the cover was a picture of an actress and her new baby. They both looked encouragingly wholesome and nice. The magazine feature that week was on fertility. At least it was less disturbing than that one on orgasm which had suggested feeling about *down there* to get to know yourself. She settled herself in her seat and began with the serial, which this time was set in Mexico. They gave you some very interesting locations nowadays, though she was quite happy just to read about them. Especially after that spicy foreign chicken.

*

Square Jaw was asked by the chap in the office next to his if anything was up.

Square Jaw said no.

The chap in the office next to his looked relieved at the obvious untruth. He closed his door. Duty done. And ceased to notice that Square Jaw looked pale as a corpse.

*

Gretchen O'Dowd was not given to dreaming, but there was no doubt that a great, red mouth, with numerous pearly-white teeth, hung above her like that cat in Wonderland. It might well be a cat, for it had a fine mane of pale hair and a neat little nose. The only discordant thing (and one expected them in dreams) was that the nose was wearing dark mirrors above it, and these reflected her back to herself. The self it reflected showed mistily through slitted eyes. She opened them wider; the dream incorporated a pair of shoulders and looked, suddenly, very real.

'Hi,' it said, with an American accent. 'I'm Rohanne Bulbecker. Who are you?'

Gretchen screamed. Appropriate in the circumstances. The cause of the scream waited until it was finished, and then smiled again, reaching out a most sinister gauntleted hand.

'I'm not going to hurt you,' said Rohanne Bulbecker, in the soft tone of one who very well might. She sat down beside Gretchen, and the mirrors on her eyes reflected a round pinky-brown face a-twitch with fright. 'Do you, by any chance, know the whereabouts of Janice Gentle?' she asked softly.

The round pinky-brown face shook itself. 'N-n-no,' said Gretchen, hoping this was the right answer.

127

'Shit,' said Rohanne, and the slap of her leathered hand on her leathered knee made Gretchen wince and jump.

'S-s-sorry,' she said, and meant it.

'Oh, never mind,' said Rohanne Bulbecker.

She removed her sunglasses and peered at Gretchen. Her peering ended at the moustache. 'Sorry to butt in on your siesta,' she said, 'but the door was open.' She said this with a smile that neither touched her nose nor reached her eyes. She looked, Gretchen thought, murderous. Gretchen gulped. And people had the cheek to comment that *she* looked weird.

'You don't have any idea where Sylvia's secretary went to?'

Gretchen shook her head.

'And you really don't have any idea where Janice Gentle is?'

Gretchen twitched negatively.

'Do you know where she lives?'

'N-n-no,' said Gretchen.

'Who are you, then? What are you doing here?'

'This is my ex-employer's office.' Gretchen attempted to sit up a little. She felt at a great disadvantage lying down beneath the gaze of this strange aggressor.

'Sylvia Perth?' The woman drew closer.

Gretchen swallowed but could not speak. She nodded.

'What are you?' asked Rohanne, desperate to discover if this person could help her search in any way. 'Chauffeur? Janitor?'

Gretchen decided to continue on the path of invisibility.

'Friend?' went on Rohanne desperately. 'Relative?'

No point her pretending. An answer was definitely required.

'Personal assistant?'

Gretchen settled for that, and nodded.

'Oh,' said Rohanne, much relieved, 'then you *must* know where she is.'

Gretchen, whose mind was as far removed from Janice Gentle as Rohanne Bulbecker's was absorbed by her, wrongly connected the pronoun to her deceased employer and thought of Sylvia.

Rohanne stared at the recumbent creature before her, willing her to know, her eyes aglow with the light of compulsion.

Gretchen went rigid, while her brain went spongy. She could not speak.

'Come on,' said Rohanne, applying wheedling tactics, 'you do know where she is, don't you?' She leaned forward and gave her a devastating smile.

Gretchen winced as all those shining teeth came out again.

'In a manner of speaking, yes,' she said, warily, thinking of Sylvia Perth, edging herself, finally, into a sitting position.

'For Chrissake!' snapped Rohanne, fixed on Janice Gentle, 'where?'

Gretchen jumped. All attempts to put it in the same poetic mode as Mr Mole went out of her head. 'Well,' she said, 'she's dead.'

'Oh my *God!*' said Rohanne Bulbecker, and she put her face in her sinisterly clad hands. 'Oh my God.'

Gretchen began easing herself off the day bed with a view to leaping across the room and out of the door.

'That's it, then,' said Rohanne, despairing, resigned.

Gretchen almost had both feet on the floor.

Rohanne looked up. 'When did she die?'

'Very recently,' said Gretchen O'Dowd, trying to sound casual and as if her body were not in a very peculiar position: both feet were safely on the floor, one buttock had slid to freedom, and her arms were poised in a prepare-to-eject position. With one bound she would be free.

Rohanne was thinking how odd it was that both agent and writer should have died at the same time. Perhaps Janice Gentle felt she could not go on without her protectress.

'Suicide, was it?' she asked wanly.

Gretchen arrested the last fractional movement which would release her.

'Heart,' she said.

'Good grief!' said Rohanne incredulously, for she knew that Sylvia had also died in that way. '*Both* of them? At the same time?'

Now Gretchen knew for sure that this person was deranged. Despite all the interesting achievements in modern surgery, people still went around with only one of those organs. You might have a kidney too few – that was possible – but you certainly never, ever had a heart too many.

'She only had one,' she said defiantly.

'One what?'

'Heart.'

Now Rohanne knew for sure that this person was crazy. Which was sort of comforting. If she was crazy (and she looked that way), she might not really know anything.

'Not two,' added Gretchen.

'You mean . . .' Rohanne said carefully, kindly even, for light was beginning to dawn – here was someone in deep distress; you could see it from her posture – 'if she had had two hearts then one could have malfunctioned, but the other would have kept her alive. Like an aeroplane and its engines?'

By now Gretchen's muddlement had temporarily overcome her fear.

'What I mean,' she said, 'is that Sylvia had one heart and she died from it. Recently.'

'Yes,' said Rohanne soothingly, 'and Janice Gentle did, too?'

'Did she?' said Gretchen politely.

It was Rohanne's turn to scream.

*

'"Man's life is well compared to a feast,"' said Janice, making her way to the top of her road. '"Then with an earthen voider, made of clay,/Comes Death, and takes the table clean away."'

Who wrote that? she wondered. One of those feckless Elizabethans she supposed. Such crude metaphor. Apt, though. Death had certainly taken away *her* table, metaphorically speaking.

Bacon, was it? Or the Earl of Essex?

The combination of the word 'feast' and the word 'bacon' worked in her head and thence downward to her stomach. She fancied a bacon sandwich, whichever poet wrote it. She almost turned round and went home again. A bacon sandwich suddenly became most pressing. And being out here on the road to Dog Street felt, quite suddenly, rather foolish.

A voice behind her called, 'Morning. Don't often see you about this time of day. Well, I must say it is *hot*, very, very hot, too hot in my opinion. What say you?'

She moved away and crossed the road hurriedly. Anything was better than walking back past that. She must take her courage and go on. Yesterday she rang Sylvia's number and, on hearing that lively voice, began talking – no, *chatting* – to it. That settled it. Janice was well aware that in some respects she was outside the rules of society, but she was not what her mother would have called *mental*. Courage it would take, but to Dog Street she must go. After all, how much worse for the pilgrims of yore? One road, thick with footpads and danger, and only the promise of sporadic inns along the way. Walking through the London of today could hardly be comparable with that . . . After all, even Madame Eglentyne, that fastidious Prioress, had travelled in the unavoidable discomfort of the age, despite her corals, furs and finery.

And here was Janice on a sunny morning, setting off in the full and comforting certainty that she would arrive, whole and unmolested, at her destination. She could hardly turn back, given those easy odds, now could she? She shook her head and set off resolute once more. Look upon this as your own little pilgrimage, Janice, she told herself, and none the less comforting for all that.

*

Rohanne Bulbecker stood on a street corner and whistled for a cab. One stopped. Her stocky and rather unwilling companion entered it glumly. Rohanne slammed the door. 'Dog Street,' she said, 'Dog Street and step on it . . .'

Chapter Twelve

MORGAN Pfeiffer stared at the photograph of his late wife and smiled at it confidently. He had just dialled London again and Rohanne Bulbecker was no longer in her hotel, which meant she must be out on the trail. He intended to keep up the pressure. There was nothing like pressure to bring results. Besides, Stoat was nearly expiring with damped-down energy. Much more of it and he'd have a coronary, and he was far too good a man to lose. Where are you now, Ms Bulbecker? he asked the ether. Where are you now?

Ms Bulbecker was sitting with a clamped smile upon her face opposite Gretchen O'Dowd, who wore an expression ghastly enough to be a death mask. Still, Rohanne continued smiling. At this stage there was nothing further she could do.

*

The Boss Masculine, having seen his wife after her operation, and having been told by her in detail how the catheter felt and what the nurses had said about her bowels and the sagginess of her belly muscles, made a very aggressive business call that afternoon. Even the Little Blonde Secretary Bird was surprised at the vehemence of his voice as it rasped through the closed door.

'I don't want fucking excuses,' he shouted, 'I want action.'

Really it was what he had wanted to shout to his wife.

The Little Blonde Secretary jumped. Normally the Boss Masculine was even-tempered to the point of dullness, and sort of spoke in a low voice through gritted teeth if he was angered. There was something quite exciting about that explosion, more like the sort of men she read about, men with power, men of ruthlessness, men who needed to be tamed . . . Surreptitiously she put away the magazine she had been reading – apparently there were creams you could rub in to stop stretch marks, and with a good nursing brassière your bust need not suffer any ill effects at all, thank heavens. She turned to her machine and finished the page of figures. Soon it would be lunchtime and she wanted to go to British Home Stores; they were doing some lovely styles in maternity wear nowadays.

The Boss Masculine, recovering from the unsatisfactory dispensation of his rage, dropped his coffee cup down his chest and lap and, giving full deep-voiced vent to his further enragement, yelled, 'Damn everything to hell!' A cry whose shocking resonance caused his secretary to feel quite fluttery as she flew to his aid. She mopped the upper half while he dealt with the bit below the belt. Automatically she brushed his shoulders free of dandruff, too. Might as well make him really presentable. Her small hands with their perfect pink nails were deft and dainty in their movements. It was a long time since he had been touched intimately. He thanked her and, as she left the office, he noticed that she had a neat little bum and nice legs. A tingling began in his groin. He turned the photograph of his wife towards him, stared at it, frowned as Crippen might have frowned, and returned it to a less prominent angle.

*

Morgan Pfeiffer had made his money in candy bars. Stoat, whom he had brought with him from the realms of gold to the realms of literature, had been his marketing giant in the launching of Brite the Booster Bite, a candy bar that was marketed as full of vitamins, energy and natural goodness – and great for your sex life. Morgan Pfeiffer had been a little sceptical about the emphasis on sex, but Stoat had proved abundantly right: everything you sold was about sex – and if it wasn't, it could be made to be. In marketing there was very little else. Stoat told him a healthy, energetic, pure body made you one of the beautiful people. And the beautiful people never had any problem getting and enjoying sex. It was only the schmucks, the ones who smoked and drank and didn't eat Brite the Booster Bite who had attraction problems. And as the first six months' sales figures came through all those years ago, proving the argument indisputable, so now, in the same way, Stoat was sure to be right. Janice Gentle with sex, so he assured Morgan Pfeiffer, made great marketing sense. Stoat had called the deceased Mrs Pfeiffer a Very Great Lady for daring to think of it; he did not say that he had suggested it to her in the first place.

Morgan Pfeiffer looked through the blue haze of smoke at the photograph on his desk and sighed. Mrs Pfeiffer, deceased, smiled piggily back at him, eyes sunk into ruddy marshmallow cheeks, chins delineated by the Bermuda sun, curvaceous arms of deep rich brown achingly seductive with their potential strength, and those breasts, magnificent things, scarcely held by the scarlet boob-tube, like pneumatic roundels of chocolate blancmange. A full-blown woman. Ah, he thought, where was there such another?

How he missed her. Dammit, that woman had an *appetite*. If he took out one more glitz-dunked sparrow and watched her push a radicchio stalk around, he thought he'd go pop. Mrs Pfeiffer might have been a woman of whom it was said that the elevator did not go all the way up, but you knew you had something when you got hold of her. And that made her a very desirable person indeed. Nowadays he was permanently seeking distractions to compensate for the loss of such tantalization. There was nothing more lonely in the world than a powder-pink, heart-shaped, double king bed. He picked up the photograph. He'd bet she was giving old St Peter a good time up there; got him off the fish by now for sure. He sat down and shook his head.

He had tried many compensations – even taking a blow-up doll of grand proportions to that pink, flouncy bed, but it lay there, with his arm around it, so mute and cheerless that he had consigned it to the trash can the next morning. He liked the rustle of candy papers in the bedroom, he liked the smell of Turkish delight on the pillow, he even – hard to believe, but so it was – liked the feel of sugar and biscuit crumbs in his bed, and the sound of a voice, slightly indistinct, mellow with pleasure, talking wanderingly as he squeezed a yielding thigh. Perhaps occasionally he wished she could discuss things other than TV and magazines and stuff like that, but in an imperfect world Belinda Pfeiffer was pretty well irreplaceable.

Irreplaceable. He had found that to his cost when he bought the services of a human replica. And the woman had looked all right. Built like a double-dose Mae West, she had lain on the bed, a pink Michelin woman, pink as the bed, and smiling in the correct porcine manner. But alas, just as he began to get a feeling for the thing, just as the squeezing of her thigh became a heightened experience where reality and Mrs Pfeiffer, deceased, became entwined, the lady of the night had – as requested – begun to talk. And alas, not only was she built like a double-dose Mae West, but she misconstrued the kind of talk required ... Mae West minus the wit. Dirty, very dirty.

He decided not to try again. No, there was nothing to life nowadays except profit and success. Nothing.

'Lust, greed, murder, betrayal,' mused Morgan Pfeiffer, 'with a moral ending.' He checked the notes that Enrico Stoat had left. 'And six sexual encounters distributed throughout the book. Sensitively handled.'

He would have liked to add, 'And a *big* heroine,' but good marketing sense prevailed. Ah well. Nothing more to do now than to sit back and wait.

Chapter Thirteen

A T Dog Street Rohanne took Sylvia's keys from Gretchen.
Gretchen was sorry about this and felt she had every right to
be their keeper, but Rohanne's air of authority made this impossible. Instead, like an anxious, scurrying bull-pup, she followed
the carapacial Rohanne into the building and up the narrow stairs.
It was impractical to ascend two abreast since the space did not
permit it, and Gretchen continued to follow close on Rohanne's
heels up to the top flight. Rohanne, feeling the bull-pup pursuit,
went at quite a lick, with the result that, by the time they
reached the final landing, both women were puffing and groaning and the inner state of Rohanne's leathers was the stuff of
which top-shelf publications are made. Unable to go up any
further since Sylvia Perth's apartment was the last in the building, Rohanne stopped suddenly, and with impromptu rigidity,
at the top of the stairs facing a door. Gretchen, who had found
keeping her head down as she went helped her breathing, was
unprepared for stopping, and, at some speed, head-butted
Rohanne in the coccyx.

Experiment for yourselves: on approaching an unknown door
that has both a lock and a separate handle for turning, you will
grasp the handle and turn it as you apply the key to the hole. You
will not expect the door to give way until the key has done its
duty, and in most instances your assumption would be correct.
But Erica von Hyatt, not having a key of her own and having
made her earlier milkmanward sortie, had forgotten to resnag the
lock – people who have lived in cardboard boxes and under
railway arches tend, on the whole, to be unmindful of locking
procedures. With the result that, instead of the cool, calm, digni-
fied and slightly menacing entrance that Rohanne Bulbecker

had planned for herself, she went into the deceased Sylvia's apartment nose first, at some speed and in a manner that the English are pleased to call colloquially 'arse over tit'. Followed immediately by Gretchen O'Dowd, who, less graceful than her transatlantic sister, though none the less urgently propelled, went in very fast and then down like a sack of potatoes right on top of her.

There are some who, upon entering a room of unknown possibilities, might feel quite philosophical about doing it on all fours and beneath the body of another. Rohanne Bulbecker was not one of these. The opprobrious messages meant for Gretchen O'Dowd, who lay across her like an iron girder on a Japanese house, were more or less lost in the thick white pile of the carpet into which the Bulbecker nose was firmly pressed. What opprobrium did escape was delivered with great authority. All the more galling, then, that the pinion should remain firmly where she was.

It was not so much the Arabian opulence of the furnishings that kept Gretchen there. Nor the yellow light that beat against the half-draped windows, bringing mysterious shadows amid the sunbeams. It was not even the heady scent that hung about the still room, nor the exotic objects scattered about. No. What held Gretchen O'Dowd in a flattened position was the sight of the room's occupant. The figure lay across the couch, asleep, dreaming perhaps, illuminated and enriched by the light that fell upon it from between the half-closed curtains. Gretchen thought that she had never seen anything quite so beautiful in all her life.

Erica Von Hyatt was still taking a nap. The Jack Daniel's mixed with chocolate milk drink was of soporific effect in its own right but, sipped slowly after a long, steamy, perfumed bath while reclining on cushions in the late morning's heat, it would have taxed the profound resolve of even Cerberus to stay awake. Erica guarded no one save herself. Erica felt safe. Erica slept. She slept the sleep of contentment. Not a hungry sleep, not an escapist's sleep, but the sleep of one who has merely chosen to enjoy the experience. And the enjoyment showed. She was rosy like a child, and her golden hair – washed, combed and sparkling in the light – streamed around her on the velvet couch. About her smiling mouth were the milky traces of her favoured cocktail. One cheek held the trace of a dimple, her pale eyelids were smooth and unmoving as pebbles. Beneath all this, sumptuously spread, was the pink gown, its heavy silver tassels scattered on the floor. This was the legend come to life, this was the dream of childhood, here was the princess of fantasy as pure and beautiful as in any fairy tale. Gretchen, immobilized, stared in wonder.

Rohanne Bulbecker, on the other hand, saw nothing but the roots of the carpet tufts and a tassel or two. What she was saying, louder and louder into the carpet tufts was not an unknown language to Erica, who – though asleep – began to register the rude and brutal message. In the Moving On of the streets, she had long learned to shift herself without wakening completely. Whoever was speaking clearly wanted her, Erica von Hyatt, off out of it, and in Pavlovian response there was nothing to do but oblige. There never was.

She rose from the couch, still half asleep, and stumbled across the room. 'OK, OK,' she muttered wearily, 'I'm going, I'm going . . .' And as she opened her eyes, she found herself impeded, and then falling over a couple of strangers who appeared to be At It on the floor.

Muffled expletives, indistinct but full of ire, rose from the one at the bottom of the pile. Rohanne got some air, gasped, and managed, 'What the hell *is* this?'

'Sorry,' said Erica von Hyatt humbly, righting herself. She took the flailing hand and pulled at it, freeing the speaker, while Gretchen O'Dowd rolled gracelessly on to her back.

Gretchen stared up at the vision. 'Who are you?' asked the supine adorer.

But before Erica could respond, she found her arm held in a tight, leather-gauntleted squeeze and the air was charged with excitement. 'Are you – by any chance – Janice Gentle?' said the mouth beneath the sunglasses.

'Why?' asked Erica von Hyatt, recognizing the desperate

urgency of the question, playing for time. She eyed the talking woman's outfit up and down. Black leather, and in this heat. It was clear to Erica what sort of thing this person had in mind.

'Because that's who I'm looking for,' said Rohanne as nicely as she could. 'I have a proposition for her.'

I bet you have, thought Erica von Hyatt.

'Well,' said Rohanne Bulbecker encouragingly, 'are you?'

The glove tightened, the heat radiated out from the gleaming black body, Erica pondered. S&M was something she had encountered before, after all, though this time, from the way the woman was dressed, it didn't look as if Erica, or this Janice Gentle person (good name, good name), was going to be asked to play the dominatrix. Which was a pity. If it had only been one of those 'Tie me up and don't give in to my pleas' situations, she would have done it cheerfully. Or, rather, with firm and hard-mouthed positivism, as she had been instructed once by a fish merchant from Hull. These S&M people never seemed to see the funny side . . .

'Oh do say you are,' said Rohanne, suddenly weary. 'Please.'

So Erica did.

With extraordinarily gratifying results. The woman in black held her shoulders and kissed her on both cheeks and went on and on and on about how glad she was to have found her, etc, etc, so that Erica got a bit lost.

'You took *quite* a bit of tracking down,' continued Rohanne Bulbecker. 'Sylvia Perth was *very protective* of you.'

Erica decided to continue along an oblique path for a time, the Jack Daniel's and the sudden arousal making her a little foggy. 'Where is Sylvia?' she said.

Gretchen, glad to have something to contribute, said, 'I think she's still with the police at the moment, but she'll be coming to Mr Mole's parlour very soon.'

Erica thought it was rather a good name for a knocking shop. She did not ask for further clarity. 'Oh good,' she said.

'Oh yes,' said Gretchen. 'It'll be a lovely ceremony.'

Ritual too, thought Erica von Hyatt with a heavy heart. 'What do I have to do?' she asked wanly.

'You don't have to do anything,' said Rohanne Bulbecker. 'Everything will be just the same – only without Sylvia Perth. We'll be *just* as protective of you. You don't have to worry about a thing.'

I've heard that before, thought Erica von Hyatt. 'You must want something,' she said.

Rohanne held up a hand and smiled cheerfully. 'Nope. Just one more' – she gave a little moue of encouragement – 'baby, that's all, and we'll do all the rest.'

Erica, still rather fuzzy and shaky, sat down again. 'You're not S&M, then?'

'Were you expecting them?' said Rohanne Bulbecker, suddenly alert for a rival.

Erica eyed her up and down. 'Well, sort of . . .'

'No, I am Rohanne Bulbecker.' She began feeling about her person, annoyed to have forgotten her card case.

Erica watched the suggestive antics and sighed. The peaceful independence had been so lovely. 'When you say *baby*, what exactly do you mean . . .?'

Rohanne laughed. 'I mean that Sylvia told me all about you. She was extremely enthusiastic about your next one. Well, we all are.'

She beamed at Erica. Never in Rohanne Bulbecker's wildest imaginings had she dared to hope her prey would be this beautiful. Just wait until she got back and introduced her to Morgan Pfeiffer and Enrico Stoat. They'd go wild. The whole project was going to be sensational.

'Morgan Pfeiffer is just going to love you,' she said.

'Who's Morgan Pfeiffer?' asked Erica, eyes widening. How many more were going to be involved for God's sake?

Rohanne laughed. 'Just about the biggest publisher in America,' she said. 'And' – she laughed again and tapped Erica's forearm teasingly – 'I guess you could call him the *prospective father* of your baby . . .'

Neither Sisyphus without his stone nor Prometheus without the eagle could have felt more relieved than Rohanne Bulbecker at that moment. She was therefore unusually disposed to banter with metaphor. 'He'll make a *great* dad,' she smirked. 'Just great!'

Suddenly Erica von Hyatt understood. It wasn't S&M at all. It was that thing called surrogate motherhood. She knew people who had done it. You got looked after while you were pregnant and quite a lot of money afterwards. Erica could see no wrong in it. If you could knit, you would make a jumper for someone who was cold, and they would pay you for it; if you could cook and someone was hungry, they would pay you to make a meal. Why not make a baby for someone?

'How do you feel about that?' asked Rohanne.

'Fine,' said Erica von Hyatt. 'What's the . . . er . . . *dad* like?'

Rohanne Bulbecker was delighted with the game. 'He's *very* distinguished, Morgan P. Pfeiffer. Very clever. *Loves* the books . . . Well, don't we all?'

'How much?'

Rohanne liked the directness and told her the dollar sum.

Erica von Hyatt was mute.

Rohanne sucked her fingers.

Gretchen, who had found the whole conversation confusing, fluffed her moustache and waited for enlightenment. The silence in the room was exquisite. She took a breath, about to speak.

'Be quiet,' said Rohanne Bulbecker. 'Janice is thinking.' Gretchen gazed at the thinker in silent worship and Erica fluttered her eyelashes with intuitive response. Beyond that, she could neither move nor speak. Gretchen O'Dowd sighed like swains of old. Erica fluttered again. Gretchen O'Dowd sighed deeper. She was, she knew, radically and for ever in love.

'Janice,' said Rohanne beguilingly, 'where were we?'

Erica was a little unsure. Very probably, she thought, where they were was in a dream.

'Well?' asked Rohanne. 'Does that figure sound about right? Of course it's only the advance and there will be all kinds of synergy, but that's the sum Morgan Pfeiffer will pay you up front. Half now, half on delivery. What do you think?'

'Sounds all right to me,' said Erica. She shrugged carefully. It would not do to look astonished or the price might drop. She couldn't, really, believe it, anyway – but she'd go along the road in case it was true. In her head she was pretending that she had just been offered a free meal. It was much easier to think of it in those simple terms. And anyway, she had already been a *sort* of surrogate mum – with Dawn. What was the difference between one made out of a mistake and one made out of a paid-for plan?

Rohanne touched the back of the couch lightly. 'And . . . er . . . how long do you think *this* one is going to take to . . . er . . . produce?'

Erica felt on safer ground but a little surprised at the question. 'The usual nine months, I suppose. Do I have to go over there and fuck him, or what?'

Much taken aback by the crudity of this, but not inclined to upset the delicacy of the moment, Rohanne smiled. She had heard that the British had a strange sense of humour. 'I don't think – hah hah – that will be necessary.'

'Really,' said Erica, eyes wide again. 'Well, he can hardly send it over by post. Can he?'

'Of course he can,' said Rohanne. 'In fact, it's already here at the bank, waiting for you.'

Erica von Hyatt had heard of sperm banks. 'Oh, I see. He's going to do it *that* way. We don't even have to meet.'

'Well,' said Rohanne, 'I think he would like to meet you eventually.'

'Doesn't this Mr Pfeiffer like sex?' Given that amount of money, he was owed a bit of pleasure and rules were made to be broken. 'He'd enjoy it. I'm quite good at all that – *if* I say so myself.'

Rohanne Bulbecker felt as if she had just arrived in heaven. 'Well, that is just *brilliant*,' said Rohanne. 'That is exactly what we want. Morgan Pfeiffer has asked for two little changes from you . . .'

'Yes?' said Erica obligingly. 'What?'

'Sex. And to make it a bit longer.'

'I've gone on a night and a day once,' said Erica with pride. 'Length is no problem. I'm *very* amenable.'

Rohanne coughed. Despite her hopes, she had not expected Janice Gentle to be quite so raunchy. There was no hint of it in her work. 'Oh no,' she said hurriedly, 'you wouldn't need to go that far. Just a little lust, the thigh beneath the silk, know what I mean?'

Erica smiled. 'I know what you mean. Something a bit classy.'

'Exactly.'

Erica leaned back on the couch and closed her eyes. She didn't know who or where this Janice person was, but she, Erica, had got in first. And just let them say she hadn't.

Rohanne Bulbecker looked at her. She could quite see why Sylvia Perth had kept her hidden. Well she would, wouldn't she? And secret from the moustachioed one too, if her expression of amazed admiration was anything to go by. Funny old devious Sylvia, thought Rohanne Bulbecker, now your secret is *out*.

'Are you recluse?' she asked the golden beauty before her.

'What do you mean?'

'Do you prefer to hide away from the world?'

Erica thought. In a big lie it was always best to stick as close to the truth as possible. She had not found the world a place in which she would choose to spend a lot of time. Not if she could live like this. This kind of hiding away seemed perfection. 'Yes,' she said positively, 'but I'm not hung up on it.'

'Good,' said Rohanne Bulbecker, 'because I'm going to call Mr Pfeiffer right away with the good news, and I just *know* he will want you to go over there whenever you feel ready to do so. Is there a phone here?'

Erica pointed to the sequinned scatter cushion on top of an inlaid desk. Gretchen lifted it. Rohanne was doubly blessed – happy are the technocrats – for behind a beaten-brass bowl that hid its undecorative outline also nestled a fax machine. 'Great,' said Rohanne, her eyes lighting upon it as one might light upon a hidden jewel. 'That's just what I want. I can send this off to him straight away.' And from the unzipped deeps of her jacket front pocket she produced the Pfeiffer contract. 'If you could look this over and then sign here,' she said to Erica von Hyatt, 'that would be great. Let me know if there are any problems.'

Erica flipped over the pages, understood nothing, nodded for authenticity and obediently took the pen. 'How do you spell

Gentle?' she asked. Feeling Rohanne Bulbecker start nervously, she quickly added, 'Just a joke.' Her eyes were heavy with Jack Daniel's. She badly wanted to snooze again.

Morgan Pfeiffer stopped listening at the point in Rohanne Bulbecker's glowing description where she said 'slender as a willow'. Slender as a willow was not what he considered beauty. He sighed. Still, the rest of the world, almost without exception, would consider it so. Certainly, Enrico Stoat, listening on the other extension, was twirling his wrist-watch and rolling his eyes in a lather of jubilation. Morgan Pfeiffer sat back in his chair and recalled the Black Sea resort he and Mrs Pfeiffer had so enjoyed in the old days. There they had recognized the beauties of real flesh. Those women had rotated rather than walked, and when they lay on their backs in water the sea had held up their breasts like ripe pumpkins – mmmm, mmmm . . .

'Sure,' he heard Stoat say. 'Get her over here as soon as possible. It's good to know she's a looker. I was shit scared she'd be some kind of freak . . .'

'Well done, Miss Bulbecker,' added Morgan Pfeiffer. 'I felt certain you would bring the deal off.'

'I'll fax the contract immediately.'

Behind Rohanne, on the couch, Erica von Hyatt slept. Behind the couch Gretchen O'Dowd stood guard. Gretchen removed her jacket because of the noon heat and, as she did so, the letter she had been handed that morning crackled beneath her hand. She had forgotten all about that. The tableau of beauty before her stirred, moved a little. She forgot about the letter all over again.

Rohanne Bulbecker began pulling out the drawers of Sylvia's desk, idly at first, then, as she began to pause and read some of the documents, her eyes grew luminous and large. She picked up several files and slipped them into the front of her jacket, pulling up the zip with a flourish. Here was news indeed.

*

144

Arthur smiled at her across the breakfast table. She caught the look, could not avoid it this time, and smiled back. There were delphiniums in the room, past their best, the colour fading to peppered blueness. They echoed her eyes, eyes which held a secret nowadays, eyes into which her smile had not quite reached.

'Perhaps,' he said, 'you should buy a hat.'

'Why?' she asked, curious despite her misery.

'Isn't that what you ladies are supposed to do to recover your spirits?'

'You're old-fashioned. All that went out with cloaks over mud. Anyway, my spirits are fine,' she said, and then, since it was patently untrue and the look in his eyes told her that he knew, she shrugged, 'Or almost fine.'

'Then, why,' he said, 'are you crumbling toast between your fingers like the despairing heroine of a Gothic novel?'

'For the birds,' she said defiantly. 'They are God's creatures, after all.'

'Shall I butter and marmalade it for them?'

Her laugh was no less dry than the toast.

He set aside the letter from their South-East Asian mission. He had been going to ask her to get the Guides to do something – less (if he was honest before his God) for the good of the mission and the Guides than to keep her occupied. Usually activity released her melancholy or defused her scratchiness, but this sad and almost total detachment was new to the pattern. It came back with her from London. He knew that she needed to take it back there if it was ever to be shed.

She put her chin on her hands and looked at him. She had begun to hate him for his ability to love her, for his clumsy attempts at gallantry, his mannered wooing. He saw the look in her eyes, somewhere between pain and contempt. He moved his head, questioning.

'It's the tea-urn,' she said. 'You know how I loathe the bloody thing.'

'Ah,' he said, 'the tea-urn. Then perhaps we should buy you a new one instead of a hat.'

'It's love–hate, Arthur,' she said. 'Take that away from me and what have I got left?' *That*, she thought, was a fair metaphor. 'Besides, as you say to your souls, if God had wanted to make things easy for us he would have taken us straight to heaven without all this three-score-and-ten fuss on the way. The tea-urn is my cross to bear.' She smiled.

Somehow, from her lips and at that moment, this was no blasphemy.

'You can't appreciate heaven until you have suffered a little.' He folded his hands together and looked over the fingertips compassionately. 'Nor choose martyrdom. Bind and loose, as Eliot would have it.'

'You look exactly like a vicar *should* look when you do that.'

For a moment her eyes were very blue again, flashing fire, angry. The red of her hair seemed to sharpen.

'And you,' he said mildly, 'look nothing like a vicar's wife when you do *that*.'

'What?'

'Rage with your eyes.'

'It's the tea-urn,' she said firmly.

'Then we shall buy a new one.'

'Oh no,' she said. 'Too easy.'

'Even Our Lord had his Simon of Cyrene.'

'The cross-carrier?'

He nodded.

'Was he willing, or was he made to do it?'

He leaned back in his chair and no longer looked at her. 'Willing or unwilling, it helped. We will . . .' – he stared at the letter from the Asian mission, then picked it up and folded it neatly back into its envelope. A child and a grandmother stared up at him warily. *Strictly* the Guildford money had been for local benefit, after all – '. . . buy a new, improved, dynamic, state-of-the-art tea-urn.'

'State of the art? Arthur, where do you pick up these phrases?'

146

'I am not,' he smiled, 'quite ossified yet.' He tucked the envelope beneath a pile of others, 'and you will go to London and effect the purchase.'

'Why London?' she said, incredulous, shaking.

'Because . . .' He reached over and took her hand. It lay limply in his, cool and unmoved, belying her face, which was flushed to rose, and her eyes, which shone. And then she withdrew it, quickly, smoothly, and began picking at the toast again. He thought of a magical experience, he thought of saying, 'Come to bed. Let us make each other happy again.' He said her name, she looked up.

'Because what?' she said shortly, afraid of what she read in his face.

'Because I believe it is in London that your best tea-urn replacement lies.' He put the magic away and got up from his chair. He spoke firmly, business-like.

'When?' she said.

'As soon as you like.'

She closed her eyes in the wonder of a doubtful prayer answered.

*

From behind her, somewhere near the window, Rohanne Bulbecker heard a terrible howl – the kind of howl that would not be out of place in Baskerville territory, but which, in a small room behung with silks and padded with cushions, was distinctly *de trop*.

'Jeezus,' she sighed. 'What the hell was that?'

'I don't think that your friend' – Erica, awakened, naturally enough, was pointing at Gretchen O'Dowd – 'likes what's in that letter . . .'

Rohanne looked. Gretchen O'Dowd was hopping from foot to foot, her face contorted with dreadful emotion, holding her letter with one hand while punching it with the other.

'I'd say,' said Rohanne Bulbecker, staring in wonder, 'you were right.' She looked at her watch. 'Do you know what I think?'

Erica shook her golden head.

'I think it's time for a celebration lunch. You choose where. You know London much better than me.'

Not the London you mean, thought Erica dryly. But she remembered that she had once had a rather good doorway along Piccadilly, not a stone's throw from its most famous hotel. She had stayed there for a number of nights and it was beginning to feel quite homey until the passers-by complained. After that they sprayed the whole area with water so that she had no choice but to move on. She had not been back since.

'The Ritz,' she said. And added truthfully, 'I haven't been there for *ages*.'

*

Janice Gentle crossed the river at Vauxhall and knew that she was passing into the dangerous world of the rich and the sophisticated. An alarming thought. She didn't mind using it in her books, but she did not want to be a part of it. It frightened her, all that class and style. She opened another fudge finger and played the game of making it last by sucking and not biting, a game she never won. Some urge always overtook her and she ended up chewing.

By the third fudge finger she had reached the other side of Vauxhall Bridge. Hitherto she had been as mindful and careful as Chaucer's Prioress, prissy Madame Eglentyne – 'Ne wette hir fyngres in hir sauce depe' – and despite the sun had stayed relatively unsullied. She had made every finger of fudge count. But now, as she surveyed the new land of Chelsea and Pimlico, she gave up. She dug into her bag any old how and chewed as she went, angry that she had been foolish enough to set out. She looked back towards dear, familiar, undemanding Battersea and felt certain that its cloistered quiet would never be hers again. She felt distinctly medieval. For so, of course, it had been for the Pilgrims. So, of course, it was for any traveller. Leaving the familiar for the uncertain always meant you were changed irredeemably. That was why she had never sought a journey beyond the enclosed world of the tube. She wished never to embark anywhere to be changed irredeemably until she was *confidently* en route for Dermot Poll. That was the only life-change she sought, and for that she had been perfectly prepared to wait. And now this. And on such a hot, uncomfortable day, too.

The Prioress, with her ingestive etiquette, bowed, gave way and finally departed in the heat of the day. She was Janice Gentle once more, afraid of the journey before her and just as afraid of the one she had left behind. She walked on. She ate. There was Millbank, the Tate Gallery, and there was chocolate around her mouth. There was Westminster, there was Churchill, and there was chocolate on the front of her beige cardigan. Her hands were sticky and grimy already with the pollution of London streets. The hot sun had reddened her face and she walked uneasily with chafing thighs. She noticed irritably that there was still scaffolding around the Abbey; it had been there the last time she visited this part of London in a taxi with Sylvia Perth.

If ever, she thought earnestly, a pilgrim was required to travel in grim discomfort, she qualified. Surely, given the sacrificial nature of her effort, she would be rewarded somehow? Something must happen after Dog Street. When she had done her kindly silencing of Sylvia Perth, something had to begin, surely *something*? And for perhaps the thousandth time in her history, she wondered where, at that exact minute, Dermot Poll might be. Her spirits lifted. If they were still mending Westminster Abbey after all this time, then what was time? He might not be so far away, after all. It was with this comfortingly peculiar piece of logic that Janice Gentle journeyed on.

Chapter Fourteen

IN Skibbereen the Saint's Day bells rang out as Dermot and his lady lay endeavouring to continue asleep. There was a little blood on the pillow, not much, on Deirdre's side. Dermot had swung rather faster than he meant to and caught her a goodly blow to the bridge of the nose.

'Would you look at that?' she said disgustedly, opening one eye and not being able to open the other. 'I shall not share this bed another night. When a woman says no, she means no, pigman, and that's the last you'll get of me.'

So saying, she rolled out of the bed, trailing her pillow behind her, and fell into the empty bed next door, the bed that had once been Declan's. 'Son, son, son,' she moaned as she drifted back to sleep, but she was not despairing. He would do fine for himself in London, Declan – with that pretty face, those crisp, black curls and the voice of a nightingale. And much better off away from here. She might go back herself one day.

Anyway, moving bedrooms was a good first step and as far as she wanted to go for the moment. She'd put a little bicarbonate of soda solution on the eye. The bells ceased and Deirdre slept, content and at peace in her isolation. She should, she thought, have done this years ago . . .

Dermot turned, felt the empty mattress beside him. A brief stab of regret at the space was short-lived. He stretched out his leg and rubbed it across the void. Then he stretched the calf, stretched the toes, and sighed with pleasure. That was better, much better, now he had room. Nice for a while. And she would be back – he knew it. 'I'll walk beside you through the passing years,' he sang to the ceiling and remembered how the ladies had loved him to sing it, how the tears had flowed and how innocent it had all been then. He would have still been there, singing in London, living well, thinking fondly of Erin's Isle, enjoying the regret with his emigré companions if that girl had not waylaid him the night Declan was born. Women, ah women! They were hell. Would a man have left him lying there in the street like that and gone off on a bus? With a policeman able to come up and find him? First the boot, then the questions. 'What's your name, son?' *Son? Son?* He'd been no older than himself. 'What are you doing out? Where do you live?' And then the goading, the sarcasm. 'Bog Irish? Crawl back into the peat, scum . . .'

Was it his fault that the bomb happened? Was it his fault that he spoke with the accent of the guilty? And was it his fault that they'd got his address and only for being drunk? 'My son was born,' he told them, but they took him, and it was six days before he got home. The neighbours had broken all the windows, Deirdre's milk had dried away and she had tickets for the ferry. 'Days of joy and laughter, pain and tears . . .'

If that colourful girl had only put him on the bus with her and taken him home he'd have been all right. That's what any man would've done, wasn't it now? Women, ah women! They were all hell. Ever since Eden . . .

Chapter Fifteen

O N the way to the Ritz Gretchen reread her letter.
'I am asked to stay on for three months in my present capacity
as housekeeper and to accept, as a gift from the estate, designated
by my former employer, the seascape watercolour that hangs in
my room.'

'That's kind,' said Erica. 'Is it a nice picture?'

'No,' said Gretchen miserably. 'I hate the sea. And the painting
is all fuzzy and peculiar.'

'What about money?' said Rohanne Bulbecker.

Gretchen O'Dowd peered at the letter. 'My wages and
something called an *ex gratia* payment . . .'

'That's not bad . . .'

'But I was supposed to inherit everything. She said so. There
was nobody else in her life so close as me.'

Rohanne took the letter. 'You could go and see these people.'

'I am,' said Gretchen miserably. 'I have an appointment this
afternoon.'

'I'll come with you,' said Rohanne Bulbecker. 'I need to do a
little investigating, too.'

'*And* I was going to bury her. Such a lovely funeral it was
going to be. Very grand. Guests and everything.'

'It is profoundly to be hoped that they have buried her already,'
said Rohanne Bulbecker. 'Ah, here we are. The Ritz!'

*

Square Jaw pulled out the box of Melanie's things. She ought to
have them back. Every time he got into bed he stubbed his toe,
and he could swear that her scent lingered in the room. He was

right. On closer inspection he found that the bottle had tipped over and leaked. There were all kinds of things in there that she must want. He touched one or two of them, familiar things. He'd ring her, offer to take them over to her, that would show there were no hard feelings, that he could be kind. Anyway, it would be all right – and he would quite like to see her again . . .

He dialled her number confidently this time, without needing a drink first. This time he had a good, solid, respectable reason for doing so – none of this being unsure what to say. She answered.

He said, 'Hi,' cheerfully.

She said, 'Hi, how are you?' With equal cheer.

That was unnerving. He had expected her to be a bit emotional. He was glad that she wasn't – and *not* glad. Confusing.

'Fine,' he said positively. 'You?'

'OK,' she said. 'How's work?'

'Not bad. Pissed off with the travelling.'

'You always were.'

'I don't like the tube.'

'Go by bus, then.'

'Worse.'

Melanie wondered, with rising irritation, why they were discussing the London transport system. *And* why he was being his usual negative self again. Why didn't he just say, 'Melanie, I love you. Come back'?

Square Jaw wondered why Melanie could never say anything sympathetic any more. She'd been so caring and thoughtful in the beginning. If she said she was sorry, it would be something.

'Did you ring for anything in particular?'

'I've got your things.'

'Yes?'

'Thought you might want them.' He attempted a joke. 'They're no good to me.'

Melanie felt the tears rise, the lump grow in her throat. 'I don't expect they are. Well, I haven't had time to fetch them. I've been very busy.'

'So have I,' he said quickly. He was *not* going to ask, he was *not* . . .

Melanie, on the other hand, tried not to and failed. 'Doing what?' she said.

'This and that,' he said.

She was stung by his hedging. It could mean only one thing, that he had been doing things he didn't want her to know about. That meant he had met somebody else. No wonder he wanted her things out of the way. Well, she bloody well wasn't going to collect them and make it easy for him.

'I've no idea when I'll have time.'

'I could drop them off,' he offered, relieved at last to have got round to what he wished to say.

'Don't bother,' she said icily. 'I'll collect them some time.'

'When?'

'When I've got time.'

'Like *when*?' His voice had risen. She could be infuriatingly obtuse. And he felt angry, put down, that she didn't want to see him.

'I'll let you know.'

'Next week? Next year?'

'Don't shout.'

'It's my bloody flat they're taking up room in.'

She put down the phone. If he wanted her cleared out, he'd have to wait – whoever the *she* was. Arrogant, bad-tempered, cruel bastard. She rang her closest girlfriend, who agreed.

Selfish, ungrateful, callous bitch. He switched on the video and lost himself in *The Naked Gun*.

*

Red Gold closed her eyes and dreamt of how it had been in the past. The train rocked and swayed, and it was almost like being held in her lover's arms already.

'I am coming to London to buy a tea-urn.' She had laughed down the phone.

'When?' he said.

Ah no, she thought, I shall be too clever for that. 'Whenever you are free,' she said.

He had checked his diary and given her a date. And today it was. This beautiful, beautiful train was taking her to him. A liaison with her lover from the past. A liaison of just one night, a night that would count for all eternity. She asked no more. Close the book. Back to Arthur and the reality of for ever with things just the same as they had always been, life going on – only she would have a precious secret to get her through the hungry winter's evenings.

After she had spoken to him, she cradled the receiver to her cheek. Her heart was racing, wanting to sing. But already the distant memory of subterfuge returned to her. She must look no different, sound no different, give no clue to Arthur that she had anything more than a tea-urn and other items to purchase on her mind. Her stomach turned, her head felt light. They would have tea at the Ritz (she would pay, she would pay). And afterwards? Afterwards it did not matter. Afterwards it would be somewhere. Her head rang with the mystery of the feeling inside her for this one man among them all. She was lucky, she told herself, to have experienced it even once. She replaced the receiver and looked through the window at Arthur sitting in the garden with his bridal class. Most people – like him, like those three young women out there – never got close.

In a painting, she thought, the scene would have been delightful. Three young women, pretty and innocent as daisy flowers, sitting at the knee of the man of God as he helped them see the pleasure of purity, the fineness of faith, the joy of married union. In reality it never reached the nursery slopes of the ideal. All the same, Arthur pursued it. He was pursuing it now with the non-painting: three unattractive young women grouped around him in the garden. The scene was perfect, it was the players who were at fault. 'Arthur's little joke with God,' she risibly called these classes, though he knew she did and laughed too. If these girls wanted to be White Queen for the day then they must be instructed in what it meant to the Greatest Husband of Them All, and the home He offered them in the Church of Christ.

Making them pay for their vanities, was her assessment. Arthur was kinder, if rigid for the rule. 'Maybe some of it goes in and remains in,' he said, if she teased him (she could call it teasing now, she had no more need to mock with her flame of joy burning inside her).

'Maybe when I talk to them about Jesus and the family and love, a little shard penetrates and stays. Think of Langland's Piers the Ploughman – how he fought back at the licentiousness of the age with stories and examples. Perhaps a particle remains.'

'Like a splinter? To irritate? To inflame?'

'Nobler than that.'

'Are you not,' she said, 'in danger of perpetrating one of your Ploughman's Deadly Sins?'

'Which?'

'Pride?'

'Tell me?'

'Pride in likening yourself to Langland, whom you call a genius? Comparing yourself with your hero . . .'

'If he was a visionary, he was also an ordinary man,' said Arthur, 'and he believed in speaking plain. That is all I do. I have no pride in that.'

'Do you have pride in anything, or are you pure of it?'

He looked her full in the face so that she had to look away lest he could read her thoughts. He smiled, amused at himself. 'If I have a pride, it is not in my work . . .'

'Then it should be,' she said quickly, 'for you are very good at it. And maybe, as you say, a little shard penetrates.'

Looking around the town, at the pasty, fat children in grubby muck-smeared pushchairs, with their blank-faced parents in Oxfam clothes, as quick to swipe as to kiss, she was not so sure. She went to their houses, she iced buns and gave them tea in the hall, smelled their smells, did their jumbles. She didn't think anything had penetrated them, nor remained. Arthur was dreaming, Arthur was living an ideal that was nothing to do with reality. The lessons on the lawn. Nothing would come of them. After the wedding, the deluge, with the frock put away – never to be dyed and worn to a ball. In Arthur's church there was nobody likely to be asked to a ball, and you couldn't wear such a gown to the disco. And *anyway* (she thought of how different her own memories of love were), discos stopped with the first baby. Indeed, the first baby was probably conceived at the disco – or shortly afterwards. The best thing a white wedding dress could do was make you net curtains so your neighbours could not see the paucity of your life; or stand you a fiver from the hock shop.

Before the three girls arrived, Arthur said that he thought he might temporarily drop the bit about 'considering the lilies of the field', since few people up here had the opportunity of choosing whether or not to toil or spin. More of the joke? She was unsure. But against all this dreariness, she, at least, had some joy in her life. Something delicious. Like eating cold suet pudding in February and finding a strawberry inside. And if it were worse than that? If it were Sin? Who did it harm? Why should she renounce it? After so long what harm could it do? Not to her, not to him, not to Arthur. None at all. If you *desired* the deed, it was, very likely, as bad as going ahead and doing it.

So she had made her date, while Arthur held his bridal class, sitting in his deck-chair, with the girls untidily kneeled around him on a tartan rug. She saw him point at his feet and then gesture a question. The girls laughed. He had got to the bit where he asked them if they would use up their best face cream to soothe their husbands' feet. The bit about sacrifices. Time to take out the cooling drinks. Those three blank faces would need some refreshment. Sacrifices were what they would do for the rest of their lives. She ran down the stairs, scooped up the tray with jug and glasses and came smiling upon the group.

'I was saying,' said Arthur, 'that marriage is a labour of love. That each of you is required to give things up to the other's better happiness. Go into it with both your eyes and your heart open and knowing that to change, to adapt, to accept, is to succeed.' He sipped his drink, looked over the top of the glass. 'Would you say?'

'Oh, certainly, certainly,' she laughed. 'Never stop working at

157

it, girls,' she instructed like a school-marm. 'Don't have too many dreams ... And keep the little niceties ...' (if they had any to keep) – she was feeling almost delirious with the bubble of pleasure, the memory of his voice on the telephone – 'the little niceties in view. Do you know that Arthur kisses my hand sometimes?'

The three girls giggled nervously. Arthur looked at her. Again she looked away. Her heart was aching for London. She should not have said that. Perhaps it was a nice image for the girls? Anyway it was too late, it was said now. Maybe he would stop doing it at last. She looked at the sniggering faces.

Later, she promised herself, I shall atone. I always do. It was the shedding of guilt. I have given him this.

'I'll get the early train,' she told him. 'There's no need to come to the station.'

'I shall walk with you when you go,' he said firmly. Somehow there was no room for the even the lightest of arguments against it.

And he accompanied her. They walked past honeysuckle, and the drying pods of the delphiniums gave off their dusty, peppery scent. The roses, heavy and full-blown, bent as they passed, still with the dew on them.

'The garden needs a good pruning,' she said. 'And the lawn's mossy again. I've let it go these past weeks. I shall set it all to rights when I get back.'

She resented his staying so close as they walked. She wanted the excitement to begin the minute she stepped out of the front door. Every minute that Arthur was with her meant a shaving of the pleasure time. What was she doing talking about horticulture at such a moment?

'Go now,' she said to him at the barrier. She said it more loudly, more crossly, than she had intended.

He shook his head. 'I shall see you on the train,' he said, and waved with cheerful greeting to the ticket collector as they passed.

On the station she prattled away brightly, hating his being with her. Her only consolation was that this was another penance for her to fulfil. A task, the kind of thing he talked about in his marriage lessons. Talking to Arthur now on this run-down, littered, grimy platform was hell. She must suffer it, though she wished him away from her with all her heart.

'I think I can hear the train,' he said suddenly, and moved towards her, kissing her cheek. 'You were beautiful last night. Come back to me soon.'

She moved away, smiled awkwardly, looked down the line, waiting with hope. They had made love. She out of penitential duty, the feeding of dues to Arthur, the assuaging (she hoped) of his watchfulness, which might or might not be purely in her imagination. She had done that, atoned in the dark. Could he not now let her alone to her pleasure? Last night she had pleasured him. Oddly she had enjoyed it, a surprise, a bonus. Her body shook with his at the end and her sigh of satisfaction had been real. A reminder, perhaps, of how she could respond, let her body delight, when she was lit from within. Then he had stayed close, his head buried in the well of her shoulder, damp-eyed, arm heavy around her waist, stifling, but she had not remonstrated. Now she wanted him gone.

The train, coming round the bend, was like a saviour. She had waved from the window, each wave representing another measure of freedom. And now she was alone, rocking towards London, a voucher for Carver's the church suppliers in her handbag, a room booked at Arthur's club for the night, and – the strawberry that nestled within it all – tea at the Ritz to come.

*

Outside the Ritz Rohanne congratulated herself on her achievement and looked about her with a pleasurable smile, which was somewhat diminished at the sight of a fat bag lady staggering towards the entrance of Green Park. She watched as a woman with red-gold hair pressed a coin into her hand and gave her a brilliant and happy smile before skipping off.

'What the hell makes people that way?' Rohanne asked as they entered the Ritz. Erica shook her head. 'She wasn't one of us,' she said positively. 'You can tell. She wasn't going for a touch at all.'

Rohanne was giving her another curious stare. 'Pardon?' she said.

'I mean,' said Erica, 'I don't *think* she was.' She decided to change the subject to something altogether safer. 'How *is* Sylvia?' she asked with a bright smile for her companions.

This time they both stopped and stared. This time they both said, 'Pardon?'

'You do . . . um . . . *know*, don't you?'

'Know? What?' Keep smiling, she told herself, keep smiling.

'That Sylvia Perth is dead.' Gretchen held up her letter and wiggled it.

'My employer . . .'

Light dawned. 'Oh yes, of course, how silly of me. So she is,' said Erica quickly. 'I forgot.'

Shame, she thought privately, but she was not surprised. The woman was a bag of nerves, really.

Rohanne's eyes widened. Even to one as tough as Rohanne Bulbecker, forgetting such an event was, well, a little unfeeling. 'Just how close *were* you to her?'

'Very,' said Erica von Hyatt firmly. 'Very, *very* close . . .' And so they had been on their one night together. Erica von Hyatt liked to keep near to the truth.

Rohanne put it down to eccentricity and the national propensity for a stiff upper lip, and they entered the building cheerfully enough for a trio so recently bereaved.

Nobody minded how they looked. Erica's pink gown and silver tassels were quite acceptable since the petro-pound had revitalized the primitive art of wearing one's wealth ostentatiously. Rohanne was not turned away for her mirrored shades and leather gear, since the petro-pound had now evaporated, and a customer was a customer . . . And Gretchen looked perfectly decent, her moustache neatly tidy.

Erica felt philosophical. It might or it might not work. She might or she might not sustain the deception. The real Janice Gentle might or might not arrive and unmask her. It was out of her hands. In the meantime she would deflect personal questioning, wherein lay discovery, and make the most of the meal. At the bottom line, which is where she felt it was always sensible to begin, she'd eat better than she had ever eaten in her life. And they can't take *that* away from me, she thought.

She smiled at Rohanne through a mouthful of bread.

'Champagne?' said Rohanne.

Erica nodded through the bread.

Champagne was ordered.

Then Rohanne sat back and looked fondly at her protégée. 'I'd like to know all about you,' she said encouragingly. 'Tell me about yourself.'

Erica von Hyatt smiled back. She went on chewing, slowing down so that the process became more like a bovine exercise. Erica's mind had gone blank. Rohanne Bulbecker, retaining her encouraging smile, had begun to drum her ragged nails on the tablecloth. The waiter intervened and poured the wine, and, without thinking ahead, Erica picked up her glass and took a gulp. Which dispatched the last of the protective bread. Now she was on her own.

'Well . . . um,' she said.

Gretchen O'Dowd was looking at her with quite as much interest as Rohanne Bulbecker. She took advantage of the silence to ask what she longed to know. 'Have you, for instance' – she shrugged as if it were immaterial, but her heart was pounding in her breast – 'ever been a barmaid?'

'Yes,' Erica said, deciding to be positive about everything. 'I have.'

Gretchen sighed. 'I knew it,' she said. Her pounding heart was irretrievably lost.

'You *have* been around,' said Rohanne, determined to think positive. Erica put more bread in her mouth, chewed and smiled gummily.

Gretchen talked regretfully of her now dashed plans for Sylvia's earthly commitment. 'Oh yes,' she said dreamily, the champagne giving her wing, 'she would have lain in the open coffin for a day and a night with candles at the head and foot and dressed in her white satin Hartnell with the rose at its breast. There would have been huge arrangements of summer flowers, including scented lilies, to hide the smell.'

'What smell?' asked Erica, interested.

'Putrefaction,' said Gretchen promptly.

'Yes,' said Erica, 'we had one of those once. When I lived under the arches at Kennington. He'd got a washing-machine box, nice and big, still with the top flaps, so he closed them up at night. It was really very private. And none of us knew for days that he'd snuffed it. It was during that hot summer. Remember, last year? Twice as hot as this. Anyway, it wasn't until this smell began to get everywhere that we realized what . . . had . . . happ-ened.' Her voice slowed and trailed to a halt as she realized that Rohanne Bulbecker, spoon to lips, was staring at her as if she had died in a box herself.

'Charity work,' said Erica promptly, remembering a November evening when their homes had been invaded by do-gooders bent on suffering alongside them for a night. 'Take me with you, Guv,' she had called mockingly after their sad-eyed leader in the morning, but he appeared not to hear.

Rohanne relaxed again. 'Just for a moment there I thought . . .' she said, and then shook her head, putting a spoon of consommé between her teeth.

'Go on,' said Erica to Gretchen. 'What else?'

Gretchen explained about the walk over the fields.

'Very nice,' said Erica.

'Jeezus,' whispered Rohanne under her breath and continued to smile.

Suddenly she felt humble. Instinct and character told her to rebel at these stupidities. Discretion in matters of business prevailed. But given the growing weirdness of everything, she broke her rule and took another glass of bubbles. Which did, indeed, make the world seem easier to bear.

Two glasses of Château Haut-Brion were brought. Rohanne herself was happy with sole. Given the nature of the proceedings, sole seemed about as much as her stomach was up to. She smiled across the sensitively arranged goujons as Gretchen described the wake, the food at the wake, the music at the wake, the dancing . . .

'*Dancing?*' Rohanne put down her fork. She could eat no more under the circumstances.

Gretchen nodded. 'Dancing. I thought that would be nice . . .'

Erica, who had been only half listening while looking covetously at Rohanne Bulbecker's still-full plate (her own having been emptied and wiped for some time), said, 'Don't you want that?' pointing at the scarcely touched fish. Rohanne watched, astonished, as Erica stretched across and pulled her plate towards her. She was even more astonished to see that while she did this with one hand, the other was furtively concealing bread rolls in the folds of her swinging pink gown. Rohanne Bulbecker shrugged. Best not think about it. Only the dessert to go, she counselled herself, and then it will all be over.

Erica requested to go back to Dog Street. She was vague about her own home and, in any event, Gretchen O'Dowd was feeling very firm on the matter of inheritance. 'Until they prove beyond reasonable doubt' – she had watched a few courtroom dramas in her time – 'that I am not her heir, you have my permission to be there.'

'Is there anything you need?' asked Rohanne.

'Well,' said Erica, 'There's not much of anything in the flat. Not even toilet paper. Pink would be nice.'

Rohanne remembered the bread rolls. 'What about food?'

'There isn't much of that.'

Rohanne sighed with relief. At least it was *some* kind of explanation. 'Sylvia's solicitors are in Knightsbridge. We'll get something from Harrods afterwards.'

'Harrods?' said Erica ecstatically, 'I once lifted four cooked chickens from right under an assistant's nose. He never saw. But when I went back to do it again . . .' – she yawned – 'they'd moved them out of reach.'

They watched her taxi move off. 'In the bag,' muttered Rohanne doubtfully. Once again she felt peculiarly alone.

Gretchen O'Dowd and Rohanne Bulbecker walked down to Knightsbridge. Rohanne had her nose deep into a pile of papers.

'What are those?' asked Gretchen.

'Oh, just a few documents I picked up at Dog Street – accounts, stuff to do with Janice Gentle, things like that . . .'

She read for a while. 'Look,' she said eventually, and she gripped Gretchen's arm so tightly that Gretchen feared very much what was coming next, 'when we get there, pretend I am Janice Gentle's American lawyer. OK?'

Gretchen shrugged and nodded. That, at least, was a harmless suggestion.

*

Janice Gentle wished increasingly that she had not chosen such a hard task for herself. She expected Sylvia's side of town to be elegant, mannerly, refined, but by comparison with Battersea it was worse than a medieval stew. It was certainly as threatening. So far (and she had only got to Piccadilly) she had been accosted by a fist-shaking old woman with a mane of matted hair, cracked shoes and the vestiges of violent action around her eyes and temples – scabs, bruises, abrasions. 'What do you want?' Janice had asked politely. 'Revenge,' said the woman, and pushed Janice over in the gutter. Nobody came to help her up, and one woman hissed, 'Drunken bitch,' as she stepped over her. Not much further on a man with dreadlocks and a prayer book was standing on a street corner declaiming on the evils of the world, while boys jostled him, shouting obscenities, pitching into him though he stood his ground. 'The day of the Lord is nigh,' he averred. 'Go back to the jungle,' they replied. The man with dreadlocks was right: the world did, indeed, seem to be on the edge of something and full of menace and despair. Less and less did Janice feel she was participating in a Burgundian celebration or Chaucerian cavalcade, and more and more did she feel she was treading the path of the post–Black Death social degeneracy.

She had parted with over ten pounds in change before she realized that she could not go on sparing a quid for a cuppa every time she was asked, and when she had refused, finally, to grant such a request, the pinched-faced young woman with a battered pushchair and two head-lolling children had rammed her legs and cursed her with cancer. She tried resting in Green Park and was given a pound coin herself by a passer-by. When she handed it on to a weird young man with a jewel in his nose, he spat (though she didn't think it was particularly at her) and went savagely on his way. Dogs snarled at her. One shop asked to see her money first and another tried to short-change her. She was refused permission to a public lavatory, and, on showing her money, was allowed in only to find it was better to risk disgracing herself in the street. All in all it was hell on earth out here. She could not wait to switch off Sylvia Perth and get back to the safety of her own little cell.

By the time she turned into Dog Street – a journey that had taken a good deal longer than it might after her A–Z had been snatched from her hand – she felt she had suffered enough, even for the noble Sylvia. The tube journeys had, at least, been contained. This – this was a rampant free-for-all, and none had showed themselves to be kind. Except the woman with red-gold hair who had pressed the pound coin into her hand saying, 'Have this for love.' But even she had wanted something in return. 'Wish me luck,' she had urged, 'wish me lucky in love.' But she was gone before Janice had time . . . If she had not looked so much younger and so much more frivolous, Janice would have sworn it was the same woman she had noticed on the tube.

Well, Dog Street at last. She looked up at the building. 'Top Flat' said the disc on the keys in her hand.

Well, it *would* be, she puffed, beginning on the stairs. Nothing seemed designed to be easy any more.

*

Unusually for Square Jaw it had been a spur-of-the-moment

thing. He had got into the car, bought a bunch of sodding flowers on the way, and driven to Melanie's place. He had put the box of things in the car, just in case she was cool, and when he rang her bell, his heart thumped, which was crazy given how long they had known each other. And after all that – *shit* – she had been out. Again. But he waited, just in case she was held up at work. He waited for an hour in the car, listening to Clapton, chewing Murray Mints, thinking each sound might be her. He felt quite at home waiting there. Like in the old days. In fact – he looked at his keys in the ignition – in fact, he still had her key on his ring. He could, if he wished, let himself in. He didn't, though. He waited through the whole of *Behind the Sun* and *Greatest Hits*, and then drove away. He felt angry, cheated. He could have left her the flowers, but she might laugh at them, or maybe she would come back with somebody *else* who would laugh at them.

He stuck them in the sink when he got home and listened to his answerphone messages. There was one from Jeremy's girlfriend. 'He's away in Hong Kong,' she said, 'and he's asked me to tell you we're having a party.' She sounded slightly peeved (he recognized that kind of tone from Melanie sometimes). 'Apparently Jeremy has got the deal and wants to have a celebration. Come around nine.' She gave him the date.

I might just do that, he told himself, but he didn't, really, think that he would.

Melanie returned with a heavy heart. Oh, the misery. Oh, the tears. It had been a spur-of-the-moment thing, creeping past his place in the car, looking up at dark windows, empty silence. So where was he, then? She was tempted to use her key, but what had once been open territory was now banned; she would be a trespasser. And if she did go in, what? To sit up there and wait for him? Maybe wait all night? Or wait and find him coming back with somebody else? She sat in the shadows, further down the street, she waited for an hour. She listened to the Eurythmics and Annie Lennox made her weep (she always did). Eventually, after 'Savage' and 'Be Yourself Tonight', she drove home, taking the river route and sobbing to the moon.

On the answerphone there was a message from a Gerald she had met with Becky at that wine bar last week. Oh, why not? she thought, but with little conviction.

*

Janice climbed the stairs. She felt philosophical about their steepness and the fact that Sylvia Perth lived – *lived?* – right at the top. What pilgrim, what traveller after redemption ever had it easy?

She puffed on.

She thought of Christine with her pen, cold within thick winter walls, writing into the night in the meagre light of too few candles.

Langland, storm-blasted on a pastureside, distilling poetry and morality from the harshness . . . Do well, Do better, Do best. 'Contrition is on his back asleep and dreaming,' Peace said. 'Then by Christ! I will become a pilgrim and walk to the ends of the earth to find an honest livelihood . . .'

An honest livelihood? Janice Gentle strove upwards though her heart was pumping and her inner thighs were raw with chafing. Would that *were* her journey's end. As it was – and at best – she would switch off Sylvia. And at worst? She shuddered. She could not think beyond the switching off of her agent's voice.

When the world seems to scorn and reject you, take the courage of Christine de Pisan's fifth spear, the one wielded by Lady Hope, who is loved by Patience and protected by the shield of Faith, she told herself.

Above her she heard footsteps, the slam of a door, the rattle and crash of breaking bottles as if scattered by flailing feet. A yoghurt pot, cracked side dripping, came bouncing down the stairs. She stopped. The footsteps descended, bringing with them an eddy of ire. Janice pressed herself into the wall as a young woman appeared, running and muttering like a well-dressed White Rabbit. 'Now I'm late. Now I'm late.' And then, 'Why me?' She stopped, wild-eyed, to ask, 'He's in Hong Kong – what am I doing here?'

Janice shook her head, trying to look like an interested party.

'Haven't *I* got a job to do? Would he come and clean *my* sink?' The young woman suddenly looked at her hands. Despite her immaculate dress, she was wearing a bright yellow pair of rubber gloves. She stared at them as if she were staring at blood. 'Look at these,' she said.

Janice obliged.

The young woman ripped one off with a loud and rubbery smacking sound, throwing it carelessly over her shoulder like a Russian on party night. 'I ask you. Would he come to my flat and do that for me? Would he? Would sodding Jeremy do *that*?' With the stylishness of a mannequin she peeled the remaining glove off slowly and let it fall, plop, on to the floor. And with a click of her sparkling high heels, she turned the corner below, and vanished.

Janice thought of the beautiful Dermot Poll, and she wondered, sadly, if he had a sink. And if he did have a sink, she wondered if he cleaned it himself, and if he didn't clean it himself, did he have anyone who cleaned it for him? It could, were things different, have been her . . .

She picked up the yellow gloves. It was all so unsatisfactorily topsy-turvy. As if she had been living inside out and needed righting.

'The rule is, jam to-morrow and jam yesterday – but never jam to-day,' said the White Queen. 'It must come sometimes to "jam to-day",' Alice objected. 'No, it can't . . . It's Jam every other day: today isn't any other day, you know.' 'I don't understand you,' said Alice. 'It's dreadfully confusing!' 'That's the effect of living backwards,' the Queen said kindly: 'It always makes one a little giddy at first –'

So thought Janice, coming upon the mess and mayhem. She dropped the yellow gloves near by and tapped at a broken milk bottle with her heel. A note rolled over, saying 'Recommence delivery from today.'

She took several deep breaths, swapped her pilgrim's wimple for the braveness of a crusader's shield, and continued towards Sylvia Perth's front door.

Chapter Sixteen

GRETCHEN O'Dowd watched and listened in wonder as Rohanne Bulbecker infiltrated the solicitor's office. She told such enormous lies that Gretchen half expected the floor to swallow them both up – but it stayed in place. 'Stinking fish,' said Rohanne finally to the man in the pinstriped suit. 'You lawyers have colluded in stinking fish, and I intend to expose it. Now, shall we talk?' The man, who had hitherto suggested that they make an appointment some time next week, blinked once, retained his expression of blank distaste and led them into his office. 'I can give you precisely five minutes,' he said. Rohanne proceeded to lay out on the desk before him a number of documents and to point to their relevant parts. The five minutes passed unremarked and led into ten and then an hour. The pinstriped man had coloured slightly but remained calm as clay. Rohanne called for tea, which came in little bone-china cups, and she was pleased to note that the solicitor's cup tinkled a little as he replaced it in its saucer.

*

Derek was holding the Little Blonde Secretary's legs up in the air after intercourse. Even he, not one to make judgements on such matters, found these gymnastics (of a purely obstetric nature) deflationary. Nowadays she was always getting him into bed with her and going at him in a variety of ways that he didn't know she knew and he didn't think she knew she knew, either, until recently.

They were trying to get pregnant.

'It's time to start a family,' she had said, and though she

had taken out her cap recently she still didn't feel pregnant at all. Well might that magazine article say don't worry but she did. And she felt that a firm hand was needed. Derek was getting altogether too tired, what with the garden fence and visiting the pub. He needed to put his heart and soul into it.

'You need to put your heart and *soul* into it, Derek,' she said. 'And eat more salad.'

He could only nod when she said this, since his mouth was full of vitamin pills and she was waiting to see him down his glass of SuperMalt.

The magazine had been very helpful. It didn't hurt any man to take good care of himself, it said, but it always seemed to fall to women to do the organizing. Very true. Look at her dad. Look at Derek. Look at the Boss Masculine.

At work she had smiled up at this latter as he passed, discreetly hiding the magazine. The Boss Masculine stopped. He did not think he had seen a smile like that for weeks. And he was not looking forward to the conference in Birmingham, either. Women's smiles were nice. They reminded him that he was (despite *her* catheters and *her* scar tissue) still a man. How nice it would be just to have someone with whom to talk over the day's business while eating a civilized meal – a female voice, a female presence, a female smile . . .

He smiled back at the Little Blonde Secretary Bird. 'Would you be able to come to the conference with me? I could do with your help . . .'

She remembered the deferential tone of his voice fondly as she watched her husband at his health-giving ritual.

'So, Derek, I checked my calendar and the conference was in my' – she lowered her voice – '*safe period*. Then I rang you. And you said yes . . .'

Derek, still swallowing, thought he would just like to have seen her if he'd tried to say no.

'And do you know what he said then?'

Derek shook his head.

'*He* said that if I'd been *his* wife he wouldn't have let me out of his sight for a moment.'

'Well you're *not*,' said Derek. 'You're mine. And I will.'

If the Little Blonde Secretary Bird thought there was something wrong with this, she could not quite put her finger on it, and she satisfied the disquiet by remembering how the Boss Masculine had compared her blushes to a little pair of roses . . . If only his wife looked after him better, he could be very presentable.

She took out her jar of stretch-mark cream and sniffed it. It smelled wholesome. Placing it next to *Getting Pregnant, Staying Pregnant* and *The Pregnant Father*, she fixed Derek with a look of firm intent. He looked back at her with as much fervour as he could muster, given the ferrous taste in his mouth. If he could just stop taking the iron he'd be grateful.

But Derek was prepared to look on the bright side. The prospect of starting a family had a positive spin-off. For, looking around the house one quiet weekend, he had realized that there was nothing left to do (the district surveyor still refused planning permission for the loft – alas, it would always be the wrong height) and his heart had grown heavy. The decorations were in superb condition, more or less brand new, and even he – who loved the feel of the paintbrush, the slither of the paste – could think of nothing else . . . But now, suddenly, he had a reprieve. If they were going to have a baby, then they would need a *nursery* . . . He had looked up 'Nursery' in his DIY manual, measured up what he might need, and set off for B&Q.

Such a lot of work, he had thought happily, pushing his trolley through the doors. Shelving, nappy-changing bench, small wardrobe, intercom. The music smoothed his way around the aisles and he fingered the pine and the melamine lovingly. He was away for quite a long time. When he returned to the house, he wondered if somebody had died while he was away. The front-room curtains were drawn against the sunshine (it was 2.26 p.m. on a Sunday), and, as he let himself into the hall, whistling, his nose twitched at the pungent assault. Rich. Very rich. He nearly choked. Sort of musky and smoky at the same time.

'Hallo,' he called, putting down the plastic bag of fixings that had been on offer and might come in useful. 'Hallo?'

'In here,' called a strange voice from the front room. A throaty voice, deep, slow, female – something akin to the exotic scent pervading the house.

He pushed open the door and entered their living-room to find her lying on the sofa. The fire was lit (gas-coal, he thought in passing, state of the art), the curtains drawn, candles alight, a bottle of wine and two glasses on the middle-sized occasional table. And she – he blinked – she was lying back, absolutely stark naked, swathed in whirls of smoke. For a moment he thought she had taken up pipe-smoking or something, so prevalent were the bluey wreaths, but – and much relieved – he saw that there were a couple of joss-sticks burning in a vase on the mantelpiece.

He gulped and he felt a cold sweat breaking out on his forehead. He gave a nervous smile, suddenly aware of his teeth, which would not retract, and he wondered if she had gone mad, got drunk or – or *what*?

'Hi,' he said, trying to sound casual. 'Sorry I was so long. Quite a queue. Found the butterfly bolts and the –'

And then he could not go on. She was smiling at him in a way he had never seen, not even in their six months of courting and during all the fumbling and panting in the back of the Escort and what not; she was smiling like something out of one of those magazines. She was smiling like those fantasies of his that surfaced now and then, and she was even – he blinked – wearing high heels. Not a stitch on, lying across the settee sporting (no other word for it) white stilettos.

And this is my *wife*, he said to himself.

And further, he thought, this is my wife with whom I have not been doing much of this sort of thing recently, and certainly not like this *ever* . . . In the pub last night, when Ken and the others had talked about garden fencing and keeping it up, someone had cracked a joke about keeping it up in other areas. He, snorting lasciviously with the rest of them, found himself wondering when the last time he had kept it up in that way had been: weeks, he thought. And now this . . .

'Why don't you come and sit down and take off your clothes, too?' she said sweetly. 'And I'll pour us a nice glass of wine. We can, well . . .' – she patted the settee next to her – 'we can' – she fluttered her eyelashes coyly – 'you know' – flutter, flutter – 'all afternoon.'

He dismissed the sinking feeling this suggestion occasioned, put aside the tantalization of the B&Q items that throbbed in the hall, and began unbuttoning his shirt in much the same way he would have done if she had told him she wanted it off for washing purposes. She put out her little hand and pulled him on to the settee. He sat very heavily, pushed off his shoes, kept his head down, and went on unbuttoning. She handed him a glass, delicately pushed his hands away from his shirt, and continued the unbuttoning herself. He sipped the wine and stared. This was his *wife*, he had to remind himself, this was his wife behaving like a . . . well . . . He drank deeply, trying to keep a smile on his face to match her smile, and his eyes met with hers, which never wavered. Perhaps it was his wedding anniversary? No, it couldn't be that, because, despite never *quite* remembering the date, he did always remember that they married in the autumn; he had been worried about the leaves in the gutter of the new house, so he was sure of *that*.

The promise she exuded was outrageous. She began running her fingertips up and down his bare breastbone. She reached for the buckle of his belt and pulled it undone. Some sixth sense of modesty prevailed and he dispensed with his trousers and undergarments himself.

'Socks, Derek,' she said, in a tone which was comfortingly familiar. But all too soon it was replaced with that same, throaty timbre.

He finished his glass and she took it from him, winding her body around his, warm, scented, yielding. Everything a man could possibly want. Except that this was his wife and he was *not* a man – he was *Derek*. She had never behaved like this before. Why was she doing it now? What was expected of him? The erection that had begun to creep up on him despite himself went down again abruptly. He put a cushion there so that she could not see, but she was having none of it . . .

'Naughty, naughty,' she said, pulling the cushion away. She stared. 'Oh *dear*,' she said childishly. 'Naughty, naughty, *naughty* . . .' And with amazing expertise, hitherto only experienced in his dreams, she bent her head down between his legs.

He was just going into stage three of ecstasy, that stage prior to explosion, when, as suddenly as it had arrived there, she took her mouth away and lay back.

'Do it to me now, Derek,' she said, eyeing him like a blonde pussy-cat, and there was a distinct edge of command about it. He felt more comfortable with that, much more at home. Though, suddenly desperate, he decided to be a bit careful, just to make quite sure of what she meant . . .

'What . . . um . . . *exactly* . . . um . . . did you have in mind?'

'Go on, Derek,' she said, a trifle impatiently, and then, as if remembering, she flung her arms in total abandon above her head and pouted.

There was no mistaking what was required. He decided not to think any more, merely to act. He jumped on top of her. He tried to forget that this . . . um . . . *whore* – ooh, aah, eeh – beneath him was actually his lawful, wedded wife – the woman he had been in Sainsbury's with yesterday morning and who had told him it was about time he knew where the margarine spreads were kept . . . He managed to forget the polyunsaturateds and her with her tartan shopper and replace them with this erotic creature instead. He held on to that, sustained it – and the joy of spasm was his.

He lay back and looked at her. He expected – what? He was unsure. They had never done it like this before and usually in bed it was straightforward. You just fell asleep. But on a Sunday afternoon, in the front room with the curtains drawn – well, much as he would like to have a little doze, it seemed wrong. Anyway, he had loads of things to be getting on with before beginning on the spare room – buckets to clean, brushes to assess, perhaps another shelf in the cellar, screws to sort. Screws . . .? He looked at his wife and wondered how long he should lie there before he could decently get up. He rather hoped she would give him the all-clear in a minute.

'Get off, please, Derek,' she said, and was wriggling out from beneath him.

He complied and sat up. He was about to apologize for squashing her when the words tucked themselves back behind his teeth. If what had just happened was bizarre, it was as nothing to what was going on now. Nervously he reached for the cushion she had tossed aside earlier, and he held it to his nakedness. What on earth was she doing? Having a fit, by the look of it. She had suddenly rolled away from him, lifted her legs in the air and begun bicycling and scissoring like a US Marine in training. He clutched the cushion even tighter and wondered if he ought to restrain her in some way.

'Hold my ankles,' she puffed.

Tentatively he reached out with one hand and circled one of her legs.

'Both hands, Derek,' she said, already out of breath. 'Put that cushion down.'

Reluctantly he did so and clasped both her ankles.

'Pull me up tightly so my legs point at the ceiling,' she said.

He did so. He swallowed. He needed an answer and he was afraid to ask.

'If you do this,' she said, cycling some more and going disturbingly red in the face, 'the ... er ... stuff ... goes all the way down.' She paused, thinking. 'Or do I mean up?'

Derek remained mute. It really did seem the safest choice.

'You go and make a cup of tea,' she said, 'I've got to stay like this for a bit longer.' She was grimacing and had turned a dangerous shade of pink.

He put out his hand to touch her breast, suddenly realizing he had not got to them in all the goings-on.

She batted his hand away lightly but firmly. 'Don't,' she said. 'Or you'll knock me over.'

He felt on safer ground after that. On the way out to the kitchen he started whistling, and, retrieving his plastic bag from the hall, began unpacking the interesting contents while the kettle boiled. Whatever was going on, some things were secure. No doubt she'd explain it all to him in due course; in the meantime, he wondered, where *were* those gingernuts.

Nowadays he had grown used to the ankle-holding. What he hadn't *quite* got used to was the scene-setting she went in for. All sorts of different variations and what she called 'games, Derek' – which were certainly nothing like those outdoor activities of his schooldays. He was beginning to feel a teeny bit, well, *used*, like he was a unit of production, but on the other hand it kept her happy. When she undertook something, she undertook to do it *perfectly* – 'one hundred per cent, Derek' – and he was quite sure that this would extend to their having children. He could follow her confidently along that path. He *had* to follow her confidently along that path, because if he didn't, she could make life unbearable. At least she had gone mercifully quiet about the Vent-Axia, because he had decided it was something worth taking a stand over. When an extractor fan went in as perfectly as that one, you didn't go taking it out in a hurry . . .

*

Square Jaw read one of the poems on the tube. It was called 'Distance'. He was not one for poetry: indeed, if anyone said the word to him, it made him think of school and boredom, something difficult and dull, and learning by rote – not something that touched things about himself. He had said that to some guy in the Indian restaurant the night he and Melanie split up. He was waiting for the take-away and he had been asked if he ever read any. At the time it seemed a pretty fatuous question. Now he read the little light verse above his head and was sort of touched by it. He knew something of what the writer meant . . .

> Were you to cross the world, my dear,
> To work or love or fight,

I could be calm and wistful here,
And close my eyes at night.

It were a sweet and gallant pain
To be a sea apart;
But, oh, to have you down the lane,
Is bitter to my heart.

He read it several times. Well, whatever was happening between them was silly. He decided, if nothing else, that he would ring her and suggest meeting for a drink. Pretending the other didn't exist when they only lived a couple of miles apart ('down the lane') was really stupid. He had thought about going to Jeremy's party tonight. In fact, he had given it a great deal of thought. After all, this was what it was all supposed to be about.

Freedom.

Freedom to be a bachelor.

Freedom to go to parties.

Freedom to go to parties and meet girls.

Freedom to go to parties, meet girls and . . .

Freedom

to

wear

condoms . . .

He had completely forgotten about those.

He shrank at the thought. The idea of falling into bed with a stranger and then having to wrestle with an unwilling rubber was hardly conducive to the *Esquire* image. And then there was all that *afterwards* to think about – the getting to know, the do you want to be *bothered* to get to know? It occurred to him, briefly, that he and his contemporaries who dismissed marriage as a trap were wrong. You could be just as trapped being single.

Afterwards . . . All that *afterwards* . . . He had done all that afterwards with Melanie. The walks, the talks, the dinners, the armpit anxiety, the breath anxiety. Facing it all with someone else wasn't exactly enticing.

He stayed late at the office that night and rang her just before he left. He thought he could collect the car from the station and drive past her place, maybe go to a wine bar or something. But there was no reply. This time good sense prevailed and he left a nice, friendly, slightly flirty message for her. He said he was sorry if he'd been a bit sharp, and perhaps they could meet up soon. He'd be in tonight. *All* night. He would, he said, be *honoured* if she would bestow upon him a little of her company. Come any time.

He flashed his season ticket with a flourish at the barrier and felt that at last he had done the right thing. '"But, oh, to have you down the lane,"' he murmured as he got into his car, '"is bitter to my heart."'

*

When Rohanne Bulbecker emerged from the solicitor's offices, her eyes were glittering, there was a spring in her step and she was prepared to love the world. Including its miscreants, of whom she now knew, Sylvia Perth had been one. Behind her, sucking her knuckles, came a downcast-looking Gretchen O'Dowd. Within her remit to love the world, Rohanne was prepared to love this woebegone part of it, too.

'Come on,' she said, tucking her arm into Gretchen's. 'Be philosophical about it . . .' And she smiled a warm and encouraging smile. 'Maybe Harrods will cheer you up,' and, dodging the traffic, she steered the unhappy Gretchen O'Dowd in.

She squirted her way through the perfumes, and they made their way into the food hall. The sight of Janice Gentle hiding food in her clothes had unnerved Rohanne. 'We'll get her everything she needs until New York.' She sniffed some smoked salmon. 'They are going to just love her there.'

'Oh,' said Gretchen miserably, 'are you taking her away?' She gave a little gulp and Rohanne saw a tear caught in the web of her moustache. It was not surprising, given the interview Gretchen had experienced with the solicitor, and Rohanne said so.

'Sylvia Perth has a lot to answer for one way and another,' she said. 'But at least they've asked you to stay on until everything is settled.' She picked up some peaches and smelled them. 'Janice is the one who has really suffered,' she said, peering at a tray of handmade chocolates. Gretchen was surprised at the look of pleasure and satisfaction on Rohanne Bulbecker's face as she made her selection.

'Flowers too,' Rohanne said. 'She must have both with what I've got to tell her.'

Much later and several bags heavier, they left the store to return to Dog Street. The Boss Masculine observed them leave. Poor sod, he thought, assuming the half-hidden Gretchen to be the husband. Poor sod to be used like a credit-carded packhorse. The Boss Masculine knew all about *that*, since his wife had been unable to carry anything for years. Never would again, he was sure. For the rest of his life he would be carrying her. He paid the assistant for the little Bruges lace handkerchief and asked her to gift-wrap it with special care. His conscience pricked him and he decided to get his wife a present, too. He fingered the other lacy items on the counter and then turned on his heel in the direction of the book department. She did a lot of reading nowadays, especially in bed. He'd get her a bloody book.

'Like I said, Sylvia Perth has a lot to answer for,' said Rohanne in the taxi.

'She certainly does,' said Gretchen O'Dowd mournfully. 'I wasn't even allowed to bury her. Her mother did it. I didn't even know she *had* a mother . . .'

Rohanne snorted. 'Even Hitler had one of those.'

Gretchen looked shocked.

'Cheer up,' Rohanne said. 'At least she left you the painting.' She tried not to smile. 'Even if you hate it.'

Rohanne sat back and closed her eyes for the remainder of the journey. One way or another she had a lot to thank Sylvia Perth for. She had died at the optimum moment, and she had been crooked. These twin attributes made life much easier for Rohanne. Janice Gentle was inescapably hers. All that beautiful, golden girl now owned in the world was some apartment in an out-of-the-way place called Battersea and her copyright – though the latter was far from certain. The solicitor had wrinkled his fine, aquiline nose as he mentioned the address in Battersea. It seemed it was hardly decent. Everything else was gone – or, rather, tied up in Sylvia Perth's estate, now Mrs Perth's estate. And the old lady was of no mind to give it back without a struggle. It would all take years to unravel. Which meant two things. One, Janice Gentle actually needed the Pfeiffer contract. And, two, there could be endless publicity over the case. Rohanne pictured it. The beautiful, golden waif of a writer, screwed rotten by first the daughter and then the mother. Why, it was the very stuff of romance itself. And it would certainly sell a few books. Janice Gentle was in the palm of Rohanne Bulbecker's hand, and each represented the other's salvation. That, thought Rohanne, was appropriate: the perfect Chinese bargain, one in which both sides have equal gain. She saw herself in the executive suite at Pfeiffer's. Part of the team. What else could she do, as she sat there, daydreaming, eyes closed, but congratulate herself? Congratulate herself very heartily indeed.

Chapter Seventeen

JANICE had no idea of what she would find in the way of interior decor behind the door of Sylvia Perth's apartment. None the less, an open mind is not necessarily a mind that cannot be surprised. And Janice was surprised. Sylvia had always complimented her on her own pale, uncluttered existence. 'Oh, *Janice*,' she would say, 'if only you knew how I envy you this peaceful environment . . .' Looking around now, Janice could quite see why.

There was not a surface left unfilled, not a colour that was bland, not a space without texture. It was like something out of the *Arabian Nights*, as if she had stumbled out of her convent and into a Moorish stronghold. Rather a fitting analogy, she thought, since she had come as a cross between crusader and pilgrim. She closed the door behind her and slipped off her shoes – whether because her feet were sore from the struggles of the day, or out of respect for this temple of the Infidel, she was unsure. In any case the pile of the carpet felt wonderful beneath her toes.

In the corner, on a desk, she saw what she had come to find: the answerphone. But on the couch, directly ahead of her, she saw something else much more disconcerting. She saw Scheherazade, she saw Criseyde, she saw *Vous ou Mort* personified, the embodiment of all that Knightly Honour could possibly desire, she saw . . . She scarcely believed it, she pushed her spectacles back up her nose, and she blinked, and she blinked and she blinked. It was only when she was quite sure that the recumbent beauty was real and breathing (and not the last and most fearful of her imaginings, Sylvia Perth's youthful *alter ego*) that she tiptoed across to the couch. The recumbent one continued unconscious. Janice waited. She went back and rustled her bag.

She returned to the couch and sighed. And still the sleeper slept. Janice coughed. The sleeper murmured, turned a little, breathed deep again. Janice coughed louder and rustled her bag anew. The sleeper moaned softly. Janice gave one more good loud throat clear and it worked. Erica von Hyatt opened her eyes, returned the blinks, and smiled.

'I am allowed to be here,' she said. 'I have the owner's permission.'

'But,' said Janice, 'I thought the owner was dead.'

'Nope,' said Erica positively. 'Just gone to Harrods.'

For a moment Janice wondered if she meant, in some poetically right way, that Sylvia Perth, who had loved Harrods as some love their country, had gone to that great and ultimate Harrods in the Sky.

'May I sit down?' she asked weakly.

'Help yourself,' said Erica cheerfully and indicated the space at the end of the couch. She rubbed her wrist across her sleepy eyes and yawned.

Erica von Hyatt felt on top of the world. Being awakened held no rancour for her. That it was a stranger and one of such unprepossessing mien held no rancour for her. Nothing caused Erica von Hyatt rancour, for Erica von Hyatt had seen it all. By the law of averages it was bound to be a stranger. After all, the world was full of them.

Janice removed several sugared almonds from her pocket and put them one after the other into her mouth. She was almost sure that this was the right apartment, because it seemed to be the very last one in the building. Perhaps she should check. She smiled at Erica and pointed upwards. 'There isn't,' she said carefully, 'anything else after this, is there?'

A religious freak, thought Erica, but she felt quite safe. She had dealt with all kinds in her time. 'Well, *I* don't think there is. Otherwise why would there be so much sodding pain in the world? Sorry for swearing. Think of all the Africans starving,' she said vaguely.

Janice preferred not to. That was what had been so good about

Sylvia. Sylvia had positively encouraged her not to think. 'Concentrate on what you want to write,' she said, 'and let Sylvia deal with the rest of the world.'

'I mean,' Janice said apologetically, 'there isn't another flat above this?'

'Not unless they like it open-plan. That's the roof.' She eyed Janice's bag. 'Need somewhere, do you?' she said sympathetically. 'You can stay here for a while if you like. I'll tell the owner you're a friend, just passing through.' She raised a finger. 'But no nicking anything, mind.' The finger wagged. 'And you've got to remember to flush the toilet.'

Janice was beyond any indignation on matters of honesty or personal hygiene and set those aside. 'This . . . er . . . owner,' she said carefully, 'you're sure about Harrods?'

'Yup,' said Erica.'

'And this . . . er . . . owner seemed . . . quite *well*?' How she longed to come right out with it.

'Think so.' Erica shrugged. 'All right after the Ritz. Talked nineteen to the dozen about the funeral. Not much to say apart from that. More the silent type.'

'Funeral?' said Janice. She sucked hard and then bit, crunch, crunch, her tongue desperately seeking out the soft, sweet nut beneath.

They sat in silence for a while.

'I'm off to America and I'm going to have a baby there,' said Erica eventually. 'Haven't met the father yet. They're introducing me when I arrive.'

Janice, singularly failing to deal with both sweet and information, began choking.

Erica banged her firmly on the back. 'You never in the least know what's going to happen in life, do you?' she said cheerfully. 'Look at me. One minute I had nothing. Now, all this. Mind you, I never trust anything to last. Do you?'

'I did once,' said Janice sadly.

'Bad mistake,' said Erica, shaking her head. 'Always expect it to end, and then you are never disappointed.' She held out her hand to shake Janice's. 'Cheer up. My name's . . .' She was about to say Erica and then realized that it was no longer her name, but since she had taken it from a handbag tossed over Waterloo Bridge and empty of all but a calling card that said 'Erica von Hyatt Design Partnership, London, New York', she felt she could abandon it whenever she chose, anyway. 'My name is Janice,' she said.

'How odd,' said Janice, taking the proffered hand. 'So is mine.'

'Oh?' said Erica, rediscovering nerve endings that the comfort of this exotic place had padded in gauze. She withdrew her hand and a shadow darkened her pretty features. 'Oh?' she said again.

'Janice Gentle,' came the smiling reply. 'I write books.'

It was the first time Janice had said anything like that to anybody. It felt strange, but rather good – and it made her feel sort of real. She smiled across at her new friend, but the new friend was not smiling back.

'Fuck you,' said Erica von Hyatt, breaking her rule about swearing in other people's houses. 'Fuck you, fuck you, fuck you.'

Janice's head throbbed. She had experienced quite enough opprobrium out on the street. That it continued indoors really was too much. If this was what it was like going back out into the real world, she didn't, really, see the point. 'Oh,' she said wearily, eyeing the answering machine as if, in some way, it retained its magical powers. *Was* she in there? Did she still live and breathe? 'Why do you say that?'

And Erica von Hyatt told her. She told her of what had been. She told her of what was to come. Or what she hoped was to come. What would not, now, be to come, because the real Janice Gentle had turned up.

'But I've got nothing to do with babies,' Janice said, puzzled. 'Apart from the fact that I call my books my babies sometimes. And I'm certainly not the sort of person to be a surrogate mother. Are you sure?'

'It's all legal. I signed some papers,' said Erica. 'Look.'

Janice looked. She smiled. 'I think,' she said, 'there is some confusion here. This is a publisher's contract. They want you – or rather me – to write a book.'

'A book?' said Erica von Hyatt wonderingly. 'What about?'

'Whatever you – or I – choose, I suppose,' said Janice.

'Oh well,' said Erica resignedly, 'it will have to be you, then. I have no stories to tell. I wouldn't know where to begin.'

Janice thought about her tortures on the Underground. 'I know what you mean,' she said, 'but they do say that everybody has at least one book in them.'

'Do they?' said Erica. 'I don't think I have. Not like the Princess of Wales or Joan Collins. Who'd want to hear about me?'

Janice settled herself next to her. '*I* would,' she said positively, surprising herself. And she thought as she adjusted the cushions around her that the couch was a great deal more comfortable than the seats of the London tube.

'All?' said Erica.

'Everything,' said Janice, who was suddenly very interested. 'Just tell me everything about yourself. Please.'

So Erica, ever obliging, did.

*

Rohanne Bulbecker stopped the cab on the way back to Dog Street and bought a huge bunch of flowers, pointing to bloom after bloom. She could afford to be generous and she wanted to be. She would break the story very sensitively and spare Janice Gentle's feelings as much as she could. Sylvia's sticky fingers had played all the balls into her court and delicacy was not hard to offer when you had gained so much. The story seemed so fantastical that she was quite relieved to have Gretchen O'Dowd as witness. Sylvia's Man and Boy had no doubts on that score. Indeed, the Man and Boy had been so absolutely convinced about her own betrayal that she had left the solicitor, with a proboscis that had once been aquiline and was no more, reclining on his office carpet, a bloody handkerchief to his nose. Rohanne had to admit that he had been somewhat perfunctory in his delivery of the bad news: she rather doubted if he would ever dare to be so perfunctory with a disappointed mourner again.

At Dog Street Rohanne Bulbecker abandoned dignity and, clutching her flowers, ran two steps at a time up the stairs, leaving Gretchen O'Dowd to puff and pant her way up, beladen with the bags. At the penultimate landing the Bulbecker legs entangled with a man wearing a pinstriped suit, white collar, navy-blue silk tie and extremely pink face; he was down on all fours mopping up quite a mess. Despite her excitement Rohanne paused at the sight. A man cleaning his own entry? Wonderful!

Gretchen O'Dowd, carrying the bags, noticed nothing and merely left a trail of footprints across the newly washed floor. 'That's right,' said the pinstripe sarcastically. 'Sure you wouldn't like to go back and try again?'

Gretchen fled. Why did everybody in London seem so angry?

Rohanne was not going to be deflected from her immediate pleasure of offering her bouquet. When that was done, she would ask what the unspeakable character sitting next to Janice Gentle on the couch was doing here. For the moment, in high good humour, she said, 'Flowers for Miss Gentle,' and was astonished to see a large, round arm, attached to a plump and sausagey hand, reach out and take them.

'Thank you,' said Janice, in a wondering voice, and to hide her confusion she buried her nose deep into the bunch.

Rohanne stared. She was not in the habit of buying anybody flowers, and it grieved her to see this caring gesture appropriated by the wrong person. *Quite* the wrong person. In fact a really, altogether *disgustingly* wrong person. She crossed her arms and looked defiantly at the body attached to the arm and the sausagey digits.

'What the hell are *you* doing?' said Rohanne Bulbecker, the shock making her forget that a moment before she had been at one with the world. 'Those flowers are for Janice.'

'I am Janice,' said Janice, quite used to such aggression since her sortie from her cell. 'Janice Gentle. I write books.'

She closed her eyes and waited. She waited not in vain.

Rohanne pointed a finger, keeping another in her mouth, tantalizing the edge of her teeth with its nail ... 'You are *who*? And you do *what*?'

Wearily Janice repeated the two short sentences. 'I am Janice Gentle. I write books.'

Once more she closed her eyes.

Once more it was not in vain.

She did not see Rohanne look at Erica, nor Erica return the look with a shrug of apology and a nod of assent.

Then it came. First an intake of breath, followed by a gurgling of a throat, and then the soft voice of Rohanne Bulbecker saying, '*Fuck you, fuck you, fuck you* . . .'

'Oh,' said Janice, suddenly very annoyed at the triple invocation of such crude Anglo-Saxon. 'I'm going home.' But the door was already barred by the pale-haired woman in black, who rested one arm across it as if she defended the very deeps of her own honour while chewing at her free hand's finger-end. Janice felt in her pocket. If all else failed, there was still that.

*

Morgan Pfeiffer and Enrico Stoat took a glass of champagne together. 'To Janice Gentle and the future,' said Enrico Stoat, raising his glass high. 'And to marketing.'

Morgan Pfeiffer sipped and looked pleased. 'I thought Ms Rohanne Bulbecker would do it. They don't come much tougher than her.'

'To her, then,' said Stoat, raising his glass again.

'To Ms Rohanne Bulbecker,' agreed Morgan Pfeiffer, and they drank.

*

The object of their praise had recovered a little. Not very much. Merely enough to form words and project them coherently.

Everything, then, was in ruins. She had been fooled by that bogus beauty, and she had trumpeted her befooled state to the Pfeiffer world. They were expecting gold and she would bring them only dross. She looked at the real Janice Gentle, who looked back at her owlishly.

Rohanne closed her eyes. 'What am I going to do?' she wailed. A rhetorical question.

'About what?' asked Janice politely.

Rohanne knew it was weakness. She knew it opened her up, made her vulnerable, allowed the listener to have something over her. All the same she could not stop herself. She needed to speak out, she needed to tell the truth. To this fat and unspeakable stranger she poured forth her terrible quandary. About Morgan Pfeiffer and Enrico Stoat and her own depressed position. There was no point in trying to hide any of it from Janice Gentle. It was far too late for equivocation.

'I suppose,' she said, when she had finished, 'that we could go on pretending she was you.' She pointed an accusing finger at Erica von Hyatt, who was sitting, serene and philosophical, next to Janice Gentle on the couch, while Gretchen O'Dowd stood behind her, uncomprehending but stalwart, Saturn and Mars.

'I don't mind,' said Janice Gentle. 'I'm not at all interested in writing any more books. I really only came here to switch Sylvia off. And to check she really was dead.'

'She is certainly that,' said Rohanne impatiently. 'And her mother has buried her.'

'Her mother?' said Janice, interested. 'I didn't know she had one.'

'Not you as well,' said Rohanne irritably.

Janice remembered the brave Christine's advice to older women in the state of virginity. Maidens should remain moderate and tasteful and never get into arguments or disputes with anybody.

Sometimes the road was hard. 'I shall go home now,' she said, and she placed the beautiful bunch of flowers on the couch wistfully.

'No,' said Rohanne Bulbecker. 'Not yet. I've just come from a lawyer's office. And knowing what we now know, I wouldn't be too sure about never writing another book again.' She looked Janice up and down defiantly. 'Not if you want to eat ...' Rohanne squatted down on her haunches and brought her face on a level with those pale, rather frightened eyes. Let me tell you,' she said, 'a thing or two about your dear Sylvia Perth.'

*

Square Jaw saw them before they saw him. He stopped the car and watched them furtively. Melanie was wearing a very short skirt – too short, far too short – and boots that came up to her knees – *white boots*, for God's sake. She looked like a tart, a *tart*. Sexy and daring. He did not want her to be sexy and daring. Especially he did not want her to be sexy and daring in the company of the bloke she was with, who looked, from the back at least, a right smooth bastard. A bright shirt, rolled-up sleeves, jeans, casual, confident – confident about what? Confident about bloody Melanie, from the look of it. He knew all those dodges. The way the bloke held her elbow as they reached the restaurant door (why that restaurant? Close to his place, a favourite, they'd walked there often enough), the way he put his hand on her *lower* back to guide her in. The gestures of possession, the gestures of *I mean to have*. Square Jaw remembered them. They were one of the reasons he enjoyed a long-term, one-to-one relationship, why despite the difficulties he had persisted in it – because he could let go of all those petty formalities, all those attendances that kept you on your toes, let go of them to just relax and *be*. That smooth bastard was on the make, moving in for the kill and she – white boots, short skirt – was encouraging it to happen. He got out of his car and stood on the pavement. He could go in there – have a pasta or something – and why not? He lived just round the corner, he had every right – more than they did. He got back into the car. *Shit*, he thought, who cares? He saw her turn and smile as the door swung to. Melanie happy. So why wasn't he? Well – he could bloody well be happy, too.

He got back into the car, reversed noisily, the power of the engine, the futile roaring of the clutch, the screeching of his tyres, the fright of the passers-by – all stupidly satisfying. The roar again as he changed gear and drove off into the twilit night, the aggression and the speed dispensing with any other feelings that feebly beat their wings. He'd show her, vroom, vroom, vroom. Oh yes. She'd be getting her presents gift-wrapped now, all right, she'd be turning the screw about flowers with somebody else, and soon somebody else would start getting things wrong. They'd hear her say, 'Well, if you don't know, I'm not telling you' – all that, all that – and he was welcome to it. Poor, poor sod, he could have her. *He* was going to that party after all. *He*, too, was embracing life. He took the amber light at sixty and the power made a knot in his gut. Hadn't taken her long to get over him, and just as bloody well . . .

Melanie sat down in the restaurant and looked at each of the tables, wondering if he might be there. If he could see how she was getting on with life, how she was attractive to other men, how she could laugh and enjoy herself, he would be stirred to do something. Her heart had been really thumping when they came in. Now that he wasn't there, she felt the pumping draining away and she just felt miserable again. She gave the man opposite her a very bright smile. Yes, she would like a drink – a very big drink, and very quickly. Of course, he might come in later, or walk by and see her inside. She must keep bright at all costs. She must look happy, relaxed, fulfilled – not like the old Melanie, not the old, unhappy, neurotic burden.

She leaned forward and put her chin in her hands, provocative, appealing. 'Now tell me,' she said to the man opposite her, 'what made you choose income tax as a career?'

Later she excused herself and went out to the Ladies'. On a whim she rang his number. If he answers, she told herself, I shall say something funny like, 'Help, I'm stuck in Popinjay's with a really boring man. Come and rescue me.' They should still be able to wear jokes like that – they knew each other well enough. It

190

was all so silly this being apart, and stupid, stupid, to pass up all that knowing for this . . . She dialled and waited. Somebody had written the line of a song on the wall by the telephone. 'Tell Laura I love her', and somebody had added underneath, 'Tell her yourself' . . .

*

'Do you mean,' said Janice Gentle, 'that I made a lot of money and Sylvia Perth spent it?'

Rohanne Bulbecker nodded.

'All of it?'

'More or less. Of course, you'll get some of it back in time.'

'How long?'

'Years,' said Rohanne. And then, because Janice looked so woebegone, she melted a little. 'I'm really sorry. Didn't you ever even suspect?'

Janice shook her head.

'Where did you think all the money went?' (Oh for a fraction of it, thought Rohanne Bulbecker.)

'Sylvia just looked after me. That's all. And there was always enough for my needs. What was left over was supposed to help me find Dermot Poll. Only there was never quite enough.'

This left the listening trio in some confusion.

Rohanne Bulbecker thought Der Mottpoll might be some kind of Germanic Mountain of Wisdom.

Erica von Hyatt thought it was something to do with the poll tax (the existence of which was one of the few benefits of calling a box home, since you did not have to pay it).

Gretchen O'Dowd thought of the North Pole and wondered what the most northerly part (she had watched many Open University programmes in her country solitude) of the earth's axis had to do with being a writer.

'Perhaps I should explain,' said Janice. 'Dermot Poll is a man.'

'Ah,' they said in comprehending unison. '*Of course.*'

For what else could be at the centre of such a muddle? Even despite the woman's grubby countenance and undesirable curves.

191

'I shall begin at the beginning,' said Janice the storyteller. And she took herself back to a cold, dark, wet February night when the whole world seemed coloured by magic.

*

Red Gold was laughing to herself as the train pulled out of the station. She had wanted to take the tea-urn into the carriage with her, but the guard hadn't allowed it. 'You can't put it on the seat, it's too big for the floor and if it falls off the luggage rack you could be killed.'

'So?' she had wanted to say. There was something recklessly bizarre and amusing at the prospect of such an apposite end. But she had let him take it away without too much fuss. What a joke. How they had laughed about it last night. Amid the crumpled sheets and her spilling hair they had howled with merriment at its absurdity.

'I shall think of you,' she had said last night, 'every time I use it.'

'Ah,' he said, laughing wickedly, 'but which bit of me?' And he took her hand and pressed it to that most private part of him, the part she celebrated knowing, the part she liked to recall when she saw him dressed in his perfect tailoring, his proper shirt and tie.

Of course, she had been lying. She knew that as soon as the passion ebbed from them and he slept.

'Once and only once, for old time's sake,' was what she had said at the Ritz.

He looked at her across his champagne, the perfectly manicured fingers holding his glass, the neat white cuff, the dark, expensive blue of the sleeve above. His eyes were intelligent, considerate, amused. She wanted to kiss them closed, touch their lids. 'Are you absolutely sure?' he asked. 'I don't want to hurt you again.'

'Nonsense,' she said gaily, 'that's all in the past. Why, this is just a bit of fun . . .'

But he already had.

He had told her in that one sentence all she needed to make her heart ache afresh. It would be once and once only. He would be able to walk away and never return, he would not be hurt by seeing her go.

'Of course,' she continued, still smiling flirtatiously, 'we are both old married troupers now. You are a cabinet minister and I am a vicar's wife. We could not do it more than once. It would not be at *all* proper. It was only a whim on my part, just a lovely whim.'

'A dangerous one,' he said.

'Not at all,' she replied.

For a minute she read his thoughts. He was weighing up the adventure of it, the heightened romance, against the risks. She knew what to do to allay his fears, and removed from her pocket her return ticket.

'I have to get the midday train back,' she said crisply, 'and I want to avoid any possibility of suspicion.'

He was seduced by that. Whereas the shadow of her curves, the message in her eyes were expendable, the promise of detachment without future responsibility won him. So she had had her illicit walk in the garden of Love before climbing back over the wall into her cabbage-patch life.

She leaned her arm on the parcels beside her and ran her fingers through her loosened hair. She cared not a damn for suspicion now. She had almost convinced herself that the old ghost was sated, the dream laid to rest, and that one such beautiful night was all she would ever ask. She must not enter that garden again, must never seek to. This was the last gate she could pass through, the key had been taken from her. Coming back, she was on her own. He had retained the key when she left him this morning. She must never enter there again. He had said so, stroking her hair, kissing her neck, his eyes dry, tears in hers.

'Only this once,' he had said.

'Only this once,' she had agreed.

Easy to say it then.

She began tucking her hair into a band, preparing to claim the tea-urn, descend the train, go back. She laughed as she looked in the mirror, and then she put her fingers to her mouth, for the laugh had been mirthless.

Arthur was on the platform, waiting, waving as her carriage passed him by, following the train as it slowed. Like a shepherd, she thought, in search of his lost lamb. A favourite text. If a man have a hundred sheep and one goes astray, does he not rejoice more for the one that is found than for all the others safe within their fold? Rather like her. With all the sheeply blessings she had in her life, still she sought and wanted the one which eluded her. She waved back. Arthur should really get out of the Bible and his precious Langland and come up to date. Did she want him to know? Did she care? Would it not be exciting to have an explosion of emotion? On her breast she bore a purpling mark. He who had been so careful had been too weak to resist her passionate insistence, too aroused to think beyond the offering-up of her flesh to be bruised. Now it was the mark of her guilt, the lover's brand on the sheep returning. She did not care.

Arthur held out his hand to help her down from the carriage. It felt like the hand of a cripple, without strength, without hope. He looked at her with an expression she could not fathom and then he released her.

In the car he said, 'Was everything satisfactory?'

'I think I got everything,' she said, brushing away a tendril of hair irritably.

'Nothing to go back for? Nothing you have forgotten?'

'I have forgotten nothing,' she said positively, 'and I got everything I needed, thank you.'

But already the slowness of the car, the bumping of the country roads, his unsophisticated hands on the wheel, even the smell of the upholstery were like a closing-in.

'Arthur,' she said, 'you haven't given a sermon on the lost sheep for ages. Don't you think you should?'

'Perhaps,' he said.

She stretched out her legs, letting her skirt ride up over her knees. 'I need shriving,' she said mischievously. 'London is such a wicked place.'

He said nothing.

'And I have entered the temptation of superstition.'

'Yes?' he said, turning the car through the gates. Rabbits in the dusk were caught spellbound in the headlights, feet up, ears stiff, noses twitching. 'How?'

'I gave a beggar woman a pound for luck instead of trusting in the Lord.'

'And were you lucky?'

'I think so.'

He smiled wryly. 'Maybe it was God's will all the time. If the tea-urn is unscathed from its journey, than we should give thanks for that.'

'Why?'

He turned off the ignition and looked at her. The lights showed her eyes wide and brilliant, unblinking like the rabbits. 'Because now it has arrived here whole, you will never need to go back for another.'

She shivered. The mischievous smile faded. She got out and slammed the door, leaving him to bring in the offending item. The rabbits, galvanized by the noise, scattered for safe haven. At the door she turned and looked back. She watched how he handled it with painstaking care and how he carried it with firm, sure steps towards the house.

Drop it, you bastard, she wanted to shout. Please, please, drop it.

*

'Suppose he is married?' asked Rohanne Bulbecker.

Janice wished not to hear. 'What?' she said.

Rohanne was a direct woman and erred on the side of insensitivity. So she spoke louder. 'I said, "Suppose he is married?"'

Janice looked at her blandly, eyes unwavering behind spectacles. 'He won't be,' she said.

'He might be,' said Rohanne. 'He might very well be . . .'

'A knight can always love a lady though she be married to someone else,' she said dreamily. 'It is allowed.'

'Nowadays,' said Rohanne crossly, 'it's divorce and alimony.'

Janice sighed. 'Then there won't be any need to write any more, and I shall retire from life completely.'

'But I doubt if he *is*,' said Rohanne, quick as a gunshot. 'In fact, thinking about it, I am quite sure he isn't.'

'Funny, that's what Sylvia said.'

'I'll bet,' muttered Rohanne.

'He could be divorced,' said Erica kindly.

'He could be dead,' said Gretchen O'Dowd with equal solicitude.

Rohanne glared.

'Dead?' said Janice, and she pushed another sugared almond between her lips. 'Perhaps *that* is why he never arrived.'

Rohanne patted her shoulder and grimaced at Gretchen. 'Why not take a walk?' she said sourly. 'Now, Janice, why should he be dead? He sounds like a survivor to me.'

'Well, anyway,' Erica patted the other shoulder, 'you will never know unless you find him, will you?' She remembered her chats in the crypt. 'Faith will move mountains,' she said, 'if you believe. And we're only talking about a man, not a bleeding mountain, fuck it.' She added this last, feeling it was justifiable emphasis.

'I don't want to find out, if he's dead . . .' Janice shivered.

'Can't stop now,' said Erica. 'Otherwise you'll spend all your life wondering. Think of the parable of the loaves and fishes. He raised those from the dead, didn't he?'

There was a short period of understandable silence after this, and Erica's small congregation appeared to be lost in thought. It *sounded* sort of right.

'And if *I've* survived, then I don't see any reason for thinking *he* hasn't . . .' she added positively.

Janice looked at her admiringly. 'There is a fourteenth-century French poem by Jean de Meun called *Roman de la Rose*.' She wrinkled her forehead attempting to remember it. Rohanne Bulbecker nearly groaned out loud with despair; her new-found author looked even less appetizing when she was pondering.

Janice brightened. 'I can remember it in a sort of hotch-potch of Old French,' she said. 'Of course, it is not my idea of the grand literary ideal – it's rather deprecating about our sex –'

'Shame,' said Erica.

'But it is not as cruel as *blastanges de Femmes*, and so we should allow its qualities. Now, how does it go?' Janice opened her mouth to speak, and then raised a didactic finger. 'Of course, the entire *Roman* is allegorical – I'm thinking of Jean de Meun's duenna, *le Vielle*, one of his characters, you know. He gives us a whole series of them before the Lover finally obtains the rose. In fact, the whole debate and symposium on love, which it is, of course, supposed to be . . .' – she looked over her glasses at nobody in particular – 'is interspersed and brought to life by their long, explanatory monologues.'

Rohanne thought Janice was not doing too badly herself in this department.

'The point is,' said Janice firmly, 'the point is that sometimes subsidiary characters are stronger and say more than the main protagonists.' She smiled at Erica. 'Which is something I am just beginning to find out . . . So' – she screwed up her forehead again so that Rohanne spontaneously buried her head in her hands – 'something like this:

> 'N'onc ne fui d'Amours a escole
> Ou l'en leüst la theorique,
> Mais je sai tout par la pratique:
> Esperiment m'en ont fait sage,
> Que j'ai hantez tout mon aage.'

'Ah, Ovid,' breathed Janice to herself. I had forgotten that –'

'What's it about?' Erica asked.

'Approximately it says this: "I never went to the school of love where they taught theory; all I know is through practice. The experiences I've had all my life have made me wise."'

'Streetwise?' asked Erica.

'Everywise,' said Janice. 'Like you.'

'Me?' said Erica von Hyatt. 'I don't know about that. But I bet I could find Dermot Poll for you if you wanted me to.'

'Look,' said Rohanne wearily, 'here's a deal. You write one more book for me and Morgan Pfeiffer. You get paid a fortune for it. You use the fortune you get paid to hunt down this . . . whatever he's called . . .'

'Dermot,' said Janice.

'Poll,' added Erica.

They smiled at each other.

Rohanne tried to smile, too. 'And then everybody is happy,' she added. 'How about it? One more book?'

'Go on,' nudged Erica. 'One for the road.' And she smiled a beautiful, golden smile.

'I don't suppose you *would* let me substitute a photograph of her . . .' Rohanne gazed wistfully at the pink, the silver, the gold. And then she shook her head and sighed. That would be taking deceit too far. In Rohanne Bulbecker's opinion, whatever life was, it was not a farce, and she was not going to begin to turn it into one now. *Why oh why* had she been so impulsive and told them all about the beauty of her quarry? *Why oh why* did she think it mattered at *all*? She couldn't possibly ring up now and say, 'Oh, by the way – small detail, Mr Pfeiffer – I got the description the teeniest little bit wrong. Mistook the identity. She's actually a little more like a sumo wrestler than I first suggested . . .' She just *couldn't*. It would be zero credibility and out after that.

She checked her nails. Pretty little baby growths beginning to herald the new dawn. And now two of those had gone already. She put the third in her mouth. Through clamped teeth she began to think wildly. Invent something, an illness perhaps, unidentifiable, debilitating, contagious – something to prevent her from holding court with the media. And which eventually made you swell up like a balloon.

'All right,' said Janice. 'If it truly means for the very last time, then I will write just one more.' She looked at Erica and smiled. 'My *magnum opus*. Free of Sylvia Perth.'

The telephone rang. Everybody jumped. Everybody listened. Nobody got up. The answerphone played. 'I'm sorry,' said Sylvia Perth's voice sweetly, 'that I am not able to take your call right now . . .'

Janice swung out of the couch and switched the machine off. She smiled. 'Free, for ever, of Sylvia Perth.' She rubbed her plump, sticky hands together.

Rohanne Bulbecker gazed at her forlornly. She was beginning to feel a certain amount of sympathy with Sylvia Perth.

'And if,' Janice swallowed, 'and if I have to show myself to the world, then I will –'

'Over my dead body,' muttered Rohanne Bulbecker, and then immediately apologized to God, crossed herself and took the words back. This was no time to be taking risks. 'That might not be absolutely necessary,' she said calmly. 'Perhaps just writing the book would do. You just get on with that and leave Rohanne to deal with all the rest.'

Janice thought that she had heard something very similar to that before.

'You can't even see the ship properly and there are no people in it whatsoever,' said Gretchen O'Dowd suddenly.

This received a similar response to Erica's loaves and fishes until Rohanne made the connection. 'Well, at least she gave you *something*,' she said, 'even if you don't like the picture. Janice here has lost everything.'

'Not quite everything.'

'No?'

'Oh no. I have my Quest and I have my integrity. Twin guides to steer me as I write my last book.'

'Not *too* much integrity?' said Rohanne nervously.

'Enough,' said Janice mysteriously. And she gave Erica a long and contemplative smile. 'And I know exactly how to do it.' She squeezed the hand of the golden girl affectionately. 'With a bit of help from my little pinchbeck here.'

Erica was beginning to feel rather important, which was very nice.

'*And* I get seasick,' muttered Gretchen. But nobody heard.

Fleetingly Janice thought of her characters from the tube train and wondered what would happen now she had no use for them. Despite the whole superstition seeming irrelevant and the travellers cardboard and unreal, she nevertheless felt regret. She had intended to order and fulfil their lives – the good to profit by their goodness, the bad to suffer for their sins. And now they must roam unchecked to stumble where they would. It didn't seem fair, for their stories would have no proper ending. She sighed. Nevertheless, she would have to release them soon to let them find their way.

Erica returned the squeeze of her hand. Misinterpreting the sigh, she said stoutly, 'You'll find your Dermot. I'm sure of it.'

'That,' said Janice, 'would be the very best ending of all. And the only justification for everything.'

Rohanne was not at all sure about finding Dermot Poll. Nor about anything being a justification for anything. But it was not, fortunately, her problem. At least she was going back to New York with the real Janice Gentle's book agreed. What she was going to tell them about the lack of the real (not to say substantial) Janice Gentle in person, she did not yet know. Something. Something strong. Strong fiction, she told herself wryly. And smiled.

There was, of course, one last hurdle to overcome. She cleared her throat, put on what she hoped was a breezy smile, and prepared to introduce the subject with delicacy.

Chapter Eighteen

'Er, Janice?'

'Yes, Rohanne?'

'One small little thing.'

Janice blinked. 'What?'

'Sex.'

'Sex?'

'Mr Pfeiffer wants sex. I mean, Mr Pfeiffer wants sex in the book.'

'Ah,' said Janice, and up went the finger of admonishment again. 'As with the Court of Gloriana – Virgin Queen, indeed – it has come to this . . .

> 'All you that love, or loved before
> The fairy queen Proserpina
> Bids you increase that loving humour more:
> They that yet have not fed
> On delight amorous
> She vows that they shall lead
> Apes in Avernus . . .'

'It's those amoral Elizabethans all over again,' she said, 'tampering with the purer beauties and the high ideals, replacing it with tabloid salaciousness, bringing sex and conceits and disgruntlement into everything.' She looked meaningfully at Erica. 'Avernus, of course, being another name for hell.'

'Of course,' said Erica promptly.

'And the hell in this case would be the hell of unrequited love, "to lead apes in Hell" being an Elizabethan term for sexual frustration. They should have stayed with the courtly ideal rather than reduce it to the lowest common denominator . . .'

'Um,' said Rohanne Bulbecker, who had become quite lost, 'I think he means something a little more up to date than that. A bit more, shall we say, *direct*?'

'You mean of an illustrative nature?' said Janice. 'Not the prose of the understood but the prose of the explicit?'

Rohanne latched on to the last word. She nodded. 'Uh-huh,' she said.

'I am afraid not,' said Janice.

'Why?'

'Integrity,' said Janice firmly. 'And because I don't know anything about that side of things.'

Rohanne, contemplating the figure before her, was not at all surprised. Nevertheless, that was the whole point of creativity – the ability to get inside and imagine and inform convincingly. Look at Frankenstein.

'You must know something,' she said cajolingly. 'Look, basically we want you to write the same kind of book you have always written. Only with one or two ... er ... updates, expansions, a slight changing of emphasis ...' She shrugged. There was no other word for it. 'Sex. He wants some of that going on, as well as all the other lovely things you write about so well ... After all, it is part of life ...' Rohanne felt her voice growing fainter as she spoke. 'People expect it. And it means that when he markets you, he has a hook. You'll sell a lot more books.'

Rohanne felt strangely uncomfortable as she said this. In Morgan Pfeiffer's office it had been a straightforward enough brief.

'What do you mean, sex?'

'Well,' Rohanne shrugged, 'you know.'

'No,' said Janice, 'I don't.'

'Do you mean that you ... um ... don't know whether you *can* write about it, or ... um ... that you ... er ... well ... *haven't*?'

'Yes,' said Janice. 'Both.'

'But surely,' she said, as evenly as possible though she was quite sure that if she looked down she would see the breast pocket of her leathers going pump, pump, pump, 'you don't have to experience everything before you write about it. What about your Eastern Diplomat? What about all those heroines of yours? You've never dealt in pictures or run an hotel, yet all those women were very real.'

'Of course they were,' said Janice promptly. 'They were all me. It's easy to pick up jargon, to do research' – fondly and fleetingly she thought of those cosy days in the library at Battersea – 'to create from fact. Just the same people but in different clothes, for there is nothing new under the sun. At our heart we all want to be loved, to belong – the thread to link them all.'

Rohanne fiddled with her fingers uncomfortably. It was all nonsense, of course.

'All my books have been about love, and I have loved. All of my books have been about love and difficulties, because I have experienced love and difficulties. None of my books has been about sex, because I haven't experienced it. When I meet Dermot Poll again – who knows? – it might be different . . .'

'Oh, it will. I'm sure it will,' said Erica rapturously, much inspired by the talk of love. 'I *will* find him for you. Yea, verily, even unto the ends of the earth . . .'

Gretchen resisted the urge to shout hallelujah, and looked at her pink-cheeked idol with silent emotion.

'But good grief,' said Rohanne Bulbecker eventually. So far as she knew, she had never met a grown-up virgin before and was, despite her anxiety, in some awe at the experience. 'Times are moving on. People want sex – in bed and in books. I mean, sex is everywhere, sex is of our time. Couldn't you sort of *think* sex? You must know what it comprises.'

'Biologically,' said Janice, 'I know exactly. But I might as well write about sheep mating or frogs coupling for all I could say. It would be dead writing, I am afraid. No feelings.'

Rohanne felt on easier ground. 'There aren't necessarily feelings behind it at all. There are all sorts of in-betweens. It's a bit like eating, really. Sometimes you have a big meal and sometimes – well, you snack, even when you're not hungry. Do you see?'

'No,' said Janice. 'I understand eating because I do it. I do not understand sex. How can I when I have never sung Hymen's song?'

'It could be arranged,' muttered Rohanne.

'The whole thing is a complete mystery to me and I don't understand it at all.'

'Oh, it's a very straightforward activity,' Rohanne replied as airily as possible. 'To do with pleasure, tension, release, head games . . .' She stopped. Janice was staring at her quite uncomprehendingly.

'Aren't you taking this integrity business a bit too far? I mean, you write about *men* and yet you've never known any – apart from Dermot Poll, and you only saw him for five minutes.'

'Half an hour or so,' said Janice with dignity. 'And that was quite enough. We can fall in love in a second, and by that falling we can know everything about the object of our love we need to know. In the main we create our lovers, anyway – invent what we want them to be, then set about looking for those qualities in them.'

'Is *that* what we do?' said Rohanne, intrigued. 'Then no wonder it always goes wrong.'

Janice paused. 'Does it?' she asked with interest. 'It doesn't in *my* books.'

Rohanne was about to say something acerbic, but diplomacy won. 'I'm sure it won't be like that for you and . . . er . . . him. But why can you write about men, yet you can't write about sex . . .? After all, you don't know how men feel . . .'

'It's my estimation that they feel just the same as us, only they express it differently.'

Rohanne Bulbecker clamped her jaws shut. This was no time for debate.

'I see,' said Erica von Hyatt thoughtfully, 'you think that they feel the same, but hide it? The strong and silent thing? Sort of more muscular about it all?'

'Men are not stone,' said Janice. 'Nor women rose petals. And there is only one ultimate, ideal desire in the world. To love and be loved back. Men are no different in their need for this. After all,' she beamed through her spectacles, 'if you prick them do they not bleed?'

'Frankly,' said Rohanne Bulbecker, 'if you went at them with a hatchet, I doubt they would shed a drop. But you have it your way and I'll have it mine.' She drummed her fingers on her teeth. 'But there must be an answer to this sex thing. There *must*.'

Outside the evening sun began to wane, throwing the room into violet shadow. In the softening light Erica von Hyatt looked more lovely than ever, Janice Gentle more gross. But Rohanne would not be beaten, she would not.

'What about reading *The Joy of Sex*? It's got a lot of pictures in it.'

'So has a book on brain surgery,' said Janice, 'but I don't think I could perform an operation afterwards . . .'

Rohanne was irritably convinced. This lady might look like a doughbag, but she had sterling brainpower. 'You could watch a film, I suppose. That might help. I could get hold of some blue movies for you.'

'Ah, now,' said Erica von Hyatt, child of the streets, survivor. She took a deep breath and out tumbled the words. 'I was in one of those films once, and the thing about them is that it's not about nice sex at all, it's about getting on with it. "Get on with it," the man with the watch and the medallion said, so you don't have time to build up to anything like you should. I mean, one minute you're seeing a man across a crowded beach and the next you're in his truck using his dick for lunch, and then it cuts to a party and he's eating your pussy for tea, and then it's two or three of you all going at it on one man, and it all gets very uncomfortable because you have to make sure your privates can be seen, and I mean, when you are doing it for pleasure, the last thing you worry about is if the camera can get a good view up your –'

Rohanne put up her hand. She had gone very pink and more than ever regretted the leathers. 'Yes, well, thanks. You have been around,' she added tersely, 'haven't you?'

'I only made one,' said Erica. 'They said I was very good, but the next one had a dog in it, and I just wasn't going to do that sort of thing, because there are limits.'

'Don't you like dogs?' asked Gretchen, part of whose fantasy for the future had included strolling through country lanes with a dog.

'Look,' said Erica, 'I've stroked dogs, been bitten by dogs, looked after dogs, I've even *eaten* dogs –'

'Please,' shrieked Rohanne, who longed even more for the comparative calm of New York. 'I don't think any of us –'

'*Eaten* dogs!' said Gretchen, suddenly feeling her affection wane. 'How?'

'With me teeth, of course,' said Erica sharply. 'I had a Chinese boyfriend, and he cooked one once.'

'Yuck!' said Rohanne and Gretchen in unison.

Only Janice listened placidly. 'What did it taste like?' she asked, interested.

'Can't remember, really. Meat, I suppose.'

'Please,' said Rohanne briskly, 'could we just get back to sex?'

'I could *show* you,' said Erica thoughtfully. 'I wouldn't mind doing that if we got a decent man. I mean, sometimes I like to imagine I'm doing it in front of a whole crowd of people, anyway. At a theatre or something, and they're cheering me on . . .'

Gretchen O'Dowd went pale. Here was the object of her desire, the princess of all dreams, offering to expose herself quite shamefully. She glared at Janice Gentle, who immediately understood. She put up a plump hand. 'Oh no, dear,' she said to the daisy-faced Erica, 'I couldn't possibly . . .'

'Yes, yes, well, well,' said Rohanne tartly, for Erica had just described one of her own pet fantasies (she favoured Ephesus, surrounded by thousands of happy tourists snapping away with their cameras), and the thought that this von Hyatt person, woman of no abode, destitute, arrant liar, should share such imaginings was distressing. 'I think perhaps the idea of watching some sort of film is best. And it had better be a fairly explicit one – given how little you know. Now, does anyone here know about videos?'

'Oh yes,' said Gretchen O'Dowd. 'I used to watch them all the time. You hire them from shops.'

'Good,' said Rohanne Bulbecker. 'Then you must go and get one.' She fixed Gretchen with a penetrating eye. 'You know the kind of thing we want?'

Gretchen O'Dowd, much relieved that her princess was not to perform, nodded enthusiastically.

'Excellent,' said Rohanne Bulbecker. 'That's all settled, then. Just make sure it's something really explicit.'

And Gretchen left, plucking bravely at her moustache.

'I am suddenly reminded of that bit in Langland – you know it, I'm sure – where the silken-tongued Friar tries to extract money from Lady Meed, she who represents the power of the purse for both good and evil.' Janice looked innocently at Rohanne. 'And because the aristocracy is his likeliest hope for getting funds, he feels bound to justify their exigencies.'

'Ah,' said Rohanne.

'So he says smoothly, "It is a freletee of flessh." A frailty of flesh, which, he says, is found in books. Interesting how seeing anything in print, even five hundred years ago, seems to justify anything . . .'

'Hmm,' said Rohanne Bulbecker, keeping her eyes wide and clear.

'And, Langland goes on to say it is a fact of Nature through which we all get born; if you can survive the slander, then the harm is soon forgotten. It is the easiest absolved of all the Seven . . .'

'What is?' said Erica von Hyatt, confused still.

'Sex,' said Janice Gentle promptly. 'Amen, and let's hope it is relevant to me.'

Rohanne found it immediately necessary to remove herself. She established that there was a video machine, a television, and that the two remaining players in this bizarre intermezzo knew how to work them. Then she made her excuses and left. She was beginning to ponder the disturbing philosophical point, 'Who is the more gross, Janice or me?' and she wished not to do so. She walked. 'Frailty of flesh, indeed!' She shook her head. The leathers felt nasty, sticky, hot. She wanted a bath and she wanted to be on her own for a while. Sometimes it was hard being the fixer; sure, it meant that you held all the controls, but it also meant that no one, ever, could do the fixing for you. Right now she would have liked to lean on someone else for a change, a requirement she knew would pass, for it always did.

The hotel was quiet and soothingly anonymous. She went up to her room and ran a bath and let the scented water caress her. She felt perplexed about something and she was unsure what. As she lay there, observing her toes, wiggling them occasionally, she pondered. And then it occurred to her. She had just been given the run around by a fat, middle-aged virgin, made to bend to her will rather than bend her to her own . . . She sat up and threw the sponge across the room so that it landed with a satisfying splat against the door. Then she leaned back under the water and laughed. I'll be damned, she thought, I'll be damned.

*

Gretchen O'Dowd was much flustered by the time she found the right sort of shop. It did not look the right sort of shop, having the latest Michael Douglas on one side of its window display and a newly cut version of *Dumbo* on the other. Nevertheless, this was, according to the taxi-driver, exactly the place. It was Erica who had suggested that a taxi-driver would know where to obtain the kind of movie they needed, and it was a taxi-driver, indeed, who had tapped the side of his nose and said, 'Say no more,' when bringing her here. She smoothed her moustache with damp fingers, squared her shoulders, took a very deep breath, which enhanced the solidity of her substantial chest, and shuffled in shyly.

'I want a video for a friend,' she said.

The man behind the counter looked knowing. 'They all say that, dear,' he winked. 'And what sort of thing is your *friend* interested in?'

'Sex,' said Gretchen boldly. And then she went scarlet.

The man recognized the need for delicacy. 'What . . . er . . . kind?'

Gretchen remembered. 'Explicit,' she said. 'Very explicit.'

The man looked irritated. 'They are *all* that,' he said.

Gretchen looked behind her at Dumbo. 'Are they?' she said.

He followed her gaze. The little big-eared elephant stared back innocently. 'But not animals?' he said jovially.

Gretchen shook her head.

'For a friend you say?'

Gretchen nodded.

'A close friend?'

Gretchen shrugged unhappily. 'Well, she may be one day.'

He raised a finger. 'And no particular interests?'

'I don't think so.'

He rubbed his hands. 'Then I have *just* the thing for you.'

Gretchen tucked the brown package into her jacket breast and hurried back to Dog Street. 'Sorry I've been so long,' she said.

'That's all right. We've been talking,' said Erica von Hyatt proudly. 'Or, rather, I've been talking. Janice has been listening. And writing.' Janice Gentle put down her notebook and took the proffered parcel. 'Thank you,' she said and stared at its plain wrapping.

'He said it was just the job,' Gretchen muttered. She set up the machine and then, taking Erica von Hyatt by the hand, she led her to the door. 'Erica,' she said firmly, 'you and I are going out.'

'Oh, why?'

'Because . . .'

'Because what?'

'Because I don't want you getting corrupted.'

Erica's laughter echoed up the stairs.

Janice smiled at the sound. Then, before pushing the switch, she picked up the empty case, considered the picture on the cover for some time, shrugged, put it down, polished her glasses, took up her notebook, and waited for the show to commence.

*

Rohanne had changed into a skirt and shirt, twisted up her pale, damp hair and scrubbed her face clean of the day and clean of cosmetics. It gave her a nice sense of innocence.

Back at Dog Street, she tiptoed in to find Janice sitting alone and thoughtful. 'Gretchen has returned the film,' she said.

'Good, good. How did it go?'

Janice smiled.'Quite well, I think. I learned quite a lot about the art of love.' She smiled. 'And it all fits in rather well with this particular story.'

'Excellent,' said Rohanne, and she hurried off to the tiny little kitchen. 'How about a cream cake?' she called. 'As a reward for effort?' And she returned with a plate piled high with Harrods' best. She held this out, and Janice was just doing 'eeny meeny miny mo', when Rohanne asked, 'Now, when do you think we can have the book? Mr Pfeiffer will need to know a deadline.'

'Oh, not long at all,' said Janice. 'I know exactly what I'm going to write' – her outstretched fingers prepared to descend upon a strawberry tartlet – 'and you can have the manuscript just as soon as *I* have found Dermot Poll.'

The strawberry tartlet was whisked from under her grasp. She looked up inquiringly.

Rohanne's smile resembled a death mask, and for a moment she distinctly heard Sylvia Perth laughing in her ear. 'What?' she said.

'Well,' said Janice Gentle evenly, 'it seems safest. Given the way I have been tricked in the past.'

Yes, distinctly, Rohanne Bulbecker heard Sylvia Perth cackling away. She took several very deep breaths. Keep smiling, she told herself. *Keep smiling.* And still she held the cakes out of reach. 'Couldn't we have the manuscript, anyway?' she asked. 'And then find this . . . er . . . Poll man?'

Janice shook her head. 'I think not,' she said. 'Once bitten, you know.' She looked yearningly at the plate.

Rohanne nodded. She understood completely. No doughbag at all. No Dermot Poll, no book. She kept the cakes hovering just out of reach.

'Otherwise there is really no point.' Janice blinked up at her. 'Is there?'

When Gretchen O'Dowd and Erica von Hyatt returned, they found the interesting tableau of Janice, Rohanne and the cakes.

'I'll bet I know *exactly* where he is,' said Erica.

'Oh?' said Janice.

'Where?' said Rohanne.

'He'll be in Skibbereen, where he first came from. You can bet on it.'

'But what about Charlie Chaplin?' said Janice, which was ignored.

'*I'll* find Dermot Poll for you,' said Erica very positively, 'while you get on with your book.'

'*We*,' said Gretchen, 'will find Dermot Poll for you . . .' She looked at Erica. 'I shall never let you out of my sight again. And I will follow you to the ends of the earth.'

'Well, for the time being,' said Erica, looking a little hunted. 'And it's only to Ireland. One day at a time, you know. One day at a time.'

'And when we return, I shall find us a little house all of our own,' rhapsodized Gretchen, 'where we will live happily after . . .' Erica von Hyatt said nothing, just smiled. She had heard it all before.

Chapter Nineteen

IN Oxfordshire Gretchen bought wool at the little haberdashery. She would knit them each a jumper. Their trip to Ireland would take place in the depths of winter and she did not want her fragile beloved to catch cold. As usual, the woman in the wool shop was very nervous at selling what she considered to be the mysteries of female accoutrement to this man who seemed not to find them a mystery at all. Macramé, tapestry, tatting – he had mastered them all, and now he was going through the pattern books as if it were the most natural thing in the world. It was no consolation to know that the Archbishop of Canterbury also enjoyed working with wool, for he had a very high voice and she had always had her suspicions. As usual, the woman in the haberdasher's was jolly relieved when the choice was made, the money paid and her customer departed. Gretchen left with a cheery bounce, elated by the singing blue and sturdy brown she had chosen for their respective jumpers, and the fact that she had the whole of the autumn ahead with her loved one in the Queen Anne house. Rent-free, which was better than nothing, though it *should* by rights have been hers. As she passed the pub, the barmaid, breasting a window-ledge, leaned out and waved. Gretchen walked on with no more than the slightest response of recognition. That sort of thing was all in the past now. Once again she had someone of her own to cleave to and care for.

As she crunched down the gravel of the drive, she saw the faerie figure of Erica von Hyatt gathering blooms until she was all but hidden by them. There was a distinctly surreptitious quality about the way the girl garnered the flowers, a constant looking over her shoulder, a nervousness, despite Gretchen's telling her that she was welcome to pick as many as she wanted. Now the house was full of blossoms, scattered around in vases and bowls, looking dumped and forlorn.

She waved. The human wall of blooms attempted to wave back. Fronds of gladioli and chrysanthemums parted to reveal that delighted, adorable smile. Suddenly Gretchen knew exactly what to do. She would teach Erica the skills her own mother had taught her. Erica would not only pick the flowers and garner the fruits, but she would learn how to display them beautifully, too. Gretchen sighed with satisfaction and gave her moustache a loving little tickle with her fingers. What could be more companionable than that?

*

The Little Blonde Secretary was feeling very put out. She had assumed that the decision was as good as the deed, and yet here she was again, checking the calendar, checking the temperature chart and preparing for yet another attempt at Making it Happen. The Vent-Axia was whining irritatingly as she bent over the basin to wash her hair, but she had put the issue to one side for the moment. A harmonious body makes a harmonious child, she had been advised, so altercations over something so trivial (and which could be removed – and *would* be once she was safely pregnant) were counter-productive. Instead, she thought sweet thoughts and continued with her toilette. Derek was hardly what you would call *ardent* any more, and she found it extremely irritating to have to make the running all the time. If he had once tried to surprise her with something like roses or bath salts, it would have made things a bit more romantic, but he didn't seem to under- stand. She had even read him out the closing passage from *Scarlet Ice* where the hero comes back to the heroine and produces a filmy red nightie wrapped in black tissue-paper, but when she shut the book and sighed meaningfully, he was already asleep.

She rinsed her hair with scented lotion and thought of one day having a sweet little girl, in her own image, holding her hand in the supermarket and being complimented by everyone in the queue. She began pinning careful little curls and dangly bits all over her head – something that the magazine article said held an enticing hint of danger about it. Her little girl would never have a runny nose or grazed knees, nor howl for chocolate buttons and throw tantrums on the floor. She would leave the likes of that to the lump in Reception, with her stodgy smile and her tight jumpers that showed every line of the growing bulge. When *she*, Little Blonde Secretary, got pregnant she would show *her* how to do it attractively. At least nobody – except Derek – knew how long they had been trying . . .

In the lounge she reorganized the growing pile of books and magazines on the subject into proper order. The ones about getting pregnant, the ones about being pregnant, the what-hospital guides and the parentcraft guides. She had built up quite a library and there wasn't a lot left to know. All that was required was the one essential; she fervently hoped that tonight would do it. She had rung Derek at work to remind him to be here promptly, and something told her – she hummed as she dotted Loulou behind each ear – that tonight really would be the night. She hoped so, because with that out of the way she could concentrate on the conference in Birmingham next month. The Boss Masculine was very keen and she wanted to be at her efficient best. Organized, she liked to be organized. And with that she began to concentrate on thinking nice thoughts. Not long now until he got home, unless the five-fifty-two was delayed for some reason . . .

In the bedroom she slipped a Barry Manilow moody-music cassette into the machine and practised turning it on at exactly the right place. Derek's lateness was most likely due to travel problems, London was chock-a-block nowadays, but she refused to get wound up about the progress of the clock. He would be here, in good time, because she had told him it was an *important* night. He had said, 'What, another one?' Which had made it quite hard to keep her smile down the telephone. But keep it she did, just.

She slipped into her filmy new nightie (*dangerously* filmy, the assistant had said), clipped on her ear-rings, wriggled her little painted toes into her boudoir slippers, and went down to the kitchen to wait. While she waited, she pottered, washing the vases, which she liked to do by hand, being careful to wear her yellow rubber gloves. The clock continued to try to make her feel cross, but she would have none of it. After the vases she washed the inside of the drainer cupboard. And after that she began on the windows. She hummed and underlying the hum was the consoling thought that he could bloody well have a sandwich when it was all over, and not the very nice fish pie and peas that were ready for heating up.

Derek slapped Ken's back, missed and, since Ken was not insubstantially built, took this as a sign that he had drunk enough – perhaps even too much. He decided not to look at his watch so that he could honestly say he had lost track of the time. He had told Ken all about the high heels and skimpy underwear and the Asti Spumante that – he had dared to say it after pint number two – caused him nothing but *dread*. After pint number four he had even dared to go further and confess that he often found the whole thing quite *deflating*, making it sometimes – well, difficult to *perform*. And after pint number six he had told him, shakily, that sometimes he *didn't* – not at all. Just grunted and pretended. Ken was unable to make out much of this last speech, but he felt he had the gist. He slapped Derek firmly on the back and told him he should look on the bright side. At least he was getting it now and then, wasn't he? Not like most husbands. Enjoy it, Ken urged, it'll be over soon enough.

When he got home he opened the front door with difficulty and had a sense of foreboding that was not entirely to do with the odd slooshing sensation in the pit of his stomach. He looked up, focused, and saw his wife. She was smiling at him, or at least her mouth was, and she looked – he blinked – she looked – well, *frightening*. The light of the kitchen behind her showed the outline of her perfect little body beneath the nylon stuff that draped it.

Her dainty little feet were encased in what appeared to be bits of fluff, and her face glowed like a film star's beneath a powder puff of blonde curls that looked as if they had exploded. But all that, disturbing as it was at whatever time of night, was nothing compared with the final embellishment, the ultimate horror, the last thing he noticed before sinking to the floor and into thankful oblivion – she was wearing a pair of bright yellow plastic gloves, and he could not, *would* not, bring himself to imagine what she might do to him with *them* . . .

It was, as she later reflected, a good job she had other fish to fry in her life. At least the conference was coming up soon and that would take her mind off things. Derek would have quite a lot of time to reflect on his naughty ways, and she spent several nights staying with her mother just to be sure.

The Boss Masculine let her cry on his shoulder for most of the rail journey. There was something really very pleasant about having such a pretty little thing so vulnerably in need. His wife was vulnerably in need, but she was neither young nor little. And, so far as he could make out between the sobs and the story, there was another vital difference: his wife cried at the very existence of sex, the Little Secretary was crying at the lack of it. Of the two he knew where his own sympathies lay. He resisted going into the buffet to light a cigarette, and put his arm around her small shoulders instead. Even when she cried, she looked pretty.

'Come, come,' he said, 'let's put it all behind us and have a good time while we are away, shall we?' And he kissed her lightly on the head, delighted to smell the freshness of her shampoo. His wife, who found bending difficult (seemed to find everything physical difficult), seldom washed her hair. He wondered if now was an appropriate time to bring out the lace hanky, but decided not. He settled himself closer. How could that ferrety husband of hers refuse her in bed? She was a sweet, dainty, delightful little creature who was crying out for love. As indeed he was himself . . .

The train sped on. Their rooms were next to each other. Birmingham suddenly held a magic for him and he felt born anew. 'Come along now,' he said cajolingly to the grief-stricken little face, 'I think what you need is a drink.'

And although she said she almost never did, he insisted.

As they swayed their way towards the bar, he took her hand to steady her.

She thought it was such a gentlemanly thing to do, compared with Derek who would probably have fallen over twice by now. As she held on tight, she consoled herself that, for the next few days at least, she was away with a man who knew how to behave properly.

*

Rohanne Bulbecker was having dinner with Janice on the following evening, and the day after that – wonderful, wonderful – she was flying home. The other two oddballs had gone to Oxfordshire. Janice was now safely back in her own apartment ready to work. And life was going to be sweet, after all. She had no idea what she would say when she got back to Morgan P. Pfeiffer, but she would think of something. It didn't really matter. The main thing was the book, and that was signed, promised and would – Dermot Poll willing – be delivered. Oddball major and Oddball minor were planning to dragnet Ireland early in the New Year, and even if they didn't find him, there was time after that for some professional detective work; Skibbereen looked very small on the map and someone there was sure to know what had happened to such an apparently talented son.

Rohanne pitied Janice this abiding dream. It was quite clear she had been duped and dumped, and to reunite her with the Poll man could only end in disappointment. Nevertheless, as she kept telling herself, it was no concern of hers. Deliver Dermot Poll, collect the book, and run. Those were the goals. The only goals. All the same, there was something altogether fascinating, remarkable – moving even – at the idea of enduring love like that. All

217

those virginal years, all that life, just waiting . . . All those books that told the story in so many compelling ways. Rohanne's business sense had momentarily become detached (she was sure it would come back) and somehow she felt bound into the tale too.

*

Melanie ducked the extended arm on her porch, swivelled to avoid the lips which were puckered into expectancy, and got inside her front door. 'Feel sick,' she said, giving a convincingly bilious groan. 'Must go.' And she closed the door on his questioning, stranger's face. She bent down, gave another solid performance of one who is *in* visceral *extremis* through the letter-box, agreed to call him when she was better, and shuffled towards the kitchen. If she didn't really feel unwell, she certainly felt a little squiffy, which was not surprising. That, she decided, as she boiled the kettle for some camomile tea (she had not been sleeping at all well recently) was the *very last time* she would go out with a dickhead. Two gin-and-tonics, a vegetarian lasagne, half a litre of house Barolo, zabaglione and free mint imperials and he thought he'd bought an all-night ticket? Huh! The kettle boiled. She poured the water into the mug that said Melanie in nursery colours, stirred the bag, removed it, picked up the mug, looked at its inscription, and burst into tears. He had put that in her stocking last Christmas. Bum, bum, *bums* . . .

In bed she drank the tea and settled her head on the pillow. Eleven-thirty-three. She closed her eyes. She wondered what *he* was doing right now.

Square Jaw drank three glasses of what Jeremy called 'quaffing wine' and left the kitchen. He had every intention of seeking out the most attractive female at the party (the shorter the skirt the better; if she had white boots, double points) and going for it.

He spotted her at once. Tall, long blonde hair, pretty profile and legs encased in skin-tight leather trousers. Having spotted her, he decided to return to the kitchen and have another glass of wine.

Jeremy was drinking hard, too. 'Bloody women,' he said gloomily. 'Work my balls off in HK. Get back ready to celebrate, and all she's done is to ring you all up, leave a sodding mess and bugger off. Nearly cancelled the thing. Saved by the secretary. What a brick.' He refilled their glasses. They were both deeply hurt men. 'And when I asked for an explanation, do you know what she said?'

Square Jaw shook his head, 'Bloody women,' he said. 'What?'

'She said if *I* was prepared to go over there and do her hoovering, she'd clean my lavatory. Do you understand it?'

Square Jaw shook his head again.

'Bloody, bloody women,' they both chorused. And had another drink to it.

He decided to be subtle and stood in the conversational group next to the blonde's. Earnestly he inquired if he might join what was clearly a deep and meaningful debate between a serious young man and woman. He had quaffed enough kitchen wine to feel he would be welcome.

'Ah,' he said breezily, 'a real conversation.' Fleetingly he thought this might be taken for the remark of a prat, but they were smiling warmly at him, welcomingly. 'That's what it's all about, parties. Meeting people and talking to them, eh?'

The couple nodded. He felt he was doing rather well. Sod Melanie. Here was life, after all.

He positioned himself so that he could see the blonde and she could see him, and smiled at his new-found companions. He kept the smile while they told him they were social workers (where did Jeremy, disciple of Adam Smith, get *them* from?) and listened politely – or appeared to listen politely.

The blonde wasn't saying much, but she looked great.

'. . . Don't you agree?' said the female social worker.

'I'm not sure,' he said cautiously, tearing his eyes away from the stretchy leather. 'Go on.'

They did.

He said loudly when they had finished, 'Since I have no wife and no children, why should I pay for all the things a nuclear family requires? Libraries? I never use them. Drugs rehabilitation? I don't need it. School meals? I don't require them . . .'

'Ever been burgled?' asked the man.

'Ever had your car stolen?' asked the woman.

'Yes,' said Square Jaw, sliding his eyes back to the blonde. Their eyes met. She gave a hesitant half-smile. Square Jaw suddenly ached to get inside those leathers.

'. . . And did you know that a high proportion of burglaries – indeed, all crime – is drug related? What price your dissociation from rehab now?'

'Ah,' said Square Jaw, 'I see . . .'

'Everything is woven into everything else. You can't cut loose. If you do, the whole fabric begins to unravel. *That's* what's happening in our society today. The poorly educated commit more crimes. Do you still say schools aren't relevant to you? Ghettos and inner-city decay create festering pustules that infect the whole . . . You can't say one bit is healthy and the rest is diseased – we're all suffering from the same malady because basically we're all *one* . . .'

Square Jaw felt queasy with the talk of pustules. And he felt uncomfortable, because if they had a point – and they might well – it wasn't a point he wanted to grasp. The only thing he wanted to grasp was standing about three feet away.

'Hmm,' he said, giving suitable pause, and then, 'I see. Yes.' And then, deciding to chance it, he changed the subject. 'And how do you two know Jeremy?' he asked.

'You might well ask,' said the serious female. 'I'm his sister. This is my boyfriend. And that blonde you're eyeing up is my flat-mate. Shall we leave the ills of society and go on to the more important issue of your getting introduced?'

Square Jaw winced apologetically.

'It's all right,' said the sister of Jeremy. 'Eat, drink, copulate and be merry, for tomorrow . . . Tomorrow, who knows . . .?'

Melanie was waiting for tomorrow, for when the dawn came she could legitimately get up and start the day. She lay there reading, which only made her mind wander. The radio played tracks to bring back memories. She turned out the light, turned it on again, twisted and rumpled around the bed for an hour or two and finally gave up. She might as well go downstairs and pace the floor as lie here pretending sleep would come. It was a relief to have given in, and down the stairs she padded, taking some comfort at the still, dark quiet of the house. She made a tray of tea and went into the living-room, noticing for the first time that the answerphone was winking. She crouched in the moonlight and played the message back. It was from him. And it was heart-warming after the pain. He wanted her to go to him.

She looked at the time. Nearly three, but he had said he would be in tonight, that he would be *honoured* – a nice joke. So why shouldn't she? After all, she still had the key, she could let herself in quietly, slide into bed beside him and – well, there really was no reason in the world why not . . .

Square Jaw was also awake. He could not move. His leg was twisted under another's and the another slept. Moonlight sent a bright whiteness across her ruffled hair, and her face looked colourless and still. A woman, he thought, a pretty woman – prettiest at the party. He reached out and touched the curve of her breast with his fingertips. But an alien woman, an alien breast. Not Melanie.

He'd been quite proud of how swiftly he had managed to chat her up. It was like diving – you just did it without thinking or you wouldn't do it at all. The success had made him feel good about himself and he had forgotten about white boots and short skirts in the recklessness of the hunt, wondering all the while he was talking to her, getting drinks for her, exchanging silly conversation, dancing with her, if she would finally go to bed with him. And she had. But now he had a sinking feeling in his stomach. He felt the sleeping thigh across his own and he resented it being there, holding him down. He wanted to wake her up and say, 'Let's be modern about this,' or something similar, but if he did, he knew it would not end there. Women were no good at accepting things at face value. If he woke her up and said, 'That was nice. See you sometime,' it would only be the start. She would go on and on. Women did. *He'd* seen *Fatal Attraction*, after all, and while he didn't have a child or a rabbit to stew, he had an ear that could be chewed off half the night. And if during the drawn-out monologue he should fall asleep? Christ, *then* didn't the shit hit the fan? And yet she knew just as well as he did, surely, that it had all been about bed? Not a tryst for life? If he had pursued her, then she had led him on. She had worn those leather trousers, which certainly did not say leave me alone. Women were hypocritical. They needed everything dressed up in love to justify it. And now here he was. Stuck.

Just about the only good thing to come out of this whole mess with Melanie was that he had got his freedom back. He thought about motor-racing. Now that he was free he could get into something like that and there wouldn't be anyone to pout disapprovingly. He could do anything, really – anything at all. No Melanie, no restriction on his life. The thigh moved fractionally. He began stroking it absent-mindedly, at the same time imagining himself roaring round the track, winning, spraying champagne, women, women climbing all over him . . . And not a Melanie in sight to say *no*.

As she drove the familiar route, Melanie thought about that twerp tonight, and all the other twerps that were likely to be on offer. She shuddered. Who knew what other groping aliens might be around the corner? Hundreds. She had already met enough to last a lifetime . . .

She felt excited, in love again. She parked the car as quietly as she could and enjoyed the thrumming of her heart. He would be in bed, he would be asleep. She might slide under the covers with him, still with her clothes on, of course, just to talk, maybe just to have a cuddle, or a hand hold – some form of contact, anyway. Anger had melted away to regret. They'd had long enough to think things over, and besides – she had to be rational – men just weren't as good as women at knowing how to behave in emotional situations. They were unformed in that department, and it was no use expecting it to be otherwise. That was like expecting a penguin to fly just because it was a bird – the breed's wings were too small, that was all. Well, she, Melanie, could handle that. A little time on her own had done wonders.

'I will be good,' she muttered to herself as she hurried up the steps to his door. The surprise would take away some of the awkwardness. She laughed to herself, happy again. Pasta and zabaglione and being courted indeed! There were things worth a lot more than *that*!

*

Janice pondered on the love that would give up a child for its better good. It seemed to her that there could be no love greater. She got out of bed, padded to the kitchen to make a sandwich, and then took it to her desk.

She began to write. 'He hath put down the mighty from their seats and exalted them of low degree.' Then she ate, and thought, and wrote again. 'Though I have the gift of prophecy, and understand all mysteries and all knowledge' – which, after all, she argued, was absolutely true of the writer – 'and though I have all faith, so that I could remove mountains, and have not love, I am nothing . . .' Indeed, indeed. 'Love suffereth long, and is kind . . .' So, so – it is so. 'When I was a child, I spake as a child, I understood as a child; but when I became a woman I put away childish things . . .'

She looked at the long row of books on the shelf before her, every one bearing her own name. Baby slopes, mere baby slopes. And through the long night, with spontaneous visits to the bread bin, Janice wrote.

*

He had won two Grand Prix, which was very exciting, and made up in part for his not being able, quite, to get off to sleep. Despite needing the bathroom, feeling thirsty, having pins and needles and a whole series of discomforts, he felt it was easier to lie there than risk waking her again. He might, eventually, get off to sleep and – who knew? – perhaps when he woke up, she would be the first to say, 'Now let's be modern about this.' Pigs might fly, but it was a comforting possibility. She moved her body fractionally, but not the leg. He began breathing regularly just in case she should be listening. He wanted to be a free man. He did, he did . . .

He looked down again. Her face was no more than a glimmer on the pillow, her breathing was even, she smelled of scent and sex and female – and she could, he thought with detachment, be anybody. He went back to Le Mans, but this time the racing itself evaded him. All he could tune in to was the afterwards, the women smiling – big teeth, big smiles, big everything. And the champagne – enormous – the neck of the bottle quite distended as he opened it and sprayed them, wetting the fronts of their T-shirts, revealing that they wore nothing – *absolutely* nothing – underneath . . .

Square Jaw shifted his position very slightly and felt her reciprocal shifting to accommodate him. She was soft against him; her breathing had changed, become shallower. He held his breath. Don't wake, he pleaded, but yet, oh yet . . . He began stroking her thigh again. Another part of him, quite separate from his brain but not his imagination, *did* want her to waken, was already stirring at the very idea of it, and she was stirring too as he pressed himself against her. Somewhere a voice was telling him *Don't do it*, but the another just urged him on. What he found himself thinking as he nuzzled her ear and stroked between her thighs was that it was unfair: they could just lie there, asleep, and still turn a man on, and then, as often as not, assume no responsibility for it, so that the poor sod with a stiffy had the choice of suffering it, dealing with it himself, or waking her up and being rejected nine times out of ten . . . All the same – he stroked on, losing care, getting caught up in the moment as she stirred and sighed and pressed her warmth against him – all the same, this one was not going to do any of those things, this one would be responsive, this was early days. He murmured her name. Might as well be hung for a sheep as a lamb. He thought briefly of Melanie, wondering if her boots had done the trick, and then he put all thoughts of her from his mind and began to concentrate . . .

Somewhere beyond the usual noises of the bed – the creaks, the sighs, the rustlings – he thought he heard another noise. Like a door, perhaps? Like a latch clicking gently? But he was being kissed and kissing back, which left no time for further conjecture.

Chapter Twenty

'I was thinking,' said Janice to Rohanne, 'of the Pardoner.'

'Who?' said Rohanne cautiously.

'Chaucer's Canterbury Pilgrim. It sounds such a lovely thing to be, a Pardoner. But, if you remember, the tale is mere crudity, vulgarized allegory, tasteless decadence. The Pardoner himself had no gift of pardon, he was a bogus, a flatterer, a fool.'

'Very apt,' said Rohanne, 'in the case of Sylvia Perth.'

Janice smiled, folding her serviette neatly. She had eaten a goat's cheese soufflé, sautéed monkfish, roast guinea-fowl, *crème brûlée* with spiced pears – and she was feeling quite benign. It was the first time she had ever been in a restaurant, and it was not, for all her fears, an unpleasant experience. On the contrary, the people who ran it and who hovered about her positively *wanted* her to eat well and enjoy the experience. Indeed, when she ordered her pudding, they had practically cheered, and the chef had come out to congratulate her personally. Stilton had been promised but was still on its way. Janice could wait.

'But even the Pardoner had the opportunity of redemption. If he so chose. If he had faith. People were closer to faith in those days. He *was* on the way to Canterbury, after all. He might not only have been going there with a view to making money *en route*. Part of him might have been hoping for forgiveness, for the lifting of his burden of sin. I expect Sylvia was a bit like that, too. Curate's egg, not all bad, but totally infected all the same.'

'I think that is very nice of you,' said Rohanne, 'but I still think she deserves a stake through her heart.'

Janice shook her head. 'Not really. She was the victim, not me. All those fancy assets . . .'

'Including Erica von Hyatt?'

'Including Erica von Hyatt. They meant nothing, really. A hole where once was a soul, never to be filled no matter how much gold she poured in . . .'

'Not to mention Chanel suits, Gucci handbags, rugs from the Orient and a country house . . .'

Janice smiled. 'But wearing a hair shirt the while. At some point Sylvia had to sit with just herself and the mirror. No. I feel sorry for her. And I'd rather be me. Soul intact.'

'And integrity,' said Rohanne wryly.

'And integrity,' agreed Janice with the slightest hint of amusement behind her spectacles. 'Sorry.'

Rohanne shrugged. 'Your privilege.' She looked up. 'Jeezus, here comes the cheese.' She gazed at it with horror.

'Judge not,' said Janice wryly, also looking at the cheese, 'lest ye be judged . . .'

An entire Stilton, blue-veined and crumbly, was set before them. Rohanne Bulbecker, putting a discreet hand to her nose, declined. Janice, savouring a morsel, said, 'Thank goodness for food. It can be such a comfort, you know. I frankly don't know where I would have been without it . . . Sure you won't try some? It's a very superior cheese, named after the town of Stilton in Huntingdonshire.'

'Er . . . no thanks, all the same,' said Rohanne Bulbecker. She leaned back, discreetly gasping for air. 'But you go right ahead.'

When the meal was finished, Janice said, 'I wonder what it was really like then?'

'When?'

'Five hundred years ago. Going on a pilgrimage. Even such a short one as London to Canterbury. Dangerous, I should think, more dangerous than now – the wooded route hiding the disenfranchised, the outlawed, the mad, the diseased, the souls with nothing left to lose. Very much more dangerous. And therefore more noble, more rewarding. I've often thought I ought to tread the path they took, just to experience a real pilgrimage. Not by train or car but on foot, by mule or horse, like them. Think of all the pondering you could do on that long, slow meander . . .' Her voice sounded dreamy, seduced. She ran a fingertip around the line of crumbs on her plate and then sucked it ruminatively. 'In a way, though, I've sort of done one. Going to Sylvia Perth's apartment was like a pilgrimage. It was certainly fraught. But it's hardly the sort of thing Chaucer's lot had in mind. I *wonder* if it could be done today . . . There must be maps of the old route . . .'

Rohanne went pale. 'You aren't planning a trip to Canterbury, I hope?' It would just be her luck if this prize of hers underwent a religious conversion.

'Oh no,' said Janice Gentle. 'Not at all. After this I'm going to stay lodged in my Battersea cell and write. A new book, a new departure. It comes to the same thing, really. And, of course, I shall be making my own pilgrimage in due course – when I go to meet Dermot Poll.'

Rohanne kept her smile bright. 'Sure,' she said. 'I wonder how those two love birds will make out.' She raised her glass. 'Here's to Dermot Poll. And here's to the new book. What's it going to be about, by the way?'

Janice raised her own glass, and smiled. 'Ah-ha,' she said. 'Wait and see.'

*

Enrico Stoat worked hard into the night. 'As if Jane Austen had lifted her petticoats,' he wrote, and he smiled at the brilliance of the comparison.

*

Square Jaw was somewhere between the desire and the spasm when a noise different from any of those emanating from himself or the alien woman made him resurface. He felt a bumping under the bed, which, he was sure, had nothing to do with what was happening on top of it. He negotiated himself into a position where he could peer over the edge and came face to face, dim in the shadows, backlit by moonlight, with Melanie's eyes.

'Bastard,' she said. 'I can't move the sodding thing.'

Not surprisingly the alien woman began to sit up and make noises of inquiry. With a reflex action he pushed her down and pulled the duvet up to cover her. There was a noise not entirely indicative of approval from beneath the bedding, but he hoped she would construe it as a chivalrous gesture.

Take this nightmare away, he begged silently, but Melanie did not vanish. She merely went on attempting to pull out her box, wildly and without success. He put his hands in his hair and hung his head. Through laced fingers and gritted teeth he said, 'Melanie, this is my bedroom. It is three a.m. What are you doing here?'

'I'm getting my things,' she said, and continued scrabbling ferociously.

He spread his hands over his knees. The nightmare faded. Now it was like starring in a very bad film. He wanted to laugh. Or possibly cry. Both, really. 'Why now?' he said, daring to look up.

'You invited me,' she said.

'I did?'

The figure beneath the duvet twitched. He felt a terrible urge to pat it and say, 'Down girl, down.'

'Look,' he said, standing up, 'I think we should go into the other room.' He could sense the rage in her, almost hear her heart thumping. He had never felt quite so naked, and he had visions of her doing him some actual bodily harm. Was he imagining it in the shadows, or were her knees twitching dangerously? He grabbed a pillow and held it to himself until in the gloom he could recognize his underpants. He picked them up and stepped into them quickly. He felt slightly more in control of things with them on.

He sidled towards the door.

'That's right,' she said, 'walk away from trouble.'

'I am not walking away,' he said, grabbing his dressing-gown, slipping it on. 'I am walking to somewhere we can talk.'

'What's wrong with here?' she said defiantly.

There was a rustling from the duvet, a head began to appear from beneath it. He grabbed Melanie's hand and pulled her out into the corridor. There were some things he was not up to dealing with. He released her hand and dived back into the bedroom. 'Stay there,' he pleaded. He tweaked the duvet cover up again. 'Sorry about this.'

'*You're* sorry!' came the muffled indignation.

'I'm dealing with it, OK?'

'Tell her to piss off.'

He was thinking much the same himself.

Melanie was still in the corridor. 'Who does she think she is? And who is she, anyway?'

He ignored both questions and, with the courage of a Wild West sheriff, turned his back and walked down the passageway into the living-room.

Melanie followed. He closed the door after her.

'Well?' he said.

'Sorry to disturb,' she said sweetly.

He sat down. 'Melanie,' he said, 'you had no right –'

'I had every right.' She raised her voice, the stridency betraying that she wanted it to be heard. 'You invited me over. You said you were in all evening. You said come any time. Didn't you?'

Once more he put his head in his hands. 'Oh God,' he said, remembering.

'Well?'

'I didn't mean three bloody a.m.'

'Clearly,' she said, with potent satisfaction.

'I think we should talk,' he said.

'Talk?' she said. 'Talk? Talk? What about?'

He knew that trick. 'Melanie,' he said, not without anger, 'why did you choose to come here, unannounced, at this time of night?'

'Morning,' she corrected.

He felt dangerously close to smacking her. Instead he got up and switched on the lamp, dispelling the shadows and moonlight and bringing sanity to the proceedings.

He looked at her. She was tensed as if under starter's orders. She was also, he knew from the line of her mouth, hurt. But over all she was *angry*, which made him afraid of her. He suppressed thoughts of conciliation and allowed his own anger in.

'Well?' he said, folding his arms like an inquisitorial father. 'Explain yourself.'

She shrugged. 'I still have your keys. You never asked for them back.'

'And I still have yours. Doesn't mean I'd come bursting in in the middle of the night, showing you up in bed with lover boy.'

'You wouldn't find me in bed with *lover* boy – because there isn't one.'

'Pull the other leg . . .'

'I just wanted my things, that's all.' She was walking round the room, trailing her fingers over objects, riffling through postcards on the mantelpiece. He knew her. She was out to irritate and she was succeeding. 'I needed one or two things from the box.'

'At three in the fucking morning?'

'Do you have to swear?'

'Yes, I fucking well do. Fucking.' For a moment he hoped she was going to laugh.

No such luck.

'Like what did you need?' he said belligerently. 'A hairbrush? Those pink socks with stars on them? Your *Wind in the Willows* T-shirt?' He laughed. 'Oh my goodness, I simply can't go *on* without Toad . . .'

'Don't be so childish. Can I have them, please?'

'No.'

'You wanted to get rid of them. You rang me and told me you did. The only phone call you've made in the whole six weeks was to say you wanted to give me my things back.' Her lips wobbled but she righted herself.

'Don't cry,' he said warningly.

'Well, it's true, isn't it?'

'It is not true. I didn't only ring about that . . .'

'Oh. Now I'm a liar.'

'Melanie!'

She stood in front of him, cocking her head in the direction of the bedroom. 'Didn't take you long. How many's that? Six? Seven? Eight?'

For a moment he felt rather flattered. He thought about looking as if it might just be true but remembered the reality of the lump under the duvet next door. This was no time for misplaced pride.

'What about you?'

'I haven't been to bed with anybody.'

'I saw you.'

'What, in bed?'

'No. In Popinjay's.'

'So? It's a restaurant, not a knocking shop. At least, so far as I know. Of course, you may know different and –'

'You were all over him.'

'So?'

'Don't keep saying that.'

'*So.*'

'Boots, short skirt – putting it all out on display. What's the matter? Didn't he bite after all? Perhaps you didn't leave enough to the imagination.'

'You bastard. Just get my things.'

He stood up. 'Well? Did you?'

'Did I what?'

'Let him?'

'Let him? You are just so unliberated. *Let* him? As if I am a piece of merchandise . . .'

'That's what you looked like.'

'We had a meal and then he took me home. And why the *hell* am I justifying myself to you – when you've got *that* in the other room?'

'Melanie, it may have escaped your notice, but I *live* here. This is my flat, my home, my bloody bed if you want to know, and you've just barged in . . .'

She was silent. Swallowing.

Very quietly she said, 'I apologize. If you will get my box, I'll go.' And she immediately sat down. 'It's funny,' she said, 'but I thought you'd be thinking things through. Instead you've been out fucking every Tom, Dick and Harry.'

'Hardly,' he said, feeling the first thaw of humour, 'I don't go in for that, remember?'

She looked at him. He nodded in the direction of the bedroom. 'Female,' he said. 'It's a woman.' He attempted a joke. 'Try Thomasina, Doreen or Harriet.'

'It's not funny,' she said. 'How many times?'

'One – and a half, thanks to you.'

'I don't mean that.'

'Just this once.'

'Did you use condoms?'

'Of course I bloody used condoms. Did you?'

'I . . . haven't . . . haven't –' She broke off, unable to finish the sentence. She stood up.

He was torn. Part of him was pleased. Part of him knew he had lost ground now.

'What? Not even once? What about the guy tonight?'

'Not my type. Would you get my box? Then I can go and you' – she looked significantly at the door – 'can carry on.'

She put out her hand as if to shake his. 'I apologize again. I just thought I could come over and slip into bed beside you.'

He laughed, forgetting for the moment the seriousness of the situation. 'It might have been interesting if you had . . .'

The laugh died. Too late. He knew, quite suddenly, that he had blown it. Quite suddenly, he knew the whole thing had turned and would not turn back. Her face had set to a ghastly stone. The hand he held went rigid and withdrew itself. He heard a choir of told-you-so's singing that he shouldn't have done that. He remembered. A sense of humour was not one of her strongest points. Oh *God*, what the hell, that was it, then; he had really done it now.

'You insensitive shit,' she said quietly. And without another word, she opened the door, clicked it behind her, and left.

'What about your things?' he called.

But there was no reply.

'Is that it?' he asked himself wryly.

It seemed that it was. For a split shard of time he felt liberated, and then from the bedroom he heard the distinct sounds of female sobbing, a familiar tune. He kicked at the couch, swore under his breath, and returned to the alien woman.

Chapter Twenty-one

THE cab pulled up outside Janice's address.

'Oh,' said Rohanne surprised. 'Here already.'

Janice laughed. 'Despite Sylvia's disapproval, the place is very close to the centre. Piccadilly to Battersea High Street is a very few miles.' She raised a finger. 'Remember the old saying, "You must go to Battersea to get your simples cut"?'

'No,' said Rohanne.

'In olden days the market gardeners of Battersea grew simples – medicinal herbs – and London apothecaries came here to choose and gather what they wanted.' She looked out of the taxi's window at the brick walls and car-lined streets. 'Wouldn't believe it now, but so it was. They used the old saying to reprove a simpleton – someone who held a foolish belief. Like you.'

'Me?' Indignation overruled politeness. 'What, exactly?'

'Love, dear. Or the virtues in the lack of it. You think I'm quite dotty to have waited for Dermot Poll this long.'

'Well . . .'

Janice raised a hand. 'Oh yes you do. Well, believe me, it is better to have hope in your heart and love on your sleeve than the freedom of emptiness.'

'It weakens,' mumbled Rohanne.

'It what, dear?'

'I said it weakens.' Rohanne was about to say, 'Look at you . . .' But somehow the equation didn't hang together.

'No, no. Good love supports weakness, draws from strength. It's a state of enhancement. In its perfect state it makes all who are held in it good. It spreads to every fibre; its strength can outwit evil. And though Perfect Love is of its nature unattainable, we can at least strive for it. I am quite sure of that. And as such it will wait for ever, even to the moment of death . . .'

'Hah,' said Rohanne. 'You really *are* in the fourteenth century. There doesn't seem to be a lot of Perfect Love about now-adays . . .'

'Oh but its essence stays the same in whatever age. Poor Ovid, happy in his lusty detachment, suddenly bewails that he has fallen in love – and in so doing he feels like a hunter who has stepped into his own snare, never to be rescued . . . Dante glimpses Beatrice; Troilus, Criseyde; Lancelot, Guinevere . . . Even Victoria sees a sneezing Albert through a curtain and loves at once. There is no age in which it was not so, no time in which lovers did not seek the elusive joy – and no age which did not set out to bludgeon the purity of Love Found.'

A little coldness clutched at Rohanne Bulbecker's heart. 'Janice,' she said, 'the . . . um . . . sex thing . . . in the book – it is . . . um . . . going to be all right for you, isn't it?'

'You mean all right for *you*, I think, dear?'

'Well, perhaps.'

Janice leaned back and smiled. 'Oh yes. Perfectly all right. No problem at all. Your . . . er . . . inventive action was' – she stifled what Rohanne thought might have been a giggle – 'just right. It fits exactly. You and Mr Pfeiffer mustn't worry at all. Sex you will have. *That*, I promise you. Six scenes, evenly distributed, just as you ask, and sensitively handled, of course . . .'

Rohanne wriggled.

The taxi-driver, too, began to show signs of restlessness. Despite the clock going into pleasant profit, it was irritating to have to sit there while two women nattered in the back.

'I should go,' said Rohanne, 'I have a plane to catch to-morrow.'

'Somebody nice waiting for you?'

'Morgan Pfeiffer,' said Rohanne darkly.

'No one else – of a romantic nature?'

'Nope,' said Rohanne positively. She thought about Herbie. 'Well, certainly not a case of *Vous ou Mort*, anyway.'

'In all,' said Janice, 'I've been in love for twenty years. It's what kept me going.'

'And *I*,' said Rohanne cheerily, 'have successfully avoided love, and *that's* what's kept *me* going.'

Janice patted her knee. 'Try it the other way round for a change. Go through the looking-glass. You never know, you might prefer it.'

'I threw a Filofax at my last lover,' said Rohanne, 'the day I came to London. It hit him on the shin.'

'Better there than anywhere else,' said Janice and, with surprising suggestiveness, she winked.

Rohanne decided that the sexy passages were probably safe in her hands, after all. And that, dammit, she thought as Janice got out of the cab, was all that mattered.

*

The Boss Masculine invited the Little Blonde Secretary to dinner.

'You have been such an efficient and charming companion,' he said, 'despite your own troubles.' He let his eyes rest on hers for a moment to give solemn weight to the words, and she blinked her pretty wide eyes in pleased acceptance of the fact. She had indeed been efficient, and she was, she knew, charming, despite Derek's silly behaviour and her resultant troubles. The Boss Masculine was very understanding and kind: '. . . And I should like to thank you properly.'

'That would be very nice,' she said, 'I'll just go and change.'

The Boss Masculine watched her pert little bottom as it stepped into the lift, and it was not only his heart that leapt a little leap. It was like being eighteen all over again. How could he have got himself hooked up with Valerie so young? He *deserved* a bit of fun. He had been faithful for years, and where had that got him but into a bed as cold as a tomb with a wife who was a walking gynaecological text book? 'Try a little tenderness,' the counsellor had said brightly, 'and the hysterectomy could be the beginning of a whole new area of sexual pleasure.' She must be raving mad.

He had only to touch his wife and she froze beside him. And she wanted separate beds. Well – he resisted the urge to reach out and pat the little bottom in front of him – she could have them now and welcome.

He turned to press the button and the Little Blonde Secretary looked up at his shoulders in their dark suit. It was such a pity that he didn't do something about his dandruff, otherwise he would be quite attractive for someone middle-aged. She had a very strong urge to reach up and brush the tell-tale white speckles away for him, but there was another person in the lift, and she didn't think it would be polite in company. You'd have thought, she mused as the lift ascended, that his wife would have done something about it. Taken him in hand. Derek used to have the same problem – he had that sort of skin – and it was so bad that not only did it show all over his clothes but it made quite a mess on the bedroom Wilton. She had been forever hoovering before she discovered Head & Shoulders, which was a very good product. She hoped she could bring it into the conversation sort of casually later.

They parted at their doors.

The Boss Masculine rang his wife. He put on his hang-dog voice, said the conference had gone well, but there was still a lot to do. As he had thought, far too much to be able to come home tomorrow, so it was a very good thing they were booked for another night. To his wife's inquiry about how the Little Blonde Secretary Bird had coped, he said (lowering his voice, looking anxiously at the communicating wall) that she had not done awfully well, that he was feeling a bit put out with her. His wife suggested that he should take the girl out for a meal and try to talk to her about where she had gone wrong. It was a struggle not to laugh. 'If you think so, dear,' he said. 'Perhaps I will.'

The Little Blonde waited for Derek to ring her but she waited in vain. As she dabbed Loulou behind her ears and put a trace in her cleavage, she observed to herself that Derek certainly didn't deserve her. He was supposed to ring at seven each night and here it was, gone half past, and nothing. And he had promised after that horrible night never to go near the pub again. Well, whatever he was doing, it could not be as important as remembering to call her. She had bought him a lovely tie in the Birmingham Bull Ring, and this was all the thanks she got . . .

She gave her hair one last riffle so that it looked just as fluffy and cute as Melanie Griffith's, wet the tip of her finger and ran it over her daintily shaped eyebrows, and smoothed her black velour frock. No dandruff adhering *there*. And when the knock came, she was perfectly ready.

'You look lovely,' he said.

'Thank you,' she replied as they entered the lift. She knew that she did.

Derek was feeling slightly uncomfortable. All right for old Ken to say that if he had promised not to go to the pub, then the pub should come to him, but they had left a helluva mess. Still, as he cleared up the tins and bottles and crisp packets, and took the take-away containers out to the dustbin to hide them at the very bottom, he was feeling quite proud of himself, too. Ken and the others had been impressed by his home improvements, and were especially complimentary about the bathroom – with good reason. Ken understood immediately when he told him about the Vent-Axia and how it had slipped in so perfectly. 'Pity everything doesn't,' he had said, and nudged him with a wink or two. Derek found himself colouring at this. If she knew the half of the sort of things they said to each other, she would – well, it didn't bear thinking what she would do. He was still unclear about what he might or might not have said to Ken in the pub on that awful night, but so far no one had mentioned ankle-holding or anything else indiscreet, so he thought he was all right.

He had showed them the finished nursery. Perfect in every respect except that the blind with the pink, fluffy clouds on it stuck occasionally. But Ken had the answer. 'You just need to adjust the fitting a fraction,' he said, and did it for him. It really did run a treat now.

Then Derek took them into the bedroom to show them the

vanity unit where the door had dropped slightly. Unless you thumped it, it swung open. She had been very critical, saying, quite rightly, that the one in the showroom had stayed shut with just a light push. 'What it needs,' said Ken, 'is taking out and realigning. The whole thing. You've set it in at a slight angle. Mind you, I wouldn't bother, personally.'

But Derek thought that he would. She liked things to be right, as he did himself. And he was working away on that, the following evening, making amends in his head for having bent the truth a little regarding the pub, when he realized that it was a quarter to eight and he had forgotten to ring.

'I'm sorry,' said the receptionist, 'but there is no reply from that room right now.'

Derek left a message. He was going to say that he had rung and would be in all evening if she wanted to ring back. But he had second thoughts, for it implied that he might have been thinking about going out on other occasions. So he settled for simply saying he had rung. And he went back, whistling, to his task of love.

The Little Blonde Secretary Bird was going to be especially charming to the Boss Masculine tonight; at least *he* appreciated her even if Derek didn't. *And* he didn't have sticky-out teeth.

'You don't mind if we dine in the hotel?' he said, touching her lower back ever so slightly to usher her in. He felt a thrill of something long forgotten, and kept his hand there all the way to the little table in the corner. She looked around her at the powder-blue velvet curtains and the flowered wallpaper with its decorative scroll lights. She approved.

'Oh no,' she said, sitting down daintily, 'and the music is lovely.'

'Yes,' he said. 'What is it?'

'James Galway, I think,' she said, flicking out her serviette before the hovering waiter could do it for her. 'Classical. It's the theme from *Doctor Zhivago*.'

He was about to ask her if she had enjoyed the film, but

remembered, in the nick of time, that she had probably been in her pram when it came out.

Ordering from the menu *en Français* was a bit tricky, but he guided her through with little squeezes and pats of her hand. For the starter she chose prawn cocktail, while he settled for soup, deciding to avoid the garlic pâté just in case . . .

They played a little game about the main course, she choosing chicken *without* the garnish, and he, at her suggestion, having the more manly fillet steak.

'You men need building up,' she said smiling, tapping his hand, trying not to look at his shoulders which had begun to go peppery again. Also, she noticed, there was quite a lot of grey dotted about, but not in the distinguished areas of the temples (like in *Towers of Steel*), just all over the place. If she ignored this, then the meal and the surroundings, with the candlelight and the wall-brackets, were not unlike that magazine picture. She gave a little shudder remembering the article about orgasms. She was almost certain that what was going wrong was that she didn't have one, and very probably you couldn't get pregnant unless you did. She drank some of the Riesling and watched him sip his dark red wine, which, she thought, showed great sophistication. He would know all about things like orgasms – being a man of the world, but, of course, she couldn't ask him, a *man*, now could she? But no wonder Derek was getting a bit, well, strung out – they had done it so often recently (apart from that one night which was, of course, the important one) he must be feeling quite bored of it all by now.

She certainly was. An orgasm was probably what was needed. But how? She sipped away at her glass, head on one side, looking prettily bright and not listening to a word he was saying. She wondered if his wife had them. Probably. Everybody in the world – she suddenly felt quite irritable – seemed capable. Why not her?

It was the first time in her life that she had not achieved what she set out to achieve and it made her very cross. Not least when she thought of that ballooning female on the switchboard who had the cheek to confide that *her pregnancy* had happened by mistake.

She ate daintily and both their bottles went down, hers surprisingly quickly. He knew exactly how to behave and was ever so attentive.

He looked at her and thought she was the prettiest, most perfectly formed thing on two legs – and the impression grew as the level of his Burgundy lowered.

She thought he was charming and very kind and so *interested* in everything. And by the time they got to the pudding, she allowed herself the indulgence of Black Forest gateau and cream. She was astonished to hear herself say yes to a helping, and to follow it up with one of her favourite phrases, 'A moment on the lips, a lifetime on the hips,' which he found gratifyingly funny.

She pronounced the gateau 'very nice' with an accompanying giggle she had not expected to give, and even fed him bits from her own plate. Thinking of babies made her stop before she had drunk *all* the Riesling. Drink could be very harmful, and she said this out loud.

'Drink is very bad for babies.'

He looked at her, startled, quickly removed the startlement and nodded sagely, as if she had expounded Plato. He did not know what to say. Eventually he plumped for 'Absolutely', which he delivered with vibrant sincerity.

She was impressed. 'And what do you know about orgasms?' she continued. 'Because I don't think I've ever had one and I really would like some help.'

His own wine having gone, he reached unthinkingly for the remnants of hers and finished it. Whatever happened, he wondered, to the need for an opening gambit like 'My wife doesn't understand me'? For a moment he felt chilled by her directness, for he had quite liked her to be a little shy. Still, you couldn't have everything, and this was as close as he was ever likely to get to a cup running over.

'Derek didn't ring tonight,' she said, and her eyes went swimmy.

'If you were my wife and away with another man I should ring you every hour.'

'Oh,' she said, 'he knows I'm not away with another man. He knows it's only with you.'

If ever he had thought to be honourable, if ever he had thought to leave it all in the realms of fantasy, the thought died at that precise point.

'Let's take a brandy up to my room,' he said. 'Shall we? I've got something there – a gift, a token, by way of a thank-you.'

She smiled. 'And I've got something for *you*,' she said provocatively.

He ignored further thoughts of his being an 'only you' – which was just the sort of thing his wife might have said – and looked at that pert little bottom again wiggling in front of him.

It occurred to him, as they made their way back towards the lift, that he had not had more than three cigarettes all evening. Which was amazing. It also meant that she was going to be good for him, too. Really the whole thing was perfectly, perfectly justifiable, and – he looked at the bottom again – a long time overdue.

'Oh, look,' he said, giving her lower back a much stronger pressure as he ushered her into the room, 'a bottle of champagne and two glasses. It must be a gift from the management.'

'Oh,' she said. 'How nice. Hic!'

He took her arm and led her towards the bed. 'I think we had better open it, don't you?'

'Well,' she said, 'just one glass. Thinking about orgasms! Oh dear,' she giggled. She had meant to say babies, but never mind, the two were rapidly becoming synonymous in her mind, anyway.

'Of course,' he said, smiling wonderingly down at her. 'Now you sit there and tuck your legs up comfortably while I pop the shampoo.' The hics continued. Cautiously he put a very little in both their glasses. It was a fine line to draw between releasing inhibitions and ending up snoring or worse. This he vaguely remembered from his teenage years. Besides, she seemed more or less released from her inhibitions already.

She watched him, marvelling at the deftness of the act, the film-star sound of the eager cork, the fancy bubbles cascading into the long glasses. He handed her one and she sipped. 'Lovely,' she said, and then she looked at the tulip shape in her hand. 'But you'd have thought they'd have given us proper-shaped glasses. Those flat ones are best.'

'Are they?' he said, and sat next to her. 'To you.' He raised his glass.

'Cheers,' she said, and giggled again. 'Honestly, if Derek could see me now . . .' And she burst into tears.

Which, from the point of view of advantage, the Boss Masculine thought pretty damn near perfect. He put down his glass and picked up a package from the bedside table. 'There, there,' he said. 'Look, I think this is the right time to give you this . . .'

She opened the pretty parcel and held up the scrap of lawn and lace. It delighted her – it was romantic, it was feminine and it was tasteful. 'Oh *thank you*,' she said, giving him a resounding kiss on the cheek. 'Thank you, it is the sort of thing I really like. Derek doesn't –' She stopped, drained her glass, and burst into tears again. 'Derek doesn't –'

'Derek doesn't what?' he asked, sliding a little closer on the bed, then kissing her shoulder.

She looked down. From where she sat she could get a really good close-up of the dandruff problem. 'Well,' she said, a little mesmerized by the extent of it, 'Derek is very practical.' She put the hanky to the corner of her eye and dabbed delicately. 'I shall always treasure this,' she said.

He put his arm round her waist.

She dabbed at the other eye and then looked at the lace admiringly. 'Mine isn't nearly so exciting,' she said. 'It's an aid, really.'

'Aid' had an interesting ring about it. He moved his arm up a fraction, towards the warmth of her armpit and other areas. 'Oh, I'm sure it is,' he said, and then, because he was unclear what they were discussing (and he was having a great deal of difficulty concentrating) he added, 'What are you . . . er . . . talking about?'

'Your present.' She sniffed anew. 'It's not half so nice as yours, and you've been so-o-oo' – she mopped another tear – 'kind.'

'I'm sure it's as enchanting as you are,' he said. 'Never mind that now . . .'

As he bent to kiss her again, she looked at his shoulder and had another terrible urge to brush him down. She moved away and stood up, swaying slightly.

'I want you to have it,' she said positively. And picking up her key she tacked across the room, out of the door, and into her own.

While she was gone, he made a hasty visit to the bathroom, squirted some Gold Spot into the further reaches of his mouth and dived back on the bed again in time to look as if he had never moved. He switched off one of the side lights to make the room more . . . intimate. He heard her turn the door handle and looked up expectantly. In she came, a little smile of hesitation on her delectable, freshly pinked lips. She crossed to the bed, sat down near him, removed her hand from behind her adorably feminine back and held out to him her presentation. Her token of esteem, her favour, her emblem of regard.

He stared.

He swallowed.

His mouth became a desert.

His stomach filled with ice.

She continued to smile her pretty little smile, pressing the gift into his hand.

'Take it,' she said, 'I sent off for it from one of my magazines.' The pretty little smile stretched like pink elastic. 'I think it is just what you need.'

The book she held out had a title, *Men: The Middle Years – A Maintenance Guide.*

He took it, zombie-like, and stared anew. 'Oh, thank you,' he said.

'Don't mention it,' she replied. 'And look . . .' She tapped a small bottle, which was attached to the cover. 'Free gift . . .'

He stared.

He was staring at a miniature bottle of Head & Shoulders shampoo.

'I think you will find,' she said happily, 'that will do the trick.' She lowered her voice discreetly. 'And there are things on the market for grey hairs, too . . .'

Bloody little tartlet, he thought, as redness rose angrily within him, but before he could tell her to leave she had reached the door and was peeping round it coyly on her way out. She gave a little wave of her hand and a rallying eye-screw of compassion. 'Enjoy!' she said. And, forgetting all about orgasms, she went.

*

Janice, travelling in the lift with no further psychological difficulties, entered her apartment. The machine sat there waiting. She ran a finger over it, remembering her characters for *Phoenix Rising*. She must release them soon. She had a compulsive urge to feed Rohanne Bulbecker into the software, too. But she did not. She felt that, perhaps, she did not need to.

Rohanne looked out at the night view of London for one last time. She was tired and glad, more than she had realized, to be going home. Mission accomplished, she told herself, always mission accomplished. She kicked off her shoes. On the small table near by was a tray, two glasses, a bottle of champagne in a cooler and a card. She opened the envelope and read, 'All my love as usual, Horace.'

Horace? *Horace?* Despite the many men in her life, she couldn't remember one of those. She looked at the envelope. Wrong room number. In her current state it would be far less wearying to take the thing next door herself rather than summon the fuss of room service. She picked up the tray, stepped into the corridor, and knocked at the suite next door. An elderly man in a silk dressing-gown, closely accompanied by an elderly woman in pink quilting with daisies, peered out from the door.

'Horace?' said Rohanne, extending the tray which he took. 'It came to the wrong room.'

'We were just wondering,' he said. 'Thank you so much . . .'

'Don't mention it,' said Rohanne, 'And have a nice . . .' She

246

was about to say 'day', but smiled and said, 'Have a nice night,' instead.

All of seventy, she said to herself, seventy if they were a day. And she shook her head. But she lay motionless on her bed and thinking for a long, long while.

Chapter Twenty-two

ERICA agreed with Gretchen that the picture was a bit basic. 'Why,' she said, 'you can only just tell where the sea ends and the sky begins. I'd chuck it if I was you.'

'I can't do that,' said Gretchen, 'it was given to me. And I haven't had many presents in my life.'

'The mean old cow,' said Erica.

'Please,' said Gretchen. 'You must not speak ill of the dead.'

'Balls,' said Erica.

Gretchen winced. Sometimes she could be a *mite* rough in her ways . . .

*

'One of the things I always thought about the ministry,' said Arthur, 'was that, like dentistry or doctoring, it is something that can be done anywhere in the world. China, India, Eastern Europe.'

'To see China,' she said, her blue eyes going dreamy.

Arthur smiled. 'We could stop off in Paris on the way,' he said, dreaming also, suddenly remembering their honeymoon. Three days in a small hotel near the Gare du Nord, lunching on a baguette and chocolate on the coldly beautiful steps of Sacre Coeur. 'There's a lot of work to be done in those places.'

'Where?' She deliberately misunderstood. 'Paris?'

He laughed. 'Even there, I dare say.'

'Claw them back from their popish ways?'

'That's a bit old-fashioned now that Canterbury and Rome exchange Christmas cards.'

She laughed, too. 'Isn't that heretic?'

'Very probably.'

'London would be nice,' she said, dreamy again, smoothing and resmoothing the tablecloth she was folding. 'London is more or less like a Third World place. Charity colder than marble there. Perhaps you should persuade them to send us to that particular outpost.'

'Do you miss it that badly?'

'I don't miss it at all,' she said quickly. 'I told you when we came here. I wanted to get far away and this' – she began gathering up the lunch things jerkily, spilling the salt, dropping a spoon – 'is perfect.' She looked up at him. She was on her knees picking up the spoon. 'Oh, but I forgot – the only *perfect* thing is God. Sorry.' She stood up.

He put his hand on her arm before she could turn away. 'So what is the flaw in all this perfection up here?'

She wanted to say, 'You, Arthur,' but stopped herself. Instead, she threw back her head and laughed.

He watched her throat move, wanting to kiss it, remembering film posters of his youth – Cary Grant or Rock Hudson bending over similarly tantalizing but willing throats. 'Well?' he asked mildly. 'Share the joke.'

'Oh, Arthur, Arthur.' She was shaking now, voice and body strung out with tension. 'What other flaw could there be up here but the damnation *tea-urn*, of course? What else?'

Her laugh was shrill in the room.

He winced. He stood up. His usually mild eyes were not amiable. 'The joke,' he said, 'is wearing a bit thin.'

She peered at him, her blue eyes sparkling with feverish merriment. She could see his distress, felt galvanized by it.

'Well, *I* like the joke,' she said. 'And I'd like to keep it going on and on for ever. *My* tea-urn,' she said suddenly, like a child. Her eyes blazed, delphiniums on fire.

He was afraid of the anger, the passion that radiated from her like a madness. He calmed himself and went to her, putting his hand on her shoulder, a gesture as if he were casting out devils. He said, 'But that's all in the past now, isn't it?' Beneath his hand her shoulder felt thinner. It was as if she were being eaten from within. 'You dealt with that last time you went to London.'

'Yes, yes,' she said gaily, moving away from him, scrunching the tablecloth anyhow into the sideboard. 'Unless it goes wrong, of course,' she said defiantly, 'and I have to take it back.'

'It won't,' he said positively. 'That one is built to last.'

She was crying. She had turned her back, fiddling with the cruet on the sideboard, running her finger up and down, up and down the bevelled edge of the oak. She made no noise, gave no sign, but he knew that she was. He put his arms round her, turned her to him. Tears were dripping from her chin, flowing down the lines around her mouth. They stood close but their bodies scarcely touched. She was aloof, alone, held in a private world.

'You're upset,' he said. 'Come and lie down for a while.'

She shook her head.

He kept his arms there this time, positive, insistent.

'You are already late for your class,' she said. 'You had better go.'

'Some things are more important than unwilling ten-year-olds understanding St Paul. I want you to lie with me now.' He touched her breast lightly, closing his eyes at the pleasure of its weight and its warmth.

She remembered the bruise that had been there.

When he opened his eyes, he knew she had flinched at his touch and it shamed him. 'Nothing will go wrong with that tea-urn,' he said firmly. 'God will protect it.' He walked away.

'Oh, will he?' she muttered feverishly. 'Oh, *will* he?'

She picked up the telephone and dialled the headscarfed one, she of the polished brasses. 'I think,' she said, 'it is time we got the Guides to do a little tea for the old folks.'

She of the polished brasses agreed.

She put down the phone and went to bathe her eyes before the Crèche Committee arrived for morning coffee.

There were twenty-three of them from Kenley Grange. She watched them as they bit into sausage rolls, the slack skin of their faces moving like colourless rubber as they chewed, their wrinkled lips hooking over the cups as they sucked their tea. She felt her own cheeks and throat, already it was there, the same dropping, the same sagging, beginning, and no going back. Arthur was talking to them, making them laugh. The sun shining down showed that his hair was thinning, she could see the scalp. Age. It was coming to them both and, until now, she had thought she could accept it. Up here it was acceptable, up here she had almost thought to welcome it. Expected. Time past, time passing, the earth and the seasons close to them.

Not like London. London was different. In London you could hold on, stop the process, like dropping an aspirin in a bowl of flowers, arrest it for a while at least. Of course not for ever – but for a *while*. She wanted, *needed* to go back there. She wanted the key to the garden of love again. Once had not been nearly enough. She remembered more and more vividly, surprised at how the details filled out with time, like a tapestry which the more studied has the more to reveal. Every nuance, every word of pleasure he had uttered that last time she relived, until she was convinced that he, too, must be pining, regretful, longing to see her, feel her, bury himself in her once more. She looked at the table loaded with thick china cups, jugs of milk, plates of baking and the monster – settled like some toad, malevolent, oppressing the surrounding crockery, shining in its newness. She hated it.

They were complimenting her on the tea. Yes, she had baked everything herself. Yes, the jam was her own. Yes, the scones. *Yes, yes, yes* to everything. *Yes* even to the bloody tea in their cups.

'My wife,' said Arthur, 'went hunting the best tea-urn in London. A little bit of pride there, perhaps?' He turned to her. 'Like Lady Fee to Westminster?' He turned to the tea-drinkers as if to include them in the joke. He had been reading Langland to them on his visits. His reading voice was very good; he had acted at Cambridge. 'Like Reason, you remember? Who says, "It is no use asking *me* to have mercy until Lords and Ladies have learned to love the truth."'

'Very true, vicar,' said an old man with a whiskery mouth.

'Yes,' said Arthur, looking at her. 'Very true.'

She thrust a cake plate at the old man, hard up against his chest so that he winced. Then she held it out to Arthur.

'Just tea,' he said. He gave her his cup and she went to fill it, stroking the toad as she milked it, thinking it was the keeper of her secret, afraid somewhere inside that she had gone mad.

When she came back, he continued as if he had waited for her.

'And Lady Peacock, says Reason, must cast her finery off and lock her furs and gewgaws away in her clothes chest.' He raised a finger. 'But even though she does that, and even though the clergy feed the poor, though the government serves the public good, though St James is sought in pilgrimage to Compostela – still there will be no pity until Fee is thrown out and Reason and Conscience replace her . . .'

'Amen,' said one of the old women nervously. It was all a touch too evangelical for her.

'Which, of course, they do,' Alice said, pushing a strand of red-gold hair from her forehead, looking at her husband.

'Which, of course, they do,' he agreed.

They stared at each other, forgetting, for a moment, the company they kept.

'Would you like it in Middle English?' he asked.

'Not at the moment,' she said.

'Not ready for it yet?'

'How does it end?'

'Everybody behaves themselves as they should. With kindness, dignity, honesty and love. And the King, counselled by Reason and Conscience, if I remember . . .'

Arthur, she thought, you are playing with me.

'. . . The King grants it will continue that way. "God forbid that we should fail!" he says. "Let us live together for the rest of our lives . . ."'

'Hallelujah,' said the nervous old lady.

'Hallelujah indeed, Mrs Bell. Would you like more tea?' He took the cup. 'And you?' he asked her.

'How can I have more,' she said, feeling like Looking-Glass Alice, 'when I haven't had any yet?'

'No?' he said. 'I'm sorry. I thought that you had.'

She went to take Mrs Bell's cup from him. He held it, squeezing finger and thumb tightly around the thick white china.

'How's the tea-urn?' he asked. 'Functioning normally?'

'For the moment,' she said defiantly.

'Good,' he said. 'Because if it goes wrong, it will be my cross to bear to take it to London this time.'

'Nonsense,' she said. '*If* it goes wrong, I shall take it myself.'

The old man with whiskers said, 'We've got plenty as can mend it up here and needing work.'

'Ah,' said Arthur. 'I don't think that is really the point. Do you?'

She went to refill the cup. The tea ran perfectly, and when she turned the handle it ceased to flow, driplessly . . . Very well, she thought, if I cannot go with you, then I shall go without you. But go I shall.

As she walked among the nodding heads, offering tea, holding out cakes, she knew suddenly, was certain, convinced, that he, the other, would like the surprise. She wanted to see his eyes light up at the unexpected sight of her, his delight at her sudden availability. She could even check first that his wife was at home in the constituency and not with him in London. He would have nothing to fear from her surprise. She would explain how clandestinely clever she had been. They could go back to the Ritz and there would be one more night. That was, she told herself, all she required to get her through. Away from Arthur reason would prevail. He knew nothing, she was merely jumpy, suspicious, bad conscience. She would return to Cockermouth again afterwards, and never leave it. By the time she returned, she would have thought of a good excuse for her sudden departure. The tea-urn, working magnificently as Arthur remarked, no longer held any hope. She would invent something else. He, the other, would help her do so – he had always been good at deceits. She would go the day after tomorrow. Why wait? Just once, once more, she pleaded with herself. Once more before she too was set for decay.

From the train the early-morning landscape was misty, the air fresh. She snuggled into her seat, clutching her coat around her as if it were his arms. The train's rhythm was a refrain of expectancy that beat out its miles in her head. She smelled coffee but could not drink and told herself that they could have coffee later, or tea, or champagne or *anything* – there was no end to what they could have together *later* . . .

In Cockermouth Arthur slid his letter into an envelope, sealed it and got up from the table. He looked out into the dark night, still and silent, waiting for the rages of winter to stir it up. He damped down the flames, put a guard in front of the fire, and went upstairs. In their bedroom he placed her secret and his on her pillow. The powder compact next to the letter he had received from Guildford – from where the pilgrims once set out, he thought to himself ironically. Beside these he opened his *Piers the Ploughman* at the page about Lady Fee at Westminster. It was poetic, after all. Then he retired to the spare bedroom, which was cold and damp, the bed like a tomb, the sheet a shroud. Tomorrow he would post the letter to his bishop.

For a while he lay awake thinking about the future. Perhaps China was the soft option? Who could know? He heard Piers's voice: 'I have never found any life that suited me, except in these long, clerical clothes. If I'm to earn a living, I must earn it by doing the job I've learned best, for it is written, "Let every man abide in the same calling wherein he was called."' Ye are bought with a price. Be not ye the servants of men . . .

He wondered if, after her journey's end, she would wish to come, too. And if so, what her price to him would be . . .

*

Janice Gentle crossed to the kitchen and swung her carrier bags up on to the table. What did it matter if the man in the corner

254

shop thought of her as a congenital idiot? She had finally achieved it – given her list of requirements and stood waiting for it to be fulfilled in absolute silence. Like a dentist probing for a nerve, he had rattled through a whole series of potential galvanizers, but she had remained mute. If the weather had cooled, so be it. If the price of cheese had soared, what good was comment? If the youth of today were ignorant and loutish, why remark it? In the end he had given way and finished serving her in silence, and only when she had paid and was half out of the shop did she soften enough to turn and say, 'It will probably rain tomorrow,' and wait for him to respond with, 'Garden could do with it,' before moving off swiftly lest he tried to take it any further with his runner beans and plagues of blackfly.

Janice felt liberated. Kindness made her regret the passing of Sylvia Perth, despite her sense of betrayal. But liberation was a pleasure. It was as if she had been reborn. And now – the ritual of the food stores in place – she could begin as a true creator, to create alone.

She smiled as she pinched the warm, doughy bread between her fingers. And she remembered, glad now that it was only a memory, how Sylvia's eyes would slit like a cat's, screwing themselves up against the cigarette smoke, and how she would say that awful opening sentence of hers, 'Well, actually, Janice, I think perhaps just *one* more should do it . . .' This time Janice had the feeling that this would be so.

Butter gleamed in a dish, the bread filled the kitchen with its sensual aroma. She dipped her knife into the honeypot and spread thickly. She knew exactly what she was going to write. She would invent nothing and had only to extemporize. Her last, her greatest, her *magnum opus* indeed. She crossed to the machine. Once begun, she must cast out those souls who sheltered within. She had no more need of them; soon they would have to wander and fend for themselves.

*

The Boss Masculine surprised his wife by producing two tickets for a short break in Tenerife, leaving almost immediately. To her protestations that she was unsure if her abdominal muscles were up to flying, he said, rather shortly, 'I'm not asking you to bloody well flap your wings,' and then immediately apologized. He flapped his own arms in embarrassment. 'It's what the doctor ordered,' he said firmly and began packing the suitcase.

She was flustered into submission, having expected him to be in Birmingham for longer, and wide-eyed with acquiescence. He seemed angry, deeply angry, and for once he did not accuse her of being the cause. She felt much better for that; it was a relief to have the guilt lifted from her for a time, like having a rock unstrapped from her back. She found herself standing quite straight, helping him with the packing, dealing with all the last-minute arrangements. She did not utter one word of criticism as she watched carefully ironed shirts squashed in anyhow and her own insubstantial wardrobe rolled up beside them. There would always be an iron somewhere. She smiled to herself, absent-mindedly brushing at his shoulders in a gesture so familiar that he did not even notice it any more. There always *was* an iron somewhere. She bet that even if they travelled to the ends of the earth they would find an iron waiting for them. You couldn't get away from ironing anywhere in the world. Wherever you went, you would always find your *bête noire* just behind. Hers was ironing. It could be worse.

'Who is looking after the office?' she asked.

'That silly bitch I call a secretary,' he answered, flinging in his shaving gear. 'Do you know what she did?'

'What did she do?' His wife surreptitiously refolded her Angela Gore.

'Hah!' he said, immediately unfolding it again and tucking it in haphazardly. 'Got drunk, gave me a book on my slow disintegration, a hint on hair tinting and a miniature bottle of dandruff shampoo!' He made a mincing little gesture and mimicked the Little Blonde's diction. 'Because that's what *her Derek* uses . . .'

His wife kept her smile to herself. Everyone has their supreme area of sensitivity, the *verboten* . . .

'And,' he continued, still punishing the skirt, 'then she had the nerve to say I ought to stop smoking because it was staining my teeth and fingers!'

. . . And some have two, she thought.

'*And* she was nothing but a tease,' he said. 'Do you know she talked non-stop about sex? Orgasms and everything. I mean, I ask you . . .'

'Difficult for you,' said his wife.

You don't know how difficult, given the state of *our* marriage, he thought, but for once he forbore to say such a thing. 'I ought to sack her.'

'You can't.'

'I know,' he said, straightening up and smiling at her dangerously. 'But I can make it hell for her.'

'In what way?' She was inching towards the open suitcase, smoothing the skirt again, closing the lid so that it could lie undisturbed at last.

'Make it impossible for her to stay.'

'How?' She clicked the latch and sighed with relief.

'Demote her.' He nodded to himself with pleasurable conviction.

'To what?'

'Well, the girl on the switchboard is leaving to have a baby. I'll put her on that.'

'Can you? What about tribunals?'

'Same pay. They can't do anything. And she'll go. No one with any sensitivity would stay after that.'

'Who'll replace her?'

He shrugged. 'Doesn't matter as long as she's efficient.'

'Or he?'

He smiled. 'Perhaps.'

'No more Little Blonde Secretary Birds?' She was looking at him very hard.

He raised both hands in a gesture of sincerity. 'Honestly, lovey' – he looked up towards heaven – 'I never even *thought* about it.'

'I believe you,' she said. 'And now I'm going to have a bit of a pamper in the bath.'

'We haven't got long.'

'Long enough for me to have a soak and wash my hair.' She giggled like a schoolgirl as she closed the door. 'Tenerife! Well, well. And I might even pluck my eyebrows.' What did his being economical with the truth matter? she thought, as she ran the water. He hadn't called her 'lovey' for years.

They flew out that afternoon. He would not let her carry any of the luggage, apart from her handbag and some magazines, and remained calm and good-humoured, save for one moment when an American girl walked across the path of his trolley causing him to swerve. There might have been a row – always a nasty way to begin a holiday – for initially the American girl said, 'Are you *blind* or something?' very aggressively, but just as the Boss Masculine was about to make an acid retort, the girl softened, put up her hand (shame about the bitten nails, thought the Boss Masculine's wife) and said, 'I apologize. It was my fault. Sorry.' To which the Boss Masculine, also changing tack, declared it was entirely due to him and he hoped he had not hurt her in any way.

The Boss Masculine's wife looked to see if there was some sparkle of flirtatiousness behind all this but could detect none. Just two people being polite. She tucked her hand into the crook of his arm but did not lean on him heavily as once she would have done. Her hand rested there lightly – a connection rather than crutch – and together they wheeled the trolley along the walkway. She asked him more about Birmingham. He shrugged. 'I didn't arrange for us to go on holiday to discuss business.' This so unnerved her that she felt almost girlish, wondering what they could talk about instead. He asked her if the walking was tiring her and how her muscles felt. She told him that *she* had not come on holiday to discuss her medical condition. This surprised them both and they continued along the walkway in pleasant silence.

When Derek met the Little Blonde Secretary Bird at the station, she was looking very pale and very tight-mouthed. 'I ate something that upset me,' she said. 'And he had to get home to his wife, who is not well.'

'If you want my opinion,' said Derek, with unaccustomed assertiveness, 'I think it's a cheek. He shouldn't have left you on your own like that.'

'He trusts me, Derek.'

'I've a good mind to go and see him about it.'

'You can't,' she said. 'He's taking her away.' She brightened. 'And leaving me in charge. He thinks very highly of me, Derek.'

'Funny way of showing it,' he said, helping her into the car.

'Don't mutter, please,' she said.

At home she unpacked. She took out the scrap of lawn and lace and waved it under Derek's nose. 'He gave me this,' she said. 'He's a real gentleman. There I was in tears . . .'

'Tears?' Derek looked surprised. 'Why?'

She looked at him pityingly. 'If you don't know, Derek, then I'm not telling you.' She held up the hanky and fluttered it again. 'It's ever such a romantic thing to give a woman.'

'Is it?' said Derek. He didn't think Ken would think so. He didn't think *he* thought so. It was all a mystery to him, this romance business. He used to buy his Auntie Megan hankies for Christmas, with an *M* embroidered on the corner. He hoped she hadn't misconstrued it . . .

'I'll make you a nice hot mug of tea,' he said.

'Cup, Derek,' she said, and, looking at the lacy lawn, she sighed. 'Tea in a *cup*. Remember?'

Pausing at the bedroom door, he turned and, looking pinkly pleased, he added, 'You haven't noticed.'

'Noticed what?' she said crisply.

'Behind you.'

She felt irritated. Her headache had not entirely gone despite the lapse of time. It must certainly have been the prawns. 'Hmm?' she asked again sharply.

'*Behind you.*'

'Derek, I am in no mood to play at pantomimes!'

'The door.'

She turned round, puzzled.

'I've fixed the door.'

259

She gave it a little push. It stayed shut.

'Well done, Derek,' she said.

He felt it was considerably more 'well done' than that stupid bit of cotton she'd dangled under his nose. 'I had to take the whole thing out.' He said. 'All of it.' He waited for her accolade.

'Talking of taking things out, Derek,' she said, 'we'd better have that awful Vent-Axia out this weekend, too. I'm sure that doesn't help the atmosphere . . .'

His pinkness turned to red. He very nearly shouted. 'But that's exactly what it *does* do,' he said. 'Without it the atmosphere would be terrible in there. Don't you understand, woman?' He was raising and lowering his arms at his side like a feeble chicken. 'If we didn't have that Vent-Axia, there'd be all *sorts* of things trapped. Steam, smells . . .'

'*Derek*,' she said warningly. 'Besides, I am not talking about that sort of atmosphere. I'm talking about setting the mood. You should have seen the restaurant in the hotel. They knew how to set the mood with atmosphere, all right.'

'And poison you,' he said huffily.

'Derek, that was unfortunate. But the setting was very romantic. And it didn't have . . .' – she began snapping, the throbbing returning – 'it didn't have a whining *monster* stuck in the wall.'

'Oh, *didn't* it?'

'Oh and also' – she fished about in her bag, taking out a small card chart – 'this weekend . . . um . . .' She ran a finger down the lines. 'It's an *important* one. All right.' She snapped her bag shut, turned to the door, but he had gone.

There was a sudden crashing sound from the bathroom. She froze, card in hand. He was *so* clumsy. She waited for his apologetic cry, which did not come. Very well, she thought, *I'm* not going to ask. But suddenly, remembering the card, she put her hand to her mouth. Supposing he had damaged something – of an important *physical* nature. She rushed to the bathroom and pushed open the door. He stood there, Vent-Axia in his hands, and without a further sound threw it down on to the black and white diamond tiles. He drew his lips back over his teeth in a curl of scorn, said, 'Happy now?' and went out. He was rather pleased at the last picture he had of her, with her pretty little pink mouth in the shape of a perfect O.

By the time they were speaking again, which in reality was by the time she was speaking to him, ovulation had ceased and the Boss Masculine had returned. Interviews were taking place for the switchboard girl's replacement. The Little Blonde Secretary Bird found it odd that she was not involved in the decision about replacing such a lowly minion but thought it was probably kindness, the sharing of burdens at this critical emotional time in her life.

Apparently the person had been engaged, but she knew no more than that. Time would tell. She was quite looking forward to it. She organized the whip-round in the office and bought the mother-to-be a pretty plastic changing mat for the baby and a boxed selection of beauty aids and bathtime pamperers for herself. The mother-to-be left clutching these to her extraordinary belly and the Little Blonde Secretary began to look forward, with interest, to Monday morning.

Derek gave an even louder whoop of pleasure than the whoop he had given when the now defunct Vent-Axia slipped into place. 'Are you quite sure?' he asked the man on the telephone.

The man on the telephone said that he was.

'And the new rules begin from when?'

The man on the telephone said, 'Next Monday. You can collect the new specification from the Town Hall then.'

Derek felt as if he were floating on air. If his wife had been there, he would certainly have kissed her – if not more. He couldn't wait until Monday to confirm the truth. The Borough Council had reduced the ceiling height for loft conversions. He would be able to add one to their house after all! And that was the first really cheering thing that had happened to him for ages. She would be over the moon when he told her. Life would get back to normal again – him doing home improvements and her being encouraging. Teamwork – that was what marriage was about. Probably better that she didn't get in the family way yet – though he wouldn't actually say that to *her* ... He wouldn't mention anything until next Monday night, when he definitely knew, had the paperwork in his hand. He didn't mind half so much about the Vent-Axia now he had all this to look forward to.

*

Dermot Poll was finding life very dull now that Deirdre had gone teetotal, eschewed his bed and refused to fight any more. As he said to her, pleadingly, 'What else is there?'

But Deirdre was not to be moved. She had taken to crocheting in the evening, perched on a high bar stool, chatting to the customers, sipping blackcurrant cordial and soda.

The only little excitement recently was a telephone call from England in which a Miss O'Dowd inquired the whereabouts of Mr Dermot Poll. It was Deirdre who had taken it and who had said, smooth as a spoonful, that she had once known a man of that name but that he had gone away a long time since. Whatever the reason for Miss O'Dowd's inquiry that particular pot was best left unstirred.

Chapter Twenty-three

Erica von Hyatt was amenable to everything. In the first days of late summer and autumn she had gathered the flowers, gathered the fruits and learned all that Gretchen O'Dowd could teach her about the art of floristry and basket-arranging. But now the garden and the hothouse were empty and damp and cold. They spent each day and each evening alone together. And Erica von Hyatt was feeling extremely constrained.

But she remained amenable. Soon they would be on the road again and that was a freedom to be savoured. In the meantime she behaved herself, biding her time. The balance of comfort and confinement was equal. Everything was fine, providing she knew it was not for ever. So she said yes to walks, she said yes to television, she said yes to cucumber sandwiches. Everything was lovely, nothing was too much trouble. They slept together, snuggled up tight in the large, snowy bed, and, even there, Erica von Hyatt said yes to everything.

'Will it always be like this?' Gretchen asked Erica one evening as they sat in the winking firelight.

'For as long as you want it to be,' said Erica von Hyatt positively.

Gretchen O'Dowd was puzzled. Somehow the answer was not as pleasing as it should have been. 'What do *you* want it to be?' she asked.

'Whatever you do,' said Erica, 'of course.'

'Do you love me?'

'Have I given you any reason to doubt it?'

Gretchen felt uneasy. She, too, began counting the days to

their journey to Skibbereen. All this acquiescence was becoming rather tedious. Sometimes they were so undemanding of each other that they ended up doing nothing.

'Which way do you want to walk?'
  'I don't mind. Whichever way *you* do.'
  'No. You choose.'
  'I don't mind a bit.'
  'Perhaps we should just go home?'
  'Fine.'
  'Would you prefer soup or a sandwich?'
  'Whichever you're having.'
  'Either is available.'
  'I'll have the same as you.'
  'I don't think I'll have anything.'
  'Fine.'
  'Is there anything you would prefer?'
  'No.'
  'Can I improve in any way?'
  'Oh no, it's all lovely.'
  'Which bit do you like best?'
  'All of it.'
  'Do you like me to do this?'
  'Ooh yes.'
  'Or do you prefer that?'
  'Ooh yes.'
  'Or this?'
  'That's just as good.'
  'Don't you have a preference?'
  'Oh no. It's all just wonderful.'
  'Do you want to go on?'
  'Do you?'
  'I'm asking you?'
  'Whatever you want.'
  'Maybe I'm sleepy.'

'Me too.'
'Good-night.'

*

Sometimes Gretchen O'Dowd would catch Erica von Hyatt unawares. She would be staring into space, or out of a window, and there would be about her posture an aura of unease, and in her eyes a faraway look as if she, and only she, could see what was on the horizon. If asked what was the matter, she said, 'Nothing.' If asked what she was thinking, she said, 'Nothing.' And always with that broad, amenable smile. Gretchen O'Dowd had once seen a programme about Egyptian and Grecian mythology – not part of her course, but she had watched it all the same, finding the androgynous nature of so many of the deities encouraging. She had been particularly interested in the Sphinx and felt rather sorry for it when its secret, its ultimate truth, was discovered and it was duty-bound to destroy itself. That seemed rather unfair. Yet the Sphinx did look a little self-satisfied – that smile was the sort of unbreachable smile that made you want to punch it on the nose. Gretchen occasionally, and with surprise, found herself looking at Erica von Hyatt's similarly Sphinxian smile in the same way, with her fist twitching involuntarily.

They were not seriously dashed by the disappointing response from Skibbereen. Erica's worldly wisdom was convincing. '*I* wouldn't admit to being me over the telephone. So why should anybody else? It'll be different when we get there. You'll see.'

Whether it would or whether it wouldn't, Erica von Hyatt was not going to lose the opportunity of getting back on the road. Despite this slavish love, she was bored out of her beautiful head. It was very hard being somebody's dream. You lost sight of your own. For a while the combination of Jack Daniel's and milk had soothed the path of the tedium, but Gretchen O'Dowd, easy in all other matters, had frowned upon the indulgence. And Erica, apparently, obliged.

'Don't you miss your Jack Daniel's?' Gretchen asked once in a while.

'Oh no,' said Erica happily. 'I'm fine with orange juice or tea, the same as you.'

'Sure?'

'Sure.'

'Fine.'

Only later, when the couple were far away and over the Irish Sea, did the removal men pull out a tinkling box from the depths of the conservatory and find it filled to the brim with miniature Jack Daniel's bottles. It was odd, they remarked to themselves, what some people treasured.

*

Janice wrote as if a fever were upon her. The words tumbled over themselves, sentences flowed, and she knew, instinctively, it was good. There was magic in her finger-ends, sorcery in her brain, and she could hear, from time to time, goading her to write more quickly, more richly, the voice of Sylvia Perth – synthetic, detached – saying, 'Not a very *nice* story, is it, dear?' It was such a profound experience that Janice could smell the cigarette smoke ribboning around the room.

Janice agreed that it was not a very nice story at all. 'Not all stories are,' she said to the pervasive Sylvia. And wrinkling her nose at the unwelcome spirit and its pollution, she looked up the definition of 'nice' in the *Shorter Oxford* and found its root to be the Latin *nescius*, meaning 'ignorant', 'without truth'. It was the understanding of the word that Christine de Pisan would have known and fitted rather well. In which case, she thought, as she dipped into the box of fondant creams at her side, it was fair to say that this, her latest, her last, and by far her best book was absolutely, one hundred per cent, not *nice* at all.

Chapter Twenty-four

MORGAN Pfeiffer, looking down, saw how casually the passers-by avoided the street sitters, as once, in more innocent days, they might have avoided ladders. Hands that shook and rattled plastic cups were invisible and soundless. Aggressive begging was now an indictable offence. Bad use of resources, thought Morgan Pfeiffer, bad use of resources. He moved away from the window, tapping the unlit end of his cigar against his teeth. It did no harm at all to observe the sufferings of those less fortunate than yourself when bad fortune hit you. He turned and smiled across the room.

'It is a compromise we have to accept,' he said. 'Nothing can be done.'

Enrico Stoat slipped his medallion into his mouth, an unconscious sign of inner turmoil. 'Everything hinges on her coming over here. If not now, when the book comes out. How can I promote it without the lady in person?'

Morgan Pfeiffer shrugged. 'You may not have to. Wait until the manuscript is delivered. She will feel differently about it all then. Writers get funny sometimes. Once a book is finished they usually blossom again. Bide your time.'

'No photograph for the jacket even? That's not compromise, it's breach of contract.'

Rohanne stood up. 'I have checked,' she said, 'and it isn't. The only breach of contract will be if she doesn't deliver the manuscript, or if the manuscript doesn't conform to our . . .' – she paused – 'To *your* specific requirements. And it will. I can assure you of that.' She picked up her briefcase.

'But we don't even have an address? We can't call her?'

'Until it is finished, I suggest we leave Miss Gentle in peace.

Anything you need to discuss can be done through me. Now, I have a great deal to catch up on . . .' She held out her hand and shook Morgan Pfeiffer's. 'Mission accomplished,' she said, giving him a bright smile. 'And I can assure you that Janice Gentle is absolutely enthusiastic about the whole idea. I know she will give you exactly what you want.' She smiled at Enrico Stoat. 'She is a very beautiful lady.' Stoat sighed with depressed fury. 'And now, if you will excuse me . . .' And she was gone.

Morgan Pfeiffer thought. He tapped his teeth with the cigar again. He longed to light it, but Mrs Pfeiffer, deceased, had always said not before noon. Gentlemen did not smoke cigars before noon, just as real ladies did not eat candy until lunch was cleared. You'd have thought, he conjectured, that given Mrs Pfeiffer *was* deceased, he could at least indulge himself over things like the morning cigar. But he could not. Somehow it still held good. He returned his thoughts to the business in hand.

'We could have suspected it, Stoat,' he said. 'After all, she is known to be a recluse, and she has never used a picture on her jackets before . . .'

'But neither has she written a sexy book before!' Stoat was so exasperated he nearly choked on his medallion. 'Not even a *Polaroid*.'

'Turn her into a mystery woman,' advised Morgan Pfeiffer. 'For the time being, anyway.'

'That just about sums it all up,' said Stoat, and the Rolex on his wrist went ping.

'Ah,' said Morgan Pfeiffer, much satisfied, 'noon at last.' And he sucked on the flame and sighed. 'You go, Stoat, and start all over again. Hell, man, it's what I pay you for.'

After he had gone, Morgan Pfeiffer went to his desk. He sat and stared at the photograph. Mrs Morgan Pfeiffer smiled cheerfully back at him and he could almost smell her fragrance in the room – a commingling of chocolate and roses and the sweet smell of cachou violets on her breath. Her very skin, warm, rich layer upon layer of it, had given off an odour of sweet delight. Something to sink your teeth into. That was what he needed, all right. He was beginning to feel as if the stuffing had gone out of him. He was lonely. He should have been forcible, cogent, as vigorous with the Bulbecker woman as Stoat had tried to be, but somehow his spirit had dried. He touched the outline of Mrs Morgan Pfeiffer deceased's solid shoulder but all he felt was the glass that divided finger from photo. Nothing. He could look for nothing more there. In which case – he stood up, went back to the window – it was merely business as usual.

*

Gretchen O'Dowd had finished knitting and she was very pleased with the result. Both the sweaters came from a one-size pattern and were large enough to fit either of them and she had chosen the colours very carefully; both would suit either. She pressed them carefully with a warm iron and a clean damp tea towel and took them into the sitting-room, where Erica von Hyatt was eating crisps. The cucumber sandwiches had long since been abandoned for snack pizzas and packets of nibbles, and freshly squeezed orange juice or tea from the Georgian silver pot made way for Diet Pepsi in cans. Nor had the dreamed-of dog material-ized. Gretchen favoured a labrador, and Erica said that she didn't mind what dog they had so long as she didn't have to *eat* this one, hah hah (there was sometimes, especially towards evening, a coarseness about Erica's conversation), but somehow Gretchen had still not got round to buying it. She was impatient to begin their travelling, for she thought that once they were free of the house and free of the past, then, as she put it, 'Life would begin beautifully anew.'

Despite the crisps, the cans and the television game show, Gretchen was caught yet again by the sight of this beauty before her. Erica lay across the couch and looked much as she had when first they met, with her streaming golden hair, her pink, half-smiling mouth and robe with silver tassels. But this time there was not trace of milk around the sleepy lips, only salt crumbs and the gleam of Pepsi froth. Gretchen advanced, stood before her, worshipped anew. Gifts to the shrine of beauty. It worked every single blessed time. No matter how disillusioned Gretchen got, Erica would suddenly come over all beautiful again and that was that. Like now. How could she be cross with a vision such as this?

She knelt and laid the sweaters one, two, across Erica von Hyatt's knees. Dutifully Erica tore her gaze away from the screen ('C'mon, Billy, give us a clue.') and looked at the offerings.

'Lovely,' she said, 'really nice.' She darted a quick look at the screen. 'Smashing.'

'Which one would you like?' asked Gretchen. Erica looked back at them both. 'Either,' she said. 'You choose.'

Gretchen felt her fist twitch. In order to overcome the twitch she breathed deeply and took the can from Erica's hand. She swallowed a deep draught. Erica looked at her with something akin to fear. Gretchen returned the can to her and said, 'I don't know how you can drink that stuff. It tastes really *odd*.'

Erica gave a little giggle and then burped. 'Whoops,' she said. 'Sorry.'

'Which sweater, Erica?' said Gretchen through gritted teeth.

'It doesn't really matter, does it?' said the girl. 'They are both really nice.'

'Choose,' said Gretchen.

'Can't,' said Erica with a smile.

'*Choose,*' repeated Gretchen.

'I can't,' said Erica, eyes back on the screen once more. 'You choose for me.'

Gretchen knew it was time to pack up and go. There seemed little to keep them here any more.

*

Deirdre had spent the seasonal period making lace doilies and her Christmas Day had passed without so much as one little drop of port passing her lips. Declan's card was postmarked 'Kilburn', which brought back strong memories both good and bad, and it said he was doing fine, planned to travel, and would write to them again one day. Deirdre went on working with her silks, occasionally looking from the card to Dermot and back again and sighing. He sighed too, but the source of his sigh came from a profound need for action. Where had the Spoon of Life gone? Declan far away, Deirdre as calm and unstirrable as a nun. Nothing was happening any more. He seemed incapable of *making* anything happen. Not like in the old days when he had merely to bang his fist on the bar, shout almost anything, and have instant turmoil.

'Jesus, Mary and all the Saints,' he said despairingly, 'if only something exciting would happen . . .'

He said this to Leary, and Leary winked. He had been a doorman at Cork Lodge Hotel for thirty years. The wink was his 'big tip' wink. 'Maybe it's another woman you need?' he said, nodding down the bar towards the deft placidity of Deirdre. He winked again. Dermot poured him a large measure of whiskey, which Leary, obligingly, downed in one. So much for the profits, but what the hell. Maybe Dermot should go travelling, too. He had always said that he would. He might have gone with Declan and showed him how to do it properly. As a father should.

*

'*Nihil obstat quominus imprimatur,*' said Janice. She leaned back in her chair, pointed a plump finger over the full-stop button, and brought it down on target. She had never enjoyed writing a book so much, though it felt strange to have abandoned the comforting shadow of Dermot Poll in this, her final work, her *magnum opus*. She put the very last chocolate brazil into her mouth and enjoyed it slowly. Well, Christine, she thought, this one is for you. It is the one you would have approved of most. *Blastanges de femmes?* Have done with ye . . .

She telephoned Rohanne, but Ms Bulbecker was out of town.

Coming back when, please?

A week. Message?

271

No, no message, but could Janice Gentle please have the address of Morgan Pfeiffer?

Sure she could.

Then she picked up the telephone and dialled the Oxfordshire number. 'Girls,' she said, 'I'm ready.'

Gretchen went into town and posted all the keys save her own off to London. Returning, taking her favourite walk for the last time, she waved at the distant farmer, who was pacing his frozen fields. 'Sylvia Perth is dead,' she called.

'I know,' he called back. 'But just see how it burgeons again in the spring.'

And she felt a tear trickle down her cheek and freeze like a tiny diamond in her moustache.

*

'I told you,' said Erica von Hyatt sleepily, 'that we should have brought the cushions.'

'How was I to know they'd be holding the Festival of Celtic Origins in the south?' said Gretchen O'Dowd, pulling the neck of her jumper up round her ears.

'I knew we wouldn't sleep in a hotel. I *knew* it . . .'

'Oh, shut up,' said Gretchen O'Dowd, surprised at how satisfying the suggestion was, and she turned her back, huddling closer to the base of the brick pier for protection.

'*And* we didn't get a cabin to cross in.'

'They were full.'

'Why didn't you book in advance? You said you would book in advance. When I asked you, you said you *would book in advance*. You insisted . . .'

'I know what I said, but there wasn't one to be had. That's why it took so long before I could get *any* booking. Anyway, we had Pullman seats.'

'Pushman, more like,' said Erica. 'Bolt upright all night with that crowd behind us on brown ale and pickle sandwiches and that painting of yours digging me in the ribs – I mean, fancy bringing that on holiday . . .'

'We are not on holiday –'

'Too bloody true.'

'And I had to bring it because I had nowhere else to leave it, and it is mine, and it is the only thing I have that Sylvia Perth gave to me.'

'Even if you hate the sodding thing . . .'

'It was her gift to me . . . And I've asked you not to speak ill of the dead, please. Anyway, it's something for you to lie on. I haven't got anything.'

'You don't need any extra padding.'

'What?'

'This jumper is sodding itchy.'

'It's best angora wool mix.'

'It's given me a rash.'

Gretchen felt a faint stirring in her fist, shades of her father calling her back. 'Take it off, then.'

'Mean old cow.'

'Who?' The fist twitched more strongly.

'Psycho Perth.'

'Sylvia!'

'Bollocks.'

'*Erica!*'

'I'm cold.'

'Thought you were a child of the streets.'

'I am.'

'It's not even frosty. The wireless in the chip shop said it was the mildest February for years.'

'You said we'd sleep in beds in hotels.'

'We will tomorrow. We'll head for Skibbereen. There'll be plenty of room there.'

'Say you love me.'

'I love you,' said Gretchen O'Dowd, but the words rang hollowly round the darkness.

'And tell me a story.'

'Once upon a time,' began Gretchen O'Dowd, 'there was a beautiful princess imprisoned in a dark dungeon from which only a Green Knight could save her.'

Erica von Hyatt snorted. 'Pull the other one,' she said, and, wrapping the *Irish Press* more tightly around her shoulders, she fell sweetly and delectably asleep.

At least, thought Gretchen O'Dowd as she closed her eyes tightly and wrapped her arms round herself, at least Sylvia used to hold on to me once in a while.

*

Janice looked in the freezer. There was little left – a packet of chocolate muffins, three take-'n'-bake rolls ... The refrigerator was almost empty too – a little butter, a little potato mayonnaise, some cream cheese. In the cupboards it was the same – a packet of milk, scoured pots of lemon curd and jam, a tin that rattled with a few broken biscuits. And the Turkish delight was reduced to granular crumbs submerged in white icing. She stood back and surveyed the debris with pleasure and satisfaction. Such perfect timing. And now, as soon as the news came through from Ireland she would deliver up the manuscript and ... She shivered. The night was a cold one, she argued with herself, no reason *not* to shiver even if her kitchen was always warm. She took out the packet of muffins to defrost, and went, smiling, back into the living-room. The screen shone soft as underwater light and she resettled herself in front of it. She remembered that there were souls inside it who had to be released.

The creator is God, she said to herself, as she called up the tube-train travellers. You have been safe, protected, secure in my green cave but now I must free you to travel where you will –

The pinger went on the microwave, the muffins were done. God the creator was hungry. She rushed to the kitchen forgetting her protected souls. For the moment the warm, moist chocolate enticed. She ate contemplatively. She would render up nothing to Rohanne Bulbecker until she was sure of Dermot Poll. Wanting to trust was not the same as conviction. And after Sylvia Perth's behaviour, Janice felt she had a right – no, a *duty* – to be wary. It was a good book. She knew it. *Quite* the right thing to bow out on. She would not change one sentence, phrase, word or letter of it. She hummed a troubadour's song.

> My lady will not speak the word
> That shines without her eyes
> Yet may she sing it pure and clear
> And save her lover's sighs . . .

*

Rohanne looked behind her at the blue-white snow, virginal save for the slicing tracks she had made. The air promised a new fall soon and then these would be covered, the landscape once more returned to its unsullied state. She leaned on her stick and thought that not all things are so easily restored. Perhaps, she decided, there was a time to fail. She had missed it with Janice Gentle, who, true to Rohanne's predictions, had succumbed, for whatever the reason, to the enticement of money. Rohanne had found no pleasure in her success, and of the whole episode perhaps that response in her was the most disturbing of all. She replaced her visor and pushed off from the mountain with all her strength, scoring the whiteness again with her skis. It was a wonderfully dangerous and slippery slope, just as dangerous, she suspected, as Janice's . . .

*

'My wife,' he said, 'that's her down there with the cherryade and embroidery kit – well, I would not wish you to get me wrong . . .'

Erica shook her head. 'Not at all,' she said.

'But, well . . .' – he shifted nearer – 'she does not . . . understand me. She does not . . . understand me at all . . .'

'Ah,' said Erica, moving a little closer across the bar. 'Surely not. And you such a dear and lovely man, too, Brian.'

'And I'll tell you something else about me . . .' He also leaned closer, and poured a sensible measure of Jameson into both their glasses. By gosh she was a picture.

'What's that now, Brian?'

He bent his mouth to her ear. So pretty, the little pink shell of it. 'My name is not Brian at all.'

'No?' she said, sitting back a little and giving him a look of perfectly delightful wonderment. 'You don't say. What is it, then?'

'It's Dermot,' he said. 'Dermot Poll.'

'Well, I never . . . You don't say,' she breathed, smiling with her glistening pink mouth.

'I do say. And I say something else, too.'

'What's that?'

Her laugh was like harebells.

'You have the loveliest ears, the loveliest eyes, the loveliest hair and the loveliest body I ever did see. Slender as a lily stalk. For I could never abide fat on a woman. Fat shows they're running to seed.' He directed his gaze down the bar towards Deirdre. 'If you see what I mean.' He raised his glass to Erica. 'You are like a pure, white light at the end of a tunnel of darkness.'

'Sweet of you,' said Erica, and she toddled down to the other end of the bar to tell Gretchen.

'You want the good news first or the bad news?'

Gretchen asked for the former.

'The good news is we've found Dermot Poll.'

'And the bad?'

'It's that slob at the other end of the bar.'

Janice sent one copy to the Pfeiffer Organization and one to Rohanne. As she went out to the post office, she could hear Mr Jones muttering to himself while his hearing-aid whistled plaintively. She no longer feared him. 'Good morning, Mr Jones,' she said to his kneeling back view, but he did not hear. He was dealing with the lift. She peered into the compartment and remembered the face that had lain there so livid in death. To be buried in Birmingham seemed a fitting bathos. Poor Sylvia, destined to lie not among the rural beauties of Oxfordshire but in the concrete shadows of manufacturing England. In a way she owed her everything – both the good and the bad – and she decided it would be perfectly fitting to dedicate this, her last, to the memory of Sylvia Perth, who had, despite Janice's ignorance, helped bring pleasure and literature to thousands. That, then, was the final part of the rebus: 'For my friend and betrayer, Sylvia Perth. Rest in peace . . .' For a moment she thought she could smell that aromatic smoke again, hear a hissing behind her. Perhaps Sylvia was not able to rest in peace. Janice smiled benignly behind her glasses. Perhaps she was actually turning in her grave . . .

The old grocer looked out as she passed. There was a metal grille in his window now and the bubble-gum machine had been smashed. 'They'll be putting wooden pips in the jam again soon,' he said dolefully. 'You mark my words. Nowadays' – he looked up at the sky and shook his head – 'nowadays *everything*'s up for grabs.'

'Well, I'm not,' said Janice firmly, and she pressed on towards the post office, the frosty February air whipping an unaccustomed colour into her cheeks. She paid the fee for express delivery, watched the packages consigned to a mail sack, and was glad to do so. It had been far too long in coming, this moment; she wanted to go full speed ahead from now on. With a lightness of step that she had not felt since that other February night, she made her way to the travel agent's to inquire about Ireland.

'Going for the Celtic Festival?' asked the man.

'No,' said Janice. 'Pilgrimage.'

*

It had been a wild and thrilling night. Looking out of her window, Janice saw a dustbin lid flying down the road, and people of quite substantial proportions being blown off their feet. It was exciting weather – if you were not out in it, and she had cause, as she pulled her cardigan round herself, to feel very grateful for her sanctuary. She took it as a sign, she took it to mean that this journey to Ireland was always meant, for she had had a very narrow escape. Thank heavens for cocoa. It was cocoa she was making when a piece of somebody's chimneypot crashed through her big picture window. A few minutes before she had been standing there, looking out, when the urge for cocoa came upon her. Without that urge she would have been dead, ribboned flesh, bleeding freely. Yet here she was, whole, undamaged. It must be a suitable omen for the rightness of her cause and she felt positively uplifted. Mr Jones came and put up brown board and said the glaziers would visit as quickly as they could come, local damage being what it was. Janice did not care about that, either. When they came, she would already be far away.

She crossed to her trunk and removed the detritus of years that stood upon the lid: yellowing papers, old magazines, a few glued china fancies that had been her mother's. She put all this to one side, opened it and breathed in the smell of lavender and camphor. She took out her coat of many colours and smiled as she examined the cloth. Neither time nor moths had damaged it at all.

Dressed, she let herself out of the flat and patted the door with a sigh. Everything was done. All over now. And she was on her way – not via Walsingham, it was true, but Heathrow Airport could justifiably be thought of as a contemporary staging-post.

She knocked on Mr Jones's door. When he opened it, muttering, irritable, impatient, she was engulfed in an odour of warm oranges. At least somebody was still making real marmalade.

'Good morning,' she said.

'Um,' said Mr Jones.

Janice handed him her spare keys and a sheet of paper. The paper contained the address in Skibbereen. Mr Jones had been insistent. 'After all,' he said, 'your windows are out . . .'

He peered at her. 'You look different.' He peered again. 'Brighter.'

'I expect I do,' she said, and swung off with her case into the waiting taxi.

*

Morgan Pfeiffer stared, his eyes misted over with rage, blinked, and refocused again. Then he roared. He roared with all the might of a jungle lion who has learned to tolerate the chronic pain of a thorn in his foot until a passing elephant steps on it. He closed the manuscript and looked at the photograph of his good wife, deceased, through a veil of pain.

His roar was not an inarticulate one. It got itself easily around the human larynx and formed the sound shape, 'Stoat!' It formed the sound shape twice more for good measure. And then he waited. There was a satisfactory explosion of activity outside his door. The roar had been heard. His secretary jumped.

Morgan Pfeiffer resettled himself at his desk, got up, paced about, sat down again, picked up his cigar, picked up the manuscript, flicked at its pages as if in a vain effort to be proved wrong, shook his head as if knowing that he was not.

'Mr Pfeiffer?'

'You did not knock, Stoat.'

Stoat stood there for a moment wondering what to do.

'Well, Stoat?'

Lunacy prevailed. 'Sorry, sir,' he said, and went out, knocked, and waited.

Morgan Pfeiffer crossed to the door in the gliding fashion that seemed to betoken calm – recognizable only as its opposite to the photographic one now deceased. He opened the door gently.

Stoat smiled and squeaked. 'May I come in?'

Morgan Pfeiffer gave an expansive sweep of his hand. 'By all means,' he said through syrupy lips. He watched Stoat enter and walk to the desk, and was slightly mollified to observe that he had shrunk by quite a few inches. That helped. It didn't make it better, but it helped.

'Bring in the Gentle contract,' he said smoothly to his secretary, 'if you would be so kind.' He noticed that she had spilled correction fluid all over her desk. That helped, too.

'Read,' he commanded Enrico Stoat, and he pushed the opened manuscript towards him. 'Read the sex scenes just to begin with, Stoat. I have marked them for you.'

Stoat did so, his mouth making silent word shapes as he forced his concentration over each page. 'My God,' he breathed from time to time. '*My God, my God, my God* . . .' His jaw dropped, his shoulders sagged, his eyes bulged, he seemed to shrink even more, and he looked, Morgan Pfeiffer thought with satisfaction (it was the *only* satisfaction), like a dying Hobbit.

'But, Mr Pfeiffer,' he said when he had finished, 'we can't use this. This is . . . well . . . this isn't *straight* . . . Mr Pfeiffer, sir, this is . . . er . . . deviant. She can't do this!'

'She can, and she has, Stoat.'

Morgan Pfeiffer's secretary entered and handed him a file. Morgan Pfeiffer took it and the secretary scuttled away.

Enrico Stoat, expiring Hobbit, felt for his medallion and wept openly.

Morgan Pfeiffer waved the contract file under his dripping nose. 'And there is nothing in here, Stoat – nothing at all – to stop her.'

'Jeezus,' said Stoat. 'I don't believe it.'

'Believe,' said Morgan Pfeiffer, suddenly and frighteningly quiet. 'Believe.'

Stoat sat down, very suddenly and without requesting permission.

'Now,' said Morgan Pfeiffer, advancing. Stoat stood up. Morgan Pfeiffer pushed him back down as easily as if he were oiled. 'Read some of the *story* line. What you like to call "ballast". Tell me whether you don't think it's an itsy-bitsy bit *chocolate* box. Hah!' He spun Stoat's chair and walked over to the window. 'READ!' he roared.

Stoat read. He stayed in the revolving chair. Permitted or not, he very definitely could not stand. 'Oh *my God*,' he repeated. 'Oh my God,' he said and looked at Pfeiffer.

'Does anything strike you, Stoat? Anything not quite right? A bit out of the ordinary perhaps for the kind of market we are after? The sex scenes, for example? Our "Janice Gentle gets sexy" scoop? Anything in particular about that?'

Stoat nodded and groaned. 'Yes,' he whispered. 'Yes, Mr Pfeiffer.'

'And *what* in particular strikes you, Stoat?'

Stoat mouthed some words.

'I can't hear you, Stoat. Speak up now. Say it.'

'Oh, Mr Pfeiffer, *sir*,' said Stoat. 'Well . . . um . . . er . . . the women, the . . . er . . . encounters mostly seem to be . . . er . . . gay . . .'

Morgan Pfeiffer permitted himself a bitter laugh. 'Lesbians, Stoat. *Lesbians!* More dykes than on a Dutch beach. Let me tell you, throughout the book there is not a desirable dick in sight.' He raised a finger. 'There is *one* . . . er . . . piece of masculine equipment offered the reader. Right at the beginning. You may have missed it. That rather over-friendly superintendent in the children's home. Remember him?'

Stoat shuddered.

'Apart from that? Not one. Dogs, we've got. Arthritic old dykes in wheelchairs, we've got. Even a kinky male fish merchant . . . We've got "home is a cardboard box", we've got a hose-down near the London Ritz, and we've got an abandoned baby. The only shopping that appears to get done is of the light-fingered variety and centres around sustenance, the only fashion notes seem to be of a hard-wearing and waterproof nature. And the sex scenes, as you say, are . . . nothing but deviant filth. *Gay.*' He leaned on his desk so that even the photograph quivered. 'So, what are we going to do, Stoat?'

Stoat swallowed. 'We'll sue,' he said.

Morgan Pfeiffer thrust the papers he held into Stoat's hand. 'Sue? Sue for what?'

'Sue for breaking contract.'

'She hasn't done that, Stoat.

'Stoat,' said Morgan Pfeiffer, 'I think you should go away and concentrate on reading the whole book. I think you'll find the main character, the story and the plot all of great interest. It's about an itinerant girl who lives on the streets, by her wits and with the aid of casual prostitution and the occasional sugar-mommy. *Mommy*, Stoat, not *daddy* . . . She gives up men for a variety of entertaining reasons, many of which will be an education to our readers!'

A small light entered the deadness of Stoat's eyes. 'Rohanne Bulbecker,' he cried. 'Rohanne Bulbecker . . .'

'Forget Rohanne Bulbecker. From now on I deal with this myself.' He picked up a small piece of notepaper attached to the manuscript. 'Miss Gentle has been kind enough to send Miss Bulbecker a copy all of her own. She has also appended her address in London. So I shall not wait for Ms Bulbecker's interference. I want to see Janice Gentle, I want to speak with her in the flesh. We'll see if she still thinks she can play this kind of trick when I'm through with her. Oh she thinks she has been so *clever* – laughing all the way to the bank. Recluse? I tell you, Stoat, by the time I've finished with her she'll wish she lived on *Mars* . . .'

Chapter Twenty-five

They have found him. He has an inn at Skibbereen! So here is the manuscript, sent with my love. I hope you like it, I do.

The little piece of paper fluttered to the floor as Rohanne Bulbecker reached eagerly for the manuscript. Whatever she had expected, it was not this. The glow of her snow-tan began to fade long before she reached the end and, by the time the very last page was laid aside, she both looked and felt quite pale. That it was good was not in dispute. That it had conformed, exactly, to the contractual requirements of Morgan Pfeiffer was not in dispute. Whether it was acceptable was not in dispute, either. It was not, and never would be. She weighed the pages in her hands, thinking. Even were she to find the best editors in the land, they could do nothing with it, nothing to make it the awaited, expected book. She puzzled over its sexuality. How could Janice Gentle have gone down that particular path? And then floating into her mind came the eager face of Gretchen O'Dowd and with it that familiar gesture of fingertips to moustache as she set off to get the video.

And then Rohanne laughed. It seemed like the best joke of all, though it was clear from Janice's writing that she did not see it as a joke, merely as a story, a good story, and one that she very much wanted to write – passionately wanted to write if the compelling qualities of the novel were anything to judge by. And what was more – Rohanne went over to the telephone and dialled the Pfeiffer number – what was more, it ought to be published. It was too good *not* to be published. And she would tell Morgan Pfeiffer so . . .

'He has gone to London,' said the flat voice.

'In that case may I speak to Enrico Stoat?'

'Enrico Stoat,' said the voice impassively, 'is no longer with us.'

*

Morgan Pfeiffer was not a happy traveller. Travelling alone and in angry mood to an uncertain destination for an uncertain and undoubtedly acrimonious meeting was not conducive to harmony. He could not even read the newspapers since there were reports on every page to remind him of Janice Gentle's nasty book.

By the time he reached Heathrow, he was ready for war. He shouldered his way through the milling airport travellers, each and every one placed there purely to annoy him. In the taxi he growled rather than spoke the address of the loathsome Janice Gentle in Battersea. When Mr Jones told him she had gone away, he assumed it was because she felt guilty.

'Where to?' he asked Mr Jones.

Mr Jones, annoyed to find that this was not the glazier, was quite short with him. 'A place called Skibbereen.'

'Near here?' asked Morgan Pfeiffer, lighting a cigar for comfort.

'Ireland,' said Mr Jones.

'Shit,' said Morgan P. Pfeiffer, and climbed back into the cab.

*

Janice Gentle sat in the plane and dreamt. She was ready now, more than ready, for love. She spread out comfortably in her seat and prepared to doze.

Skibbereen.

Gretchen said Dermot Poll was alive and well and living in Skibbereen. Janice asked no further questions. 'I am coming,' was all she said.

It was curious that, after all, she had not needed to write this last book. The money was quite unnecessary. In the end his pursuit had cost very little. Yet she had enjoyed the work, given of her best, enjoyed writing of a heroine other than herself, to control the experience rather than be controlled by it. Once she could write only her truth, now she had written the truth of another. She was sure Erica von Hyatt would be pleased . . . '*Who would be interested in me?*' Janice smiled. Quite a lot of people would be now . . . She felt a little regretful that this was her last book, but she shook her head free of the thought. She had but one goal to achieve, which was now attained. She had found Dermot Poll. That was the peak, that was the pinnacle. *Vous ou Mort*, and she needed nothing more. Assuredly, assuredly, she was ready to yield unto love.

As her eyes grew heavy, she remembered she had still not released her tube travellers. That was unfair. She had no more use for them, yet still she kept them captive. I shall do it just as soon as I get back. I will. I promise . . . And, so saying, she pulled her coat of many colours about her ample form and fell comfortably asleep.

Chapter Twenty-six

THE Celtic Festival was causing an interesting confusion for travellers in Ireland. Rohanne reached Cork railway station after a train journey which would have made a sardine blush, and was swept out into the street by the noisy, anxious crowd, all of whom were determined to travel onwards that night and few of whom had forward-planned the means. Coaches, buses, taxi-cabs, private cars, motor bicycles and horse-drawn carts all turned up for hire by the throng. Irish, Manx, Welsh, Cornish, Breton, Scottish showed their blood bond and helped one another. Rohanne, who was determined to reach Janice before Morgan Pfeiffer, to warn, to protect, to defend her, lied about her origins, invented a grandmother from Wales, and was put in line to await whatever transport became available. It would not take long, she was assured, by a man with a lilt in his voice who was organizing the snake of waiting travellers. Rohanne believed this. She still clung to the belief several hours later.

*

Morgan Pfeiffer saw a deliciously fleshy pair of legs beneath an extremely bright coat disappearing into a taxi-cab. Since it happened to be the last taxi-cab available, on a freezing February night, this merely seemed more of Fate's ill will. He made a half-hearted attempted to run through the crowds towards the cab and its tantalizing occupant, but failed. Instead he leaned against the station doorway and allowed his anger with Janice Gentle to warm him. If she thought that running away to this obscure place would save her, she had reckoned without *him*. Morgan Pfeiffer was stirred from his suffering widowerhood, the sleeper awakes, and he responded with joy to the fire of the fight in his belly.

'Is it always like this in Ireland?' he asked the sky. 'And how the hell do I get to Skibbereen?'

He was brought back to earth by a man in uniform standing at the station entrance. 'It's the Festival,' he said. 'And the only thing that'll get you there is money. There's not a piece of public transport left to be had.'

Morgan Pfeiffer indicated that this was not a problem and sat waiting on a dusty window-ledge, pulling his coat more firmly around him. The cold whipped his wrath. When he got to Skibbereen, he would bring Janice Gentle to her knees.

The man returned, looking a little less confident. 'We'd a truck going out with Celtic crosses, bound for a mile or two the other side of where you want, but it's gone. But we may be lucky. If Cake and Confectionery is still in the Tabard finishing his stout, we can get you in there. Wait now.'

Morgan Pfeiffer lit a cigar, but the aromatic smoke gave little comfort in the bleakness. Cold, he thought, and no room to go to.

*

Janice asked her driver why everyone was journeying towards the south-west.

'A spiritual journey,' he said. 'And yourself?'

'The same,' she said, and settled back to dream.

'That's a very fine bright coat you are wearing,' said the driver conversationally. 'I like a bit of colour. Sometimes it seems to me that the world is in mourning for something. Black, brown, grey – the colours of dirt, the colours of decay – and you in yours so bright, cheerfully dazzling in the night . . .'

'You sound like a poet,' said Janice. 'Are you?'

'Of course,' said the driver, amused, 'I'm Irish.'

'Ah, yes,' said Janice dreamily. 'So you would be . . .'

*

Dermot Poll eyed Erica. Erica eyed Gretchen. Gretchen eyed Deirdre. And Deirdre eyed Leary.

'Time to go,' she said to him eventually. 'Residents only now.'

Leary swallowed and winked and let himself out.

'Snag the lock,' she called after him, 'when you have relieved yourself.'

But he forgot.

The only light came from the reddish glow of the oil-lamp and the flickering flames of the fire. The room was warm, closed in, as if separate from the world now that Leary had gone and the door was shut against the wailing night outside.

'Just hark at that wind,' said Deirdre. 'I wouldn't be a traveller on the road tonight.'

'Oh, I don't know,' said Erica von Hyatt. She was drawing rings in the wetness of the bar top, and Dermot Poll, hunched on his elbows opposite her, watched fascinated. He leaned forward and whispered something in her ear.

She stopped drawing and looked at him incredulously. 'You have to be joking,' she said loudly.

'Dermot,' said Deirdre, without looking up from the difficulty of turning the heel on a burgundy-coloured sock, 'leave the girl alone.'

He shrugged, yawned, rubbed his chest and reached for the whiskey bottle. He winked at Erica as he poured two substantial refills. Erica sipped it unenthusiastically and Gretchen O'Dowd, winding wool for Deirdre around the back of a chair, looked at her lover and sighed. She couldn't remember the last time Erica had taken a cup of tea.

Dermot began to sing. Softly at first with a crack in his voice, and then gradually, with each change of song, the sound became more beautiful, more musical. Deirdre closed her eyes: if she closed them and no longer saw him, then she could enjoy the beauty of it, she could let the music enfold her as once and long ago. She thought about Declan and a tear or two escaped from beneath her closed lashes. He would be fine. It had been the right thing for him to leave. All the same, another tear fell on to the half-turned heel. All the same, she missed him. She felt an arm slide around her and herself pulled towards a solid breast. She smiled up at Gretchen through her tears, keeping her eyes closed, and laid her head against the body that was offered.

'Ah,' said Dermot Poll, pausing between songs, looking down the bar, at the pair of them. 'Isn't *that* sweet now?'

'Yes,' said Erica. 'It is.'

And he began to sing more softly, like a piece of silk twining itself around the room. 'I'll walk beside you through the passing years . . .'

*

Morgan P. Pfeiffer rested his head against a stack of Double Flavour jelly babies. The packages were comfortable, and, if required, he could make a couch from nougat, toffee-chip block and cellophaned sugar almonds. There were heart-shaped boxes of chocolates and other fancies neatly piled about him. It was like heaven lying in the sweet vanilla air. As transport went, it was not uncomfortable and they were going at a steady pace. The driver said he knew a short cut. Some of his anger had melted into the confectionery cloud, and he was content to sit there, basking in it, waiting for the driver to stop at Skibbereen. The rolled-up manuscript knocked against his fleshy ribs, a reminder of why he had come. And the sugary air reminded him of joys once known. He was not going to have either his past or his future betrayed by Janice Gentle and her degenerate tale. He had paid her good money up front and he wanted a return. He would get it, too.

He breathed in the sweetness and took heart from it. To her knees, all right. For Mrs Pfeiffer, the Pfeiffer Organization and the Readers Out There. She'd capitulate. In the end nobody could resist the force of money. People had mortgages, people had families, people liked to pay their bills and keep the heating on. He could do it. He *would* do it. He brushed the sweet, white powder from his sleeve and then tentatively licked his fingertips. The taste of love denied.

*

The Celtic crosses were polystyrene sprayed with grey paint and were very cosy, especially after Rohanne's long wait. The driver had pulled a tarpaulin cover over her and she lay back, bumping against the squeaking totems, looking up at the stars. The wind howled, the trees swayed and it seemed that the very elements were angry and urging her onwards, but the truck just crawled along. Without her Janice would be bullied, hammered, squeezed into shape. She would be unable to defend herself against the might and the wrath of the publisher denied. Rohanne must step in, put up that shield of faith, uphold Janice Gentle and her book, protect that synthesis she had helped to create. 'Faster!' she cried, to the swirling universe above, *'faster . . .'*

*

Janice Gentle stood in the moonlight before the door of the inn and stared at its peeling paintwork, enraptured. Behind her the trees were whipped to a metallic fury, and she could hear, far off, the sea breaking and crashing in its hunger to be fed. Janice recognized that wild water's need in herself, but, despite its thrall, she was sure that she really *could* hear Dermot Poll singing. The door creaked and swung to and fro a little, its old hinges resisting the urge of the elements to thrust itself wide, and, as it moved, it released and recaptured an angle of reddish light that spoke of warmth and the hopeful pulse of love. Her heart beat steadily. She had always known this moment would come and she knew she was not dreaming, but awake and ready. She took the rubber band from her hair and shook it about her face, then she removed her glasses and smoothed away the rain speckles on her skin. Thus prepared, and feeling suddenly beautiful, Janice Gentle pushed at the door and went in.

Chapter Twenty-seven

Erica von Hyatt emptied her glass. Dermot Poll was still singing as he refilled it for her. It was strong stuff. It *needed* to be strong stuff. Here he came again, thrusting his face at her, all stubbly jowls and bloodshot eyes. If ever there was a lesson in the evils of drink, here it was. It was no good. She could not respond. Not even to convince Gretchen O'Dowd that she was not a princess after all and no better than she ought to be. She sighed and drank deeply. Gretchen O'Dowd was honourable and probably *would* follow her to the ends of the bloody earth, exactly as she threatened . . .

Here he was again. Hand on chest, wet lips wobbling as he sang only to her. He placed something on the bar and gestured with his hands that she should take it. She looked. It was a heart-shaped cake.

'I'll look into your eyes and hold your hand . . .' He picked up her hand. 'Be mine, Valentine,' he sang.

Deirdre looked up and, seeing the cake, shrieked with rage. 'That's *my* present from Declan. Came in the post today. Oh you *pig* of a man. I'll give you *Valentine* . . .'

Dermot Poll smiled at Erica. He reached out his arms and enfolded her. He placed his lips to her hair and swayed as he sang, his voice rising still. And then he bent to kiss her, whispering, 'There now, little queen, come along, ah, come along, for I used to be irresistible to women . . .'

Several things then happened, all at the same time, as occasionally several things will. Gretchen, moving like a rugby ace, ran the length of the bar and delivered a stout blow to Dermot Poll's already strawberry-like nose, which brought about the release of Erica's hand quite nicely but, alas, did nothing for the pretty little cake into which Dermot immediately slumped.

'Thanks,' said Erica. 'Hic!'

'He had that coming to him,' said Deirdre peaceably. She trailed a ball of wool behind her, curving, stylized like a line of blood upon the floor, and drew near to peep at her husband. 'Is he dead now?' she said wonderingly.

'No, I am not dead,' said a voice much muffled by the bar top and the desecrated sponge.

A door creaked shut behind them.

'Oh, why has he stopped singing?' said the newcomer's voice.

Half hidden by the women, he of the copious nosebleed looked up. 'Madam,' he slurred, eyes glazed, lips trembling, 'I should have thought it was obvious.'

Deirdre automatically took the burgundy sock and pushed it on to his weeping nostrils. It was a good colour for it. She then remembered that she could not stand the sight of blood and slumped to her knees in a faint. Dermot Poll, seeing his wife take the easy way out as usual, chose to follow her and slid, as easily and naturally as a cut string, out of sight behind the bar. Taking the remnants of the cake with him.

Gretchen blew on her knuckles and blushed, pushing them out of sight behind her back. 'Janice!' she said brightly. 'You are here! We have found him for you. Here he is on the bar.' She gestured triumphantly, though not without embarrassment, to what had been Dermot Poll's resting-place.

Janice peered round Gretchen O'Dowd's square form and stared at the counter. It held nothing but a half-finished sock of burgundy-coloured wool and a little blood. Janice put her fingers to her mouth. For one extraordinary moment, for one *very* extraordinary moment, she wondered if Dermot Poll had been turned into a sock. And, accordingly, was speechless.

Erica, finding the silence oppressive, and feeling something was required, said, 'I love your coat. You should wear bright colours more often.' Whereupon Janice, still staring at the sock, burst into tears of vexation.

Deirdre groaned from the floor.

293

'Where is he?' whispered Janice, rubbing at her eyes. It *was* him. She would have known his voice in a thousand. 'Is this some kind of joke?'

Erica shook her head and slid uncertainly from her bar stool. She pushed Gretchen towards Deirdre. 'That's where you belong,' she said firmly. Then she took Janice by the hand and led her around the corner of the bar and said wryly. 'And this is where *you* belong. There he is. Dreamboat.'

Janice knelt down behind the bar and stared. She felt for some comfort within her pockets, but they were bare. It had been a long, tiring taxi journey. Oh for something to suck.

'*Ecce homo*,' she whispered, touching the bloodied nose, picking away pieces of cake from his ears. '*Ecce Homo?*'

But this was not Dermot Poll at all. Only the voice she had heard was his, only the dream of him. The rest – she removed a lump of icing from his hair – the rest was – She recoiled. Had she not passed this way before, all those years ago?

She knelt there, staring, speaking low. '"*Mulier est hominis confusio.*"' And shook her head regretful, sad but firm,/That Dermot Poll had turned out such a worm.

> '. . . And curses on us both,
> And first on me if I were such a dunce
> As let you fool me oftener than once.
> Never again, for all your flattering lies,
> You'll coax a song to make me blink my eyes;
> And as for those who blink when they should look,
> God blot them from his everlasting Book!'

'Quoting poetry again,' Erica announced. The hiccoughs had ceased and there was a certain dignity in her bearing. 'Frankly,' she said, 'if this is normal life, I'd rather have the street.' She looked swimmily at Gretchen O'Dowd. 'I am going out. I am going out *solo*. And wherever I am going, it is my business, and mine alone.' She tossed her head. 'Right?'

'Not *quite*!' boomed a thunderous voice.

Deirdre jumped, finally jerked back into full consciousness.

Gretchen held her solicitously. 'Who said that?' asked Deirdre, trying to swivel her head and see.

'Don't move,' said Gretchen O'Dowd.

'But it's after hours,' said Deirdre, sitting up. She stared at the large man in the camel coat.

He was extremely angry.

So was she, what with one thing or another.

'Who are you, and why are you here at this ungodly hour?' she said, pulling her skirt back down over her substantial knees, which he seemed to be eyeing despite his high emotion.

'Morgan P. Pfeiffer,' said Morgan P. Pfeiffer, 'and I have a few things to say to Janice Gentle.'

He advanced towards Erica von Hyatt, bringing with him the strange, engulfing odour of sweetness. Rohanne Bulbecker's description of her was exact. Blonde, blue-eyed, unappetizingly slender. He pointed at her accusingly. 'Janice Gentle,' he said. 'Your novel will not do. I asked for romance and you gave me dirt. You have taken my money under false pretences. You must rewrite it or face the consequences.'

'I am not —' began Erica von Hyatt, but Morgan Pfeiffer held up his hand to silence her.

'You most definitely *are*, Miss Gentle . . .'

'I am not —' began Erica even more indignantly, thinking, Look where it got me last time.

'Very well.' Morgan Pfeiffer was beyond good sense, beyond reason. 'If you continue to refuse, I shall break you. You will never work again . . .'

'I don't much now,' said Erica, and hiccoughed a smile.

He removed the large manuscript from his inner pocket and began flicking through it. 'There are acceptable targets of normality, Miss Gentle, there are concepts of the understood. When I said I wanted sex, I did not mean this kind of sex. I meant acceptable sex. As you very well knew. *I will not tolerate this!*'

He banged the manuscript against his hand and a little puff of white vanilla-scented powder flew out. 'Decent sex is what I have come here for and that is what I want! A decent, straightforward, love story with sex – sensitively handled. Not this deviant *trash . . .!*'

He advanced towards Erica. He smiled. Suddenly he changed to wheedling. 'For your readers, Miss Gentle. For your art. Please?'

Erica stared, unable to make head or tail of it.

'Will you clean it up? Your public awaits . . .'

Gretchen and Deirdre looked at Erica with wonderment.

Erica shrugged.

From the damaged nose of a supine man came the rasping drone of a snore. Nothing else could be heard in the room.

And then . . .

'Just a minute!' said a voice from the other side of the bar. 'Just a bloody minute!' And Janice Gentle, bathed in the only bright light left burning, stepped out, radiant, wrathful, as immense as an avenging goddess. The hand she extended was plump and white, the finger she pointed was rounded and dimpled, the legs on which she stood were as solid and firm and curvaceous as those marbled calves of antiquity. Above the short hem lay treasures of roundness: a belly full and ripe; the push of breast swellings that held no quarter with angles; a full chin; a veritable orb, like a marshmallow, for a face; and eyes that flashed from the depths of generous sockets. Athena, Demeter and all the warring, fructifying sisters of the world burned forth out of her.

Morgan Pfeiffer's spine tingled. His heart pumped painfully. Such a vision, even here in the land of them.

Deirdre and Gretchen were quite still. Erica was almost still, save for the gentlest of swayings as if she were caressed by a breeze.

Janice Gentle looked magnificent.

'Who are you?' said Morgan Pfeiffer.

The vision was solid. It moved. It put down the finger and advanced its whole form towards him. 'I am Janice Gentle,' it said. 'I wrote that book. And I will not change one word of it.'

Samson in his chains was no more helpless than Morgan Pfeiffer. He looked from Erica von Hyatt and back to Janice

Gentle. Something by way of explanation was required. 'I thought this person was you,' he said cautiously.

'They all do at first,' offered Erica kindly.

Janice continued to advance but was suddenly stilled by a long snore that turned into a groan of agony. It came from behind the bar. The terrible and monstrous sight of Dermot Poll rose above the wet-ringed woodwork. He looked about him and blinked. He groaned again. Janice turned.

'Dermot Poll,' she whispered, staring at him, attempting again to find in the bloodhound eyes and folds of chin flesh the beautiful young man of the past. 'Dermot Poll,' she said louder, 'I have come looking for you. Do you remember me? . . . St Valentine's Eve, a wet street . . . "O Lady of Colours" and "a picture made of jewels"?'

Dermot Poll stared. There *was* some dim remembrance — something in the shape, something in the coloured coat, something of red satin hearts and rain in the air. Declan asleep at a breast, a bus and the boot of a policeman. He put his hand to his nose, which felt like hell. And his head ached. Was it not from her that all his ills befell?

'Perhaps,' he said cautiously. 'But you've aged very badly.' Humour, savage and vengeful, welled up. He laughed through troubled teeth. He glanced at his wife. She was staring at him with that look which said the world and all its troubles, including hers, were *his* fault. She, his wife, had also aged badly. He looked back at the colourful woman. He sniggered through his hurt nose. By golly, so she had. He dimly remembered her mysterious young face in lamplight, aglow with admiration. There was little of that commodity about her now. He stared. The savage and vengeful humour welled up . . .

'Do you remember me?' repeated Janice, rather afraid.

. . . and overflowed. 'I do,' he said. 'And by God, I could wish you had stayed at home. For you've turned to fat and are amazingly ugly.' He looked pointedly from her to his wife and back again. 'And I've no time for women who let themselves go . . .'

Straight away he knew that it had not been a sensible thing to say. The large camel-haired shape lunged towards him. The moustachioed woman lunged towards him. He knew what was about to come, it would be his tender nose again, and he ducked. Swiftly he ran the length of the bar, lifted up the counter flap, and scooted out into the night. It was wild and cold and wet. Behind him he could hear shouts, commands, an order for him to return and make apology to the ladies he had insulted. Well, he thought, bugger to that, and he ran off over the fields and down to the hungering sea. A little salt water to his stinging face, a moistening of the already drying blood, and he'd be right as a rat. He scudded over the dunes, pounded towards the water's edge, and thrust his face at the flying foam. The wind dragged him towards the pull of the breaking waves. He was in further than he had thought to be – ah, but the cold sea spray felt good. He closed his eyes. Neptune roared the hunger of his belly across the boiling emptiness, and with one great motion swept him into his pot, washed clean of the world.

'He'll be back,' said Deirdre, drawing strength from his departure and going through to the kitchen. 'I'll be wetting some tea if anybody wants it.'

'God,' said Erica von Hyatt, 'I'd give anything for a cup right now. But first I'm going out for some air.'

'I'll go with you,' said Gretchen O'Dowd.

Erica smiled at her, quite kindly. 'Yes,' she said. 'Come and walk along the beach with me a little. It will be for the last time.'

'Oh?' said Gretchen, looking from Erica to the swinging kitchen door and back again.

'I need to be free,' said Erica. 'And you'll like being here.'

Chapter Twenty-eight

THEY were alone. Morgan P. Pfeiffer stared at Janice Gentle, who in turn stared at him.

'Thank you,' she said, 'for being so gallant.'

'Any man would have done the same,' said Morgan Pfeiffer.

There was an uneasy silence.

'So,' said Morgan Pfeiffer eventually, '*you* are Janice Gentle?'

'I am she.'

'And *you* wrote this . . . er . . . book?'

'I did.' She smiled. Suddenly she felt as old as the universe itself. She smiled again. 'And you are Morgan Pfeiffer, the man who is going to publish it.'

'I am?'

'Why, yes.' She blinked her pale eyes, round and distant in their unfocused mistiness. 'Of course. It is very simple. You wanted me to write you a book. And I have done.' She pointed with her plump finger again, a finger that looked infinitely suckable to Morgan Pfeiffer. He could almost imagine its cushiony flesh pressing on his tongue. '*Ecce liber*,' she said, 'as Christine de Pisan told her queen some six hundred or so years before, and on this very saint's night, too. Behold my book. With which I *honour* you. *Fidem servare*, Mr Pfeiffer, *fidem servare*.'

He thought about the marketing department. He thought about the Moral Majority. He felt he had commissioned a swimming-pool and been given the unbiddable sea.

'You were magnificent,' he said. He moved a little closer. He touched her hand, lightly and fleetingly, to be sure she was flesh. She *was* flesh. 'Miss Gentle?'

'Mr Pfeiffer?'

'I don't suppose . . .' – he held up his forefinger and thumb to indicate a tiny mote – 'I don't suppose you could see your way to changing a *fraction* of it?'

'Not one whit, sir,' she said, and shook her head. Her full, white neck shivered as she did so. 'Mr Pfeiffer . . .' she said, sniffing the air, drawing even nearer. She was sure, she was positive, that she could smell chocolate and Turkish delight – with perhaps, just perhaps, an underscent of jelly babies. 'Do you happen to have anything of a *sweet* nature upon you?'

And he, with the delight of one who has waited too long, withdrew from his pocket a handful of sugared almonds. In another pocket he had a heart-shaped box of chocolates and jelly babies, but he would save those for later.

'Oh,' said Janice Gentle lasciviously. 'Oh oh oh.'

He held them out, then withdrew them slightly. 'Not even one very small fraction of it?'

'Oh no,' said Janice. 'Not one particle.' She took a sugared almond, placed it on her tongue, smiled up at him with pleasure.

Morgan Pfeiffer knew that he was sunk.

Above them someone gave a satisfied sigh. In the firmament, Christine de Pisan relaxed back into her couch of clouds. Never underestimate, she wrote, the value of both the strength and the weakness of women. Here was her sister scrivener, susceptible to sweetmeats, rock-like in conviction, ready to be loved. The Perfect Triumvirate, the Golden Ideal. Well – she yawned, feeling pleased – she had never really doubted the outcome. So now she could go back to her real task in hand, which was, as always, to defend women against defilement of their essential qualities, which, sad to say, still seemed to occur . . . She had learned a new phrase in her heaven that day, from a new arrival, a Ms Sylvia Perth. 'Sleeping with the enemy,' this woman had said and had got very hot under the stomacher (or whatever they called those garments nowadays) about it. Christine had listened, as one should, and then used one of the words she had come to learn and love just recently. 'Bullshit,' she said.

The woman, who had expected her companion to say, at the very worst, '*Non Blastange!*' was surprised into silence.

'Bullshit?' said the young woman eventually.

'But you might prefer "Cowshit"?' asked the unblinking Christine. 'Hmm?'

'But why?' said the woman, who chose to ignore the suggestion.

'Because sleeping with the enemy is a no more substantial notion than the dew drying in April sun. The enemy is first within ourselves. It is ourselves who must stand firm. After all,' she said finally, 'I have seen little change down the centuries. No, no. Go for love, my dear. Love, after all, is truth.'

Reminiscing now, Christine de Pisan smiled. The newcomer would change in time. There was nothing like living in an atmosphere of absolute equality to purify belief. We are, after all, but one flesh. Get that under your girdle, she thought, as she swished off to Mr Ibsen's eyrie, and you are free to explore much more interesting paths. Christine herself was almost up to date – only the twentieth century left to go. And then what? she wondered. What then? Another form of looking-glass to distil the age?

*

Rohanne Bulbecker was asleep when the truck reached its destination. The driver let her rest while he sat having a smoke, safe and warm in his little cab, looking out on to the seething darkness. He could just make out the ramshackle public house. He had always thought of it as a quiet place, but tonight it took on the activity of a shaken ants' nest. First had come a wild man running down the path, over the fields, shirt-tails flapping, hand to his head, going as if the banshee itself were after him. He was followed through the broken gate by a large man in a pale coat who called and hollered and raised a murderous arm. But the fugitive ran on, away to the sea. Then came two others, walking slowly, deep in conversation, seemingly indifferent to the winds that whipped about them. He watched them disappear into the darkness, and then climbed out of his cab, stretched himself, and shook the sleeper awake.

'Journey's end,' he said.

Rohanne Bulbecker got down from the truck and looked about her. It was as if she had reached the edge of the earth, empty of everything but the roseate light from the pub. The storm was dying, and the clouds, moving on, left behind them tranquillity and starlight. In the distance another bank of clouds rose up, slow-paced, ready to cover the firmament, but for a time there was the moon to guide her. She breathed deep and, whispering to herself *Vous ou Mort* for courage she did not feel, walked up to the half-open door. She would defend Janice Gentle to the uttermost. From now on Janice Gentle would be hers.

In the warm light of the room she saw the writer and the publisher in apparently harmonious debate. Janice looked up, her face smiling with surprise, her eyes alight.

'Rohanne, my dear.' Janice extended her hand. 'Are you, too, here to berate me for what I have written?'

'Certainly not,' said Rohanne. 'I have come to defend you.'

'There is no need,' said Janice simply. 'I have defended myself.' She took Rohanne's hand. 'Did you like my *magnum opus*?'

'Like it?' said Rohanne. 'Like it? Mr Pfeiffer, if you have any principles, you will publish and be damned.'

Morgan P. Pfeiffer looked at Rohanne. It was not the look she expected. It was an acquiescent look, the look of a conquered man.

'Oh,' said Rohanne Bulbecker, setting aside her shield of faith, which was, apparently, not required. 'You are?'

'I am,' said Morgan Pfeiffer.

'Have a chocolate,' said Janice, offering the heart-shaped box. 'Everything is going to be perfectly all right now.' She smiled a little wicked smile. 'Just like in my books.'

Rohanne took a chocolate. Outside snow had begun to fall, covering the land in a blanket of purity. 'Well, what do you know?' she said, biting into the rich, dark sweetness.

*

Erica stood looking out to sea. The snow fell in soft white lumps that melted in the churning water. She felt very small and very ordinary despite the fact that a whole book had been written about her.

'I am not anybody's princess,' she called to the waves. 'And I am glad of it.' She laughed and threw a pebble into the sea. Her eyes, screwed up against the cold spray, were mischievous. They had all believed that bit about the dog – every one of them. She thumbed her nose at the waves. As if she *would*! You had to make *some* things up now and again, didn't you? Otherwise it would all be so dull. And, anyway, it only went to prove that you couldn't believe *everything* that was written in books.

She wondered if one day Dawn would read it, and if so, what she would make of the tale. A tear joined the foaming sea. Well, at least she would never know it was her own mother who had professed to having eaten dog. Janice said Dawn might trace her one day if she left word of her address with the authorities. Another tear fell, plop. What address? Care of third cardboard box, South Bank? It was even more impermanent now they had started recycling the stuff. Quality cardboard was not what it used to be. Nowadays it just fell apart. Ah well. That was life. They were saving the planet, but who for and why?

She turned to follow Gretchen O'Dowd's footprints back towards the pub. She could murder a cup of tea. Bugger the drinking, she thought, and never again. Free once more, Erica, she told herself. Free again.

Her foot hit something soft. She looked down, screwing her eyes against the darkness. Dermot Poll lay on the wet sand, in the purpling dawn. He looked very peaceful, with snowflakes covering his nose, quite at rest, not moving at all.

'A terrible night,' said the officer who took charge. 'Did he often go walking like this?'

Deirdre buried her head in Gretchen's shoulder.

'He liked to go out and sing in all weathers, officer,' said Janice Gentle, replacing the covers as she knelt on the sand. 'This was not the first time.'

The officer looked down at the motionless tea towels and sighed respectfully. 'Maybe not,' he said softly, 'but it'll be his last.'

Chapter the Penultimate
And a tying of ends . . .

JANICE lay in an almond-scented bath in the sugar-pink bathroom of Morgan Pfeiffer's suite. Outside the door, Morgan Pfeiffer paced, listened, paced some more. He looked hungrily at the ruffled bed. He wanted to keep her in beautiful surroundings with silken sheets the colour of apricot jam (Janice had specified this) and walls the colour of pistachio and mint. He wanted her there, always, ready to entertain him, to fill up his gaps – available, loving, eating, grateful, existing solely for him. He wanted her seated at a table full of good things, smiling benignly on his guests as she played queen to his king, and later, when alone, he would wrap his arms around her melting extensiveness and sleep the sleep of a couple's harmony. He heard the water running away and the sound of his lady singing as she made herself ready. He put his ear to the door, for she was singing very low.

'I have a gentil cock
Croweth me day;
He doth me risen early
My matins for to say.

'I have a gentil cock
Comen he is of great;
His comb is of red coral
His tail is of jet.

'I have a gentil cock
Comen he is of kind;
His comb is of red coral
His tail is of inde.

'His legs be of azure
So gentil and so small;
His spurs are of silver white
Into the wortewale.

'His eyes are of crystal
Locken all in amber
And every night he percheth him
In my lady's chamber.'

Impatience made him peevish. Songs about poultry at a time like this?

Janice gave her powdered flanks one last pat.

Morgan Pfeiffer, ear pressed to the door, closed his eyes in anticipation. 'What are you singing?' he called.

Janice smiled and came out of the bathroom in a vapour of scented steam, padding through the doorway, a sweet, damp-scented serving of comely melting flesh. Morgan Pfeiffer licked his lips. He was ready to adore. She smiled more wickedly. 'Just a little Middle English rebus,' she said, 'that I had forgotten I ever knew . . .'

He embraced her and she was like the sweetest fruit on earth.

'So much more vigorous than those shallow, affected Elizabethans, don't you think?' The warmth of his naked skin was pleasing. Instinct told her this was no time to discuss medieval riddles. 'Proserpina, indeed,' she muttered. 'Who needs *her*!'

He had no idea what a Middle English rebus might be, nor Proserpina, nor why the strange song pleased her. But he thought she would probably teach him in time. He just hoped that Mrs Pfeiffer, deceased, would understand why her commemorative imprint was publishing the sort of thing she would have found offensive. 'Forgive me, Belinda,' he murmured into Janice's soft neck, 'but I have to.' And, after all, he had been very good about the cigars. Never lit one *once* before noon. 'A man cannot mourn for ever,' he murmured, as he led Janice Gentle to the apricot ruffling.

'I think,' said Janice dreamily as she sank like a soft fondant cream into the centre of the bed, 'that in my new book there will be lots of *lovely* sex. I shall make it a celebration of the act ...' She reached out and riffled her fingers in a box of chocolates placed enticingly on the pillow. Morgan Pfeiffer was entranced. She placed a walnut cream deep into the recesses of her mouth and sucked hard. 'Mmm,' she said, 'I can't wait to begin. And Rohanne Bulbecker is going to look after me ...'

'New book?' said Morgan Pfeiffer, suddenly anxious, for he saw the vision of his king to her always available queen fading.

She rolled over on to her stomach. He touched her gleaming contours lightly. Here was his ideal, here was perfection.

'Now is not the time,' she said. She sucked the tips of her fingers and looked at him with eyes that yielded up their innocence. 'Is it?'

Already she was dreaming of Dante and Beatrice, Laura and Petrarch, Michael and Rosalla, and the countless others who had been consigned to an eternity without the delights of the love bed. She thought it would be nice to put all that right. Release them from their purity. Once she had experienced such a release herself. She imagined how the entire canon of literature would look if Dante and Beatrice had coupled, if Laura and Petrarch had known more than acquaintance. And supposing Theseus hadn't abandoned Ariadne but married her? Just *think* – no Catullus, no Ovid's *Heroides*, no Chaucer's *Good Women* ...

She crept her plump hand along the coverlet, over the apricot-ruffled hills, towards him. And she sang again, '"I have a gentil cock, Croweth me day ..."' as her fingers drew nearer and nearer ... And Morgan Pfeiffer was forced to agree that this was no time to discuss the future of books.

*

Gretchen O'Dowd looked out from the shore of Skibbereen. The sailing boats gathered the wind in greedy mouthfuls and sped through the waves, looking quite as buoyant as she herself felt. During the last few months she had grown very fond of this view. It was never the same twice and she was no longer seasick at the sight of it. She began to understand the fascination of mariners for their calling and to look upon the painting Sylvia Perth had given her with much more affection. Indeed, it hung above their bed on a fresh white wall and looked rather fine – homely, as if it, and therefore she, belonged. Skibbereen had begun to feel curiously like home. But then, as Deirdre said, it was hardly surprising given her surname, now, was it?

She sniffed the salty air and felt at ease. Nothing on earth, nothing in the water, was going to trouble her now. In her pocket she fingered the Gold Barclaycard, symbol of so much. And it was true: once you had such a thing, people left you in peace, they left you *deferentially* in peace, or hopped about doing your bidding if you so wished. Good old Sylvia. She hadn't been quite so bad, after all . . . Gretchen slitted her eyes against the sun's misty light – there was something of the effect of the painting when you did that. Sylvia's own little memorial triumph . . .

The day after Dermot Poll's funeral (she sighed at the happy memory) Gretchen had taken Deirdre to the Antiques Roadshow, which was visiting Skibbereen, thinking it would be an acceptable form of fun for a new widow. To give the visit some point they took the seascape painting along. And there was a most gratifying moment when the languid assessor with monocle and the upraised nose of an Afghan hound fell off his stool with shock. J. M. W. Turner was, apparently, a much sought-after painter of the sea and its ships, and this appeared to be one of his works. With *that* kind of security, a Gold Card was easy.

She smiled and looked away from the water towards a black-clad figure sitting on a rock further down the beach. The distant figure looked up and waved. Gretchen kissed her fingers to the waver and then stroked her moustache. Deirdre was fond of this silky growth and quite often touched it and said so. It reminded her, so she said, of her mother who had cut cabbages all her life, died doing it, a woman of considerable strength and loyalty, who had never once seen fit to pluck a hair from her body in the name of conformity. She was sure Gretchen was no different.

Indeed, as Deirdre said to still the tongues of idle gossips, where would she have been without Gretchen O'Dowd's comfort and help in this most trying of times? Gretchen had arranged the funeral, *everything* – the flowers, the coffin, even the wake with its food and a ceilidh. Deirdre said to those same wagging tongues that Gretchen O'Dowd had handled the whole thing as if she had been waiting for just such an event all her life. And where she slept was nobody's business . . .

Gretchen, enjoying the peace, heard a noise on the beach behind her. Before she could turn to look, she felt a resounding thump in her lower back – so forceful that she was nearly felled by it. The watching figure on the rock laughed heartily and the sound of her laughter came clear across the breezy distance. Gretchen O'Dowd turned. She refused to smile though the urge to was strong. One of them had to be firm . . .

'Down, Sylvia, down,' she said sternly. 'Good girl. Down, girl. Sit . . .'

*

Erica von Hyatt felt anxious. To overcome the feeling of anxiety she put the key in the lock, turned it, opened the door, removed the key, stepped back, closed the door and repeated the ritual several times. It always cheered her. She spent quite a lot of time going out and coming in again because the pleasure of putting her own key in her own lock was irresistible. What she was not so happy about was going out of the building and into the streets, for no matter how she devised new routes, there was always some living reminder of her past. Today's had been more telling than usual because it was a girl she recognized. Erica had walked past with her eyes fixed unseeing, just as passers-by had once done to her, but it made her feel sick to do it. The girl would not be a survivor. Some fought and won through, some decayed and faded away. So what good, she said to herself, would my parting with a pound have done her? What good would my giving her a room have done her? What good the coat from my back? There are too many of them and I can do nothing. She put to the back of her mind a voice that echoed, mockingly, 'They all say that . . .'

After a few more goes with the key, and feeling better, she entered the apartment. It was full of flowers and greenery – jugfuls, bowlfuls, jam jars of them – and littered with half-made wreaths, bridal sprays, dainty table decorations and fan-shaped bouquets. Some days there was scarcely enough space for all the outwork the florist sent to her. She gathered up an armful of lilies to move them out of the sunlight, turned, found no free surface, and replaced them. It was absolutely no good, that television thing of Janice's that was not a television would have to be moved. She was sure Janice would not mind if she just unplugged it and put it on top of the chest. She would tell her when they next spoke. After all, she would have little use for it now she was in America and never planning to come back. She pressed a switch and the screen startled her by bursting with light, but she could see nothing within, only green emptiness. Nothing there, she decided. Nothing to worry about.

She would put it on Janice's clothes chest. Erica never used this, and all it contained was the pink gown with silver tassels. She couldn't quite bring herself to throw the gown away, though she did not know why. Perhaps because it had made her feel like a princess when she wore it, the kind of princess found in books, the kind of princess that children loved to draw, the unreal princess of a thousand fantasies. The princess Dawn would have wanted her to be. So she kept it. It did no one any harm.

She had thought that perhaps she would wear it for revisiting the crypt – just for a bit of fun and because it would surprise them. But she had never got round to it. Part of her wanted to see the priest who had told her about the different kinds of love, but an ever bigger part of her wanted to stay away . . . She was on the other side now, she was straight, and she certainly didn't need reminding of Before. She was content, quite happy with what she was doing, and she was waiting for the day when Dawn would become eighteen and get in touch with her now that she had a place of her own. After all – she picked up a lily and breathed in the scent – after all, the years would soon pass. She didn't mind the waiting. And if she shopped mostly at the corner shop in future she would avoid the unhappy reminders she had experienced today.

She unplugged the machine and lifted it on to the chest. Then she placed a tea towel over it to save it from getting dusty and began weaving the lilies into a wreath.

Chapter Thirty

SQUARE Jaw is holding on to the strap in the carriage and hoping the lucky band of seated travellers will shortly reach their destination so that he can sit down. He is avoiding the small printed poem above his head which begins:

> They are not long, the weeping and the laughter,
> Love and desire and hate:

He does not want to read it. Look where reading poetry got him last time.

He thought he had done so well. The alien woman told him *she* thought so, too. She said, after it was all over and he had crawled back into bed, that he had dealt with the situation very *sensitively*, very *correctly*, very protectively of *her* feelings. Basking in the praise, and needing the comfort of her arms about him, he did not correct her and say that, really, he had not given her a second thought but considered only himself and, to a much lesser extent, Melanie. She, the alien woman, had not featured in his consciousness at all.

The alien woman clearly believed that she had. Pressing his head to her bosom all the harder, she reiterated this and he, allowing his cheek to lie there and his ear to pick up the soothing sounds of her heart which pumped away with steady calm, did not point out the error. Months on now, today, he wished he had.

What was it she had said to him this morning as he shuffled around looking for shoe number two? 'You loved me so selflessly at the beginning and in so few months it has come to this . . .'

To this what? he had wondered, moving her rowing machine, stumbling over her long black boots, opening the cupboard for the third time to look and this time finding. As he sat on the bed to do up his laces, he heard that unmistakable sound, felt that unmistakable movement: she was sobbing into the pillow and he had a meeting at nine. Why didn't he say, 'Go on, get out of my life. *Go!*' He turned. There were those naked shoulders, there was that small neck, the curving breast, the clenching hand, the outline of her bottom under the duvet as she lay on her belly and sobbed, and sobbed, and sobbed.

He sighed, reached out, accepted his defeat. 'I'll come over to your place tonight and we can look at the brochure. OK?' He patted the bottom and stroked the neck. The head turned. The wet eyes no longer looked as if he had taken a hammer to her. A nipple peeped above the scrunched bedding. Pink and sweet and innocent of anything, it winked at him. He pinched it. She smiled. Wanly, but she smiled. And then she nodded. Out he went, dressed for life. And all *that*, he thought, as he gave the door a harder than necessary bang, because he had clung to a straw of independence. He had arranged to go on a motor rally with a chap from work. That was all. You'd have thought he had suggested going for a fortnight of exotic lust in Bali the way she carried on. It was hardly disloyal to take twelve days in June to go to the wettest part of Ireland and drive a Ford Escort roughshod with Adam Barnet, who had no hair to speak of, a very large nose and about the pulling power of Gandhi.

It was now or never, he thought fiercely as he made his way into the Underground. Stand up for your rights, man. An invitation to breakfast was not meant to be for life. So what if she *does* want to go to a villa in Rhodes? He wasn't stopping her. But he *didn't* want to. Why should he? He knew it had been a mistake that night. He should have just marched back into the bedroom after Melanie left, told her he wanted to be alone, got her a cab – and, bingo, *freedom*. But now, months on, here he was – fucking well *committed* again. And this one hadn't just moved in her make-up and her books and the odd item of clothing. *She'd* brought things like a rowing machine and pot plants and even a bloody Magimix . . . He wouldn't be able to put those into a cardboard box when the time came . . . If it ever did.

He sat down thankfully, finally turning his back on the words of the poem, 'They are not long . . .'

It was all right when he was away from her, but when he saw her it was hard to resist. And he had his suspicions. If he knew anything about anything, she was now pregnant . . . And you couldn't put one of those in a cardboard box along with the mascara.

He stood up. He sighed. Suddenly he felt very middle-aged. He prepared to get off the train and take up the cudgel of reality. He turned the corner, oblivious to the short skirts and snappy ankles and wide, red mouths that used to delight his short walk from tube to office.

'Hi, Adam,' he said, as he turned into the building. 'About that Irish trip. Afraid I don't think I'm going to be able to go, after all. Sorry. Something's come up . . .'

That was true, he mused painfully, thinking of little friend penis. If that hadn't come up, then he would have been quite safe, for none of this would even have begun.

*

She has trampled the flowers underfoot so that their blueness lies crushed in the dirt. Dead rose heads hang on the uncut bushes and last autumn's chrysanthemums point dry, accusing fingers at the sky. She has neglected the garden as if it were herself. She made it a mad vow when she returned the last time. She told it, without reservation, that she would not do anything for it unless *he* did something for her. He had not. And so the garden must suffer, be punished, for something must. 'I gave you your chance,' she says silently, looking out of the window, 'and you did not take it. Very well. On your own head be it. Not a blade nor a weed shall I touch, you unkind, miserable, ungenerous creature. Not until you show me something in return.'

The damp, northern air chills her fingers this morning despite the early summer sun, and she fumbles with the toast, which will not fit into the rack. As she pushes at it, it cracks and breaks, as she feels she might if touched. He picks up the bits, places them on his plate, reaches for the butter, reaches for a knife, everything so normal and ordinary and as it was, as it always will be – unless, unless . . .

'Your letter, Arthur?' she says. 'The London one. Is it . . .?'

He looks up. He is chewing. How can he eat? How can he chew food? How can he continue and be so ordinary? The toast crunches in his mouth. He has God on his side.

She has made her confession, she made it months ago, and not with a hung head and mumbling voice either, but out loud, ringingly. *'Yes, yes, yes,'* she avowed, 'this is what I have done.' She had picked up that little gift laid so accusingly on her bed and cradled it against her cheek in front of him. She wanted to be as cruel to him, as he, the other, had been to her. So she caressed it and said, again, 'Yes, monster that I am, I did that and all for nothing. I did it for Love and he did it for Romance. Here I am again. The same woman. Newly fallen in your eyes but anciently fallen in my own. Now what? Do you throw me on the streets? Do you scoop me up in your infinitely compassionate arms?' She had begun powdering her face, manically, laughing into the mirror, seeing how the light, pink dust removed all the signs of the country ruddiness. 'Look.' She turned, blue eyes bright with goading. 'Where is the vicar's wife from Cockermouth now? Where has she gone? Where will this powdered hussy be, this one who has replaced her?'

He sat very still in the bedroom chair. He did not answer. Frenzy drove her.

'Where? Where? Where?'

He stared at her, still unspeaking. She thrust her face closer. He saw how the powder caked little fine lines in her face, how the flesh around her eyes had slackened, how there were tracks at each side of her mouth, runnels for the tears which he expected would come. Suddenly he felt safe. She was ageing, she was fading, and because of this she would stay with him.

'How about,' he said quietly, 'China?'

Of course it had been an absurd proposition. But for a time it had held them together. He saw himself atoning for the provincial ease, for the fireside comforts of the manse. Sloth. The most invidious of the Seven. Langland's lines: ' "Do you repent?" asked Repentance, but at that moment Sloth dozed off again.'

She dreamed the days, weeks, months away. Walking through the dream, feeling untouched by the world around her, yet still seeming to participate. The seasons of the church represented themselves in colours and flower arrangements, not done by her, but admired by this other self. 'Well done', heartily, to Mrs Brown, whose Chinese lanterns hung their orange heads amid the dried poppy husks and fiery beech leaves. 'How bright' to Miss Lane, who polished brass and silver as if the Devil himself goaded her.

And she waited. All these tiny people, all this tiny island, her tiny marriage – soon to be free of it. She saw herself in the harsh landscape of some remote Chinese community, stricken suddenly with illness, dying gradually, pale against the pillow. She would instruct Arthur to take the small package she held out to him and send it to the other. And somewhere, as her spirit left her body, she would wait to see how the gift was received. He would open it alone somewhere private (knowing the handwriting), and he would find the little compact and a lock of her hair and the imprint of his and her lips on a tissue they had used after eating pomegranates. She would take a text, as Arthur took texts: 'And wherefore have ye made us to come up out of Egypt, to bring us in unto this evil place? It is no place of seed, or of figs, or of vines, or of pomegranates; neither is there any water to drink.' He would keep these things, he would weep a little, for he was Romance, as she was Love, and in this way he would never forget her.

She held this picture so tight to herself that it carried her through the the dreary days of reality. The upping and the being and the doing – only she baulked at the garden. She would not do it, for a vow taken must not be undone. The headscarfed ones of her world could look askance, could offer help, but she would have none of it. Let them peer over the wall with their beaky noses and pale, watery eyes, let them point and purse their lips. The garden waited for him to show a sign. If he showed a sign, she would transform it into a magical place. Until then, not a blade would she touch – more, she would defile. She trod and trod and trod until the delphiniums lay crushed, the blue in the dirt as sightless as she wished her own eyes. She was waiting, waiting for the change to come, for the new to begin. She cared for nothing else.

Arthur watched her. He knew. He kept the flame of the idea alive long after his bishop had told him it was inner cities or nothing. They were happy with him where he was. Did he have to change? There was a wry smile. Did he think he had suddenly been called by God to fight Confucius? The port wine flowed. He had no true zeal for the arguments. He was as phoney as the tea-urn. Escaping not confronting. She was being stifled by the wide-open skies, the swelling seas, the Siberian winds that battered their northern outpost. Perhaps she needed to bask in the teeming claustrophobia of urban decay. Their garden was a symbol. He understood that. It would never be a garden again – not for them. He nodded – both at the decanter and his glass, and at what his bishop was saying. 'Yes,' he said out loud. Inside he thought, God's will be done? Or hers?

And now the moment to decide had arrived. If he could go on eating toast and not ever have to speak again or open the envelope, he would do so. But she stood there, tense as a bird. He had been careful, reached the post before she did, hidden away the London letters, the official envelopes that betrayed something was going on. He could no longer do that. This was the last post, quite literally. He allowed himself a small smile at the pun. She was dreaming of Beijing, Shenyang, Lanzhov, and he could offer her Leeds, Wolverhampton, Stoke.

He could feel her breath on his cheek as he slit along the top of the envelope, feel it quicken as he took out the letter. Not Leeds, then. Nor Wolverhampton. Not even Stoke.

London.

Whose will? Maybe hers. Maybe God's. Not his.

She saw it as a sign. Joyous news. Not the garden, then, but the whole of this place, sacrificed. She was going back. Joy flowed through her.

He saw it, knew why, took the blow and said nothing.

The pain of sharing her bed became acute, but he would not relinquish it again. Like her, he made promises to himself. When he got to London, when he was renewed in some other place, he would conduct himself according to his heart's dictates. They would have separate rooms. Since she had told him, with fire, with urgently demented need, that their coupling touched nothing in her save the physicality of nerve endings, he had no need of it. And he would destroy the package she had hidden away, his devious red-gold squirrel, he would burn it, make a pyre. And he would tell her he had done so. After that she had her choices. He despised her. He despised himself. If he could wear a hair shirt, if he could be publicly flogged, if he could renounce every ease and comfort, he would do so. But that was too easy. That was not God's way. Instead he would be given a cosy little house, with a cosy little study and a cosy little car, and he would have to go among the destitute, the malodorous, reeking throng, the vicious, the lost, the desolate, innocent and depraved – not to kiss their running sores but to administer advice and hot soup (keep religion to the *absolute* minimum) and then return to his cosy little hell.

She rang the number. A woman answered. 'May I speak to your husband?' she said. 'Tell him it is Alice.'

He came to the phone. He said hallo, cautiously. She said, excitedly, muddling her words at first, 'Arthur and I are moving back to London.'

'Excellent,' he said in the same recognizable tone she used for headscarfed ones. 'You must both come for dinner in town. Haven't seen Arthur for years . . .'

'Will we meet?' she whispered, knowing the hearty tone was for his wife to hear.

'Nice man, Arthur. What's he doing back in the metropolis?'

'We're coming down tomorrow to make one or two arrangements.'

She did not say that she had begged to come, that Arthur was seeing the committee, that she had no role nor place in the journey except her desire for time spent with him. One more time, one more time. She could seduce him again, she *knew* she could seduce him again. They could start afresh. As if she had never been away.

'I will buy pomegranates,' she said softly.

'What? What?'

'For tomorrow.'

'Yes. Good luck with all that,' said the dismissive bellow.

'Will we meet?' she said, louder, more urgent.

'No, no,' he said cheerfully, 'I don't think so. Good wishes to Arthur, then.'

She would not let him go. 'If not tomorrow, will we meet when I am there for good? I long to see you again, I *have* to see you again, I –'

'No, no, I don't think so. Regards to Arthur. I must go. Stephanie's waiting to drive me in. Bye.'

At the steps down to the Underground she faltered.

'You go,' she said to Arthur. 'You go and do the things you have to do today and I'll meet you later somewhere. Day Return. We want to get the sixish train. Meet at five, then? Where?' (Not the Ritz . . .) And then he was gone, down into the echoing tunnels, waiting for the lonely train. And she, hunched, despairing, so old she felt now, walked slowly in the direction of Green Park, where she would sit, and wait, and think, and remember the coin she gave to be lucky in love.

*

The Little Blonde Secretary Bird reads a magazine advertisement about dental correction and notes the name of the private clinic which offers consultation and service. When she gets to the office she will ring them up and make inquiries. His teeth are not going to get any better as he gets older and he *is* getting older. His hairline is definitely receding, and he was born thin in that department, anyway. At the back of her mind is hair transplanting – but that will come later. For the moment teeth are the issue, and even if it is going to be a bit expensive – well, they have only themselves to think about now, haven't they? (She is not altogether convinced that Derek's teeth are not in some way linked to his obvious lack of virility. If he had nice teeth and could smile into the mirror without feeling – as he must, though he never says so – ashamed of their prominence, it might gee him up a bit.) Why should she take all the trouble with herself and have him go as you please? Besides, he really did have to do something about his teeth *now*. And it was not her fault it had come to this, so he might as well have the full works.

The clinic is in Harley Street, so it will be quite all right. Yes, yes, she will telephone today. That is *one* advantage of being on the switchboard. And actually, there are others. As she told Derek, there is no more important job than being the first voice to be heard when somebody rings a company. Anybody can do secretarial duties (as, indeed, the anybody who has been brought in to replace her does, and oh, those hips), but not many people can be peppy and alert and informative at the end of a telephone. Also she meets all the clients and visitors before anyone else does and has a good range of conversational topics for them. The weather, their health, the loft conversion (so nearly complete now), the price of everything nowadays, and lots more. She engages them all in exchanges like this, which, she feels, puts them at their ease and gives a good impression. And the more unforthcoming they are, the harder she works (and it is work, as she tells Derek; it's called 'interfacing' and is very demanding), aware that such reticence is often a sign of stress, which talking can help. If she had more qualifications, she would apply to be one of those counsellor people (There was a piece about therapy last week, everyone should have it, the mind can be sick just as the body can – not *hers* but certainly other people's. She had seen it.), but as it was she was enjoying herself and wasn't likely to change.

Switchboard and Reception left you plenty of time to read, and she even managed to knit things (had knitted something for her predecessor's baby in a nice lemon-yellow), so it had really all worked out very well. She thanked the Boss Masculine only the other day for entrusting her with the special responsibility. *And* told him he looked stressed. 'About time you had another holiday,' she said, but privately she thought she wouldn't much want to go on holiday with the frump of a wife he'd got.

She put the magazine back in her bag and checked the contents. Hairspray, perfume spray, deodorant spray. She had to carry these about with her nowadays, as she had actually found the Hips borrowing this latter (she always seemed to be perspiring), which used to reside in the ladies' loo. If she put them in her desk, she quite often forgot to take them with her, whereas she always took her bag when she set off for a tidy, so it was no hardship. It was nice to have these small things worked out. As she said to Derek, get the little things ironed out and the big things will follow. She was more and more sure that was true of his teeth, anyway.

He had been very happy lately due to the building work – whistling around the house, replastering the hole where the Vent-Axia had been (*and* apologizing, at last, which she had been waiting some time for). He never went near the pub now or that horrid Ken, who winked at her at the firm's Christmas dinner dance. She didn't mind the wink so much (after all, she was wearing her clinging pink velvet), but when he danced he pinched her bottom, hadn't got the consideration to wear aftershave, *and* carried on a conversation with the couple next to them. Not a very nice conversation, either. And Derek had been sitting next to the store manager or some such, drawing diagrams on the back of napkins – staircases and window recesses and the like – so he hadn't even bothered to look at her and see – well, frankly, how lucky he was.

It was all very well when the advice concerning the problems between her and Derek was to 'Woo Your Partner'. But she had grown sick of doing it all. And he just fell asleep. If she attempted to resuscitate past success – as that Sunday when she stripped off in the front room – he had so much to do upstairs that she was left holding a glass of Asti and a wicked pose while he said he had to crack on. 'Rev him up, dear,' said the agony aunt on the radio phone-in. 'Go up to him and *plunge* your hand into his trousers. After all' – embarrassingly raucous laugh – 'what he's got is half yours, you know. And that doesn't just mean the house. Hah hah . . .'

Well, against her better judgement it was, and against her better judgement it should have stayed. She had chosen the moment as best she could: after they'd stacked the dishwasher and *The Archers* was over. He looked relaxed enough, standing with his back against the kitchen door, ankles crossed, tapping those teeth of his with a screwdriver while he checked something in the plumbing manual (he was putting a shower and WC up there – said it enhanced the investment, which didn't *quite* sound right, because, as she replied, it was supposed to be their child's play area). And given the relaxation of the moment, she had snapped off her gloves with what she contrived to be a romping motion, thought flamenco, and, advancing towards him, reached for the place suggested, señorita-style, pulling at the zip with dramatic perfection, getting it down in one.

It had been done stylishly and with a knack she did not know she possessed. She had felt quite frolicsome, but it came to nought because Derek's yell just about split her ear-drum. All right, it was true that there were several hairs caught in it when she looked. But then, as she said, mopping at the blood from his lip and vainly looking for the chipped piece of tooth, it wouldn't have happened at all if he had learned to pull his underpants up properly . . . And she was kind enough *not* to say that, given the prominence of his teeth, it was stupidity itself to put a screwdriver anywhere near them . . . They didn't seem to have made much headway since then. But they would. She was determined that they would.

She prepared to stand up. The carriage was pulling into her

station. She checked the bag once more: all correct. And she smiled happily as she trotted up the steps, for she had remembered that there was something else in the bag, something she was really looking forward to, something that she had been waiting to read ever since she heard there was a new one out. She had the new Janice Gentle book in hardback (to show she was a connoisseur), and more than anything she was looking forward to being transported to how people could be if only the world didn't have so many nasty elements in it. She wondered what the hero would be like in this one. She wondered what the heroine's job would be. Did she live in a London flat overlooking Regent's park, or a houseboat in Chelsea, or even another of those large country houses where she had horses and dogs? The man would be handsome, of course (no dandruff, no sticky-out teeth, no lack of aftershave), and virility would not be an issue. The jacket description looked – well, *interesting*. A little bit of a departure, but you could trust Janice Gentle.

She hurried down the busy London street, stepping round the beggars, grimacing at their pleading, shifty eyes, recoiling from the smell in doorways. What would it be? she wondered, as she clattered up the steps of her building. Some beautiful orphan saved from the horrors of the streets and all those nasty people by someone rich and kind? Yes. That'd be it. With the orphan no longer poor and homeless and alone, the book would end happily. Right would have been done, love would have been declared, and the future would look all golden and rosy, like a newly picked pomegranate.

Have I spoken too much or not enough of love?
Who can tell?

But we who do not drug ourselves with lies
Know, with how deep a pathos, that we have
Only the warmth and beauty of this life
Before the blankness of the unending gloom.
Here for a little while we see the sun
And smell the grape-vines on the terraced hills,
And sing and weep, fight, starve and feast, and love
Lips and soft breasts too sweet for innocence.

And in this little glow of mortal life –
Faint as one candle in a large cold room –
We know the clearest light is shed by love,
That when we kiss with life-blood in our lips,
Then we are nearest to the dreamed-of gods.

READ MORE IN PENGUIN

In every corner of the world, on every subject under the sun, Penguin represents quality and variety – the very best in publishing today.

For complete information about books available from Penguin – including Puffins, Penguin Classics and Arkana – and how to order them, write to us at the appropriate address below. Please note that for copyright reasons the selection of books varies from country to country.

In the United Kingdom: Please write to *Dept. EP, Penguin Books Ltd, Bath Road, Harmondsworth, West Drayton, Middlesex UB7 ODA*

In the United States: Please write to *Consumer Sales, Penguin USA, P.O. Box 999, Dept. 17109, Bergenfield, New Jersey 07621-0120.* VISA and MasterCard holders call 1-800-253-6476 to order Penguin titles

In Canada: Please write to *Penguin Books Canada Ltd, 10 Alcorn Avenue, Suite 300, Toronto, Ontario M4V 3B2*

In Australia: Please write to *Penguin Books Australia Ltd, P.O. Box 257, Ringwood, Victoria 3134*

In New Zealand: Please write to *Penguin Books (NZ) Ltd, Private Bag 102902, North Shore Mail Centre, Auckland 10*

In India: Please write to *Penguin Books India Pvt Ltd, 706 Eros Apartments, 56 Nehru Place, New Delhi 110 019*

In the Netherlands: Please write to *Penguin Books Netherlands bv, Postbus 3507, NL-1001 AH Amsterdam*

In Germany: Please write to *Penguin Books Deutschland GmbH, Metzlerstrasse 26, 60594 Frankfurt am Main*

In Spain: Please write to *Penguin Books S. A., Bravo Murillo 19, 1° B, 28015 Madrid*

In Italy: Please write to *Penguin Italia s.r.l., Via Felice Casati 20, I–20124 Milano*

In France: Please write to *Penguin France S. A., 17 rue Lejeune, F–31000 Toulouse*

In Japan: Please write to *Penguin Books Japan, Ishikiribashi Building, 2–5–4, Suido, Bunkyo-ku, Tokyo 112*

In Greece: Please write to *Penguin Hellas Ltd, Dimocritou 3, GR–106 71 Athens*

In South Africa: Please write to *Longman Penguin Southern Africa (Pty) Ltd, Private Bag X08, Bertsham 2013*

READ MORE IN PENGUIN

A CHOICE OF BESTSELLERS

Temples of Delight Barbara Trapido

'Trapido's superbly smart novel . . . a baroque romance of untimely deaths, orphan babes, stolen novels, canny nuns and dark, forceful lovers' – *Company*. 'Confirms Trapido as one of our most beguiling literary comediennes' – *Independent on Sunday*

The Prince Celia Brayfield

Richard, second son of Queen Elizabeth, is the most eligible prince in the world. Courageous, intelligent, devastatingly handsome, his will be a fairy-tale wedding – but who will be the bride? 'Her blockbuster novel . . . is as enjoyable . . . as Miss Brayfield's last bestseller, *Pearls*' – *Daily Telegraph*

The Reckoning Sharon Penman

Concluding her magnificent sequence of novels on the death throws of independent Wales which began in *The Sunne in Splendour*, Sharon Penman evokes all the passion and politics, divided loyalties and abiding faiths, of the thirteenth-century world.

The Wise Woman Philippa Gregory

A disturbing novel of passion and betrayal in Tudor England . . . 'The first lady of intelligent historical fiction' – *Sunday Times*. 'Compulsively readable' – Andrea Newman in the *Sunday Express*

The Tale of the Body Thief Anne Rice

Vampire-hero, rockstar and seducer of millions, Lestat is an immortal extraordinaire – but he yearns to be reborn a mortal . . . Erotic, terrifying, enthralling, *The Tale of the Body Thief* is the fourth volume in Anne Rice's bestselling series The Vampire Chronicles.